Execration

Lula Lucent

Ghost Festival Press

EXECRATION

Part of the Graveduggery™ series, Book the Second

Published by Ghost Festival Press

Cover art by Les Solot

ISBN: 978-0-9906078-1-6

First edition: August 15, 2021
Duggery Day

Printed on Earth

For Leila, wherever in the silence you dream.

My memory of yesterday is ashes, and of tomorrow nothing. The bonfire's crackle fades, far beyond the hills we have already crested and left behind, dulled beneath the murmur of the cart's unstopping wheels. I stare into the emptiness down the corpse road while my darker mood lurks beside me.

"Lethean, go to sleep. It'll gloam soon."

The sky yearns to embrace the growing shadows. I turn to look at Euly, once more unsure if her tone is affection or dismissal. She stares back until I break my gaze. In the rough silence that squats between us, my sight drifts from what I really see to images that likely aren't -- now painted in cobalt flames that provide no warmth. This road runs on: rutted, threatening, ceaseless. When I finally relent and lean against her rigid shoulder, she fidgets without pushing me away and I snuff myself, but still she flickers.

#

"There is comfort in mindless repetition. An unspoken false promise that a person's brainless day-to-day leads to more brainless day-to-days." Euly flicks on her torch and fingers her scar. "But the fact that these corpses have to be dug up and reburied, when someone else will lie in here soon enough, proves how replaceable everyone is."

The trees and I shrug.

"No one gets to rot anymore," I say.

Euly waves her torch at me, an admonishing finger. "A luxury of yesteryear."

Despite her poetic spin, I have trouble accepting the sentiment. The markers we pass are etched with names I forget the instant I look away, yet they were real once and exist like you do. Some of the gravestones carry our trademark X, though none carved by my hand.

We break through the treeline and the scrubby brushland extends before us, a perpetually fall-colored carpet littered with weeds and divots. Such an unkempt condition betrays its designation "Unguarded" as the wild retakes what we once borrowed for our dead. The sole tomb that juts unceremoniously at the edge of the graveyard is devoured by doom-creepers and sunset ivy.

This is a relic, sad to say. Plenty of corpses rest beneath our footsteps, but I've heard rumblings that this whole place is going to be repurposed as a training ground for the new recruits. Someone else told me we were planning to convert it into a honeypot trap for diggers, but he's an idiot and doesn't understand the scope of our financial instability.

Oh what lovely times these.

"Hrmm." Euly stops at the pit and lowers her light.

I inspect the waiting corpse: a light layer of dirt covers its body while the head remains mostly buried. Fair work for a first-timer.

Standing up straight as a bolt, arms crossed, smug as fuck, and I ask her. "Well?"

"Here we go, the self-satisfaction. One of those nights…"

I wait in silence under the glare of her torch.

"It's fair work."

"She's a natural."

"Yeah, yeah. Your fledgling is a natural, you should be very proud."

"Lay off it, Euly, you should be too. You taught me everything."

"Never taught you to be the annoying prig. You picked that up somewhere. Wasn't me."

I hop into the grave. "Was you, actually."

She clicks her tongue, but leaves the topic on the brink of that familiar argument, and carries on. Checking the ledger, torch precariously wedged underarm.

"Last one." And scratches an X.

"Ready?"

Stashes the ledger away, spills torch light full on me, and idly places her palm on the hilt of her blade. "Go."

I jam my blade straight through the neck of the corpse and quickly twist. Its spine *shlorps* and *pops* as the vertebrae are separated.

"Done."

"Hey! Amazing job, Leth! You're a blazing natural, you are!"

"So done with you tonight, partner."

"Bind it and let's—"

A rustle of grass cuts off our playful bickering simultaneously. Euly imperceptibly arcs her torch towards the tomb behind us, the source of the disturbance. Nothing moves, except her finger silently tapping the air once, twice...

We dart in a pincer attack at the spot, leaving the opened grave gaping as a makeshift pitfall for anything that takes our bait and escapes between us. I flick on my torch. Euly unsheathes her blade, blurred desperate pounding and me vaulting over a headstone, but not her, no, she springs against the side of another, hangs like a suspended dagger in the air, then launches at her prey full force bloodlust.

And we stop.

She pants a breath until it immediately dissolves into a frustrated sigh.

"Waste of energy."

A lumpy bunny stares at us, absentmindedly chewing the overgrowth from the tomb.

"Bugger off," I tell it. The rabbit ignores me and rips off another clump. "I'm stronger than you. You must do my bidding." I pick it up and place it outside the torchlight. All the while Euly fusses. "We're jumpier than a bunny," I say, "but at least it was no big deal."

She squats at the base of the tomb and sighs again. "No, it is. Look at this." Gestures resignation at the hole burrowed under the stonework, big enough for a person.

"Damn it," I mutter, more to myself than her, knowing where her single-mindedness is about to take a night that was nearly done.

We peer inside, heads pressed together, seeing the hole open into the tomb itself. She runs her hand along the stone floor's edge. Smooth break. Probably a burrower. Or…

"Someone who knows what they're doing," she voices my thought aloud.

"Maybe. Not recent, though. This isn't on the list. We'll come back." I don't even know why I bother to waste the words.

And Euly already wriggling inside like a stupid possessed rabbit. I glance over at the bunny I dropped off, seeking a fellow in commiseration. But it's gone now too.

She's quiet inside. Her dampened torch is a whisper as she creeps around. Each step of a soft-soled boot is an exhale and I'm sure her heart beats as carefully. I stare at the hole, watching that amber glow fade into nothingness.

It is well and truly the end of summer. Under the lingering scent of the storm that passed through only last week, I can almost smell the withered leaves crumbling to dust. Soon will come the cold, the frost, those damn harbingers of deepness.

But not yet. I smile.

As if the moment waited for that slight showing of emotion to buoy my heart, she sings. A wordless tune, low and deep, echoing up from the darkest places in the earth: a tone that hinted at gradual impermanence.

As if...

As if...

The very center of the world was a tomb. Who lay there? I wondered. Maybe not even a person. Perhaps a slumbering concept, or the cobweb of a thought, or a fleeting epiphany that fizzled like a raindrop on the edge of a steaming brazier. How long a sleep that must be... How forgotten the interred... Euly's voice dredged it all up, an unremembered truth that pulsed in the night when there was no other sound save her voice in the dark.

She faltered.

The spell was over. I opened my eyes.

Shifting, pitching higher, she hums aimlessly.

"Doubt the singing helps," I say.

"I do it because I like it," she says. "Why don't you?"

"It'd be rude to kill the dead a second time."

"I'm certain you wouldn't be *that* atrocious."

"Yes you are."

"Heh. Yes I am. Toss me a drill bit. I'm out."

Start rummaging through my pack. "Uh, don't... think I have one."

Light returns to the hole, flaring reddish. "You're kidding."

"I'm looking."

"Look faster."

"I'm looking."

She sighs.

I find the strange drill bits at the bottom, wedged beneath my own torch, and still attached to their brass housing. Five broken capsules on the unit are stained bright putrescence. Only one left.

Euly drops her drill in the hole. I distractedly grab at it while steeling myself for the inevitable stench. The drill screws into the bit with ease, tight and secure, and I hold the housing... ready to snap it off.

Krrrk!

The end of the bit momentarily burns green, then dulls to the color of scorched moss. In spite of teeth gritting and breath held, it slithers down my throat.

"Here," I gag.

"Yeah. Thanks."

After waiting a minute for her report, I ask, "Anything?"

"Nn... sorry, hold on." She fiddles with something. The shadows whip back and forth, as confused as she sounds. "Nnnh... this is an absurd angle..." The shadows freeze in place. "Okay, got it." Sharp inhale. No exhale. And then: "Someone's in here, Leth."

I start getting my equipment in order. "Right. What are we looking at? Vault? Coffin? Sarcophagus?"

"Eughh, don't even joke about that. No, it's a coffin. More than half of it's gone porous."

I stop, scowling at the tomb's wall as if it's my partner's face. "Fuck no."

"Okay, hold on... gonna... I'm gonna need—"

"No," I tell her, "no way I'm letting you do that. We'll seal the hole up and—"

"Hell, man! I already bored into this! It obviously didn't go perfect, alright?"

"In that enclosed a space?"

Her voice drops an octave. "We've done worse."

"Can you open the doors from in there?"

"Naw, it's sealed. I checked that first. It's sealed, we're not gonna get that to work."

I crane my neck over at the dug grave. This happens *every time* we're sent to a weedy plot. "Euly, we've got one out as it is. This is stupid."

"I know, I know, but this is what I have to do. I'm fine, we're fine. Right? You go finish up with that one and—"

"I'm staying with you."

"Well... go tell them to get to it then. And, ah, I won't work until you're back. Deal?"

"I can *hear* you chipping away."

"Geh, Leth, what do you want from me?"

"For you to get out of there before you -- or it -- do something stupid."

"And then what. We hug until you feel better?"

"You know, it really pisses me off I don't have anything to threaten you with."

"Leverage is a bitch," Euly clucks. "Speaking of, I'm not sure how best to crack this open." Thinking with the stamp of her foot. "Gonna yank it out, I think. Legs first."

"Your final vestige of reason says: 'if the coffin is that close to crumbling, you should leave it.' But since you aren't going to, what do you need from me?"

Her head pokes upside-down out of the hole. "Lethean."

I sit down, fists cradling my jaw. "Euliae."

"I appreciate that you care about me."

"Do you?"

"Yes."

"Okay."

"But I don't appreciate that you don't appreciate that this is important to me."

"Understood."

"Give me all your kindling."

"All of it?"

She nods, which looks weird from her position.

I never use the things, so when I offer a handful of the cobalt wedges, it's literally that. An excessive pile, but she seems equal parts satisfied and frustrated. Times like these, it's best to let Euly do her thing and pick up the debris later as needed.

"I'm lighting them… now."

At first, I think it's an explosion. Intense light surges from the hole like a sustained blast of lightning -- the sound of each square of kindling sparking to unrestrained life, fizzles, hisses, with the same intensity -- staining everything within my vision the brightest blue I could never imagine existing, an unsettling cobalt hue that seems darker than the shadows twisting around me.

But then comes the bitter, unsympathetic cold. It feels as though I am submerged in an unfathomable, hopeless depth and everything in my body begs me not to breathe, screams in the rush of blood in my ears that there is no air in this remote and sodden grave, only liquid death.

And I gasp.

Choking on frost that isn't there.

When I regain my composure, a new express terror grips my spine.

I scramble to the hole, ready to dart inside and drag her single-minded ass out, while she silently curses me and my disrespectful existence, from that icy cavern. Instead, I see her fist hanging there, shaking and dripping blood.

Grabbing it.

No acknowledgement.

I squeeze. It seizures.

Force my fingers in, pry the clenched fist apart. Not even the fresh blood feels warm.

Euly's fingers grasp mine. Fervent.

::Cold:: She stutters the reply, tapping and stroking the word on my hand.

::Can feel out here:: I sign back, shivering somehow worse than her. ::Euly okay?::

::Euly lives::

::Overkill. The all them::

::Necessary. Sorry::

::What hiding from Leth?::

::Coffin abnormal. Stone-rot what caused? Abnormal. Distrust normal way. In durance::

::Durance?::

::Insurance. Sorry. Cold spasm::

::Understand::

::Tend to unbound corpse. Staying still minute::

::Promise::

::Euly promises::

::Okay. Back soon::

::Will wait. New friend will too. Tiny laughter::

::Eye roll::

::Leth. Hurry::

#

"She wasn't telling me everything," I mutter to the corpse I straddle. Bind its wrists tight. "Again." Bind its ankles tight. "Stupid woman will get us killed one day." Jam stoppers into the mostly-rotten eye sockets; the remnants of whatever's left in there squishes like soft eggshells.

I stand, arms crossed.

No, it's obviously worse inside the tomb than she's letting on. Using all the kindling was an extreme that even the most paranoid Executioner would rarely consider. And she's no paranoid. She's a professional.

Now the question is what I do with this one.

"You have it easy," I tell the bound corpse. "To think us living need to waste our precious time on you lot."

It's not worth consideration. I leave it there and sprint back to Euly. We've been gone long enough that the others will take notice. It's true I told them to stay put and not shadow us, but... well... either they follow orders or bend them when circumstances arise. One way or the other, before this night is through I'll learn what kind of professionals they'll be in the future.

Thankfully, she meant what she said about waiting. I squeeze her hand; she squeezes back and gets to work.

#

Having nothing to do is the worst part.

I sit in front of the hole, idly plucking ivy off the wall. In such a confined space as this tomb, my being inside would be a liability. And so I prepare myself for every given scenario: the quiet and uneventful execution; the slip-up that is fixed quickly; and the pell-mell catastrophe where every possible thing goes wrong. Haven't had one of those yet.

I'm overdue.

Tink. Tink.

Ah…

Tink tink tink.

She's gone with the hammer and chisel then. Unsurprising, given how cautious she's been up till now. I imagine she won't bother changing equipment until it's done. Still… if she intends to lug it out from the base…?

Tink tink. Tonk.

Painfully long silence.

Tink tink. Tink tink tink.

This will be a while.

#

An hour passes of me eating jerky. My jaw hurts. And I'm running out of jerky.

Euly's maddening chisel-work has ended.

Ssssff. Sssffff ffffff.

She's pulling out the corpse.

Sfffffffffnnnn.

I really should be in there for the next part. Can't imagine it wasn't an awkward position she was forced into… and the risk of dropping that thing must be high. But…

Trust Euly.

Sssffnn.

She's the best.

Sfffffnnnnnn nnnffffffsss. Sssffn.

She's the best of us.

Thud.

Shit.

I risk peeking. The cold light stabs my eyes.

Euly's shadow shivers on the wall and crouches atop the unseen body. It clutches her insubstantial blade in both its ethereal hands, raised high -- like some horrible supplication -- and plunges the steel through the neck, and twists. The shadow repeats this action for each elbow and knee.

Now she stands. Rigid and powerful as any marble statue.

I make room as she drags the body over. First I see hands, shriveled and dry, all but skeletal save a few patches of flesh. I take hold of the better-maintained wrists and tug. Not the best method, to be sure, but based on the size of the aperture to girth-of-the-corpse I see why Euly stabbed the limbs too. We need as much wiggle room as possible.

With a little careful effort -- and avoiding any study of its death-howl mask of a "face" -- I manage to yank the interred back into the realm of the living.

Euly clambers out behind. "Finish it," she pants.

Bind the hands, bind the ankles, stop the eyes.

"Done," I whisper. "Good wor— Shit!"

"Ffff-fine, I'm f-fine," she stutters.

But she's not. Her cheeks are flushing pink, stippled with burst blood vessels, the contours around her eyes dark blue, lips chapped and cut, to say nothing of the rubbed-raw discoloration covering any exposed skin. She falls against the tomb, drowsy and slurring any attempt to waylay my concerns.

"I swear, you're a lunatic. Come here." I pull her close and hold her tight, rubbing her back continually.

"Guess yyyou got… th-that hug yyyou wanted," she quips, mirthlessly.

"Shut up and rub your hands together."

"… yyyeah."

11

She rarely emits much warmth, but once she stops shivering she pushes me away lightly. Even Euly, headstrong to the point of stupidity, understands her limit. What makes her different from the rest of us is her rabid desperation to redefine it, to shove it back further and further, daring the darkling world to fight her for every heedless inch.

Her weak smile is genuine. When she squeezes my hand, it is a simple request.

::Help Euly carry::

Somewhere in that thick skull of hers, I hope she knows: I always have been.

#

Arroyo wordlessly hurries past us when I jerk my head back the way we came. Her partner follows after, a bit laggard. It's fine. Arroyo is clearly a leader type.

Euly and I pile the corpse in the slightly-too-full cart. Once we finish situating it, the Arroyo duo return and we wedge in our final charge.

I look around at everyone. They nod back. Our work is done at last. Euly hops up in the cart's front seat and wraps her clothing a little tighter. I vault next to her while the other two take up positions behind the yoke and begin to push. Arroyo takes the spot in front of me.

Euly stifles a sneeze, then pulls out her ledger. Begins scrawling a new page entry about the tomb. Her fingers pause in thought.

"Did you mark that grave?" she whisper-asks me.

"Got that done, Boss," Arroyo whispers, silly pride lifting her voice, confirmed with a glance back at me.

"Then it's marked."

"So she says," I smile.

Arroyo's shoulders pin back as we pass around the bend. I watch her strain against the load. I listen to the soft moan of wood moving through well-worn ruts. And then feeling

Euly's body succumb to exhaustion, sliding back into the seat and into an awkward yet comfortable position.

A cold night presses in on four Executioners traveling within its tunnel of darkness, seeking a place of repose.

For the living. For the dead.

\#

Morninglight is bleached and lifeless as a slack, emotionless face.

Like the one Euly wears.

"What…"

She stares up at the guard leaning over the battlements.

"… the hell."

The guard swallows hard under her scrutiny.

"We're closed," he stammers, trying to maintain his resolve and the party line.

"You aren't a bleeding pub," she says, flatter than the edge of the precipice this kid is on. "You're Crypt Dun."

"Even so."

"… 'even… so'?"

His face drains of any remaining color.

As much fun as this is to watch and finally not be on the receiving end, it's time to intercede. I stand up in the cart, feeling my spine pop in a mixture of pain and relief, and press Euly's shoulder down the instant she starts to rise with me.

"Jasset, right?"

"Jasper," he corrects.

"Jasper. Do you see how laden we are?"

He hesitates. We both know my obvious angle. "… sure."

"And do you know who we are, Jasper?"

"Yeah. No. I mean, yes, by way of the docket. Plus, you were on the schedule." Then he foolishly adds: "Though a week late."

I press Euly down again.

Her breaths are ragged and staccato.

13

"We've been out a month and we need to drop the cart off. That's the end of it."

"Le—" He double-checks his papers. "Lethean. I mean this: we're full up. I'm not authorized to let anyone else pass."

"Who else is on the docket?" I ask. "Coming this week or next."

"This week is empty. Three next week. One as far as Crossroads."

Arroyo frowns at our load. "If someone's coming from Crossroads, they'll be packed as us." Her voice wavers at a noncommittal threshold: too low to be confident of her own importance in the conversation, too high to simply be talking to herself.

"They've set up a temporary waystation at Pauper's Pit for incoming," Jasper explains.

"Pauper's Pit!?" Euly bolts upright, slapping my hand away in the ascent. "Are they mental? Who approved that!"

"Krohn."

"My ass she did."

"Ordered it after our break-in."

Euly may as well unsheathe her blade for all the threat pouring from her tongue and eyes. Good thing the kid is out of reach. "If you tell me Crypt Dun has been compromised, I'm going to cut off your balls."

He says nothing.

Euly whips her attention to me. Pinprick pupils.

"Hey. I want to keep my balls too."

"Where. Is. It." Euly demands of him, continuing to hold my gaze and causing my intestines to strangle various organs in their upwelling anxiety.

"Around the... back."

"Stay here" is all she barks at everyone: myself, Arroyo and her partner, the dead in the cart, and the growing number of Executioners shitting themselves along the wall.

I don't blame them.

I am too.

#

"Can't believe it," Arroyo tells her partner as they push the empty cart onwards. "Another break-in! And Crypt *Dun*? Wow!"

"Not actually another, is it?" he asks.

"Well…" she thinks. "Technically no. That first group was found out. I think while sleeping in the cart?"

"Yeah. Wait. It was a group?"

"Wasn't it?"

"I thought it was three people."

"That's a group."

"Pff, yeah, barely."

"Either ways, I meant a bigger group than that. Than the first time."

"Oh okay. Even if you say that, I don't think it was that many. What about this time?"

Arroyo jolts from a shiver. "Yeah! Boss?" Looks back at me. "How many this time?"

"… and it seemed fine," Euly is telling me in low tones, seemingly choosing her words extra carefully not for my benefit but for herself as she pieces this catastrophe together. Or emotionally processes it. "I mean, it's been a week. Mm, sorry." Pinching the bridge of her nose. "Week and a half. The damage is pretty extensive. Shattered vault covers everywhere. Some vaults themselves broken enough that they shouldn't be fixed. Absurd risk." Thin whistle of a sigh. "The rubble has mostly been cleared. Mostly. But that's not the worst of it."

I hunch down, elbows on knees and chin on hands, mirroring her own gargoyle pose.

"Course not. Nothing is ever easy anymore."

"Ssss… he says it." Leans in, knocking heads gently. "Forget the initial explosion, concussive force, whatever.

That's obvious." Her deadpan whisper is a red-hot breeze against my ear. "Long and narrow tunnels running everywhere. Sudden blast, sure, but then... the shockwave. What does *that* mean, dear Lethean?"

My expression answers for me. The end of her lip curls a sardonic angle.

"Cracks could be *anywhere* now," she finishes.

"How far has the inspection gone?"

"Not very. In fact, I'm sure no one has thought of the worst-case scenario I have. They're too busy picking up the pieces and not knowing if anyone is missing or not."

"How could they not kn—"

"Shit record-keeping. Someone got sloppy. Some corpses may or may not have been transferred to the very back because they were being noisy and upsetting the others."

"And this can't be confirmed?"

"Not yet. I'm gonna raise hell and blood when we get to Overlook."

"You shouldn't have forced them to take our load."

Pulls away from me, shaking her head resolutely. "I'll take the blame. Dun is still the best place. Not—"

Dreadful silence cuts off the thought.

"Boss?" A tentative Arroyo.

"Hmm?"

"How many?"

I look at Euly.

"We don't know," she answers. "Two gravediggers breached the atrium, hiding under a cart..."

"Farther than the first lot," Arroyo's partner mutters.

"... but it sounds like they had help. Maybe with busting through the backside of the Dun, but definitely with fleeing."

"They got away?" Arroyo blinks rapidly, nearly tripping on a pothole from inattention.

The cart shudders.

"They did. But one probably died. Flagons of blood are up in the shrine. Hard to think anyone could have survived that much bleed-out."

"Then…" Although Arroyo has turned away, I can tell her brow is furrowing. "Where does that leave us now?"

"Same as we were." Euly hops out of the seat and helps push. "Going home."

#

We stopped for a late breakfast along the road to Overlook. Small food stall. Cheap and filling. I barely noticed the few customers hurriedly swallowing their meals and leaving with agitated glances over their shoulders. I'd like to think it's our smell, but it's more primal than that.

We're dangerous mysteries with authority.
Watch out.

We might bury you early.

Stealing

your

loved ones

in

the night.

NECROFIENDS

and

CORPSE-LOVERS

and

BLACK-BLOODED WIGHTS

(yeah right.)

Some silly shit like that. It's almost cute.

And yet…

"Whatever," Arroyo grumbles at her poached eggs. Stabs them with a spoon and stirs the golden goo until the rice is supersaturated in the best way possible. She hesitates. Trembles. Then holds the bowl out in both hands, amusingly apologetic, to the chef. He adds heaps of diced, crispy bacon.

The reality is we're hungry bastards like you who sometimes like our jobs, sometimes not.

"Here."

"Huh?" Arroyo blinks at the pitch-dark bottle I pass.

"Don't you use it?"

"Um." Pops off the cork and sniffs. Warily. "Eeef! That's salty!"

"You do realize… salt doesn't smell like anything."

"Really? It's unique?"

"No, I mean, salt has no smell."

"Oh. Well. It's super fishy. I can't do it." After she recorks it, she pushes it away. But only an inch. Too polite to move it farther.

The four of us eat wordlessly at the counter, Euly and I competing on seconds. This street can scarcely be called busy, but the sounds of business, birds feigning to care about their half-remembered and constantly-interrupted strains, the workers clattering on scaffolding and hammering repairs that deepness will tear down in the passing of a single storm…

"It's so loud," Arroyo says at her empty bowl.

#

The final hike up the craggy hill can be invigorating or annoying, depending how long we've been out on assignment. Or if we're starting the day or ending it. Was better when there were pine trees up here, but they're dead and their syrup-sweet scent gone and buried.

Arroyo and partner excitedly chatter about something not work-related during the ascent.

They're too new to remember what that was like, how the shadows of branches scraped across the mottled stone throughout the day. And when torches were lit at twilight…

But it's happening all over. This… *wasting*.

"No, stop! Ease off, ease off, woman!" Metal screeches torment, a thousand deaths compressed into a single second. "Aagghhh, my ears! Asshole! I told you to ease off!"

18

Off the trail, high up on a boulder, someone is clutching their head, clearly in excruciating pain.

"What did you say?" Someone else appears next to the other.

"Just *stop* it! I didn't calibrate the distance."

"But it worked!"

"And stop talking to me. I'm deaf. I have no idea what you're saying besides dumbass crap that— aagggggnnn, this *really hurts!*"

"S… sorry." The newcomer tries to comfort the other with awkward pats on the back.

Euly points at them. "Who's that?"

"No idea," I say. Not wearing our colors at all.

I think to hail them, but they disappear behind the towering rocks soon after. Though, honestly, they don't seem nefarious.

Farther on, our proud standard comes into view: that black banner cut through from top to bottom with a single line of crimson. It trembles from a gust, then stands still. And there, right past the symbol of our organization -- same as we bind around our arms -- a brilliant light sparkles off a glass dome.

Overlook. Our strange and rough-hewn home on the edge of an abyss.

Built partway into the rock itself, jutting out and hanging down from the cliffside like petrified moss, all concrete and glass. Despite my core of weariness at having been away for so long, this sight gives me a second wind.

"Finally," I say without thinking.

Euly looks back at me with a smirk. "Sentimental Leth. Hellishly adorable."

I roll my eyes.

She laughs, and it puffs out in little wisps of teasing fog. But, coming alongside her, I notice the same glint of light from the dome reflected in her darkling eyes.

#

The front desk is deserted when we arrive. Burning coals crackle within the small steel heater next to the unoccupied chair. She can't be far…

And she isn't.

Naj pops into her seat with a jump.

"Hey guys! Welcome back."

"Thanks, Naj. How're things?"

"Lame and same. You?"

"Fine."

"Tired."

"Hungry."

"Also tired."

Comes the chorus of our voices in fusillade succession.

"I'll check you in." Places four baskets in front of us. "You know the drill."

We stow our equipment and weapons.

I gesture at the unfamiliar tents lining the walkway right outside the main entrance. "We have incoming?" I ask.

"Hmm?" she considers. "Oh. No, nothing like that. Some, um, Technocrat friends are visiting us." Naj stacks the baskets into a precarious tower, hoists them up, and cradles them in both arms. "Quartermistress isn't in yet. You need these returned soon?"

"Hope not," Euly shrugs. "Have to debrief with the Crone. She around?"

"Last I checked. See y'all." And off she tramps, struggling not to drop her charge.

"You two are free to run away now," I tell Arroyo and her partner.

"Forever?"

"Forever until we have orders."

"So, probably, a week," Euly states.

"Good enough," they chime in unison, immediately doubling over in laughter like the dumb kids they are.

"Aw man, I'm showering for days! My poor braid..."
Arroyo strokes her thick auburn hair, lopsided and frayed
and uncoiling. "De-stroyed."

"Go revive it," I say to her.

"Eeesh. Our most difficult assignment yet." But her
cheery amble speaks otherwise.

"Shower does sound good," I remark, dripping in
subtextual hints.

"Does," Euly agrees, "but we aren't off the clock yet."

"According to our friend at the Dun, we were off the
clock over a week ago."

"Come on, man. Don't start with me."

She doesn't wait, stalks up the spiral staircase towards
Krohn's office, leaving me behind. I shake my head and
hurry after. At the top, the hallway splits off towards our
dorms, the offices, mess hall, and common rooms. We spend
pitifully little time in the former, used mostly for clonking
out the scant hours or masturbating.

After a minute traveling down hallways of stone and
concrete, fitted together at hard angles with the occasional
circular window gawking out at Old City to break up the
claustrophobic monotony, we arrive. Executioner
architecture won't be winning any accolades for beauty, but
it certainly makes up for it with harsh unique aesthetics and
strict practicality.

Euly raps on the opened door to get Krohn's attention,
then promptly closes it in my face.

"Okay then," I tell the polished oak and its innumerable
knots. "Masturbation it is."

#

"I won't do it!" Euly's muffled shout.

And then she bursts out the door, slams into my shoulder
and disappears around the corner, leaving behind a frigid
sheen of silence. Krohn and I stare at each other. Her
weather-wearied face gives nothing of their obvious

21

disagreement away, instead regards me with the extent of warmth our overseer is capable of. Waves me in.

"Hello, Lethean," she says, voice of fissured granite that always reminds me of the mountains far north of the city.

"Good to see you, Krohn." I take the whiskey-spiked ginger tea she offers.

She knows me too well.

Or our circumstances.

If nothing else, she's a woman who understands the reason for the existence of booze.

"You needn't give the rundown. Euliae was quite thorough." Sits back in her creaking chair, studying me under an asymmetrical cut of short white-on-gray hair. "But of your overall assessment?"

I finish the tea. She doesn't offer more. Her chair has stopped creaking.

"Far too quiet. Made me wonder if we were unearthing the wrong corpses."

"You have your doubts," she comments.

"No," I correct. "None. Like I say, it was just a feeling. But everything went smoothly..." Hurriedly adding: "And the only reason for our lateness—"

Krohn raises a gloved hand to stop me.

I try to ignore it. "Targets of opportunity that we—"

"As I say, she was quite thorough. You needn't defend Euliae."

"Not defending her."

Krohn looks out the window behind her desk. The lake spreads in a wide, welcoming embrace and even the terraced ricefields are visible. "Beautiful day, and I'm stuck up in here because of the dismal cold out."

I can hear the wind beginning to pick up. A thin howl, probing the window's edges for entry.

"It is bracing," I say.

Abruptly, she stands. "Walk with me."

She carefully chooses the hallways we take, deliberately avoiding the ones filled with noise or conversation, cocking her head at an intersection, then darting into silence and space void of presence. It's a roundabout path, but eventually we reach the glass observation dome above a vacant common room.

I'm fond of my dorm's view of the city, but I never tire of this overlooking panorama.

A single pane of unbreakable glass is veined with sickly, irreparable cracks: an irony not lost on me, nor is Krohn's resolute refusal to ever replace it.

She sits below it, cross-legged, on a squat comfy ottoman. Hands folded. Eyes closed. Shattered rainbows crisscross her.

"Are we still debriefing?"

"One must learn to let go and... sod inflexibility." Opens one eye. "Wouldn't you say?"

I laugh at her offhand, casual dismissal. "I don't think any of us have any idea what we're doing in life."

"Ohh, but the rigid ones *break*," she nearly cackles. "Those obdurate, thick-trunked trees with their vaingloriously, self-satisfied 'deep roots'. But we willows?" Opens the other eye, piercing me with cold blue-gray intensity. "Do we not dance?"

"I try."

"Not unnoticed. And you do well enough, I think."

"Thank you."

"Of course." Nods twice. "Then, to your assessment."

I drag a chair across the room. "Well, if you already know everything..." Drop it, and myself, before her. "I fear the quiet wasn't good for Arroyo or her partner."

"Explain."

"They're sufficiently aware to not let it lull them into a false sense of oh-this-is-how-it-always-is. But this was routine for us. We know the exceptions. The times everything goes to hell and there isn't time to think, or plan for the best idea. Just... react. And don't die."

"Cynical."

"I disagree. Survival is survival."

"No," she gestures idly, "what you said before. The not knowing what we're doing. That's your youth talking. We are learning, bit by bit, even now in these times."

"I won't deny I'm often naive."

"Still." Straightens up, hands clutching the cushion. Arcs her back, forcing me to glance momentarily away from her prominent, unashamed chest sticking out -- *kkkrkk-pop!* -- and then her whole body relaxes. "I suppose that's the zeitgeist we're buried in."

"Some more than others."

"Executioner joke." Smirks. "I get it."

"Overall, it was a beneficial experience for them. Duration, I mean. If nothing else. They can deal with it. Won't go stir-crazy."

"Good, good. They are our newest and youngest. I wanted to know how stern they could be."

"Pretty damn stern. Arroyo especially."

"And how is Euliae?"

"You'd know as much as I would."

Scoffs. One of those actions only an older woman can do effectively. "Please. You saw how she stormed out. Her preferred goodbye of late, if you've been paying attention the last year." Leans in at me. "You're her friend, Lethean."

I look past Krohn at the indistinct bump that is Crypt Dun at this distance. "Not sure she has any."

"Ahh. I both admire and detest you dolts at once." Squints her eyes at me, good as her word exhibiting those competing emotions. "Your *partner*, then."

"Takes everything too seriously. All the time." I hold my arm up, tight and unyielding. "No good will come from that."

"'For her' is how you mean to end that sentence."

"I didn't say that."

"Hardly had to. Written all over your face, as much as hers with that damage. You'd think the idiot girl would learn."

"You keep pushing her."

"*I'm* not the one pushing her."

Dread silence. I don't think either of us were planning to get pissed off today. Especially not at each other.

"Krohn?"

"Hm?"

"What the hell happened at the Dun?"

"Wish I knew. We're piecing it together. No aftermath yet. I can't be certain there will be any. Is the Sovereignty going to cut our funding? Doubt it. Who else would they turn to? No. Nothing is changed. The game remains the same: our board, our players, our move. Euliae asked for the job of hunting down the burglars." Cracks her wrists. "I denied her."

"Is that what your argument was about?"

"No," she says with a finality that brooks no follow-up questions.

"I imagine you already have someone assigned to the investigation. Or you're doing it alone."

"There will be no investigation."

Her face has become a statue's.

"You can't be serious."

"Your friend gave me a lot of shit today -- a lot of shit, Lethean -- about my call on Pauper's Pit. I'm taking risks where I have to, where *we* have to because funded though we remain, we are none of us wealthy. A description, you'll agree, that hasn't been attributable to anyone going on thirteen years.

"Now, I can sit here again and play the pedant and waste both of our afternoons until the sun bleeds out or my wits do, or we can agree that life is, these days, as you noted: a bit fucked." She pants, seeming as though she ran up and down every flight of stairs in Overlook. "Damn it, that felt good."

"Welcome to the world of us groundlings, dear leader."

A long sigh escapes her, taking away the force of her indomitable form.

"Life... was never simple," she says at the floor. "We labored, as we do now. Then came the collapse, the intercession, the abdication. You aren't so young to not remember, I realize, but ours truly is a different world. At least back then, life was life and death was death.

"You knew what you could and couldn't heal. But today? Today you water a flower and it might perk up in seconds or wither by nightfall." Hands outstretched, she turns around the concept like it's an invisible object only she can touch, one about to fall through her fingers if she isn't careful. "I used to rely on the laws of nature."

"Careful, ma'am, your profession is showing through your fangs."

Frowns at me a villainous glower. "There was a story I used to love, *The Fallen Champions*. You probably know it by a different name from that overrated playwright's adaptation." I shake my head, oblivious to both references. "The world in turn belonged to the benevolent, and then the wicked. Every one hundred years it cycled, and the champions that ushered forth the world to light were destined to return the next century to blanket it all in darkness." A pause. "Remind me the name you lot call me behind my back."

"The Crone."

"Yes," she shivers, "yes, that's a good title for my character. Krohn the Savior Tyrant returns as The Crone, Destroyer of Healers. Will that happen to me, do you think? In this dead world of ours?"

"No."

"Good. Who would want to return to all this useless toil. If they were alive, my husband wouldn't, nor my wife."

The wind is moaning.

"Krohn, are you stepping down?"

The glass creaks.

"Oh dear, you're picking up on my wistfulness. How embarrassing." And steps away from the ottoman, stands at full height, such grace and power that she appears younger, wilder, more alive than I'll ever be. "No, Lethean, I remain until I too am interred -- if interred I am to be." Her booming voice. "After all..." Spreading arms, as if glorifying in a sudden downpour, and looking straight at me. "I do so love this new, strange world. Don't you?"

The unexpected constriction in my heart, a jumble of confused emotions that have no words, that to define would dilute not their purity but their realness and immediacy. I can only watch her and hope she can read the meaning in my glistening eyes.

Her first, true smile of the day comes with a shudder.

Willowy.

Satisfied.

#

I hadn't forgotten my yearning for a shower. Hurried over straightaway once Krohn and I had finished. New assignments would come soon, she said, and gave us the week to ourselves. Felt like she was bending over backwards to avoid her customary inclination to run us ragged out of necessity -- but our younger charges can't withstand that yet, and I think Euly's physical appearance tipped matters far in favor of rest.

Still human, our Crone.

Arroyo was in the showers when I stepped inside. Half expected her to be fighting with her eternally-unruly hair, me lobbing another joke suggestion that it needed to be chopped off for violating regulations, but... she just stood there, probably becoming a prune all over, in such quiet reverie. Not above wrecking a moment for a playful jab... and it was surely tempting...

So tempting...

I abstained.

And by the time I left, she remained rooted to the spot while the pouring steamy droplets made her look a wilted bloodthistle seeking redemption in the spring.

#

I ate dinner alone.

Traded friendly words with some friends, and Naj dropped by briefly to have a snack of chocolate and to professionally laze for a spell, but mostly I sat apart. Everyone here understands the need for solitude.

Staring out at long-shadowed buildings, mechanically shoving spicy pumpkin stew into my face, until night fell and the city winked on one candle at a time. In spite of a second coffee, I felt dead weary.

Drift down the corridors. Feel the rough yet smooth bite of wall against fingertips. The door swings open. Shuts. The dorm, dim room lit with an indigo glass orb on the windowsill, as remembered.

He climbs up the ladder to the loft, each rung pulling him deeper into himself, a secure comfort. Divorced from unfulfillable wants and contradictory bullshit.

So there lies she, messing everything up.

Like always.

#

Fully awake.

"Unnngg. This is where you've been hiding."

Euly moves the notebook aside to peer at me, then returns to reading without so much as a greeting or apology.

"Of course you'd be here."

I'm trying to figure out what would happen if I grabbed her ankles, threw her down the ladder, and tore up her precious ideas. Dumped them down on her, so much illegible snow.

At long last, she deigns speak. "Need to stay over tonight." Fingers rustling the pages, searching a specific thing out.

"Or you could not hide from your problems all the time."

"I don't hide from you."

"Funny."

The pages stop turning momentarily. "… heh."

"Go to your room."

"No."

"Get off my bed, then."

"I'm comfortable here."

Too exasperated and used to this crap to even sigh. I go back down the ladder and return with a spare quilt and blanket over my shoulder.

"Why aren't you at a tavern or something, screeching like a crow or banshee or whatever?" I ask, making the demi-bed.

"Mates don't know I'm back yet, though I sent a message on over to 'em." Flips a page. "Besides. Not going anywhere looking like this."

"I have seen livelier corpses."

"Right?" Flips a page.

I finish the bed. "I'm sleeping now," I tell her.

"Got it." The candlelight moves. She doesn't.

I crawl atop her, then over her, then start shoving her off the bed. "Good. Move it."

"Hey! Hey! Stop— stop touching me!"

"Sod off my bed and move it."

"I was here first!"

"Off."

"Fine! Fine fine, nnnngggn, stop kicking me, I'm off, I'm off!"

I toss her a pillow.

"Said I'm off, didn't I?" she protests.

"That's for you."

"Oh." Stares at it. "Other one's better, but fine." Makes herself comfortable enough, although her feet stick out from under the quilt. "This bed's not as warm is it? Not as... comfortable."

"Go to your room, then."

"No." As close to pouting as this ass of a woman can get.

My pillow smells like Euly. I flip it over. Too cold. I flip it back, and settling in with a long exhale, watch her read.

After a minute passes: "Stop staring at me."

"So what did she say that angered you?"

Hides her face with the notebook. "I'm busy right now. Be quiet and sleep."

"What did she say?"

Frustrated growl. Slaps the notebook closed and lies down, curled up on her side, squeezing the pillow and watching me watch her.

"What did who say?"

"Krohn."

Stops breathing. Blinks. Really does look completely screwed up: scabbed lips and peeling skin all over both cheeks. Then, a sharp inhale. Rubs the old scar that bisects her entire face as if rubbing sleep from her eyes.

"Wants me to test some new tech. I refused."

"Reasonable."

"I'll do it later in the week."

"But you said you refused."

"I did," she maintains, tugging the blanket to hide her mouth, "but I'm the best, so I have to."

"I thought you were mad at her."

"I was!" Sits up. "I was furious."

"But you say you're going to do it now."

Lies back down. "Yeah, I am. I have to."

"You never make any damn sense. Just tell her that, then."

"No." Hides under the blanket again.

"Is that," I ask, "what the Technocracy is here for? The ones camping outside. They have new toys for us?"

"Uh uh. That's some sort of transport system. For moving heavy stuff up and down the hill."

"Hardly exciting."

"Hardly." She yawns. "Can we keep the candle lit? Or is that gonna keep you up?"

"It's cute when you feign to care."

"Whatever. Candle fine?"

"Sure."

Turns away from me and retrieves the notebook. But even as she reopens it, it's clear she isn't reading it at all. Can't tell if the idle page flips are for me, or for her. "I want to go after who did this. Those gravediggers. I want to inspect Crypt Dun. I want to seal Pauper's Pit for good this time. I want to train the others, to do what I can do. I want to scout the land. What does the rest of the province look like? I want to see it. I want to root out the places we're missing. Fill in the gaps. Build the barricades. Dig the graves. Burn what can be burned, inter the rest, and stop running ouroboros and write a song that will make us all rest in peace."

If there was wind outside, it stopped to listen.

"I want to fix everything," she says. "But my body is spent, and my mind won't stop thinking, and my skin hurts, and my face is cracked in half and the pieces don't fit anymore."

The silence. A new, uncomfortable quilt that wraps us. I know she isn't waiting for an answer I don't have and can't give, but I also know she's waiting for it all the same. I reach out and squeeze her hand.

::Euly not broken::

She neither responds nor lets go of the notebook lying partially on the pillow, and it's only when her breathing whispers evenly that I know she sleeps.

I light a second candle. Burrow under my blanket. And leave one hand outside the covers between my bed and hers.

#

Deflagration consummation arcing high over an Old City enervates. Presence un-receding and *swish srish*. A stick ticking down to doom, that heralded pendulum behind our eyes. *Srish krish*. Straw bundled broom, she truncated the edges and smiled all melty marrow and crimson blood. And I was black.

Smolder relic, inferno without clouds. Douse myself and die. I fall into my grave. The skeletal hand grabs my shoulders, and pulls.

Skriss skrish.

The shrine maiden cocks her head.

"My, you're just as vague, aren't ya?" She sets me aright and roughly pats me on the back like we're old chums and she's proud of me.

I know you.

"Well!" She beams. "Beating you to that one too, fella! I figured that out not so long ago." Beams so much she emits a soft glow. "Got my name back too! Can you imagine?"

Why is the city dying.

"Oh, that." Coughs. "My fault. Kinda... fucked off for seven years. Reasons, you know?"

Unhelpful antipathy passes for knowledge, but then he swallows and returns to form and asks dead set: this is my fear.

"I... wouldn't worry about *that*. See, look." And I do. The flames turn smokeless and azure. "I'm not scared anymore. This is... totally, completely manageable!" Smiles wider, all baseless confidence and self-assurance lunacy. She's an idiot. I'm in love instantly. "Ha ha!" she exclaims.

"You're an easy one. I like you. Nice to have a visitor after… well, all this time. Even if a stranger."

Then, we don't know each other.

"Do any of us know anyone, I wonder," she mutters.

"Leth!" A call over her shoulder.

She turns. Sweeps away some papers that have Euly's face inked on them, but someone else's name.

"Well! Don't let me keep you," she tells me over her shoulder. "No one ever wants me around anyways!"

But though she says so, she laughs.

#

Gray smudge wan shelter but warm and warmly turn. Reach ungrasped too unended and not starting. Ever. Took another hour, compressed to five minutes. It was enough. We start here.

And when I awoke at false dawn completely, Euly was gone. All I found of her was a note and a toilet full of unflushed piss.

Gone few days. Gig at Sutherlairn if you promise not to bother me this time. I mean it. Don't come if you're going to be the Crone's sphincter-puppet. But the afternoon after that, meet me at Sunner's Hatch please.

She could fuck the hell off about the gig insult as I crumble throw flush the note to darkest depths of vomit, blood and shit known only to city engineers. But of the last part, I stilled my annoyed pulse and crossed my arms against a word she never uses. Takes and breaks, pisses and leaves, plays willful ignorance a more passionate instrument than her wailing cry.

And yet… asks.

I want to pretend she means it, even as I pull myself up the ladder and roll up the empty bed. What happens when the hollow puppet sees its strings, but needs the dance?

This is a music that shouldn't be, but is.

#

Sunner's Hatch. Far more gloomy and smokey than the name suggests. Feels like a morgue filled with a constant somewhat jovial wake. Hate the place. Reminds me of work too much, so what's the point?

Euly is taking a shot of thick brown liquor. Grimaces when she sees me. "Leurhhghnn!" and slams her fist on the countertop. Glasses all the way down the bar rattle. "Grrenhnnn, gross!"

The bartender shrugs. "Works."

"Yeah, I know that!" Euly frustratedly gestures for a second. Pounds it. "Grlllnn, krgfff! I... yeeeuchhh!" Gags. "I made the recipe, didn't I?"

"Only one that orders it too."

"I'm tempted to order a Euliae's Bane," I say, sitting down.

But she promptly pushes me off the stool. "You aren't staying."

"Heeyy, I like that. 'Euliae's Bane'!" Bartender starts scrawling it flowery and colorful-like on a chalkboard. "We can make it like one of those 'challenge meals', yeah? Oh right." Rubs a cheek, smudging some makeup. "Can I use your name?"

"Fine, but misspell it on purpose." And dragging me out the door.

"Yu-Li-Ay... 'Yulley'? Or... 'Eulaye'? Hmm..."

Outside, she isn't fast-walking like she's drunk. In fact, she's more alert than ever and as purposeful as a starving rabbit. I have no idea what's spurring her, and it's only when we traverse whole districts we have no legal passes for into areas crammed with warehouses that I start growing unnerved.

"I get that you never keep me informed of anything but—"

Euly spits. "Hate that drink. Do you know what it is? Rancid combination of flavors I detest. Pound that crap, suddenly doing things I don't want to do is more palatable. Geh, I need help."

With hair uncharacteristically messy, I can't see her expression or what's in her eyes.

"*This* is why you ditched Overlook and made me suffer the fact everyone sees me as your keeper. Even though I'm not," I say. "It's true, isn't it?"

"Which."

"Both."

"Yes."

"Figures."

"Worse for me, the way they ask where you are."

"What's that mean?"

Ignores the question.

"We're testing out Technocracy stuff today. It's…" Trails off. Apparently Euly Bane, alcoholic or not, is no true panacea. "Seen the schematics. Something the Crone and I brainstormed a long-ass time ago. I thought we were faffing around to get some further funding." Wiggles her fingers side-to-side. "You know, request X when you're secretly gonna use it for Y."

"Like requesting Lethean for help when I'm secretly going to be used for… why?"

"He's smart, this one. Angels save us from this clever lad." Finally looks at me. Dead sober. Probably caffeinated. "Leth, don't look for depth from me this afternoon. Or tonight. Or at all for the next twenty-four hours. In fact, it's probably better that you treat me like furniture and ignore me."

"Or sit on you."

"Don't sit on me."

Looking away. "True. Your bony ass would be too uncomfortable."

"What? I can't hear you when you turn away like that. You always do that…"

"I said, your bony ass wouldn't be comfortable."

Stops. Feels herself up and almost has a horrified expression. And I think she means it. "I... did get bony, didn't I?" Is she upset? A quaver, distinct and abrupt. "Need to start eating more food again. Remind me. If I forget. Or feed me later. Yes, feed me."

"You aren't a child, Euly."

"No. I'm not," she says, but the powerlessness bleaching those words makes me wish I knew how to reach out to her, and kills the mood.

Assuming there was one.

#

"I think this is it. Is this it?"

"Don't ask me. I've never been down here."

"Um. I... would agree with that. Huh."

Euly has led us to a nondescript steel door built into a metallic building so angled it appears to have been partially absorbed by the ground. Like a half-hearted faceplant. If this is what all Technocracy structures are like, it makes me wonder how bizarre that lot is. I only know them by reputation and the equipment they periodically provide.

I knock.

"Geh! Might not even be right, man!" she says.

Shrugging. "We'll find out."

Minutes pass. I knock again. Still nothing.

"Shall we move on?"

"Erhhh, geh. Fine? I guess?"

But then something clangs from inside and increasingly louder footsteps follow. The door opens a sliver, only enough for a face with thick goggles to be visible. It stares at us for a while, eventually settling on the black-and-crimson tied to our arms.

"Ah! You're here, that's great. Can I get you to go around to the entrance? Take a left and wrap around to the front. It's all open for you."

"Will do," says Euly.

"Thanks." And the door shuts.

"See? Wasn't even the entrance," Euly rebukes.

"Hey, this is your thing. You lead. I help."

She stows her huffiness behind a cracking veneer, agitation showing through every chip and flaw in the mask. Maybe that drink she had wasn't exactly a smart plan. But the instant we see the wide warehouse gate gaping, her spine solidifies. Shoulders back, chest out, combs hair with frenzied fingers and, taking one step forward, she returns as Euliae the Executioner.

I guess whatever she sought at last kicked in.

We pass a massive glass window fused to the steel wall; neither material seems to start nor stop at any specific point. Hell, maybe it doesn't. The Technocracy is more opaque than we are, but whereas we announce ourselves and our intentions with as much transparency as possible to ride that razor edge line between comforting the public and stirring up mass panic… they simply are the penumbra of society, cast by… I'm not sure what.

Mysterious benefactors, propping up a dying civilization of a dead world with even more mysterious technologies. As though the quiet, sentinel-like angels that populate our graveyards at once decided to offer more than tears or pity. Whether propping up the corpse that is us will truly work…?

No clue.

But it's impossible to be in this profession and not believe there's still a chance.

"Feels weird to actually meet them," I say.

Silence.

"It's only their shipments that connect us," I say.

Silence.

"Okay, I get it. Psych yourself up. I'm your shadow."

A brief nod is all I get.

And we enter the world of Technocracy.

#

"Yo, over here!"

A short woman with a tilted grin and explosion of freckles hurries over to us. A grim-looking, heavy-set man tromps behind her. They both wear bronze goggles and garb dyed teal and goldenrod, cargo pants filled with a myriad assortment of tools. They're so damnedly normal it makes me wonder what I expected.

"I'm Abi!" Nudges the goggles up to her forehead, grin tilting higher, and rapidly blinks ice blue eyes. "Oof, bright out. Are you Euliae?"

Euly nods, a little stilted. Tries to smile. Doesn't work. Abi hardly notices.

"Awesome! Super nice to meet you." Extends a huge russet glove that looks like a fist despite being open. "This here's Gorge. I know we look identical, but we just work together."

She sounds serious, but they look nothing alike. Except the same shade of straw-colored hair.

"Kinda my boss. Kinda?" she asks him.

Gorge shrugs.

"Oh hey wow, you're an Executioner too?" Abi asks me.

I nod, surprisingly at a loss of voice too. It really is like meeting a living legend, shaking hands with a Technocrat. Floating half outside the moment, sweaty-palmed, try not to make an ass of yourself. "... partner," I mutter, low enough that I don't even hear it.

"Cool!" Claps her fist-glove hands together. "Long day today will put us all through the paces. Ready? Let's get started!" she cheers, so brightly and excitedly, so incongruous to the seriousness of our daily lives that I feel torn from my world instantaneously: a banner ripped from its moorings, soaring away and staring dumbstruck at a Euly that's flying in the opposite direction.

But she's gripping her blade's hilt like it's my hand.

#

The warehouse is filled with Technocrats, dashing around like swarming, attention spanless bees. A hum of machinery, a deep rumble that I can feel more than hear. Skylights illuminate all manner of things I don't understand. Some machines are active -- doing nothing I can know -- others are being dismantled and taken outside and away.

"Is this your headquarters?" I ask Gorge.

He shakes his head no.

"We don't exactly have one," Abi answers. "Kinda spread everywhere. Also, we move around a lot. Like..." Absentmindedly taps a wrench sticking out of a pocket. "I spend a lot of time at Foundry. Oh, ah, that's our place where we do metalcrafting and such. Not honestly my specialty, but I'm trying to learn more to be well-rounded."

"What do you specialize in?" The vigil of Euly's muteness ends.

"Making stuff move," she says cryptically. "Everything else I pick up as I go." Starts walking backwards and takes the sight of us both in. "We all are, aren't we? Stay here a sec." And up a spiral staircase she runs, wrapping around a small tower positioned at the interior's center. Tubes snake out of the top, up to brass horns hanging from the ceiling.

"Yo, guys!" Abi's tinny voice trumpets from above us, echoing slightly off the walls. The Technocrats slow their work and look upwards. "Our guests have arrived for the test; let's kill the volume."

And silence descends. The machinery quietens to nothingness, the Technocrats cease their chatter and shouts, and all that is left are Abi's boots clanking back down the metal stairs and that same rumble underfoot that vibrates my bones.

"You should have heard the racket last month when we moved everything in here. Had to wear earmuffs!" she giggles.

By and by, we're led into a cloistered room built partially underground. Gorge stays outside, sitting at a desk that overlooks the transparent ceiling. Abi waves up at him once we enter. He lifts his hand in acknowledgement. Two other Technocrats join him: one taking notes, the other manipulating a set up cranks.

Across the room, a platform lowers with a dummy. A shadow person. An approximation of someone's form if I had asked the night to carve out of itself a man or a woman.

My heart starts picking up pace.

"Emergency stop is that bright red circle on its chest. Got it?" Abi's tone is no longer friendly. It is frost.

My throat is drying.

"Understood." Euly unsheathes her Executioner blade.

My hand unconsciously grips my hilt.

"It won't hold back." Abi's eyes are ice. "I built it that way."

My back is clammy.

"Understood." Euly plants her feet in a readied stance. Blade gleaming under sunlight, poised and unmoving.

My heart is pounding.

Abi puts on her goggles, flips a switch on the dummy's back, and runs like hell.

There's only one thing that makes me feel like this.

The dummy's head twitches.

A cursed.

#

Dead driven corpse stalked its prey hating light hating sound hating us seeking silence always silence screaming in a moonless night with wordless voice with unbreathed breath with no sound seeking silence always silence the sound of its feet the only noise it made drawn to our noise drawn to our flickering shadows and crackling campfire drawn to hatred's hollow abyss at the bottom of which was nothing what it sought seeking silence always silence why didn't it flee and seek its desire elsewhere in the quiet solitude of unclimbed mountains in the depths of motionless sea couldn't imagine the reasons couldn't imagine we were right all along always hoped it was a lie to nurse the dying child back to health but it was true save us seeking silence always silence we were dying it was true save us seeking silence always silence the world had ended it was true save us seeking silence always silence we had a goal unreflected in the hollows of its eyeless face in that pit was the void and the abyss it sought was the chasm we had to build over if we wanted needed desperation wanted needed to keep going one more decade one more year one more month one more second seeking silence always silence we want need desperation want need to live survive live breathe no breathing it ran at us no pause seeing sightless screaming soundless moonless night seeking silence always silence and it came to create the silence it sought frenzied shadow dead driven corpse fell upon its prey hating sound hating us seeking silence always silence.

Euly screamed in the moonless night.

But never again.

After that night…

#

… only her blade screams.

A slash, a stab, making distance from momentum. After all, the dummy can't feel pain. It won't stop and, based on Abi's admission, won't stop itself.

But Euly is testing. Learning. Every fight is new. Cursed never act alike, as individual as the individuals they used to be. *Are*? This feels authentic. Such that when Abi extracts a notecard from her pocket that reads *Don't make ANY noise*, and holds a finger to her lips, with Gorge above me mimicking with a finger to his lips, it's wholly unnecessary.

From the way Euly tries to throw off its attention with a loud stomp then lightly hopping away, it's clear this disturbing doll reacts to the slightest disturbance.

41

And then she dashes in, lets a flailing limb slam into her back, and stabs and twists the kneecap. The puppet reacts to the clang of its own body weight impacting the floor by striking all around with its remaining leg and arms.

I swallow a disgusting taste.

How…

How the fuck did they make this thing so real.

Euly tries to get another limb. Instead, she spots a readable pause in the manic swinging. Its neck, vulnerable.

Stab! Twist!

The limbs stop immediately. Limp. Not dead, but disabled. The switch on its back resets with a *shhhngkk*!

Abi hops up, grinning gleeful. "Incredible!" Gives a thumbs-up to Gorge, who returns it. "Did you see all that?" she shouts at him through the thick glass. Shakes his pages of notes at us. "Yes!" she cheers.

"… not enough."

"Huh?"

Euly doesn't turn around. "It's not enough. That was too easy."

"Wow. Genuinely?" Abi pulls out a pocket notebook, writing implement at the ready like a bared fang. "Please describe."

And Euly echoes the thoughts and feelings I hadn't yet molded into words. The flailing was too mechanical, predictable. It didn't whip its neck about like a mace, didn't use its head or chest as a weapon either. Wasn't fast enough.

Wasn't nearly fast enough.

"Got it." Abi puts away the notebook, takes out tools and opens the puppet's chestplate. "I can't do anything concerning the other points without redoing major parts. Or without killing the failsafe. But I can increase speed." Looks up at Euly, then back at me. "Would that be sufficient?"

Euly isn't talking. Eyes locked with mine. Adrenaline drops, and she's sluggish.

"I'm being perfectionist," she tells me, but it's also a question.

"You are," I say. "But hiding over here in the corner..." Knocking on the shield in front of me for emphasis. "Still scares me. Up the speed."

Our Technocrat jams tools inside the puppet and starts dialing and cranking and levering esoteric adjustments. "So... more?"

"More."

"And... got it. Okay, let's reset and try again!"

#

Stab wounds the air. Over and again. Duck jump roll stab. It pivots darkly above her, menace dive and swinging. The ground shrieks in strike, Euly gracefully half-flying half-rolling over it, setting up, it spins, one limb, two limbs, she rushes it, taking arm impact and thrusting twisting popping.

The puppet collapses.

"More."

#

Death's dance records the seconds. One. One. One. She dodges, stabs, dodges, stabs. Swing, slam, rake, rend, beat, break. One. One. One. Both knees disabled, it flops and beats the ground and seethes unheard and still it comes full terror and but and she stabs twists pops.

The puppet shudders.

"More."

#

Breaker of bones. Strike her and tear muscle from skeleton in your collision. Flense her arrogance into humble strips of skin. Beat the skull until the brains are liquid impertinence. Spit on them. Shit on them. Fuck the lesser beings. STAB TWIST POP.

The puppet spasms.

"More!"

#

Reaper chorus silent screaming wailing against her body the floor the walls all around the bloody vengeful harrow's reckoning. Silence the torment. Silence the torment! Always silence always silence!

Bruises welts bones flesh everything Euly takes them unflinchingly, blade stabbing deflecting dancing, eyes unblinkingly possessed and sense is gone and left: reaction and training and a sanguine kind of unfelt bloodlust as it drips down her arms and back and chest.

She snarls.

Tenses, and unspools herself at last.

Euly darts off the ground, flies at the wall, pivots, crouches, springs off and at the puppet. Knocks her away. Again. Again. Again! Nothing. Its limbs are frenetic shields and Euly is bleeding more and more.

She edges away. Backwards. Sideways. Quiet, always quiet. The puppet rushes headlong, akilter: an opening. Euly charges, jumps when it reacts, plants her feet on its shoulders and vaults into the air -- suspended like an icicle overhead -- slams her feet into the ceiling, fracturing it the frozen lake of glass, and shoots down a hellbent wraith, blade serrating the exposed neck through and through.

Euly pants, sweating like mad.

"That! Was! Amazing!" Abi starts running out of cover.

Euly's eyes are bright red, completely bloodshot, when her head whips around. "Stop!"

Abi is heedless.

The puppet stands.

Euly swings at the emergency stop, is knocked away, rushes after its speeding form at the Technocrat whose wide-eyed wonder ablates to wide-eyed horror as the cursed puppet careens at her diminutive, trembling body.

I hurdle over her, as heedless in killing intent as she was in rapture. Blade already unsheathed, drawing a shimmering

44

trail behind my back, and then piercing the neck and twisting the hilt in perfect succession.

The puppet lies still.

Euly, looking dead to all the world, falls to her knees right behind its crumpled form. Drops her blade, clutching her stomach, continues panting loudly.

"Are you okay?" I ask her.

Nodding. "I'm fine," she lies, blood dribbling out of her mouth.

Abi is far more honest. "I-I-I…" she sobs, huge tears streaking, thick snot leaking. "I didn't know. I didn't know! I had no idea they were like that," she bawls. "I had… no idea you could move like that. I didn't know. I didn't know!"

Gorge and his crew rush into the room, but stop after breaching the threshold. What must they think of the sight of us? What a broken, dismal tableau are we.

I kneel beside Abi, feeling the warm puddle growing beneath her legs as it soaks into my pants. She seems even smaller a person when I wrap my arms around her.

And she returns the embrace, tight and frantic. "Thank you," she cries. "Thank you for protecting us from them." Keening for what was left of the world.

Or its wretched inhabitants.

\#

We waited in awkward silence outside the test chamber while Abi recovered and the crew cleaned up the damage. I helped bandage a distant Euly who stood transfixed by some point in the ground, some target deep beneath the floor and beyond my vision. The salve I rubbed into her pink, raw, blood-stippled limbs would reduce the swelling, but not much else.

She'd be sore for weeks after that beating.

I tried to tend to the gash on her forehead, but she kept knocking me away.

"It's going to scar if we leave it," I tell her.

Her eyes scream murder at that unseen target.

"Bear with it."

Hits me again.

"This isn't like last time. It'll heal."

Hits me even harder.

"Euly," I say. "Fucking stop fighting me."

I forced my ministrations on her until the pointless resistance ended. She bit her tongue, furious at the thing only she could see. And after compressing the gash, winding bandages tight, I knew her skin would forget this wound as would she.

Never thanked me, of course.

But that's not what I wanted.

Gorge came out first. Checked on us, obviously satisfied with my work given the profound way he stroked his short beard while looking Euly over. And before Abi trotted out after, he held my hand briefly, strongly, and bowed his head. I smiled up at him, taking in his boulderous girth and tightening my grip to match.

"No problem," I said.

Abi was back to sorts, minus the boundless enthusiasm. Expressed a wish to use me as a variable in the experiment, but admitted the dummy had sustained enough of a beating to warrant diagnostics and repairs. Which might take upwards to a month. Besides, they had plenty of data to work with for a while.

We said our goodbyes, but when we finished I saw that Euly had disappeared.

#

"There you are."

Euly keeps walking.

"It's late. Lunch?"

Keeps walking.

"My treat."

Walking.

"Euly, talk to me."

She grips a lamppost, shudders, then vomits blood everywhere. I rush to her, clutching her shoulders to hold her upright.

Spits the taste away, expression more disappointed than pained. "Tried to hold that in longer. Ah well." And doubles over, puking again. Less blood, but more bile and acid. "Euughh…" Spits. "Damn it…"

"I really wish you'd stop pushing yourself."

"When have I— rehhhp!" Dry heaves. "Cared about your wishes?"

"Never. Can you stand?"

"Give her a second. She feels rotten."

I sit in front of her.

"You're sitting in my blood and sick," she leans against the post for support. "Weird lad."

"Not the only thing that needs washing off me today." I wipe the flecks of spew from her chin. "Why? Could have switched out with me anytime."

Shakes her head, licks her lips. "Had to know. It's a good…" Spits. "Good analogue. We can train with this. Tell the Crone that, if I pass out."

"Sit down, woman, and relax for once."

Flops down without hesitation. Blood splashing when her ass slams into the pool. "I did push myself too much, huh."

"Darting off the walls and ceiling like an insane spider. And after your first few bouts? Come on. None of our bodies can take that kind of strain."

"… might have to," she mutters. "What if they get faster than us?"

"Deal with it then."

"And what if they get stronger than us?"

"They already are."

"You know what I mean."

"We evolve. They don't." I cast the idea aside with a backhand of dismissal.

"I'm not the Executioners' darling because it gets me off, man."

"I know."

"It doesn't."

"I know, but you always act like it does."

Lifts her hand as high as it can go. Which isn't much right now. "Euly's up here. You little buggers are down here." Drops her hand. Probably way more than she meant to. "I set the standard. That... puppet-thingy. Also a standard. Euly approves."

"Done puking?"

"Probably."

"Good." Handing her a vial of pink liquid. "Drink."

"... my bile tastes better, thanks."

"Drink it, mistress furniture."

"Give me a break..." Uncorks the vial and shoots. Grimaces and gags. "Can't tell if I love it or hate it that you always remember absolutely everything I say." Throws the vial away. Then starts laughing, but carefully since it obviously hurts.

"What?"

"In this position," she shakes, "looks like my period exploded out of me."

And I'm the weird one, she says.

#

Night had fallen when Overlook came into view, warm welcoming light streaming out its windows and the dome bright as any beacon. Euly was glum, could only keep down thin potato leek soup, whereas I had had seared boar sandwiches with apple chutney.

A better friend would have felt bad.

But the boar was too juicy and good.

I shall not apologize.

Cold breezes usher us up the trail towards home. A pity that lift system isn't completed yet... but Euly soldiers on, arms crossed and shivering the whole way.

At the top, I see our Technocrat guests playing some sort of board game next to their campfire. One, gloriously defeated, makes an exaggerated show of agonizing death, then yawns, and tramps off to his tent.

Naj dozes at the front desk.

"Want to check us in?" I ask her bobbing head.

"Ch... ch...?" Eyelids flutter, then droop completely. "Choco...? Mmm..."

"Nevermind." I write us in the logbook, then stow our blades in baskets marked for Quartermistress. "Want to try to eat again?"

"Naw, I'm good. Let's clonk out." Stalks away towards the promised beds. Barely awake herself, she lists back and forth like she's on a sinking ship. A sidelong glance at the oversized calendar in the common room rouses her violently. "Oh, come on!"

Krohn had scheduled a meeting for everyone not currently on assignment. In the morning. At daybreak. Promptly. Pain of death, et al.

"Are you seeing this?" Hauls me over, nearly shoving my face into the wall. "Pretends she's not a withered old corpse! Masquerades four times less her age!"

"She's a fiery dame, our Krohn."

Stalks away towards the tainted idea of beds. "This is why I scheduled my debrief for the afternoon. But she knew that," she grouses, "and it's totally why she did this."

"To get at you."

"Yes!" Grits her teeth. "And it's working."

"Sleep in, I'll cover for you."

Silence.

"You mean that?"

"Of course."

"Fine." Takes the corridor for her dorm. Stops. "Hey." Turns, but doesn't look at me. "Got any more styptic?"

"Yeah. Don't you have any in your room?"

"Give it to me."

"I barely have any. Check with Quartermistress."

"Come on. Give it."

"Why don't you have any?"

"Didn't say I didn't."

"Acting like it."

Scowling at my feet. "Can I have it or not?"

I dump two vials into her demanding palm. "Go get checked out if you're still feeling sick. Self-medicating is for retards."

"Thanks, dad."

"Yeah yeah. Goodnight, Euly."

She leaves.

I watch her for a moment, snort, then walk away.

"Leth…"

I pause.

"… goodnight."

Turning back, but she's gone. And, now a shadow without something to follow, I drift my own way towards sleep.

#

Attendance, as huge as it is mandatory, meant we had to shift our meeting to the other common room beneath the dome. Few people were bleary despite the early hour. That's the way of it: either everyone's sleep schedules are inverted from the norm and they're still awake, or we're so used to minimal and interrupted snoozing that it scarcely matters.

But I yawn anyways, hiding in the corner and chewing a soon-to-be-stale biscuit while everyone gets situated.

Krohn waits until the mass of us stops shifting around and chatter lowers to a murmur, then silence. Hardly takes long. She has that kind of countenance.

50

"I won't be brief and I think you understand why," she opens, hands on hips, striking an imposing posture in front of the sprawling map of the province and other faded territories beyond. "As you probably know, I've been in and out of Overlook for a while, dealing with the Sovereignty. Gotten sick of traveling to Old Kingdom, but couldn't be helped after the Dun incident."

"Call it what it is," the spiteful voice of Regin gouging the words. "The Dun clusterfuck-up!" Scratches her inky hair, staring Krohn down, and the way her teeth grind makes me think sparks will shoot out and kindle the room to inferno.

Krohn doesn't flinch; neither does Regin. I haven't talked to her, because I avoid her, but I hear she's... worse... since returning home.

"Semantics aside, Regin, yes. No one benefited from that 'clusterfuck-up'."

"Your flawless plan better take *them* into account," Regin says. "Because *I* have a mausoleum to fix that should have been sealed *this summer*. And now, fuck it all to ashes: winter is quickly creeping up on us, and deepness follows with it."

"I'm going to round up every gravedigger and throw them down a well," Krohn retorts. "Is that what you want to hear?"

"I think it's a start."

"Well that's nice for you," Krohn says, taking a step towards Regin. "But we have more crucial matters to tend to, rather than nuisances to chase."

"They break mausoleums! Hardly minor inconveniences. And now the Dun? The pox-fucked *Dun*!?"

"Gravediggers are weather. Sometimes the rain will pass by in the night. Others, an errant hunk of hail will crack our window." Krohn cocks her head. "Want me to predict the unpredictable? Or focus on executing what I can?"

Regin has no response.

Krohn refocuses attention on the map. "Over the last year we've secured the better portion of burial spaces." Pauses. "I realize that's the incorrect word because many, expressly, aren't secure. But this... *this*," slaps the map, "is our foundation.

"The Sovereignty won't be killing our funding. That's the short of it. You all continue to have jobs and resources. Rejoice."

Silence.

"Good," she says. "Stay grim. I need that. Expect it." Walks over to Regin, grips her shoulder. "I like your determination. It suits you."

Regin makes a funny face, blinks rapidly.

Krohn returns to the map. "We can't do everything, people," she says. Lets the theme descend, seep into our skin. Waits for it to harden into an armor of despair. "But that doesn't mean we can't do anything.

"The next few hours, I'm going to laundry list your tasks. And I want you all to hear it. Each of us needs a unified view of what's to come. Because we all have a part to play in reshaping Old City and on out.

"Firstly, the Sovereignty will be conducting outreach on our behalf to the citizens. Warnings on what cursed tend to look like and especially how they act. The accusations that some people were lobbing around at each other last year were, frankly, unhelpful and dangerous. But I get it: they're scared.

"Next, I want us to engage with the Watch with regards to the gravedigging situation. It would be nice to disinter everybody, take their offerings, and tell our nighttime cousins 'we won, go home', but that's obviously too scorched earth a policy. We can, however, and we will, instruct the watch officers how to be more vigilant. Which they'll need to be because I'm pulling all guard duty from cemeteries."

That gets us buzzing. If she's culling our biggest low-key method of catching a breath after carting, what raging current is she about to plunge us into…

"Lastly, we're allying ourselves closer to the Technocracy. Their primary focus is, and will continue to be, supporting and improving infrastructure as well as recultivation of barren lands."

"Is that working?" Plaintive. Hopeful. Anyone could have asked it.

"No." The word drops like a sledgehammer.

I try cussing under my breath, but nothing comes out.

"One of our joint ventures," Krohn continues without faltering, "is a new training regimen. They've prototyped an artificial cursed, I suppose we can call it. Target practice. And I believe we've completed the first live test. Euliae? Your assessment please." I search the sea of faces. Krohn does too, scanning everyone. "Euliae?" I can't spot her. "Lethean!" I jolt, rigid as the half-eaten biscuit in my fist, and her piercing eyes flare threateningly behind pale strands of white-on-gray.

And suddenly I'm drowning in a room of eyeballs.

"Where is Euliae?" she demands.

Standing at attention. "Indisposed," I tell her. "The testing took a lot out of her. But it's got her nod of approval and I was present. From what I observed—"

"Sod observation, I want a firsthand account. I want them," claws the air at everyone assembled, "to hear it firsthand. Go get her."

"Euly would be the first to say—"

"*Immediately.*"

In life, I find, I'm wedged somewhere between Krohn's intractable and Euly's furious nature.

#

I rush into her dorm without so much as a knock. "If you aren't awake, wake up now." Bathroom and living room unoccupied. "Plenty of coffee in the mess. Hate me later, but hate Krohn first." Whole place pulses with emptiness. Did she slip out? Of course she did. The selfish woman.

I shoot up the ladder.

Euly lies in bed, wheezing, soaked in blood.

"Shit! Hey, hey, are you conscious? Fuck fuck fuck, Euly, what the hell." Nightshirt, covers, floor, pillows. Everywhere, it's fucking everywhere. I take her pulse. It's weak. "Euly, Euly, talk words at me. Come on, wake up."

"Thought I..." Slurs. "Said... goodnight?"

"*Morning*, Euly, it's morning. Shit... you vomited all this up? I told you to— Are you in pain right now?"

"All... what?" Tiny smile, eyes drooping. "Ffff-feel fine. G-goodnight good morning."

I slap her face hard.

No reaction. Opens an eye. "O... oww."

"Damn it, Euly. What happened? When?" I cast around for anything that will visually tell me a story.

There!

One vial, empty. One vial, untouched. I cradle her and inspect her face. Blood coats her mouth. Feels dry, aside from the drool.

"Is this... sexual harassment?" she huffs.

"Shitty sense of humor doesn't mean you're not dying in my arms. Can you tell me what happened or not?"

"H-honest... ly. I'm okay, I'm... fine. Think I'm waking up, you... startled me and I... all groggy and..." Shudders hard. "... stuff."

Looking hard into vacant, foggy eyes. "Yeah, and it's that 'stuff' that's worrying me."

"I... was going sleep and was warm and then I..." Singsong voice. Even drunk she's never like this. "Belly hurt when I pissed although it didn't work and... came back to bed, and— really hurt, Leth! But... um..." Sad sniff. "What was I talking about?"

"After peeing, you came back to bed. What happened next?"

"Ohhh, oh oh. Oh." Frowns. "Puked." Grimaces. "Four times." Blinks rapidly. "And then I drank a styptic passed out and now you say it's morning and Euly confused."

"Why are you talking like that?"

"Like... what?" she asks. "I'm me."

The instant I lay her back down, she starts fussing. Tries to sit up. I press her back, all the while she whines and struggles. Were she not so weak, I'd be the one getting bruised by her. But she won't quit: pushing me, pushing me, trying to push me off.

"Leave Euly alone!"

"Stop it!" I shout an inch from her face.

Stock-still. Paralyzed expression. Terrified whisper. "Don't hurt Euly."

Letting go of her wrists. "I'm not hurting you."

"Are hurting. Don't. Always doing... things against me like that."

"What are you on about? I'm your friend."

Clutches the blood-stained sheets. "It hurts again!"

"Then please stop wriggling your blasted body already! I don't even want to move you to the infirmary." Snatching the unopened vial, holding it out to her. "I'll get someone, but for now: a precaution."

A hesitation, fleeting yet significant. But she complies, shaky fingers encircling the glass and trying to pry it from my grip. I continue to clutch the vial tight. Her look is one of bewilderment and betrayal.

"Promise you drink this and stay here."

"Euly promises."

"You better mean that."

"She does."

"If you don't, I'll beat your ass so hard you won't want to shit for weeks."

"Mean."

"Then don't break your promise to me."

"Mean Lethean."

"So, what are you going to do?"

Scowled silence.

"Take a nap or prepare your ass?"

Tugs the bloody sheet over her mouth. Exhales long and sharp through her nose into the bloody pillow. "... naptime."

"Good girl." Relinquishing my grasp, she takes the vial. I wait until she swallows it before I scamper away, though not before lingering at the base of the ladder. Listening... Listening for movement: the subtext of which is *I'm-a-liar*. Satisfied, I rush towards the infirmary.

#

Of course it's been vacated. Everyone's at the meeting, I don't know why I thought an attendant would be here. Not like anyone is injured and needs tending, save some stupid woman hellbent on suiciding in the most narcissistic way possible.

The cabinets clatter open in my hunt.

Extra bandages for changing... drugs... a random load that I'll have to itemize later with retroactive requests or else incur more Executioner wrath. Way things are going, be surprising if I don't back myself into a corner where everyone's barking at me about something else.

#

I'll return to the common room to fling a heads-up over at Krohn, then ditch back Euly's way before getting hit with reprisal. Happy boss, best boss.

Or something like that.

Either way, she'll be neck-deep handing out assignments. The scornful eye will pass over me... and I can read the docket later, absorb that overview she wanted of us.

"I daresay we'll want to commission a dozen given our numbers, else ask for a staggered shipment to account for wear-and-tear. Rather ripped the crap out of the prototype myself." Euly taps the bandage on her forehead proudly. "Though not before it gave me a good knock, too."

Everyone laughs. The jest even eliciting a half-smile from Krohn.

"Ohhh that blasted sense-forsaken, accursed parasitic—" I seethe, only running out of words from lividity's sake.

"Pretty exciting, Boss!" Arroyo edges through the crowd to me, failing to keep her voice as politely low as she surely intends. "Jeeeealouuus. Love that the speed is variable so a nub like me won't freak out and curl into a ball. Ummm, what's with the med supplies? You hurting?"

"My fist is about to."

"Boss?"

"How long has she been prancing around up there?"

"Euliae? Ah, a few minutes I guess. Interrupted Krohn's assigning work something grand! You should've seen it." And then downcast. "Didn't get to me yet..." Glances up shyly. "Hope we're working together again."

"Turns out I might need a new partner soon. Rush funeral tonight." I *know* she can see me. I can *tell* she's purposefully avoiding my sight as she whips up a detailed account of the events, her thoughts, her feelings, her—!

"Eeef. You guys fighting again?"

"In conclusion," Euly flourishes, rustling a handful of papers, "I'm spending the day transposing my illegible notes. But what I saw yesterday was very, very promising."

Excitable drone from the crowd. Definitely offset from the mood we opened with earlier.

Krohn is pleased. Basking, I'd hazard. "Very good, Euliae. Thank you. I look forward to poring over your report in full tonight."

Euly makes a salute with the papers, then bleeds back into the crowd. Clearly of the intent to flee.

"Now, let's return to the former matter," Krohn says.

When Euly is in range, she flashes me a brilliant smile. All teeth. My fingers bite into her bruised arm and rip her out into the hallway. Arroyo dithers in my passing, torn between staying put or chasing after.

Probably better she doesn't hear this. I'm rarely venomous.

"Give me *one* reason why I don't cane your ass to bleeding and a darker shade purple than the rest of your ravaged body!"

"Enough with the irritated partner schtick. And let GO!"

Jerks away and rubs her arm. Following me, but at a pronounced distance.

"Do promises mean nothing to you?"

"Given or got?"

"Nevermind, I'm sure it's all the same to you," I snort. "Well, Krohn seemed happy."

"True, though she was surprised to see me," Euly says. "Did you tell her something?"

"Said you were indisposed."

"You what!"

"Well, yeah."

"Fool!" she shouts. "In front of them? You said that?"

I stand in her way. "Okay, that's my line."

But she walks around without pause.

"Fool!"

"That's it then, huh? Going to studiously sit at your desk the rest of the day like nothing happened, beautify your notes there?"

"No, I'm gonna dictate because the bogus papers in my hand are blank except for the random scribbles on the first few pages." Chuckles at her rampant cleverness. "I'm good."

Bitter laugh. "Did you forget everything? What happened yesterday? How you were this morning? That's magically gone, is it?"

Rounds a corner, far from the common room and any other room for that matter. Stops. Leans against the window. Outside, the clouds are roiling.

"No, Lethean. I haven't." Deep breath. Long, long sigh.

I take a moment to calm down. Finally one of those respites when we can stop crashing into our assumptions and talk, and listen, and actually reach one another.

"I'm not your enemy," I tell her.

"I know," she says, nodding.

"And I'm not attacking you. I want to understand you," I tell her.

"And I get that," she says, folding her arms.

"So, do you want me to ignore you when you're actively slitting your wrists? Or are you content to slash them open, then have me rush over in blind panic, and bind the wounds while you pretend you're indestructible."

Sardonic smile. Fingers the scar cut through her face. "Not indestructible, my man…"

"But you know what I mean."

"Yeeahh…" Another deep breath and sigh. "I know what you mean."

"So, which is it?"

Slaps the papers into my chest until I take them. "Look. I was planning on hiding in bed all day, alright? And have you take the notes. If you bring me soup, I'll be a good lass and obey you, and only ask for a heavy late dinner tonight of red meat and cookies to replenish the blood loss, which I'll concede was…" Pauses. "… waiting over here for your snarky adjective, I know you have one."

"Worrisome," I tell her.

Jolts a bit. Expression softening. "Really?"

"Yes, really."

"Oh. Well. I guess… I can see that."

"Yeah."

"I'm sorry I worried you," she tells me.

I shrug. "It's okay. Do better next time."

"Not gonna lie, I am ready to drop. Phew. Once I woke up fully, it was pure adrenaline. Heh." Weary, but radiant smile. "They were majorly excited about that puppet-thingy. I felt the whole room lift up!"

"I'm sure it did. Arroyo was pumped."

"Yeah," she says. "Yeah! I was thinking about her. Whoa…" Steadies herself against me. "Really felt that, we should hurry."

"I've got you. You're okay."

"I feel cold."

"It's okay, I've got you."

"Phew. It… it passed, but let's hurry."

"Bed, soup, visit from nurse, nap, and then notes later. Agreed?"

"Agreed, but remember the dinner plans."

"I do. I will."

"Thanks."

The sound of our footsteps echoes through the corridor. A little halting, but close together and resounding their own intertwined pattern against the solid stone.

"And thanks. For…" Voice trailing off. Instead, she takes my hand for a few seconds.

::All things::

#

Over the week, my partner and sometimes friend Euliae improved. I won't say recovered. Don't trust her enough to know if the outward gilding ever reflects the inner core. But she clearly needed the time to sort out unspoken turmoil as well as the obvious battering she had sustained during the test.

Tonight she stole a self-proclaimed "free day" from Krohn's plan -- which had never accounted for Euly's willful downtime to begin with.

But then… they never do.

"Ehh, what's another day matter? It's not like the world's ending," Euly smirks as she slips out the entrance.

Overlook was hollow. Everyone gone on assignment, aside from a skeleton crew. They too would slip away soon, once the final group -- us -- lit out into a land growing colder by the day. Regin was definitely right about that: winter was stirring, vexed prematurely from torpor as if by some unknown, unknowable hand.

So much for fall.

Arroyo is braiding her hair. I finish a thin, milkless hot chocolate and stare at the glowering northern range out the dome.

"Not the same, is it?" I ask.

Eyes her own untouched mug. "Rations eat my ass."

"But," I tap her shoulder, "field rations are ironically better."

"Oh geez, you're— No. Just… no." Takes a sip. "Wefff, unimpressed. It's easy for you to say. Vet and all."

"None of us are veterans." My lower spine pops when I stand and make for the stairs.

"Heard that, mister vet."

"Har har," I say. "My bones crack if I haven't moved much. Not an age thing, they've done that since childhood."

Peers at me over the balcony. "Sounds like a crossbow blast to me."

I lift my leg dramatically, bend the ankle. *Krkkknkk!*

"Gross," she says, but then laughs delightedly. "You're weird, Boss." Drinks deep. "Hahhh… but anyway, *you* can say that being used to it. Fact is, no more hot meals. No noodles. No rice. Or grilled meats. Fresh veg and fruits are out. Pastries, a fading memory on an unending, dried meal breeze. Listen to it blow. *Fuuuuuu. Fuuuuuu.*"

"Not like we're hiking across the Gap. There will be towns. Fresh food."

"Maybe, but like you say. Not the same, though, is it?"

"Won't you miss adventuring with your partner?" I call from the kitchen, scrounging for anything with actual taste.

"Sure, he's fun. But I get it. We have different skills and he's needed with his new group." That's how the words come out, but she sounds depressed. Hopefully this is just Future Arroyo pining for meals-long-past.

Fallout from the meeting was simply this: Krohn was shifting all the pieces on the board because in her arrogant presumption, and she's very probably right, she believed she could single-handedly orchestrate controlling the entire map.

Newer recruits, and those with less physical aptitude, would stay around Old City and Old Kingdom. That latter group would involve plenty of skilled Executioners, so the inspection and maintenance of Crypt Dun -- as Euly fearfully noted as critical -- would go forward. Krohn was going to see to that personally, I heard later.

Pauper's Pit, its unnamed dun, as well as Parkside Dun and Sepulcher Hill would receive like treatment; the only addendum being that everyone heretofore assigned to the Pit would stay on with the additional hands.

The open secret of it was...

The open sore of it was...

The open wound of it was...

... that Pauper's Pit remained the clusterfucked imminent catastrophe we've always known it to be. I'm sure we've one of our ranks playing historian down at Archives to uncover who first dug that place. Too late to kill whoever it was, but hey, we could at least spit on his or her grave, right?

Even so, we might see a scrap of hope of sealing that particular tragedy away for good soon.

But the rest of us...?

We're Krohn's vanguard.

(the Savior Tyrant's scalpel)

We're the Crone's pallbearers.

(the Destroyer of Healers' tourniquet)

"Boss?"

Wow. Someone left behind a spiced apple.

"Deep question time."

Damn. This is good. Why is stolen food so good…

Winding my way back upstairs. Victorious. I drop next to Arroyo, who hasn't found the nerve to pretend that liquid masquerading as a drink *is*.

"Shoot."

Asks it point blank. "What are we even doing here?"

"I'm assuming you aren't asking about the Euly running away thing, hence," I gesture at us, the otherwise vacant room, "and I'll guess this is no existential crisis either."

"Us. You and me. All of us, Executioners and the friends helping us on the outside. What's our objective?" she asks.

Mulling it over. "Fighting death."

"… we can't fight that."

"Of course we can. We're really good at it."

"Boss, we have thousands and thousands of death sleeping scant miles away in a broken Crypt Dun. That's not fighting! We're just…" Drowns herself in dilute chocolate. "Aw heck, we're just putting our faith in practices we *think* work and hoping they stay asleep. How's that being 'really good at it'?"

"What's your chocolate doing to you?"

"Bumming me out."

"What's this stolen apple doing to me?"

"Eeef, you stole that? Don't steal, Boss. Gravediggers do that."

"All I'm suggesting, Arroyo," I reply, "is that we're fighting death every moment. Food pushes away starvation. Exercise kicks back disease. The myriad things that sustain us -- physically, mentally, emotionally… things so minor on their own they're basically meaningless -- these myriad motes of dust are holding back a tidal wave of oblivion. Every single second."

Her nose fidgets.

"Well, okay, but that wave is gonna engulf everything one day. Already has!"

"So the bitch is tenacious and *wins* a battle against a shriveled prune with bad eyesight, worse hearing, and no ability to get a boner." I toss an apple seed over the railing. "What zealous victory is that?"

Barks a laugh. "Oh man, I hadn't thought of it quite that way before."

"I know it's different now. It's worse."

"It really is, Boss..."

"Life has changed, but living hasn't."

"... living hasn't changed..." she repeats to herself.

"But we're still here."

"We are, aren't we?"

"And I know it hurts."

"It really does, Boss..."

"You asked me... a question I ask too, but one I ask differently." I swallow the flesh of the apple. "The impossibility of it. Of *this*. This consciousness that is me. The consciousnesses that we choose to call Arroyo and Euliae... The odds of everyone, their chance impossibility that should not be yet is. What are we, who shouldn't exist, even doing here?"

Arroyo bites her lip. Looks down at her folded hands. Nods once, nods twice, and promptly chugs the chocolate. "Fighting death, Boss!" she cries.

"Hell, this thing we're fighting, maybe in a queer way we're birthed out of it. It's our perverse mother that desperately wants us back in the womb."

"Mom really *is* a bitch."

"Screw you, mom."

"Leave us alone, we're not done playing!"

"Do your own damn chores!"

"Whoa, did you say that to yours?"

"Nope," I smile. "What's the worst thing you ever said?"

"'Fuck you, I'm joining the Executioners 'cause I believe in them and myself. Unlike you. So fuck off forever!'"

I'm waiting for the punchline.

Arroyo brushes a loose hair out of her face.

I wait in vain.

"Wow," is all I can muster.

"Mmhm."

"Never knew you had that in you."

"Yeah, me neither, Boss. I never use that kind of language, but I guess when our backs are up against it… we push through to the other side."

#

Departure.

Arroyo was up at false dawn, pacing outside my room until I eventually came out, half-asleep, to ask if she sincerely wanted to evaporate the goodwill I currently bore towards her personage.

"Go back to bed" -- the words that bled out.

Her excitement insisted "go time!" and rather than ignoring my command she was completely oblivious to it, tramping on in, gathering things that I don't believe I asked her to gather for me while I continued to explain to her the premature interruption she had caused and that she needed to take responsibility as any adult would.

"Seriously, go away" -- the words said.

She didn't.

#

I yawned at the door. Arroyo knocked lightly. The result was immediate: Euly threw it open and came out, backpack hugging her shoulders. All ready.

"Morning!" Arroyo bounced.

"Good morning, Arroyo," Euly smiled softly. "Morning, Leth."

Desperately rubbing sleep away. "What is with you ladies this morning…"

"Places to be, man," Euly says, checking pockets by tapping them like a drum.

"Loading up on supplies is fun," Arroyo explains, leading us, constantly hopping around, walking backwards and chatting, very nearly a pirouetting top.

And it's as effective a stimulant as it is charming and infectious. At breakfast when I reach for the coffee, I instead pass on by and pour pulpy juice.

This will be my last straight sugar for a long while.

Might as well make it a thing.

#

Quartermistress gathers our things the instant we enter her station. Without a word of greeting, she sorts through a chaos of paraphernalia strewn about opened cabinets, pitched-over barrels, and all along the well-loved repair table. Although years old and rarely given downtime, her esoteric tools and mechanisms gleam untarnished.

Out of everyone at Overlook -- scratch that, out of everyone in our organization -- I've tried the most to befriend this aberration of humanity.

Nothing about her belongs.

Anywhere.

For anything.

Skin mottled and discolored, pronounced by the harsh light she insists on surrounding herself in. An ad hoc blindfold, wrapped around her head without care.

"Never have slept," she told me once, randomly. I wondered what she was referring to. Herself? Perhaps it was the extent to which she was capable of communicating emotion. Neither appearing tired nor alert, she simply existed in one unending moment.

"Everything in order," she proclaims, filling baskets Naj had stacked neatly atop the counter.

"Ahh, my love~" Arroyo says, stroking the returned blade. Euly and I stifle our shared laugh: those two, still on honeymoon.

While we arm ourselves and fill our backpacks, Quartermistress nudges a basket towards Euly. Pensively. Carefully.

"New blade and hilt," she croaks.

Euly makes a face. "I thrashed it that bad? Unnghh, feels gross."

"Your grip…" Pantomimes claws raking, then squeezing the air as though an unprotected neck. "Very damaging. Specialized hilt, different design and material. Will compensate."

"Are you sure? This is a liability if we get into it straight out."

"More liability to not adapt."

"This is like telling me to write with my left hand. I can't do it."

Quartermistress puts the baskets away. Not stacked, or together. "You will. Better design. You'll see."

"Come on, give me my old one as a spare. I was used to it."

"No. It's no good."

"I can switch when it snaps."

"No good. No good."

"Fine." Euly sheathes it. "Unnnhh, it even *sounds* different."

"Quieter."

"Looks like we're outfitted," I note. And then to Quartermistress: "We'll need replacement kindling."

She blushes. Adjusts the blindfold, her one cloudy eye darting everywhere. "Supplies exhausted." Motioning awkwardly at the wall. "Gave them out. Final shipment went missing."

"Missing? How's that possible?" I ask.

Quartermistress raises shoulders and then drops them noncommittally. This might be the extent she can offer a showing of being upset. "Stolen."

Arroyo isn't having it. "But it's worthless to anyone not us!"

"People get desperate," Euly taps on the counter, monotone. "I could see thieves selling it to anyone cursed-panicking. 'Throw this in your lantern at night!'" Mimics a hawker. "'Keep your family safe throughout the dark times and deepness!' or something."

"Perhaps," says Quartermistress. "Troubling to happen before everyone left."

"Any other acts of thievery I don't know about?" Euly presses.

"No. Isolated incident and one safeguards are being made against."

"Fair enough, but that screws us. You have nothing?"

Quartermistress spreads her arms weakly, as if to invite us to scrounge around like famished rabbits should we be so moved.

"You shouldn't have used them all," I say.

"'I told you so, Euly, you idiot-child,'" she mocks, mimicking my voice now. "Yeah, I shouldn't have. Man, always something hitching us…" Turns to me. "It'll be out of the way, but let's drop by Pauper's Pit." And to Quartermistress: "Can you sign off on that requisition?"

She thinks. Cloudy eye darting again.

"Yes. Krohn will need to sign it too."

Euly fumes.

"What did you expect," I say.

"Yeah, I know, I know! Just… don't want to see her. She always finds a way to spoil the joy of setting out."

"It's because she loves you so much."

"I don't want love," Euly says. "I want to be ignored the way this one does." Takes the signed requisition form from

Quartermistress who has already busied herself with some abstract repairs.

The long road south.

If you take the correct unmarked sidestreets, technically it's possible to walk all the way from the corpse road where Crypt Dun lies and reach one of the entrances to the Royal Catacombs way down in Old Kingdom. Assuming you have legal passage, of course, which nowadays would be us and us alone.

This is one of those repetitious thoughts I think whenever I walk this route. Reminds me of how I started in the Executioners.

Reminds me how interconnected we are to the city.

To each other.

"How was your gig last night?" I ask Euly.

"Hmm?" Lost in thought. "Oh. It was good."

"A final celebration before the quiet of the outdoors."

"What?"

"A final celebration," I say. "Before we set out."

"Oh. Yeah, basically."

"You should announce them!" Arroyo chides. "I'd love to go, but I never know when it happens."

"Aw, you're cute."

"Not being cute. I mean it!"

Euly chuckles. "I know, but it's cute. Aw, you can come. I'm not gonna make an announcement though."

"Why not?" I ask.

"Why not?" Arroyo echoes.

"Ehnnnn. Kinda… don't want anyone there, to be honest. From work, I mean. It's my downtime. People have an infuriating tendency to not divorce one from the other… when it comes to me."

Embarrassment. "I only did that once."

"Not talking about you, man."

"Who's bothering you?" Arroyo asks.

"Ahhgngnn," Euly growls. "I hate talking about stuff like this. No one gets what I'm saying."

I glance at her.

"So, say it then."

Silence.

"Wanna let go," she says. "Briefly. Of everything." Makes as if to kick a rock, then stops herself. Instead, she veers off the thoroughfare and away from the market stalls and food carts.

The alleyways are damp and mossy. A warren of rabbits parts lazily for us, most too engrossed with pruning the walls to take any notice. It's peaceful when we near the widening edges of the city, broken only by our boots and the passage of a message-runner going in the opposite direction.

And over that threshold where the city ends and the wide world truly begins, we tramp out into rolling, roiling grasslands.

Without Arroyo.

Hands folded, she regards the division between this from that. "Suddenly, I feel naked... without a cart. Is that weird? Feels comforting... protective... behind that yoke. I mean, everything we've done has been... carting. That's been my world since I joined. But... now..." Expression crushed beneath the growing expanse of horizon. "The world is my world."

What could I possibly tell the girl?

What could Euliae?

Arroyo's recognition is an awakening we all stir to eventually. Life exposes itself to us; the recognition is made. The choice, if there is one, is to drop our defenses and allow it to do what it will. She won't change in this moment. But Arroyo will finally be on the path towards it.

Quick-minded person, it dawns on her instantly:

"We're on a journey."

It came with a single step. With a gentle rustle of grass. The wind paused, listening. Arroyo, our youngest Executioner, crossed the threshold and entered into the world.

#

"Asking for the impossible, Euliae," the sour and distracted Executioner is explaining, unfortunately for him in that kind of pedantic tone that makes her murderous. "We're getting the newcomers ready as we speak. Hell and cinders, I need to get down there right now myself."

"Quartermistress." Euly nearly pokes a hole in the requisition. "The Crone." Each poke threatening to rip and make the authenticity questionable.

"And I'm telling you, it's not a matter of the order. We're running low."

"Rabbitcrap, man! You incinerate more kindling in a single day than the three of us ever will in our lifetimes!"

Carts are rolling in ceaseless procession from Pauper's Pit to the nearby dun while the sky is overcast. If it remains that way, the carting will continue far into night and on into the next day, and so on. Even under daylight, the dull smolder of cobalt that pulses out of that colossal, gaping pit is hypnotic.

The breeze it emits is a frigid winter blast.

Arroyo shivers.

I'm glad she wasn't assigned here. Unless we extract all those corpses perfectly, this will be ground zero of Old City's destruction. And as much a transparency-maven as Krohn is, *that* is one trapdoor of information we don't want cracking open beneath us.

In the deepest, longest portions of night, I have watched the lights of Pauper's Pit. It feels as though the gateway to a distant, ethereal land where we do not belong. A doorway we should never have opened.

Wasn't us that cracked it, though.

Nor left it ajar…

The cowed Executioner relents, leaves for the pit with the requisition begrudgingly tucked in a voluminous pocket. He returns fifteen minutes later with a packet.

Euly tears it open, counting each piece like a miser. "Seriously!?" she snarls. "Ten? Not even, this one's busted! Nine. You're sending me off plague-knows-where with nine!?"

He pockets the broken kindling, then exchanges it for one of his own. Wipes his hands dismissively. "We done?"

"Ten... Ten..." she grouses, passing out three to me and four to Arroyo. "I hope I get to inter that punk one fine day."

"Hey," he calls after us.

Euly catches the torch midair, barely looking. "Don't need another."

"Flick it on."

She obliges, twists the base, and with a sly hiss an azure flame bursts silently out the other end. "Huh."

"The Techs, they called it a prototype for a much larger system. We aren't using them yet. Untested and probably unreliable for a few iterations. Still."

Euly stows it. "Fair enough."

And now, after this detour, we're setting out. Our normal lives behind us. Shouldering provisions, livelihood clinging to our backs, and we go.

Into unprotected reaches.

Into the wild emptinesses, autumn's coming weeks beating like an unheard death knell somewhere below the horizon line for which we aim.

Such an ugly thought it's almost beautiful.

#

Our goal sits not in the midpoint of the province, but the dead center of what territory is actually under Executioner control. Had last year's efforts not been hampered by an early and brutal deepness, the various random disruptions inherent in life, and gravedigger problems at home and surprisingly around Crossroads, those two geographic points may have been the same.

But they aren't, so we make do.

And our new home?

Echo Downs.

An unassuming city by both name and location, but the hills that border it are rife with quality stone. The kind that makes us salivate... more enduring than what gets colloquially labeled as "Executioner grade" and claimed, by Technocracy testing at least, to become mostly transparent under certain, measured conditions.

I'm badly quoting that last bit.

Sounds like too much of a good thing to be accurate, still... whenever I give them the benefit of the doubt, those goggled weirdos never fail to impress.

With a population second only to Old City itself, Downs proved too great the temptation to Krohn. So she sent her most belovedly hated daughter to lay the foundation of a new burial network that would stretch across all our territory.

A new hub for the world of the dead.

"This is a plan I can get behind," Euly replies to Arroyo's question about her unusual heel-turn, considering her fury when we learned about the Dun break-in.

"Given the not inconsiderable and, um, inexhaustible list of things to do around the City?" Arroyo hops over another dandelion in her path.

Euly laughs. "Listen to this one, Leth. She totally wasn't ready to leave."

"Was too."

The unconvincing grumble.

"Krohn just wants you gone," I tell Euly.

"Oh please."

"Throws us out in the middle of nowhere."

"I'm the lynch-pin!"

73

We share a stupid look and start laughing. Arroyo, not really getting it, tries to share in. But she doesn't understand our complicated relationship or its friction. And neither do I. And neither, I suspect, does Euliae.

"But in all seriousness," she tells us, glancing first at me and then Arroyo, "she will by the time we're back when she learns I forged her signature."

"Holy crap, you did *not*!" Arroyo blanches.

"Of course I didn't," Euly smirks, "and there's your plausible deniability."

"Holy holy crap, Boss, this lady is *a menace*!"

"I'm sorry you got thrown in with us subversives, Arroyo," I say in approximation of how an apology should be formed.

"Ehh, wait. Did she? Or didn't she?"

"I didn't, I didn't. Don't wanna give you any impression that's permitted." Euly goes stern and teacherly. "Be a good girl, Arroyo."

"I am!"

"Good, keep doing that."

"Even if you say so... feels like you guys are bullying me."

"A little," I say. "Mutual abuse is the hallmark of deep affection."

"*What*!?"

Euly hits my chest. "Ahhh! Now I understand why you're such the glutton for punishment. It all makes sense!"

Our orders were fluid. We'd take over from the several dozen Executioners stationed in Downs and... start mapping and allocating resources for a web of corpse roads? Burrow out a maze of catacombs to rival the depth and breadth of Old Kingdom? Or would we, piling hubris upon hubris, figure out a viable way to deliver on Krohn's wet dream: a monumental underground corpse road that crisscrosses the entire province?

Hard to say.

These are the questions that will occupy us the long month of many footfalls to come. For now, we can enjoy the chill air and irreverence of camaraderie. The forest has come into view, sanguine scarlet and pumpkin orange, a joyful riot. Autumn's staggering display, the final middle finger jousting at the nostril of winter's upturned nose.

What color will these same trees be when we return home next year?

Difficult work surely lies ahead, but I look forward to the autonomy. Though she'd never admit the comparison, Euliae will shortly be a new Crone of her own running her own little Overlook. Just as fired up, self-righteous and bitterly indignant that no one is as perfect as she.

You'd wonder who these madwomen -- and madman -- were if you saw us, trudging across the land as we are seemingly without a care. You mightn't recognize us without a cart: the metonym of our trade. But the black-and-crimson scarves tied around our arms always give us away.

Although...

Skulking about graveyards usually does too.

Which is how everyone tends to view us.

Kinda sad.

I trip on an exposed root when we enter the forest, the jolt shocking me from the maze of thoughts I spiral into. Euly snorts good-natured derision.

A carpet of dead and dying leaves becomes our path, as we meander deeper in and farther south than I've been in years. Streaming sunlight is cracked by the roof of branches overhead -- the resulting fractures playfully wavering back and forth on us, fueled by an ignorant gust.

The first night out always falls quickest. Arroyo's slumping shoulders and her sudden loss of pep signal this fact an hour before gloaming.

"Not yet, I can keep going, Boss," she pouts.

And so she did until we made camp a few hours later, nestled within an ancient oak hollowed by lightning. She was asleep before she hit the ground.

"Poor thing," Euly clucks.

"Nfffff ahhhhn ffff," Arroyo breathes fitfully, then stops squirming.

Silence.

"Long day," I say.

"First of a longer line," Euly says, lighting the fire while I roll out sleeping bags.

"We're making a bee-line, then?"

Her look: pure ridicule and faux seduction. "Oh hoh, dreaming of your long-lost love? Your sweetest honey?"

"Puns don't become you, Euly. You're no poet."

"Whoa!" Taken aback to the extent that hurt flashes. "Hey. Hey. No. You did *not* say that."

"You are not punny. Ever."

"Oh no, oh no no no. I'm not letting you sneak away from that stab. You said I wasn't a poet! I heard you."

"But you aren't."

"Shouldn't have got that kindling when I can just use you…" she mutters. Then snarling: "Lethean!"

"Yeah."

"That was a real shitty thing to say. To me."

"You seriously style yourself a poet?"

"I don't *style* myself one, but I use poetry all the time."

"Well, I'm not saying you don't do that."

"Oh." Finishes setting broken hunks of bark around the flame, sits back. "I thought you were sniping at me, or something like that."

"I basically don't," I say, "though I probably should start. Why are you on edge?"

She thinks. "Ummm. Dunno. I feel…" Flops back, legs spread. "Distracted. Oh, right, yes, because we are bee-lining -- what is wrong with you that was a good joke you're so sensitive -- and I'm not planning side trips." Kicks at the slow-starting fire. "I guess you expected me to… roam?"

"I wondered."

"Not this time."

"Good."

"You think so?"

"I know you'd work yourself up into a lather and go insane."

"I wonder…"

"We're not on an interment trip. Not yet, at any rate."

"Ah. I don't think you're being very fair to me. That was that, this is this."

"You conflate those a lot."

"Do I?"

"A lot."

"I… guess I might. But we had the extra room."

"Barely."

"And it felt dangerous. Anyways. Bee-line." Flaps her hands spastically, replacing the mask of faux seduction. "Buzz buzz."

"So we'll hit Downs in a few weeks."

Her eyebrows raise. Then she wrinkles her nose, an expression that makes her face gnarled and ghastly. But that's her scar's fault. It used to be cute when she did this. "A month. And a week addition, maybe. No need to rush."

I chuckle and she dons that offended scowl again. "You hate winter. Summer is your season."

Starts chewing on rabbit jerky. "Summer *is* my season. I'm a sunny woman." Chews in thought. "It makes my heart sunny." Swallows. "I think I get seasonal depression. Like you."

"I love autumn and winter."

"Serious?"

"You obviously weren't listening when I was explaining it."

"Sounds like me." Swallows another mouthful, then shoves more in. "Whaf waf if?"

"At the end of the day," I explain. "About half-an-hour when the sun is going down. My energy slacks, not exactly melancholy, I'm... not... there. Unless I'm working. But even so, once it's nighttime I'm fine."

"Weirf."

"Yeah."

"Alwayf wike dhaf?"

"Yep."

Swallows, searches for a drink. "Huh. Interesting."

I get up. "I don't think that's enough wood for the night."

"Huh? Oh. Okay, thanks."

When I return, arms full, she's staring up at the flickering shadows on the branches. Not trying to sleep yet, just watching. I'm about to start up conversation again when she starts humming to herself, periodically singing a phrase or a lone word between breaths, her scratchy voice softened by the low, quiet intensity.

"... darkling weighted world... she's adrift... hmm hmm hmm~ far afield and roaming... something something mmm mmm~ things... painted things... No. Pained things? Woeful? No, that's a dumb word." Settles back into the pillow. "Hmm hmmm~ weighted world... she's adrift... hmm hmm hmm~ things... fall..."

I listen while I drift away -- while we both do in our own wont -- and linger on the sad notes she whispers at the deepening night, wondering... wondering why a grief supersaturates every word this furious, sunny-hearted woman composes, every melody she ever sighs.

We search the graves of the world for the cursed.

Perhaps she casts down into her heart for the right words, the right melodies, that will sing a song of joyousness. But instead this... *this* is what she dredges back up out of the thick filth and piling rot of existence.

And yet, she reaches.

It continues to elude her.

And yet, she reaches.

I suppose... we're both obsessed... I suppose... we're both reaching for a thing we cannot grasp we cannot keep...

And yet...

(... and yet.)

"Things fall apart," she sings.

\#

Arroyo always led. As days piled into the first week, she was the first one awake and munching down breakfast, the first on her feet and charging forward into the blighted unknown that had, so briefly, balked her for that one solitary pause.

No matter now. She hops along to the irregular beat of her own gleeful heart.

"This stuff smells *great*!" she announces, squishing a mossy collection of forest matter underfoot. She is a city girl, but her spirit is dyed the color of nature. Font of energy as she is, it's clear that the further we travel off the well-worn paths, the more enraptured she becomes.

At a time when no one travels anymore, Arroyo's bounce... her pirouettes... her arms-spread-wide glory... I stop seeing the girl herself.

I see a fleeting image of a tomorrow where everyone is as her:

Free.

Of grief.
Of despair.
Of resignation.

In this instant, she is renamed:

Hope.

::Leth did good::

I'm not sure Euly registers my shocked expression. Surely I misread that. But before she lets go...

::Thanks:: I sign back.

"Yep," she says.

#

Arroyo violated travel protocol.

"If certain someones can forgery…"

"Totally didn't."

"… then *I* can bring these!"

"How did this recalcitrance rub off on her so easily?"

"She's a sponge."

"A menacing sponge."

"No! *She* is the menace. I'm keeping our spirits up!"

And it worked.

While we chatted idly during the day amongst ourselves, or debated the finer points of our looming work, Arroyo taught us a card game and board game she had smuggled in her backpack.

"Eeef. Didn't smuggle it," she laments, "I snuck it."

"How is that any better framed?"

Throws arms up in defeat. "Boss, if I'm gonna get caught I might as well own it!"

Euly quietly reads the instruction paper, whispering the odd word to herself.

"What are you so intent on?" I ask her.

"I'm going to win," she says to herself, but so flat is the emotion and adamant the confidence that even Arroyo unexpectedly wilts.

"Okay, let's do a quick game first. This one's easy." Brushing braid over shoulder, assumes the aspect of teacher. I won't mention how uncommandingly adorable the attempt. "We each get our leader card and three spell cards. Then we go around drawing troop cards and personality cards, which have both merits and demerits. I like to call them 'quirk cards'. Spell cards are exhaustible and don't replenish; be careful using them. Also your leader can be used to take damage from other leaders or troops, but…!" And her silly

80

flourish forces me to stifle a laugh because she's clearly being deathly serious. "If your leader dies, you lose!"

I lose a lot over the coming evenings, though I finally start eking out victories once I grasp how to strategically place my cards on defense. Euly tends to fling her spells around like they're trash she can't rid herself of soon enough, an aggression that has her winning more often than not.

Her insistence on beating me first is pretty damn annoying, too.

"I'm not even a threat to you," I complain.

Euly scowls. "Yet."

And so I find that, unless I'm lucky and draw the angelic leader card, defeat yawns its jaws in my direction.

Master of *Fateful Order* I'm not likely to become anytime soon, but I do marginally better with *Sneaks and Scammers*.

"Ohhh, I like this one." Arroyo wiggles, setting up the board and accidentally knocking pieces to the ground in her excitement. "It's really interesting 'cause, okay get this, there's a built-in rudimentary intelligence! The guards act on their own based on what we're doing."

"This is *cooperative*?" Euly's utter disappointment.

"Mmff, there's a versus mode, but it's like… kinda broken."

The object of this particular game, rather than bringing destruction upon each other's heads, is to slip from shadow to cover, pilfering goods and money from various environments. Which was all good clean fun until I drew a special card ironically named "Respect for the Dead".

I clear my throat. "Arroyo…"

"Yeah, Boss."

"Is this game pro-digger?"

"Uhh."

"Is it?"

"Uhhhhhhhhh…"

81

Euly seizes the deck and sorts through everything, flicking offending cards out into a worryingly sizeable pile.

Arroyo regards our stern faces, at first shrinking from the sorted cards then snapping back. "It's not propaganda!"

"I don't like that it makes a game of it," Euly says with finality.

"But it's *just* a game!"

"None of this shit's a game."

"You don't have to tell me that, ma'am..." Arroyo's head drops.

"Maybe some other time, Arroyo," I offer. "It's a fun game, but it's late and—"

"I know I haven't seen it yet." Arroyo says this so faintly, we would have missed it if not for the absolute silence of these uninhabited woods. "I've seen them from a... distance, well, we all did during training. But... but... *fuuu*. You two are... *good*. Cursed get dispatched instantly when you're around. There's no time to... haaah... I don't know, don't know what I'm saying." Quick glance up at Euly's steely eyes. "I know it's serious. That's why... I'm here."

"You don't understand how many kids I've seen, hell, supposedly mature adults too, who want to play adventure. Swords and glory, or some historical fantastical bullshit. The idiots desert and the fools die."

"Arroyo isn't remotely like them, Euly."

"No. It's okay, Boss. I got this." Arroyo packs the game away. "Euliae. Ma'am. You're stuck with me. I'm not budging until we see this dross to the end, whichever way of it. I like playing games. Real games, not work stuff. I like our work. I have fun. But that fun is way, way different than the kind we were playing at before. So I don't appreciate you getting mad at me, but I respect it and where you're coming from. And I hope you can pay me that courtesy too. 'Cause I'm on your side." Finishes buckling and tightening her backpack. "Both you and Boss."

"Dang," Euly breathes. "Wish you could teach Lethean half your spine."

"Hey."

"It's true, though, this girl ain't flinching."

"I flinched a little." Rubs her freckled nose. "Plus, I'm sorta just quoting things I've overheard Boss saying to you. Mostly. But I mean them."

"Well. Okay then. You've always been attentive. And I believe you. Sorry if I was being a bitch."

Silence.

"Teach me how to get her to say that to me," I tell Arroyo.

"Fuck you, Lethean."

The tension cracks a bit, thankfully.

"What is the worst thing you've seen so far?" Euly asks Arroyo. "Probably should have asked you that before."

"Haven't," Arroyo admits. "Heard real scary stuff though. Like, one time before I joined you guys, I stumbled upon someone being killed by a cursed."

"Where was that?"

"Crossroads. I was all gung-ho enthusiast about joining. Set out to reach Avershym."

This is news to me. "Why Avershym? We barely have anyone stationed there, even as of last year."

"Sure, but I didn't know that. I thought if I could prove I could get all the way out there, I'd prove my resolve."

Euly smiles. "Honestly, we would have taken you anyways."

"Way to crush an old dream, ma'am."

"Welcome. What happened next?"

"He was screaming and I could hear him being beaten... so loud and hard, each impact silenced him a split-second. Not ashamed to say it scared me so much I ran back home and didn't stop 'til I passed out on the front porch."

"You ran through the night?"

"Turns out I have crazy stamina when my own little life is coming to an end." Shakes herself. "Know what? That's not even what scares me the most. It's that *silence*. The fact that cursed make *no noise*, just that... *sllllp slllp slllp* of their feet as they 'walk'."

"Yeah..."

"What's the worst thing you've seen, ma'am?"

"Unnggh." Euly spits into the campfire. "Probably the first time Leth and I crashed into one. Or, vice versa in truth. Looking back, it wasn't the worst, but... the shock value, right?"

"Right," Arroyo agrees.

"But I have a story that's even more frightening... Should I tell her? This is still classified, I think."

"Technically," I say. "Open secret like the Pit, more or less."

"More or less," Euly says, stoking the guttering flames to flaring. She adds another log. "You better start eating your dinner, Arroyo. This... is a bit of a tale."

Euliae tells it true, as much as any of us know. Originally it came from Krohn -- who was there -- and now no one else is left to corroborate its authenticity. I have no reason to doubt the story though, and no inclination to find out either.

"The Executioners didn't appear overnight. Even so, people like acting dramatic that we rushed out into the night like unleashed beasts. Maybe it's a fair view from the public, who knew nothing of anything until the proclamation. But that came only when our methods were field-tested, successful enough to warrant funding, and the Sovereignty was finally convinced that this new... challenge... was utterly beyond everyone."

The firelight shines in Euly's unfocused eyes.

"As Krohn tells it, the first observation she and the original founders made was how indestructible a cursed is.

Those were autopsies that never were: they couldn't even penetrate the skin. The skin! How are we to learn anything if we can't get inside?"

"Did they know how to stab them correctly?"

"Naw. That came way later. At the time, it was about locating them and not waking them up. Our backup plan is to attack; theirs was to flee. But they used the, heh, *best* science and logic of the time to figure that bones can't move on their own... so if there was a way to strip away the flesh, sever the muscles and tendons and all the rest of it, they'd have an inert corpse." She smiles. "The way it oughta be, right?

"They learned early on to close the charnel houses for good. Would've made the fight easier, wouldn't it? Too bad for us. And too bad for what came next that they didn't realize they were repeating the same idiotic mistake by a factor of I-can't-count-that-high...

"Called it... a flesh-eater. Gross phrase, huh? An eater of flesh. Imagine that. Predating the true Executioners, in a time when the Technocracy wasn't a bubble on any dreamer's lid."

"The Sarcophagus," I say.

"Yes. A special, horrible kind of stone coffin. *Sarcophagus*. Gives me chills saying the word. I think, deep down, Krohn is hoping to find a way to make one that works. Like I said, though, too easy an answer. So we won't find it. Besides, we've... learned the lesson not to seek for simplicity where there is none."

Arroyo lowers her piece of unchewed jerky. "It didn't work?"

"Ahhhh..." Euly traces unintelligible sketches in the dirt with a finger. "How lucky for them if it hadn't worked... But it did work and awoke that cursed so quickly, so ardently, that the damage isn't done yet these many years later.

"It broke through the Sarcophagus within seconds. No one had time to react. And within a few seconds more, everyone was dead: their gore caking the walls and hanging from the ceiling.

"How did Krohn escape such speed? Luck. She and another fled, sealing every exit behind them and never looking back. The... other person disappeared. Suicide? We don't know. Whoever it was... up and disappeared."

The log on the fire splits open, scattering sparks in a fiery ephemeral plume. Arroyo flinches.

"But the echo of that one mistake *hasn't* disappeared. That cursed is down there. Beating on the walls, breaking stone and barriers. Hopefully blind and senseless enough to dig itself deeper into darkness and never reach the surface again. Who knows?"

"If we know where it is..." Arroyo starts, hesitantly.

"That thing is wholly on another level. Sarcophagus didn't piss it off like fire does... made it... *exalted*. I wouldn't even volunteer to take it down. Best to keep sealing layer upon layer, hope the silence lulls it to sleep one day."

"One year," I say.

The hush surrounding us presses inwards.

"It's not all bad..." Euly says with fake cheerfulness, brushing up against the muted weight. "If not for that failure, our vaults wouldn't be so strong today. While it's true that that cursed cracked the Sarcophagus, as Krohn says: it took several real seconds. Taught us we were on the right path to Executioner grade stonework. So there's that..."

"Doesn't feel like much recompense."

"Does anything?"

"Well, yeah! If that death resulted in learning how to destroy them. Or discovering material they can't break. Something like those would be. Geez..."

Euly shrugs. "We can disable them. We can seal them away. It's fine for now. Maybe *that*," and she shakes a finger at Arroyo, "can come later."

"And it's still down there?"

"Still down there."

Arroyo stares at the forest floor, all dirt and castoff needles. She can barely lift the thought that's dragging her down. At length, she asks it.

"What the hell is waiting for us beneath the ground…?"

"More than we know," Euly says simply.

"More than we can know," I correct.

#

Another derelict town, a few days later. These are common markers of places where life used to be, one-time tamed pockets of security in an otherwise inhospitable land. Creepers and moss and lichen infecting the remaining structures sing the world's same refrain:

We reclaim our own.

Worthless as they are now, no one notes these spots on any map. Not us, not the message-runners, and doubtfully none but the most masochistically despairing and obsessive cartographers.

Not much shelter, but when we stopped for the night it provided a perfect eerie backdrop for telling more cursed stories and scaring each other. Which gave me the idea for a new game…

"This sounds like training!" Arroyo says.

"We've been hiking since we left. Our muscles need the monotony broken up," I say.

"I loved training!" Arroyo, in delight.

Stated plainly: I took the premise of her temporarily banned board game and converted it into real-life format. Euly and I would patrol the area, torches alight, while Arroyo dashed around and played the part of the sneakiest shadow this side of midnight.

And, yes, we do similar training with our recruits, though with more of the intent to make them adept at silence. If they can traverse a room without us hearing, they're well on their way.

"I feel like you're coddling her," Euly says, watching her dash away to a starting position.

"You were too hard on her and soured the start of the journey."

"Me!? I'm being frank with her. And I have trouble holding back with people."

"No! Do you?" Mock astonishment.

"We are not doing this right now, fool." Growls a few more choice words under a breath. "Can never hold back with *you...*"

"You know that's contributing to the assumption everyone has that we're a couple."

I lack words to describe the menacing visage that follows with a finger jabbing at my ribs.

"Go. Get. In. Position." The menace deepens to a cliff's edge of the homicidal. "Before I do something I will like."

I smirk at her retreating raised hackles. Honestly, I'm doing this more for her. She's gone into Euliae Mode far too early: on edge, sharper fanged, finicky. I'll get her to release the tension, even if that means it gets aimed at me.

Arroyo fails miserably the first time out. Too damned excited to take it seriously. I spy her stealing one of the targets only five minutes in. She does better the next session, nabbing five of seven before Euly takes her down.

"Wefffff, so close!" she wails.

I take a turn and was doing well enough until my counterpart -- lying in wait and cheating at the final target -- pounces on me and punches my chest.

"Gotcha, thief!"

Rubbing my bruise-to-be. "Tone down the enthusiasm."

"Okay, now it's my turn. Gonna show you noisy clodhoppers how it's done."

Later, Arroyo and I commiserated by the campfire. Our arms were crossed as we stared Euly down -- and her seven pieces of chocolate. She crossed her arms too, leaning back in such a way to emphasize her plump breasts sticking out such lewd, smug self-satisfaction.

"… a menace," Arroyo whispers to herself.

#

A perked-up Euly leads us across the stream, splashing raucously through the frigid waters. Sings a song, all vim as she, stopping only to consult our map. But even then, she barely drops the tune.

All through the day we tramp, slinking under the towering tree roots, having vertigo out in the wide-open clearings, back and forth from cloudy sky to branch-latticed roofs, and well on into night.

"Ah! Perfect camping spot!" Euly declares of a tiny glade, stars shimmering above.

Arroyo crumbles, yawns.

"We'll need a bigger bonfire if— shh!"

"If what?"

I mouth the words "shut up".

Cocking my ear. Dead silent, all around. But I know I heard something. Arroyo stands slowly. Euly starts to take a step towards me, but I stop her with a raised hand. I didn't catch the direction… where was it… where did that sound come from…

I need not wait. The rustle repeats, followed by a warbled snuffle.

"Burrower," I hiss.

Wide-eyed, Arroyo diligently assembles her crossbow while we keep watch. If we make a racket, we could frighten it off. Although, that would create a whole new problem if it isn't alone…

Carefully, carefully, Arroyo pulls back the steel-wired string. It moans in tension, then catches in place with a stark *click*. Euly stiffens, her face contorts.

And the little bastard rushes us.

Arroyo takes aim. *Twang*!

The iron bolt plows through its snout, scattering teeth like pathetic fireworks, and splitting its head from top to bottom. A hunk of brain matter squirts out and flies into the shadows.

Shadows that begin to churn, then fulminate in roars.

"No time!" I shout at Arroyo who had started to reload.

Euly yanks her to her feet and away, and we fly towards the treeline, while the unseen horde tramples its fallen underclaw. More in front, we arc, angle, dash through, on and on slavering chorus drooling desperate.

The land is too flat, too fucking flat, no way to slow them and why are they here the blighting little bitches it's too lush and the numbers for all hell the numbers. The gaping jaw is the only entrance!

Euly stabs it and vaults over. But the perforated ground impedes us with its roots, highborn wiry impediments cornfieldingly annoying and rigid as bone.

"Climb!" I shout.

Arroyo draws her blade, stabs a hungry snout. "Too thin, they'll break!"

"Damn it!" I unsheathe my blade too.

But it's useless. Useless useless useless with this swarm, this bloody damned swarm, pincering us, leading us nowhere but a bad end and trapped bleeding of these swaggering fanged animate carpets!

I stab, miss, and two snap at my hand. Jump back, hit a root, another falls on me. Its belly, exposed, slashes like a soft potato and spills its slippery innards vomit everywhere.

"Leth! Where are you?!"

Kick it off, stab an eyeball, then another eyeball. They scream, this anguish this pus-filled anguish this hunger this dead lament sanguineous pallbearing fury. Matching and livid, boiling and livid, I flense any nearing flesh and make of the ground a canvas of vile rendings and pockmarked staccato stabbed drippings.

"I'm surrounded, don't come!" I cry out.

"Boss, get out of there!"

Slash, *skrish*, kill them all the fucking little blights for hell and then -- they pile in, become a wetwork of wounds. Not enough, it's not! "Where!?"

"Leth, we're still... DIE!" An eruption of death rattles made flesh inert meat screams screams screaming a fountain of screaming. "We're still right here!"

Can't keep this up, this avalanche flood landslide. I kick the root shatter break, drag it down, and manage to climb one foot -- it's enough! -- and jam my foot into the tree trunk and fly off. Horrible plan horrible execution wouldn't work on anything higher than one foot off the ground as these wretches, but it does.

There! Euly and Arroyo, pinned down, trying to reach me. "Leth! Come to me!" Euly is a butcher. None of the blood drenching her matted hair sharp scar clawed fingers is hers. Ahh, let me reach you, my wild calling and favorite friend.

The ground is alive, filled with snuffling burrowers everywhere. They nip at our legs, then pounce at our faces. Lunge bite scream, it's not even a fight, they're so damn low to the ground and too awkward to kill until the split-second instant before they bite our faces off.

This is a retreat with nowhere to go.

"Eat these!" screams Arroyo, throwing sizzling kindling in a semi-circle.

Ffffssss-tchhhkkk!

The pop momentarily blinds me, vision snapping to darkest black then back. All the air around seems to evaporate to vacuum, freezing emptiness expands, and our flaming torches dim. The burrowers squeal and wrawl, two erupting in terrifying, cobalt, living infernos.

Krnnn-nnn-nnn-nnnnkkkgggg!

Twang!

Arroyo's bolt penetrates the burrower the third kindling had missed, skewering it to another one just behind. They both writhe, torturous spasms and bloodcurdling cacophony.

The momentum of their attack weakens.

"Arroyo! Climb!"

"The branches are too high, Boss!"

"Spring up! Off those two trunks!"

"Fffff, dammit, Boss, I can't do those yet!"

"Euliae!" I don't have time to argue. I dive into the thick of the roiling furry mass, buying us a few more precious seconds. If we can't ascend, we're dead.

"You can do this," Euly pleads. "I've seen you!"

"Once, ma'am! I can do it once, not twice!"

"They're about to charge again, Euly!" I shout back, gutting another fucker.

"I'll... I'll try, please guard me!"

I hear Arroyo running forward, all speed and grace, and then a grunt as she jumps. I risk a glance. She flies at the tree full force, slams her heels into it, pivots an instant, and shoots off and up at the other trunk. She slams her feet into it, pivots, and screws up immediately slipping twisting plummeting.

"EVERY CUNT-FUCKING TIME!" she howls.

Two more cobalt blazes explode forth amidst the onrushing beasts. Euly's buying us more time, making a path for Arroyo to flee and try again.

"You were close," Euly says. "Now, once more! Go!"

"I can't!" Arroyo wails. "This plan eats my ass!"

"You must! Go, Arroyo!"

"Ma'am, please! We gotta run!"

My blade speaks my frustration and ire in every strike. "Arroyo, we're surrounded and—"

"NO DUH!"

"—and running's not an option! You're an Executioner. Prove it!"

"Do not play with my pride, Boss, you jerk!"

The trees had to be too far apart, didn't they... if only we hadn't come to the glade and instead stayed deep in cover. Too late for that. Nigh too late for anything.

I scan above in a circle one more time, spiraling, hacking any burrower in range. Too high, all the branches are too high. Ah!

"Arroyo! Lob a bolt into the tree, make a lower branch!"

The burrower snaps its jaws at my crotch. I pierce its brain and kick it over. A short distance away, Euly and Arroyo are getting overrun. And they're separated.

"Can't! Too busy stabbing!"

"Euly, you do it!"

"Not happening, Leth!"

This is so screwed, and then I have the stupidest plan. There's yet a path between us and the target trees. I can make it. If I break off, I can make it... but there will be one less blade down here... the more we retreat, the more pressure on the rest of us...

Arroyo can't survive alone.

Euly could.

I go, building up velocity, dashing over burrowers, and cutting a line straight through Euly and Arroyo.

"I'll be an anchor!" I shout at them. "Arroyo comes next, then Euly!"

"What does that mean!?" Arroyo cries.

But Euly understands. "Do what you did before, after Leth gets up!" she shouts over the din. "I've got you, Leth. Go!"

I spring at the tree, same as Arroyo, and bounce off to the next. Arcing, arcing, higher, higher... no pivot, no pivot... now! I jam my blade into the thick wood. Bark shatters, great splintering crack thunder and damnation -- and I hang there, suspended, digging my feet in.

"Arroyo! Come on!"

I grit my teeth when I see her hesitate, but then she's off. Leaving Euly behind. My stomach moans like the tree I cling to, but I can't watch her. Have faith. Euly is Euly. Euliae is the best of us.

Euliae, my better half.

Need to focus on Arroyo. And she slams into the tree again, pivots, and flies at me quicker than thought. It's a bad angle, I knew this was stupid, and her blade is still in hand. This won't end well there is no happy ending here why are you looking for it's ending it's endless a pit and black she will scream in the end and cry and sprout wings that take her nowhere but ground and grave we grab each other's wrists clinging, and I let out my breath.

"Secure?"

"Yeah, Boss."

"Euly, get the fuck up here!"

She requires no more prompting. Like a banshee of blood she flies out of the pellmell bestial storm below us, impacts our tree, it shudders, we shake, hold firm, and she springs to the next tree, impacts, hangs in midair, and soars up above us into the branches: a dancer in the dark.

Euly is the only one of us with a torch, our others dropped with the swollen snouts that bite impotently in our direction.

"Okay, Euliae... shit," I pant, gathering myself. "How thick are the branches? Can you move about?"

"Yeah, man, it's a highway of sorts when you get high enough."

"Okay... okay, good." I swallow. "Rather than risk another plunge, can you carefully get to the tree you jumped off of, then fire some bolts into the trunk above me?"

"I don't... I... I don't..." Euly is completely despondent. "I don't think I can, Lethean."

"Make a... ladder... is what I... nnghffff..." Getting harder to hang here with Arroyo. "A ladder, what I mean."

"N-no… Lethean, I'm saying…"

"Sure, I know you'd rather… heh, skewer my brain with one, but hold off… until… Arroyo… nfffff, ya… ffgnnnn… know?"

"… saying I don't… have…"

She doesn't have her crossbow?

"… my cross… bow…"

She doesn't have her crossbow.

"You…"

"… I…"

"You selfish, egotistical, emotionally-fragile asshole!!!" I scream at her. The manic, primeval, horrified wrath blinding my eyes tears her voice away like it was a gossamer veil in a windstorm.

Neither of us have ever reacted like this before.

And now that our options are culled a sliver close to oblivion, never again I suspect.

Arroyo sheaths her blade. "Boss, no worries. I'm an Executioner, right?" Freckled grin and a wry squint. Her grip on my wrist tight, reassuring. "If it's once, I can do this."

Before I can protest, she pushes off, using my arm like a pendulum, one hop, two hops, three…! Arroyo crashes her heels into the wounded tree -- I choose to let go of her -- and she speeds through the air up at Euliae's awaiting, outstretched, pointlessly contrite hand.

But too low she ascends.

Too slowly she flies.

So soon, she plummets.

And there's only darkness below. In the depths. Between the trampled torches as trampled as hope ever is.

Who watches on at us poor fools who watch on as sweet Arroyo falls? Where are those mythical angels now? What cloud do they perch from, gawping at we who tread a ground six feet above which we'll sleep tomorrow.

Arroyo hits the ground, submerged in fevered morass.

I jerk at my blade, desperate to rip it out. Stuck fast. Paralyzed, hopeless metal lodged in wooden flesh. The tree's wound, a mock: hold fast my son.

And Euly, what of her? If she drops down, can she even get back up?

Arroyo screeches murder, punching and kicking at the sea of snapping snouts and famished grunts. I see a limb… a leg… where is she?

I strain against the blade again. "Use the torches!" I shout downwards. I don't think she can hear me. "Euliae, wake up!" But I don't think she can hear me either. "Fuck damn this rot!"

And I leave my blade behind, kick off and up to Euly. Grab the branch and whip up next to her. She grips her weapon, ready to plunge two storeys.

"I can't…" She's a statue. "… find an opening."

Rip her blade from her trembling fingertips. "Get my crossbow," I order.

All else unresponsive, she complies, pulls the parts from my backpack without a sound and holds them passively.

Plaintively.

I trade Euly, slapping the blade into her grip without the delicacy with which she offers the crossbow.

Arroyo isn't screaming. I wish she was so I'd know she was still alive. Time to time she breaks the surface, but ineffectually.

"How many bolts have I got?" I load the first.

"Standard."

"And how many do you?"

Silence.

"Should lodge the first one up your— Hell…" I drop my aim. "Three isn't enough for a ladder. This plan, it…"

Arroyo yelps, swings a recovered torch back and forth. Crawls on her back along the roots, kicking, cussing, her back now pressed firmly against the tree trunk.

"It won't work…"

"Get OFF!" Arroyo wails.

"We need to get down there," I say.

"How do we get away," Euliae asks.

"I said OFF!"

"I have no idea."

The burrower ocean is cresting, is about to crash and subsume our friend.

"We can't stay here," Euliae says.

"No, we can't," I say.

We don't move.

"OFF OFF OFF!"

Arroyo… what am I supposed to do…

"PLEASE!"

What am I… Arroyo…

"I'LL KILL YOU!"

Arroyo… what… am I?

Twang!

Skewered the head of one lunging at her exposed neck. A droplet in a storm, it does nothing.

"StopstopSTOP!"

A burrower finally grasps her ankle in its jaws and clamps down. I can hear the crunch of bone from here. She shrieks in agony. I reload. She kills it. I fire. I kill another. She bawls. I reload.

"What if I shoot the other torch!?" I demand of Euly.

"Nothing," she moans. "It won't explode. There are… safeties…"

I fire at one lunging for Arroyo's other leg, while she cradles the break and stares up at me through tears. Such a helpless expression I never want to see again. She knows. She knows that was our last bolt.

"Give me your blade," I say. "I'm dropping down."

Then a new look overcomes Arroyo. Utter despair at understanding what I'm about to do, and loathing for herself.

"Wait for me, Boss!"

The instantaneous resolve crystallizing in her voice, her face, her standing, her disappearing into the shadows away from the torches, from us, from salvation, is as awe-inspiring as it is heartbreakingly-excruciating.

Arroyo sacrifices herself...

Limping off into the night...

And its multitude of delirious maws...

Her scream pierces my guts deeper, more thoroughly, than every crossbow bolt the whole of us have ever fired at anything. And it grows in sorrow and torment to a deafening level, rising and rising to drown out the tide of burrowers and their strident hymnal of ignorant starvation.

One.

Final.

Crescendoed.

Ordeal.

And stillness, silence, for a beat, before Arroyo flies back into view and hurls herself headlong heedless at the tree. Her fractured ankle cracks against the trunk. Hanging, pivots, jumping. Darting through the air, high above the many-mouthed death snapping at her building momentum. Her cracked ankle shatters against the trunk. Hanging, pivots, jumping. Soaring high, so high, enough to surpass our waiting arms and land with enough impact against the treetop that she probably destroys more bones yet falling into my arms ossified delight and passing out for exhaustion agonied relief leaking tears and a tiny smile.

I hold her limp body. I shake in overwhelming undefinable emotion. What was lost, returns. What was broken, mends. And it will mend. In time. If we're strong enough, if we're fast enough, if we -- like Arroyo -- are resolved to force anguish on ourselves in order to reach that one splinter of hope...

There are no happy endings. But this was not an ending.

#

What follows is anticlimactic.

Euly and I were high on adrenaline, wide-eyed and unblinkingly gaping at the seething forest floor the rest of the night. We huddled in the treetops, nestled against the trunk, while the shadows shifted restlessly underneath. An hour before dawn, they scuttled away and sunrise shone over a battlefield of scattered bestial corpses (some of them charred), puddles of blood, and flagons of excrement.

A going-away present, to be sure.

I lighted down. Scouted the area. Retrieved our lost equipment, shut off the torch that had been scorching a root the past however-many hours, and satisfied myself that -- while I've never known burrowers to be pack-minded -- at least they remained nocturnal. When Arroyo awoke, sobbing in pain, we managed to secure her to Euly's back and get her safely to the ground.

Her destroyed ankle was three times the size it should be, purple to the extent that my thoughts said "lividity" and feared a need to amputate. Regardless, the poor thing needs surgery. And we're stuck out in the middle of nowhere.

We were generous with the painkillers. Too generous, considering who knows what other complications lay between us and a doctor. But the involuntary, wordless noises that escaped Arroyo's throat were so pitiful, I couldn't bear forcing consciousness on her.

"What if we double-time it?" I ask Euly.

She doesn't answer for a long moment. Stares away from us and out into countless trees ahead. I'm about to ask again, when she says soberly, "Two weeks. But we… can't tarry. We'd have to be off at false dawn, camping up in the trees by sunset. No more risks." And she hands me her full supply of painkillers. "No more risks."

I'd dole it out, keep Arroyo in a blurry state of half-wakefulness outside mealtimes.

Later:

"Whad wuz… ai…" Arroyo wobbles, "finking…"

"That you wanted to live," I say, passing her some food. "Chew carefully. Small bites."

"Ffffiding deaff, Bozz~!" Arroyo salutes.

This would be cute in any other context. Euly was silent. But that was fine. None of us had much to be talkative about. Not yet, at least.

"Dser," Arroyo states.

"What?"

"Dert!" Arroyo demands.

"What does that even mean."

Throws a drug-induced hissy fit.

"Drt! Dirurt! Sssss!!"

"What the hell is she on about?" I ask Euly, who then hands her a hunk of chocolate. Arroyo cheers and wobbles again, though now in glee.

Much later:

"Does it hurt?"

Arroyo hums. "Wha."

"Your ankle. Can you feel it?"

"Ttttrrrr… tobbing."

"Throbbing pain?"

"Uesh."

"Too soon for another hit," Euly whispers to me, or herself.

"But it hurts?"

"Nnnnfff. Onl… pessur."

"Only pressure, okay. We'll hold off until bed?"

"Uesh."

I pat her head. "You did good, Arroyo. You're doing good. I'm proud of you. Just sorry you have to suffer."

Arroyo titters about. "Uesh uesh, Bozz luffs, Royo praiz uesh uey!"

#

The first days were the worst. I obsessively cleaned, bandaged, checked, cleaned, bandaged, checked her ankle over and over compulsively. If the wound became infected, we were very much fucked.

Fortunately, they must have been stone burrower variants because it didn't seem like the bite had penetrated that deeply. Had they been grave burrowers or corpse burrowers, that would have been a different problem altogether.

Always take the bright bits amidst the squalor of circumstance.

We plow through forest as uneventful as we need. Euly shies clear of glades, especially when the sun dips. Days pass. We pass Arroyo back and forth, taking turns carrying the half-awake dreamer. Weeks pass. We pass into a marsh not depicted on our map.

"Why is this here?" Euly asks of her map, aghast at its stark refusal to answer.

The soggy, sodden ground extends in all directions. Dead trees claw out of calm russet pools, desperate to graze the blue sky their roots cannot hope to see. It is a watery wasteland.

"I could scout down south, or north. Find a way around," I offer.

"We need to stay together," she says. "I don't trust this. And we're late and running out of... everything. No time, there's no time, Lethean."

"Hider in dem... trees," Arroyo crests lucidity. "Nuffin changed. 'Cept smells... ickff." And plummets back into reverie.

"We're days out if we plunge straight through," I say.

"And longer if we wrap around."

"Okay, so, we're doing this?"

She thinks. "Yes" is all she responds, and her boot sinks ankle deep in mud on the first step.

It's not this unexpected obstacle that makes me suspicious, nor the fact that it hinders us so close to our goal and haven. It's the lack of life anywhere. No insects, no birds, no fish, no critters. And of the foliage? None of it is... correct. It's like... it's like the edge of the forest pissed out a lake that's having an identity crisis. The water isn't brackish in the slightest.

"This is... new," I realize.

"Right?"

"But why is nothing else here?"

"... biome changed; local optima haven't reacted yet."

"Now there's a bookish reason."

"Better than the one I'm actually thinking."

"Which is?"

"New natural predator killed off everything else, and the remnants are smarter than we are."

And those were the last words we spoke aloud for days.

\#

We were all on edge, Arroyo especially once she somehow came to the same conclusion we did. The boughs of the squat, tortured trees provided decent crow's-nests and later cradles in which to sleep.

But what slept beneath us?

Mercifully, we never found out. And maybe nothing else did. I'd like to believe the only living creatures in the whole of that marsh were three Executioners trudging from one edge to the other.

At the end of the journey, on the verge of victory, this is how we were: one of us broken; one of us mute; one of us fatigued; and all of us frazzled and stressed out in our own ways. It was with great relief once I felt the land dipping down, the ground firming up, and a chilly breeze puffing clean and crisp against my face.

My haggard smile lingered long past its welcome when I saw Echo Downs flooded and entirely underwater.

#

I pace.

Said I'd scout a ways down the strand, let the girls rest, of which Euly looked grateful, but I pace for minutes on end more than I hike the perimeter. I needed to clear my head. How many supplies do we have left? Rations? How close is the nearest town?

There isn't a point to this... but my feet start dragging me on again, until my heels dig in and turn me around.

"Alright, stop it." I don't. "Stop." Still pacing. "Stop already, Lethean," I say, channeling Euliae.

Only the tallest buildings of Echo Downs break the surface, the rest exist unseen in the depths or as roofs ineffectually grazing, yet never penetrating, the quivering silver waters. Towering above them all is the grand Windtower, its face a derelict hole and so much of its structure beaten and ripped lengthwise, a finger flensed nearly to the bone.

And I go back.

Arroyo dozes on Euly's lap. In my time apart, I calculated nothing except: painkillers run out in three days and I can't remember anywhere closer than a week out.

I drop next to Euly. She stares out at the lake, out at the city, out at nothing. When I blink, my eyes take so long to reopen.

"Hey." When I squeeze her shoulder, her face grimaces as though my mere touch lances searing needles through her hunched frame. "Hey..." It passes, but her gaze remains fixed. "Rest with Arroyo. I'll start a fire and then cook dinner after nightfall."

The flames kindled easily, seemingly eager to erupt and hiss out the wetness of the wood and fight back the cold air marching off the languid waves. Darkness came. I mixed some of our rations into a semblance of a chili, though the rabbit jerky's texture was off-putting. We huddled around the jumping amber glow, eating and no one talking except for the occasional soft moan from Arroyo. Euly never had to sign what I knew she would have, had she not been transfixed by the gloom out over the waters.

After dinner, Arroyo laid back down and finally so did I. I stretched to full height, bones creaking popping, and settled against the weedy hillside. As I sunk into myself, I thought on the gray tomorrow, and sinking knew that I was now asleep.

#

Bfffffl

    a breeze

                  Boffff

    a breath

                             Bzz

    an inhale, sharp

                                  "Stob ib!"

Arroyo cries aloft the floating Euliae Euliest I sluggishly rising waters to sitting Purple ankle pinioned and she weeps reaching for driftwood away the song drifts away No not like this this is not an ending this is

                                "Wuwy! Stob!"

I cry it out too, but it doesn't

                                "Uu ged hurp!"

              Wake up Lethean she's going to die

                                "Bozz! Bozz!"

Pitiful drops liars eyes gleaning nothing gleaming in the pinprick torchlight on quay remote and's forgotten shadow with Euliae unblinking at me agape not for my sake but a world gone and unburied the blood leaks out first specks of ash sparks and then streams rivulets waterfalls bleeding from those dark sockets

                                "Ged Wuwy!"

Eye stand watch body refuses to decide even when my mind now ripping out of subconscious images the visual lies worse than hers because the nightmare was when she said "I'm not waiting for you."

I know, but I am.

"Stob!"

Because I'm an idiot.

"Stob!"

Who wants to drown.

"Stob!"

Wake up, sweet Lethean.

And I do.

Arroyo's head lolls towards me, and of Euly? She isn't out beyond our reach in the sunken city hell or floating on a hastily ramshackled raft, nor are her eyes bleeding out a cask's worth of blood -- or at least, I can't tell from this vantage.

No, she's slumped over her knees, sitting where she was before, only now snoring lightly.

"Wuwy sweepings," Arroyo whispers.

"Not you, huh?" I crawl over to Arroyo.

"Naff. Dwuggies skew wiff meh skedul. Royo okay."

"That's good to hear," I say, image of Euly slipping away from us hovering in my unseen imagination.

"Bozz okay, too?"

I stay silent.

"Bozz…"

"No."

Arroyo frowns. "Wad can Royo do?" A pause. Too wisely pregnant for her age I notice. "Or Wuwy?"

Biting my lip. Sardonic chuckle. "Premonition."

"Bozz…?"

"Are you hurting?"

"Hmm? Naff. Bwurwy. Why?"

"Going to build a raft. One that will work safely and not be a frantic labor of desperation that gets someone sodding killed…"

"Ehh?"

"Sorry. Still waking up. Can you help me bind logs?"

"Wehhhh…" Flexes her fingers. "Be swoh. Ah meah, modoh condro kind skewy."

"Don't worry about it." Jerk my head the way we came. "Plenty of broken wood around. I'm gathering. Scream if you need me."

"Or Wuwy does zomeding duhpid."

I pat her messy braid. She titters lovingly. "You're too damned astute for your age."

#

The look of concern with which Euly regards my raft is, if I'm being… *very* giving, rather critical.

"It's safe."

She looks away.

"It's *safe*," I maintain. Arroyo vigorously and wobblingly nods undeniable confirmation.

Euly rolls her eyes. I get it: her own unbreakable sanctimoniousness versus the word of a drugged girl and… me.

"Let's go and get this over with," I say.

Arms crossed. Rigid shoulders. Such scowling.

"Wuwy, wez go." Arroyo tugs on her sleeve. "We godda know." Tug. Tug tug. "Godda see."

Euly whispers something to herself that sounds like "old messes".

I don't understand the stonewalling front. Why she's gone more than taciturn, why she's not the one screaming murder at us for daring to rest before considering a scouting expedition. And the more I think on it, the more I think she's just pissed at me for lashing this together before she could do the same and slip off to oblivion.

A story as old as hate: one friend trying to help another.

Eventually, we coax her aboard. She and Arroyo hold torches aloft while I row. Off we float out towards the heart of the drowned city, our campfire crackling in desperation for us not to leave its safety -- yet we must. Far too soon its lullaby deadens and its flicker fades.

Alone.

Gray waters below, depths I cannot fathom, and my oar penetrating only the surface sings a solemn, unending dirge. Of unreachable homes and rusting lampposts and streets never to be trod again and beneath it all the bloodlet veins of sewers. Call imagination the only color in this incalculably deluged grave out of which the most storied buildings loom as portent shadows at the edge of sight and the thickening mists.

The raft skims a roof. I push off and leave it behind.

I stop rowing. So quiet. It's so quiet. Nothing flows, or drips. Muffled emptiness. A hollow space divided from the known world. Darkness, felt more than seen. Experienced in a manner that none should. I shiver, and row once more.

It's only when we pass the first structure that juts out of the water -- the tip of a windmill's blade -- that I feel the loss of the city as a mattock wedged dead-center into my breastbone.

How can we come back from this?

How do we rip this dead weight out and keep going?

"Should we turn back?" I ask, but I'm not really asking.

Silence.

Arroyo's voice. "We can't."

I row.

Because we can't.

I row.

Because we can't.

Because we can't.

We row.

We can't.

We row.

We can't.

107

Euliae lurches, nearly pitching off the raft. Rights herself, gripping the edge, and points her torch commandingly at the rooftop in front of us. Yeah... yeah... The height is enough, we can dock there.

We climb the concrete, drag the raft up and over. But Euly keeps going, drops the torch midstep, ignores it, grips her forehead, stumbles, keeps walking, spasms, ignores it, and stops.

Mouth slack, lips peeling and stretching backwards into nothing I wish to recall now or ever. Her eyes, poor Euly's eyes, even wider than those exsanguinating empty sockets from my nightmare...

Above her dwarfed form -- in heavy judgement -- ruined buildings now become memorials seem to regard the penitence of the tiny, unimportant creature we choose to call Euliae the Executioner, and then they turn away in distaste.

A reedy, unending exhale escapes Euly's throat until she drops to her knees at the edge of the waters, covers her eyes, and vomits out a paralyzed gout of bile-saturated anguish into the liquid shadows of the deep.

Arroyo buries her face against my chest. Only when the hellish chill of the mist pinpricks my body to shivering untold minutes later, I realize she's there, and realize further that my hand is stroking her frayed hair. But Euly... Euly...

Soundless keening crescendoing into the silent choruses of excruciation, all wails unheard. Somewhere in this remaining world of ours is a mouth that was opened and will never, never close again. Tonight, it borrows the mouth of my partner, my ally, my friend. What sullen mundanity,

in voiceless screams and unshed tears.

Hours could have passed. I think, maybe, it was a single day. I can no longer tell time. Stretched to infinite thinness by our slog into the unknown. I know it's coming. That sealed vault that I know well. Ahh, death, has it come around at last to embrace me? I hope... I hope when I reach it, I have the strength to claw my way back out. My arms covered in someone else's scratch marks, each nail bit so deeply in the ridicule of love I was always reaching the wrong way for. Ahh, what a fool. *Are none like me?* These will be her words, but... mine now, for this last instant, to ask anyone: *are none like me?* I hope they aren't for their sake, and hope they are for mine. Please. Please know, I wish them peace. I wish them *peace*.

I kindled the campfire.

And we sat there. What else could we do?

The flames were warm. I felt nothing.

We wouldn't be able to linger. Lack of wood to keep this going. And yet... and so... this vigil.

For no one.

For everyone.

For you.

For me.

But then, just then, a shining from the blackest horizon. Our fire reflected on a mocking mist. I relax my shoulders. But then, just then again, a glinting along the trembling of the waters. And I stand.

"Hallo!"

The ferryman glides to a stop before the rooftop, presses a boot against the stone for stability, and pulls back the hood of her amber cowl.

"Phew, live 'uns!" she cackles with perhaps the most genuinely happy grin in all existence. "Case yeh han't heard, this ain't no place fer the livin'." Pauses. "Ha!"

This feels like a misplaced joke and yet I'm suddenly gripping her into a fervent, desperate handshake and asking twenty questions all at once and her laughing and Arroyo almost bouncing for joy despite the ankle and oh hell we have to fix that and Euliae timid in approach and constantly her laughing shaking hands and finally, finally, finally: "You're alive? Who else is alive?"

"Not a lot," she admits, sadder smile, "nossir, not a whole lot. Enough though, ain't it? As many as could." Looks us over. "This all yeh? No 'un left ashore?"

"This is us."

"Aight, can take this many. Shall we off?"

Surreal. Absolutely surreal. She helps us embark, taking particular care with the wincing Arroyo. And when we're situated, she flashes her teeth.

We're off.

The streets lap against us. A single candle in the ferryman's lantern lights our way. I look up into the sky and see nothing, not even the outlines of the places we pass by. Her bent form silhouettes a soft ghostly glow and the long oar that rows with even measured beats. Slosh of the water, wind high above us, my own calming blood and pulse, but when I begin to sink into peace, the candle's flame rouses a dusty memory and I find myself wide awake once more.

But then a greater light ahead beckons. The darkness is peeling back, relegated to stark-edged shadows plastered along the clustering buildings and disembodied pillars. We pass under an arch, weathered yet still striking, and what remains of Echo Downs passes into view.

"Welcome to Drowns," our guide intones. And I sense pride peeking out from behind the casual tone.

I expected, when I learned of survivors, nothing more than a paltry refuge of huddled masses. Insufficient food, inadequate space, all grime and mold, an air of inconsolable suffering. Bluntly: a few poor sods who escaped calamity only to wait to die.

Nothing about this abiding city is ramshackle.

Normal citizens walk the roads, now lain atop roofs and connected by stone bridges. A man, clad in a billowing cloak, leans against the bridge's railing and waves us in. Street lamps are shining an unwavering, welcoming gold along the edge of every building. Many of these have high storeys that have been repurposed, no doubt their lower levels remain unusably submerged, but those that don't -- that crest just above the waterline -- have altogether become the unlikely foundations to new structures.

And the windows that dot this sunken courtyard? Most with curtains drawn, others with dancing candlelight muted by thick coarse glasswork. This could be a tranquil evening view back home for all the lack of outlandishness.

Our ferry rocks, reminding me this is not a stroll.

"Are you nocturnal here?" I ask.

A nod, deep enough to be mistaken for a bow. "Some, aye, self included. Takes an effort t'run our home fer ever'un. Wanted t'meet yeh, we did." Shoulders shaking. Laughter? "We... we been waitin'. Long time." Shoulders stop shaking. "Long time, 'ad it..."

The man who waved pushes an oar against the ferry. "Slow down, Megrit."

"Woohp! Sorry, sorry. My bad," she chides herself. The ferry slows, coasts a final few inches and collides with the small driftwood dock one solid, hollow thunk.

The man helps Euly out first, then me. I kneel down and extract Arroyo, whose cautious steps seem to test the ground for proof of materiality. Satisfied, she offers me a careful smile and holds on to my belt for support.

"Hup!" The ferryman hops out, sets her oar against a bench, and beams at us. "Ah right. I'm Megs, I am. Good meetin' yeh!"

There weren't many people about, but everyone converges on us. Tittering. Whispering. Leaning in. The atmosphere bursting with an expectation I fear is stillborn, an unspoken feeling of hospitality and invitation uprooted when I notice the man frowning openly at my arm.

"Three and yet too many," the man says, a voice that starts ponderously, a boulder on the precipice of irresistible momentum. "Executioners."

I wait for Euly to make introductions. But she merely ignores the swelling scene, blank-faced mask, a puppet of ennui. Arroyo's previous grin is fading fast.

"We are," I state, introducing myself and my comrades in turn. I want to believe it was only my anxiety that thought the murmuring of the gathered crowd had abruptly ended, yet when I clear my throat and hear nothing but my own unwelcome grunt, it's obvious to everyone that it did.

"O-oh," says Megs.

Her companion continues to eye the colors bound to me.

"Well." Megs shrugs at him meaningfully. "I mean. Makes sense amirite?" Nods encouragingly around, but no one picks up her attempts to rekindle the extinguished spark. "I mean. Who else..." An uncomfortable laugh. The cheerful facade disintegrates, and all on stage -- Megs especially -- shed their roles and blocking and cues, and cast away every illusion of a fourth wall to the unsubstantial house floor. "Who else would they send...?"

"... we." Arroyo's face is averted. But she says it to me, more than anyone, her lucidity dropping the following words like a trapdoor. "We weren't sent for."

"That doesn't make sense."

"Impossible."

"Could they—?"

"Of course not. After all this time... after all—"

"Shhh, it's okay."

"Forgotten. Like ashes."

"It's not like that."

"She just said it was!"

"Did she?"

"Calm down."

"It's over then."

"Don't say that."

"You're right. It is over."

"Stop saying that."

"Why isn't he saying anything?"

"What else is there?"

"It's fine. We were resolved."

"I wasn't."

"Now we know."

"Nothing has changed."

"We can keep going."

"Nothing ever changes."

"But I had hoped…"

"This is too much. Throw them out."

"They're here to help."

"Idiot, she said they *aren't*."

"Throw them out!"

"Where are the rest of them?"

"This means they died."

"Or no one cared."

"No one is that heartless."

"But it still means they're dead. Dead!"

"Did no one listen?"

"It's not that."

"Couldn't be."

"They simply… didn't…"

"… make it."

"…make it."

"Yeah…"

"We're alone."

"Then… throw them out."

"Yes, throw them out."

"They don't belong here."

"… *Enough*."

The man sets his jaw in an implacable line. His salt-and-pepper beard, immobile granite. "Enough," he intones once more. "Megrit, you have work."

"*Megs*," she insists. "And that can wait!"

"For?"

"They're from outside, ain't they?" she snorts. "Yeh actin' like that's nothin'."

"It is exactly what it is. Raise your celebration if you feel moved and let them that want join you."

"Feck!" She shouts the incisive invective. And then to the agitated crowd: "So we ain't saved from our tiny hells. Who the frig is!?" Then, to us: "Hey, I'm sorry. This is piss yeh don't deserve. Thanks fer comin'. Okay? Mean that."

I'm not sure how to answer that, so I nod with what I hope is magnanimous authority.

"We'll get yeh a place t'stay and food. Right?" she demands of the crowd.

"There's ample space at Crow's Rest," a haggard woman says after Megs' question goes unanswered for awkwardly too long. "I could fire up the kitchen early," she adds.

"A room would be plenty sufficient," I tell her. "We haven't had a proper bed since setting out."

"Old Kingdom?" a young, pouty-lipped boy asks.

Shaking my head. "Old City, but technically yes what you mean."

Silence reigns, always the patron ruler of humanity trying to reconnect to itself.

"How is it… The City?" an old man asks.

"How bad is it?" the old woman beside him asks, their hands clutched like twisting, dried leaves.

"You make me play the message-runner," I chuckle lightly. "What is their phrase? 'All is well'."

"No plague?"

"No. None."

"Deaths?"

"Average. Nothing outlandish."

"The crops?"

"Not great. Not horrible."

"So, no starvation…"

"No one is getting complacently fat, but no one is going without," I tell them. "There were some moments of rationing this year, but… that ended quickly, thankfully."

"That's good."

"Thank you."

"For what?"

The teenager tears up.
"I… I'm not sure," she says,
turning away and hurrying
perhaps home,
likely somewhere
that is nowhere.

"Cursed?" a voice presses in on me.

I glance at that same stolid man whose warmth had gone from waving and gripping my arm and yanking me upwards, to standoffishness with as much resolution as the grave. Scrutinizing one another. Sizing each other up. He's bigger than I am. Not a dire accomplishment. The majority of Executioners, at least those out in the field, are fit and slender -- though I've always been a bit scrawnier: Euly says "emaciated".

I wonder what his hardships have been to bring about this stifled resentment. Did I inter your wife? It happens. Get over it. She was *gone*. I'm setting the corpse in a hoped-for final rest. Hahhh… such a thankless occupation.

Could probably drop him easily.

"I don't know how much you know—"

"Nothing," he replies, "outside a year."

One year… one year… that's a lot of news to cover. And do they *need* to know about the Dun?

"Transparency," Krohn murmurs from behind her desk, cracking her fingers, then putting leather gloves back on.

"Yeah, but—"

"Transparency, Lethean!" she barks at me, slamming a fist down and rattling the overfull teacup.

"Crypt Dun was compromised," I relent.

Ah.

So this is what it feels like when message-runners carry ill news, a contagion in their hearts that, when delivered, disperses to the inexorable wind. It is an open flask the recorking of which is moot.

'All is well'...?

Some message-runner I am...

The man is unmoved. "Did the cursed do it?"

"No. Someone else. It was deliberate."

"Gravediggers?"

Nodding. "Or thieves, likely."

"You don't know?"

"I don't."

"Does—" he stops, shifts his stance. "Do the rest know?"

"We don't. Not as of last month when we left."

Stiffening. "Old City is unsecure."

"Incorrect," I say. "We've secured the site. Our best people are on it."

"And clearly sent their second-rate to the edge of the wild world and back..."

Arroyo growls. "Not second-rate."

"... if they come back at all."

He doesn't even acknowledge her non-threat. Probably picks out the obvious physical pain hidden behind each irate syllable. Enough of this farce. We have priorities.

I have priorities.

"I'm happy to field your questions." *Judgements accusations belittling puerile dick-measurings.* "Any of

116

yours," I announce to the group. "There is, depressingly, a considerable amount neither of us know about either of our cities—"

"Why in plague's name are you here?" the man presses.

"Why are you?" I snap.

"Ooookay, cut this crap." Megs steps between our rising temperatures. "We're human beings tryin' t'get through each day and I ain't havin' this. Ever'un get on with things. Dunno where or whichways our guests have come, but they lookin' mighty daggered. No reason fer us t'blow our wigs, 'ad it."

"Finish your rounds," the man says, leaving for the nearest bridge.

"I am, damn it!" she spits back.

The rest dither momentarily, then leave us be. When Megs approaches us, she's the friendly version we had met on that first roof. But clearly a little wearier.

"I *am* sorry 'bout that."

"Not your fault."

"We... han't much order here'bouts no more."

"You came across as pretty leaderly."

"I came 'cross as pretty cross." Laughing a dead weight a few inches before it settles back in, then sighs. "Not much the former. Nossir."

I try not to sound pissed off -- not sure why he was getting under my skin -- when I ask: "Who was that?"

"What, him?" Points at the broad back of the man. "Ricken. He's not usually a bastard, but..." Shrugs at the surroundings.

"You're in the thick of it."

"Aye. In the thick'a it," she agrees, gathering her oar.

A light thump. Arroyo leans against me. "Boss..."

"Shit, are we late?"

"Y-yeah, Boss..."

I rummage my pockets for the painkillers.

"Yeh hurtin' real bad, Arroyo. Is it yer leg?"

"Yes, ma'am."

Megs cringes, laughs without levity. "'Ma'am', huh? Not m'night." Grips the oar tight. "Yeh need a physician."

"And a surgeon, probably and unfortunately," I tell her.

Arroyo frowns. "Shattered the bloody hell out of my ankle. Very literally."

"Please tell me you haven't lost your doctors."

"Nay, we got what yeh need."

Relief unwinds my unease. A bit. "Good... good..." I breathe deep. "Ahh, hadn't struck me that you may have lost— Who can she see and when?"

If ever there was a definition of an ironic grin.

"Oh." Arroyo's eye-roll is audible. "Figures."

Megs is pointing, once more, at Ricken.

"Who else?" I ask.

"Trust me, she wants Ricken t'check it over."

"But do I really?" Arroyo wonders.

"I don't trust myself with him," I say, acting as Arroyo's crutch, "but if you insist. Let's go."

"Boss, I can't walk that far." Wriggles her nose. "And I don't want to be held like a baby anymore." Clears her throat. "Even if I like it."

Megs' face softens, remarkably serene. "Yeh two got a good relationship," she says. "But if yeh'll give me leave, I'll take her. Never lose a charge. I'm a ferryman who knows the business."

"Suits you?" I ask Arroyo.

"Mm." Nods her head twice.

"I'll depend on you, then," I tell Megs.

That lights her up. "Perfect! And don't fret 'bout the tense atmosphere. I'll settle it with him. Yer friend will be in good hands." Which is abundantly clear from how gently she aids Arroyo's descent into the ferry, keeping the vessel from rocking as she settles into a comfortable position.

I toss a pouch at Arroyo, who pockets it without so much as a thought. "Get a refill while you're there."

"On it, Boss."

"Good luck."

Arroyo salutes.

Megs lightly steps down, agitates the lantern to flaming, and pushes off. "Crow's Rest is the small residence constructed 'round that stone tower. Normally our lighthouse, but… well." Smiles away the negative subtext. "We'll be talkin'. Right?"

"Agreed."

"Bye, Boss. Bye, Euliae," Arroyo yawns. "Try to get some sleep instead of fighting."

Our guide pulls her hood tight against the growing chill and paddles quietly out into the open. Her wake leaves a dark, dispersing line stretching from me to somewhere out in the vast wreckage of Echo Downs, now the flooded city of Drowns. She becomes a shadow's shadow and the glimmer of her candle off the waters the only sign that she is passing.

"Time to turn in," I say to Euly. Without a grunt, she shambles the way towards lodging.

We spy Crow's Rest on the other side of a long stone bridge in a remote and silent corner. Flanking us, the water is black and stilled. I crane my neck, taking in a view of the unlit lighthouse. In a strange way it's reminiscent of an abandoned Overlook, except purpose-built and yet somehow lonelier for having sloughed that original purpose.

I lower my gaze by degrees until only Euliae fills my vision, her hand running absentmindedly against the railing.

"You okay?"

No answer.

I wait. In vain.

Slipping my fingers into her palm.

::Euly okay?::

No answer. I let go.

Sometimes she can be reassuring when she's anything but. Though, truthfully, I'm not sure if that's accurate at this moment.

A single candle slumped upon the windowsill by the front door is the strongest light around. Aside from the glowing outlines of curtains in a dozen odd windows, the surroundings are completely black. From the name I had assumed an inn: a wooden carving of a dozing crow, squeaking in thirst for oil against a rusty chain.

Too soon I forgot the aberration of this ad hoc settlement's survivalism.

There will be no architectural flair here. Only a visual hymn to carrying on with an undercurrent -- the repeated chorus -- of paths of least resistance.

I push the door open. The woman from earlier offers a wan smile -- but seems to mean it. A speckled handkerchief covers graying hair. She dips her head, a modest bow, and ceases to clean.

"It isn't much, I'm sure," she apologizes, setting the mop aside. Eyelids puffy and pink, very nearly able to hide the dark circles underneath. "I try to maintain it as much as I can. But it's not," a tremor runs down her arm, "important work."

"Not at all," I say. "We're in your debt."

Her shoulders spasm, more self-deprecation than a shrug. "It's hardly anything. Scarcely anything at that." Searches for the words. "A room. It's... a room." Reaches as if to take up the mop once more, catches herself, and lowers her hand; it grips her apron's pocket instead. "Honestly, it isn't trouble, I can heat up something for you. I shouldn't have welcomed you that way, terrible of me, but my cooking is quite good. I'm never... modest about that..."

I'm not a wise man.

And, you should know, that's not Euly's constant belittling finally seeped into the porches of my mind and clogging all the veins. I know what I know. I can tell when someone wants to feel useful.

How much of that emotion could possibly exist in a home such as this?

"By all means." I spread my arms. "Though promise me you'll hie yourself to bed right afterwards. I'm sure you've had a busy day."

Her laughter is brittle glass, chipped yet still polished. "I haven't. But you're sweet. Lethean, wasn't it? Yes. That's a fine name. Let me show you to your quarters. Please, follow."

Shuffling along, mounting the steps to the third storey, carefully, shuffling down the hall, and stopping at the end. This floor feels unused. Is this for our privacy? Or can no one suffer a nearby Executioner? But no, as I glance out the window beyond the door she creakingly opens, it's... because it has the best view.

Such simplicity is touching.

But when I make to enter, Euly brushes past me, pushes me out into the hallway, and shuts the door.

Krikk.

Locking it fast.

"Seriously, this is what we're doing?" I tell the door who, clearly Euly's newest friend and accomplice, responds with nothing.

And with Arroyo herself stolen away, by now probably lying on a slab, being looked over by some supposedly knowledgeable asshole?

Sod this.

I'm hiking.

"I don't suppose you can prepare the food to take with me?" I ask of our host.

#

My angular shadow stalks me the final steps to the top of the lighthouse. I pause, fill my lungs with midnight, and...

121

let it go. Deciding in the last second that shouting wouldn't satisfy me after all.

I sit over near the ledge and eat.

Triple mushroom stew, plenty of stout and caramelized onions making up its base. Salt and black pepper. A brief sharp sting. Ah, red pepper too.

"I like this."

The bread is thick and dark. Molasses? Blackstrap. Fantastic. Crispy outside, moist inside. The perfect pairing with a whiskey. Which I don't have.

"That would be good, though."

Up here the breeze is a constant whispering threat of frost, the lantern light beside me meagre, and everything is solitude.

"This sucks."

But the vista is something special, certain to be equally informative and depressing at dawn. Pinprick lantern light as though earthbound stars... marking makeshift tenements, bridges, and perhaps docks. I can barely make out three separate ferries crossing the void between spaces.

I look up.

Nothing.

Another void. Cloud cover a curtain drawn against the heavens -- or perhaps an eyelid shut to the sorrow of Drowns. I suppose it's good we hadn't arrived during the day. To have seen the full extent of the destruction...? Better to shut my eyelids too and behold the reveal gently, tenderly.

That's my role. To watch.

While Arroyo can't.

All of it.

When Euly won't.

Until it's time to act.

And then...

And then...

What happens then?

I don't know.

Our strategies. Our backup plans. They echo in my mind, such empty tall tales -- what ambition! -- told around the successive string of campfires lighting our way from home to where we ended up. All those flames are doused, crushed underfoot, scattered, buried, left behind. What campfires light our path home now? Where can they be seen?

More of the city is lit than I would have expected before mounting those steps and looking down on a loss I can neither fully see nor comprehend. It heartens me, to what extent it can. Which of those lights down there will take us home? That light upon the bridge? Or those by the dock? Over there? Or there? In that ferry or that one? Or must it be that we, like always, must spark a pyre to inferno and illuminate our own way through more underbrush, untrodden ground, and no assurances that where we aim is where we're bound.

Perhaps none of these.

I notice that the lights abruptly cease at this derelict lighthouse and do not cross into the deep waters beyond. It could well be that this is where our journey ends. And this.

This.

I extend my hand, reaching for nothing.

This is our high-water mark.

#

"Yer li'l friend is restin'," I hear a voice say when I return to the kitchen to grab more bread.

Megs is perched on the countertop of a miniscule bar, watching red wax dribble down a candle in front of her drained glass.

"What's the diagnosis?" I drop onto the nearby stool.

"Threw me out a'fore he'd say." Taps the counter with the edge of her glass, causing the expanding wax puddle to tremble. "Wants her t'sleep the night through. Poor tyke's exhausted, 'ad it. One good sleep a'fore testin' and bein' pained, y'know?"

I examine the bottles along the wall.

Difficult to tell if any single one is full. Might all be dregs at this point.

"Well," I breathe, "if we set her bones wrong, one day won't change that."

"Aye."

"All the difference between if she can walk normally again versus do what she has to do with us. Hell."

"Hell," she repeats. "Now that's a thing. Not that I know what y'all do much."

"What do you think we do?"

"Bugger corpses."

"Besides that, obviously."

"Oh, *besides* that," she chortles, snatching a nondescript bottle from the lowest shelf. "This is the one y'want."

"Thanks."

"Besides *that*..." Nudges away her glass with a single finger, apparently done drinking her own woes to throbbing non-silence. "Caretakin' this world a'fore we leavin' it."

"Nice. Krohn should use that for public relations."

"'s't work?"

"So far."

"Han't been to Ol' City myself. Hear that Dun a'yers is a right sight. But it's broken out'a?"

"Into."

"Well, there's a thing too. Better keep a record, you and me, a'fore the night is out we'll have ourselves a dreadful tally."

I raise my glass of rye. "To broken homesteads."

"And the constant mendin'a," she states solemnly and raps a fist against my drink.

"I suppose you know my next question."

"S'pose I do."

"And if I read the mood when we arrived, you haven't told this story yet to a single soul."

"All Executioners this masterfully astute?" she asks.

"Only the ones smart enough to drink instead of sleep."

"He's in good company then…"

She slides off the bar with a hop, lands in the stool beside me. And leaning against the countertop, chin resting on her hand, she's all flirty simpers and raconteur anticipation.

"And…?"

"This is a game," she drawls. "You have t'say the words."

Silence.

"Megs."

"Sir."

"What happened?"

The playfulness stumbles to sobriety with one solitary, hollow laugh.

"What'll happen to ever' city eventually. Echo Downs was simply the first. That we know 'bout…"

Here was a tale one year in the making -- and what a year it was. Dreadful, was that Megs' omen? Barely penetrated the surface more than my paltry oar did the lake by comparison. Drop by drop, my drinking companion, the girl with haphazardly-chopped hair -- as if done in a raging mania -- who is both victim of unleashed tides and ferryman for others, clarified that liquid tragedy is what flows beneath us. Water is merely the metaphor.

"Lived all my life in the city, I have, one way or the other," she says, easing into it. "Started out in the pastures, inched deeper and deeper as time went on, followin' schoolin', family, odd jobs, flings with boys I thought was love, until one day I was alone in the heart a'this bustle and realized my li'l shadow had been engulfed by the Windtower's such that I couldn't see mine no more.

"Where did I stop and the city begin? Or vice versa, 'ad it. Lonely, but it was my loneliness. Not happy, not content, but... not displaced.

"Then comes last autumn. Real cold, maybe should've made me nervous for winter." Resigned shrug. "Threw more wood into the fire. Bought thicker socks. Extra cups a'tea at night. Normal stuff, y'understand."

"Sure, no reason to overreact."

Bobs her head. "Aye, none a'that. Then comes scamperin' in a boy with the brightest bluest eyes y'ever did see. Ah, wanted t'snog him but good and finish off a bottle from lip to heel. Terrible, I am. Dang but if he wasn't gorgeous.

"Rattled off somethin' 'bout graves and the dead and yeh lot and the government and didn't seem t'have much t'do with me. Said his piece, passed out some papers. I took one so as we could chat. But ignores me, kept passin' and then so did he, dashin' through the streets and on out into who-knows-where east."

Our timeline starts to make sense with this foundation. "Winter came next."

"Sure did. And the deepness with it, faster and fiercer'n ever a'fore. I tell yeh, stand on the road and stare up at the highest spires and y'could see the frost freezin' up there! Windtower quit workin' good, too!"

"Can't imagine that went unacted on."

"Nossir." Proud grin. "Was one a'the few sent up t'clear it off. Nigh died three times."

"That thick, huh?"

"That *frequent*," she boasts. "Sent us up those three times over two weeks, 'ad it!"

I knock back the rest of my drink. "Dismal up Old City way, Old Kingdom too. Fog and all that follows." Pour a few fingers more. "But that came after the new year. You're talking earlier."

"'Bout year's end," she starts again. "Fierce rain. Dread fierce. Wouldn't stop. Felt like an ocean sky was dumpin' on down and soon that would be drier'n dirt and we'd be under. Funny how errant thoughts become the thing what happened. A wretched time. Feels like such a nostalgic thing t'say. Storm moved north and we thought it was over." Shakes her head. "Not over. Buildin' up, bidin' its time, and then… And then."

Reaches over, borrows a deep quaff from my glass, hands it back. I refill, then pass the bottle. Sharp fingers jump out, but… ultimately relent. There's a point where the alcohol does nothing.

"We don't assuredly know what happened. Sometimes, stuck in the present, past don't matter much a lick. Storm made a lake? Or another storm we never knew 'bout did it? And our storm doubled our nothin'? Whatever it was, when the deepness crashed down on us with hail big as wagons, must have done the same up north and the dam, whatever that dam *was*, broke.

"No one down in the streets survived. Few on ground floor did either. Survival rate increased the higher y'were." Another resigned shrug, though less committal. "Hardly a guarantee. I was atop Windtower when…" Blanches, clutches pain for a protracted grip, at last cramming the distilled finality of disaster into a single utterance: "Deluge."

I wait until she can go on.

"Never was close to the family, but my brother, we at least… sometimes, y'know, and I… Ahh. Aaaahhhh."

"You were the lucky one to have been up in—"

"Oh, aye! Aye! Lucky t'seen that feckin'…! All rollin' over the hills I used t'play in, carryin' a battery a'trees I likely climbed a'fore I first bled, all that pox-of-it-all just… just floodin'! Floodin' into ever' empty space until there were no space no more!" Covers her face briefly, then slaps her hand down, accidentally sending the bottle careening.

I grab it in time. "Lucky! Yessir, lucky t'have clung to the scaffoldin', cryin' nuff tears I ain't got none no more, pissin' m'trousers so thoroughly almost slipped on the puddle t'my death once the lake had settled into its new home a'Drowns, though maybe then I'd 'ave been yer 'lucky'!"

I might feel ashamed of my choice of words were I not an Executioner. But...

"Death used to be an end," I say. "Don't know why that changed, same as no one knows when it did. Or why it is sometimes and not others, nor why it is for someone and not another. The natural order is not... ordered. Not anymore."

"That meant t'comfort me? Cuz I mostly want t'kick yer teeth in."

"You haven't seen a cursed yet," I reply. "Once you witness that horror, its unnaturalness, you recognize we've crossed a bridge that's been burned. And being alive in all its ordinary glory is a blessing." Smiling. "Kick my teeth in for saying a phrase that pedantic and trite if you must. But when we Executioners confront the true face of this new world, and subdue it, and seal it away... feels like hope to me."

"Han't felt that silliness fer a time now. If yer right, then maybe it's worth bein' somewhat grateful. Though fer me... don't know where I should go now. So, I ferry them that do. That's m'chosen lot. Only way I can help anythin'. Assumin' that's a help."

"We're all trying to help each other. It's sad it took the end of the world for us to finally do that."

"True words," she nods meaningfully. "But yer wrong 'bout one thing, sure as shittin'."

"That is?"

"Seen the cursed. All the time."

I put the bottle away and don't finish my drink. "I know."

"Not the way y'have, I bet. But... seen 'em. Know they're there."

I've held off long enough.

"How many people inhabit the city today?"

The number she says is pitiful.

I don't want to know, and yet…

"How many people inhabited the city last year?"

The number she says is…

"Where is yer hope now, Executioner?"

I have no answer. There is none.

None.

"… we went a year, not knowing this? Another city. Another *city*."

"Tried t'get to yeh."

"Did you?" I stare through the wall.

"One group in the deepness, out a'desperation. Then another in the wane a'winter. Then a smaller one in spring. By summer," she says, "we gave up."

"We didn't know."

"Did they make it?"

"We had no idea."

"Maybe… maybe if trade between us han't up and died a decade ago. No communication. No message-runners, save m'fantasy beau." Stares through the wall with me. "Hope he's okay."

"They're hard to kill."

"Like us?"

"Yeah. He'll be fine."

"Like us?"

"Yeah."

Looks at me hard. "Yeh truly believe."

"In?"

Smiles. Relief? "No. Yeh just… truly believe."

"Sorry we failed you."

"Y'ain't a city. Yer only one man."

"And two women."

"Aye. And y'all mean t'help?"

"Somehow."

"Goin' t'have t'forgive me fer not countin' on that."

"You don't have to until you see it," I tell her. "And then I'll forgive you."

Hops off the stool, facing the doorway. "Yeh sleepin'?"

Shake my head. "Nah." Eyes darting at the stairway, then away. "Planned to hike around."

"Brilliant. Yeh want the grand tour?"

"Offering?"

"Aye. But I need t'doze fer a few hours," she says. "Don't sleep much, but I do need it when I need it."

"Sounds like a plan."

"I'm off, then." Waves. "Catch yeh at dawn." Pausing at the doorframe. Lips curl in mischief. "Or an hourish later."

"'Ish'," I echo.

Flashes her teeth.

The door shuts. My hip bones pop as I vault to the floor and crack as I mount the steps to our room. Still locked, of course. I check the room next door. Storage space, but there's a pallet and blanket inside. More than adequate for someone used to passing out on the barren ground next to a cart of rigid corpses.

Soft. Warm. Comfortable. Surprisingly tough to fall asleep on. Before oblivion claimed me, I realized one fact omitted from our talk: every Executioner stationed here had drowned.

#

Horizon is trapping a face, warped from extreme angles, curving away, a giant black void of an eye the mountainous sun engulfing the point where sea and sky meet and die. Together, we lost. Together, we yearn. It spasms, longingly, to speak. The jaw is broken.

"I cannot reach," the jester puppet says.

In the ferry, I cannot row towards her. My arms are bone.

#

When I blink, sunlight is stabbing through the uncurtained window into my eyes. Megs is surely waiting. I gather my things… and then leave them. I need some time away from this… and then regather them anyways. This isn't the time for a break. Stupid to be unprepared. We're down one of us as it is.

Frowning at her door. Long seconds of expectation and debate. *Walk away*. Frowning more. *Stop it*. Raising fist. *Stop it, Leth*. *Walk away*. I knock. *Idiot*. I knock again.

Weight shifts on the floorboards within. Silence. Thump. Silence. Shuffling across the room. Silence. Thud. The door shudders into stillness.

"Ferryman is showing me around."

Sliding, haltingly. *Sss ssshh. Ssshh ss*. The door wobbles. *Sss… sss… shhh*. Thump. The door stops vibrating.

"Let's get going. Busy days."

Nothing. Not a grunt. Not a snort. Not even a fart.

"You know we can't lollygag."

I'm talking to myself. This is cute. Or delusional.

"Is this listening-to-me mode or ignoring-me mode?"

Sitting down, back pressed against the door. She's probably sitting in the exact same manner.

"You're not exhausted. Hell, if you were, you'd adamantly refuse the rest. What's going on?"

More nothing compounds itself.

"If you're overwhelmed, tell me. I'm here to hear that and help carry the burden."

Nothing.

"Megs wants to show us the city during the daytime. It's important. I know you want to scout."

Scratching. Frantic. Sharp.

Sssttstttt.

And then she scampers back into the room, loudly disappearing. Annoyed, I rise and…

See the paper she slid underneath the door that reads:

"It's weird how closely you monitor me."

Monitor...?

What the actual fuck.

No. Of course. I'm horrible. Checking on my partner, what a fiend. How could I have been this arrogantly foolish. To think that since I know my companion's desires, I anticipate them and let her know things she'd want to know. These same things she'd otherwise not know. I'm sorry. That's the correct phrase, right?

"Didn't sleep none?" Megs asks, bit of boredom creeping out of the words.

Figuring I'll misplace my mood and lash out at the wrong person, I simply tell her: "Good morning."

"Such as it is such as I can be," she says. "Shall we ride or yeh still fer that hike?"

"Moving my legs would be preferable at the moment."

Secures the oar and ties up her ferry to a post. With an encouraging gesture, she beckons me to follow over the bridge. I resist the impulse to look back at the Crow's Rest. The stones under my feet feel more stable.

#

Returning to the watery courtyard of last night. Now under the blunted gaze of morning, the remnants of the city appear vaster and more preserved than shadows and imagination had foretold. But it's... an appearance. Most of the spires, roofs, or bits of artistic architectural flair are uninhabitable.

I hope Megs will illuminate the extent of survival.

"This square here is our hub. Come together fer big decisions, talkin' and fightin'." Fixes me a serious stare. "But good fightin'. Tryin' t'help ever'un kind a'fightin'." Nods. "Market is here. Festivals too, though that takes up the islands there," pointing one place after the other, "and there, there, sometimes that one too."

"Pretty extensive."

"Think that now, wait till we tour them. Bigger than they seem. We... got good at maximizin' space."

"How does the market run?" I ask. "Clearly you have a job."

"Han't no economy, Drowns."

"Really."

"We manage without," she admits. "Ample food t'go around. And water. Heh."

Over the stone bridges, on every "island" as she calls them, we bump into people chatting, fishing, carrying boxes back and forth, maintaining and repairing stonework and woodwork. And far off, a small fleet of ferrymen coordinate some great endeavor at a resurrected tenement.

"You make it sound like thirteen years ago."

"Aye," she drawls somberly, "Ricken had a hand in that. Right lucky we was as he had settled in here not long after. He's an insight and a right blessing, 'ad it."

"From the Sovereignty, then?"

"Can't rightly say none. But definitely close enough t'understand how t'keep a community goin' when capitalism goes t'rot." Grins. "Lot does nowadays, y'know?"

"More than most," I sigh.

"Not a scant hike we got, grand tour and all that. Hallo!" Waves at a middle-aged, distracted shopkeeper over his counter. "Three a'those. Yeah, thanks. And... ah, gimme a bag a'mixed veg. Hey, got any baked potatoes? Not yet. Aight, we'll double back 'round later. Thank yeh!"

Unconsciously, I start to reach for a pocket with money. Ah. Right. "I'll never get used to this," I say.

"Plannin' on stayin'? We can getcha nice accommodations. Life ain't s'bad."

I don't think she's serious, but the importance of that question gives it substantial heft. What *are* we going to do now?

"I should check on Arroyo..."

"With some restful hours between the two a'ya, meanin' Ricken, maybe y'all can stow yer surly swaggers."

"He was lusting after a fight."

"Aye," Megs says, "and y'were more'n happy t'oblige." Points out a small alabaster watchtower. "We're that way, then. C'mon." Shrugs her shoulder-slung bag to comfort. "Ain't blamin' yeh. Y'seem a tolerant sort. But e'en yer like gets frayed ends, 'ad it, 'sides y'all didn't know Drowns was drowned. Silly fer anyone t'not sympathize with yeh. But I found y'all. Despairin'." Shoves hands in pockets. "Shred a'pity yet left in me."

We climb up the spiral staircase.

"I didn't lose anyone here, though," I admit.

Silence until we crest the top. On the landing, we find a narrow rope bridge extending from here all the way out to the next island. On the other side, another alabaster tower awaits.

"Course yeh did," Megs says over her shoulder, then slogs off nearly without me. "We're yer brothers and sisters, too."

I grip both sides of the bridge as we go, reassured only by Megs' confident, nonchalant gait. Unperturbed by the gusts that rock us to and fro, she is someone who understands the roads she has walked over one thousand times -- or has finally run out of shits in life left to give.

We cross another two tower-bridges before descending onto a seashell green rooftop with a mossy brick building built over at the edge. Four more rope bridges stretch out from that final landing, making this something of a crossroads. I wonder how extensive this network is. The more I see of this place, the more I discover how much remains -- to whatever dismal magnitude -- populated.

Megs knocks on the door.

"Ah crap!" Shoots me an embarrassed face, then knocks again more softly. "Sorry. Habit."

After a minute, the door creaks open. Ricken shoves his face out, gravely. "Yes."

Megs, nodding. "Oh nice welcome. C'mon, Ricken, lighten up and smile once in yer life, 'ad it."

"The little one is slumbering. You might try later in the—"

"Am not!" Arroyo bellows.

I can't help but smirk.

He stands in the doorframe, hand on the lintel, a veritable blockade. I fully expect my charge to come soaring out, knocking him into the water, or myself doing something similar. But he recedes.

"Arroyo!" Surprised at the volume of my own enthusiasm when I see her.

"Hey, Boss!" Waves at a funny angle as best she can.

The poor thing is on the side of the workshop, flat on her back in some sort of semblance of a bed. She scoots over, insisting so noisily with beating hands atop the cot that to not sit there would be the highest affront imaginable.

"How are you?" I ask.

"Sad."

I stroke her hair. Completely destroyed, without a hint of a braid. Ahh, it's like the loveable wight has died... Where has my Arroyo gone?

"Why's that?"

"Fighting death had consequences." Somehow manages to squish her entire face over to one side. Ahh, there she is!

"No doubt."

"You hadn't set the bones correctly," Ricken tells me.

Arroyo seethes. "Boss did too!"

"You hadn't set them correctly," he repeats, "or else she put pressure on it regularly or at significant, forceful intervals."

"Did not."

"We carried her," I say, voice lowering defensively.

"So you say. Left untreated, she will walk without difficulty, but in high likelihood with a limp. The angle and height are a bit off. She might compensate. I wouldn't know the result until it happened. By then, it would be far more insidious to fix," he says. "Depending what your definition and intent of the word 'fix' happens to be."

"I gotta be at one-hundred percent!" Arroyo protests. "More than, if I wanna surpass Ms. Euliae."

"She's an Executioner. We need her perfect. I want that. She wants that. Simple."

"No. Not quite as simple as you assume. Her ankle was completely shattered," Ricken says.

"Yeah, I know that. I was freaking there," Arroyo snaps.

"What is healing is not healing this 'perfect' that you seek. You wish the pitiless truth of the matter?" Ricken asks. "I'll have to go in and shatter it again: what is healed and what hasn't yet. Then carefully set the pieces. In that, no guarantees." I glower at him, but he glowers back more deeply. "I feel as if you need to hear how brutal I'm going to be..." Jerks a thumb over at an immaculate, sterilized workbench. "I'll need to saw out her bones -- above and below the damage -- and redo everything. This child's bones turned into a magnificent puzzle. You want this?"

Megs' laugh is dull. "Way t'dampen the blows."

Arroyo's face is full of passionate intensity. It's obvious what her answer is.

"You give me two answers, doctor," I say. "Risk her supposed imperfection later, or depend on your artistry and increase her suffering now."

"In principle, yes."

"I'm not letting you scoop out her damned bones," I snarl. "I set it. Euly checked and double-checked and triple-checked. We have never, in our lives, been this meticulous and certain about anything. *Anything*."

"Deciding for her out of distrust," he muses. "I see."

"The opposite. I *trust* Euliae," I say. "I don't know you in the slightest."

"And yet you allowed her to be parted from you."

"Because she's not a child, you bloody stonewall, and I knew she needed an examination over putzing around with me. I was worried about her. Still am."

"Guys," Arroyo interjects.

"You'll have to clarify the nature of your angst. What or who is your enemy at this moment in time? The world, this girl's bones, or me?"

"One foot on 'land' and you've had nothing but bile for us. Look, I appreciate you looking over Arroyo; I'll thank you for it. But you... you have this unspoken dagger aimed at us. Had we been refugees, I imagine the tone would be lighter. I have to ask then: what is your damn problem with the Executioners?"

"Guys."

"You've given me too much to choose from," he says. "You're likely to get either everything or nothing, and I certainly can't do everything. I'll try not to do nothing.

"Shall we start with the absurd idealism? The utter cessation of the aftereffects of death, or if I'm being conservative: its physical manipulation. How droll. Using carefulness as a lever, instinctual dread as the fulcrum, to uproot the very tree of life itself. And what to do with this 'husk'? Why, hide it away from the innocent, shunned eyes of the populace. To wit, concealing what is presently the foregone conclusion when every daybreak is memento mori? How scrupulous indeed."

"Sure. Fine. I'll grant you that," I say. "Then we should do nothing? Let it spill into the streets?"

"Have you, by chance, considered the possibility that you've made a mistake? That there's a better way forward yet you flail down the only corpse road you've ever known, ever traveled?"

"Burial becomes super-duper burial. Yeah. I get that. And transfers from Pauper's Pit to its dun are moving one problem to another. I'm not a cynic, but I *think*."

"Then you imbeciles have started excavating...? Of course. Of course you'd be that idiotic. Ah there it is: again the clarifying of why I left that corrupt city. It is a crutch made for a grandsire who no longer exists."

"Ricken, I am not planning on cozying up with the dead and letting this story end. Moreover, we've proven as a society we can keep going."

"There are four conditions under which a kingdom can be said that its permanence is over: one is repeated swapping of ruling caste; one is messing around with systemically-installed and untested technologies; one is harboring provenanceless organizations without democratic oversight; and one is transparency -- which if you follow through with the convention means you have to act, you're mandated, to prevent civil upheaval."

"You're willfully ignoring—"

"The Sovereignty had broken all four. More than once."

"Guys!" Arroyo shouts, breath arcing high-pitched in pain. "Ain't on meds right now, am I? Stop fighting! *Please*. Dr. Ricken: stop arguing philosophy with Boss, it's boring, and saw out my cunt-fucking ankle already!"

"If you are saying it with witnesses this time, very well," Ricken's voice rolls out. "But refrain from 'doctor'. Technically, it is only something I picked up." Offers me a weary side-glance. "Professional dilettante. If you like."

"I don't," I bark. "Arroyo—"

"Boss, no." Punches my leg without energy or malice. "You don't get a say in this."

"Damned if I don't. I'm watching out for you. To speak nothing of being your friend."

"Boss, that loyalty of yours gonna get you killed one day." Arroyo covers a smile, but it's still there when she moves her wrist. "Okay. You get a say. But you don't get to decide, right? It's my body."

"If you're sure," I say. "I'll be at your side."

"The work will be tedious. I'd prefer not," Ricken says. "It's quite evident we don't get on."

"I won't be getting in your way."

"Perhaps not, but I would likely get in yours."

"When can we start?" Arroyo asks, blunting the next row.

"Once you've had your movement and haven't drunk for several hours."

"Well that was blatant." Arroyo screws up her face again, then settles down. "You don't gotta stay, Boss. But sure be nice if you and Euliae were around when I woke up."

"Deal."

Ricken leads us towards the door. Megs scampers away first, pops an olive-stuffed loaf from her pack and leaves it on the converted kitchen's countertop. He and I are alone for a few seconds.

"Listen," I lower my voice. "I'll un... bare my fangs if you'll sheathe the claws."

He emits a deep, earthy, nonplussing "Hmmm."

Megs dashes the moment to dust by slapping his oversized shoulder blade. "We're in yer care, Ricken."

"Finish your rounds, Megrit."

"It's 'Megs', yeh damn tool. Get it right, 'ad it..."

We go.

"You can loiter outside until she stirs."

I turn, but he's gone.

Perhaps the start of a ceasefire. Though the unclosed door gapes devoid of reassurance.

#

My guide takes me across the network of rope bridges, to islands near and far, some stretching plaintively an extra storey high -- an extra two storeys -- out from the waters.

But most, ahh… what a completely inadequate word… barely reach the level atop which we walk.

Megs' boots splash with every step.

"We subsist," she says proudly and, seemingly about to say more, moves on.

#

My guide takes me to the roof of yet another alabaster tower as indistinguishable as the rest. But she exhibits a specific sense of peace here, shoulders lowered, leaning over to me. I accept the bundle: olive-stuffed bread and unfamiliar vegetables that taste of lemon and wine.

"Dead center a'the city," she says, "or leastways what was a'it."

#

My guide takes me to the summit of a hill, one that would be an impressive dun in a different life, one that may have been planned as a dun in Krohn's fantasies, but now only the top third is visible.

A gate is burrowed into its side. She opens it, and I behold layer upon layer of marvels.

Every floor we descend is devoted to a different type of food, an entire hill hiding stacked farms of wheat and barley, potatoes and carrots, apple and persimmon trees. And yet this is not what amazes me. Golden, pulsing webs cover every ceiling, emitting soft light that is the perfect level of warmth. An eternal spring.

"This is Underground," she says, "and the spider gossamer keeps ever'thin' growin' all the year 'round."

#

My guide takes me to the base of the Windtower, a heavenward spire that rivals the antiquated clocktower in Old Kingdom even in such rampant disrepair as this. Climbing and looking down would give a supreme vantage of the flood and the surrounding hillsides, though I'm loathe to subject myself to such masochism.

The only thing to be gained here is a perspective to crush my already shaken, strained, professional confidence.

"Can't be helped," she says. "Place is literally crawlin' this time a'day. It's bad season. For the spiders, I mean."

#

And when my guide returned me back to our lodgings, she untied her ferry, and waited solemnly. It felt like a funeral was set to begin and, looking back, perhaps it was. I entered, sat, and she rowed... straight for the empty mass of water behind the forsaken lighthouse.

I heard it long before I saw it.

> Her oar gently kept its pull at bay.
> A brushing back of death:
> > not yet
> > not yet

"Maelstrom" is all she intoned, a single finger pointed outwards like a compass needle drawn in a direction it must never go yet is eternally compelled to seek.

The arms and legs of the cursed dead broke the surface and crashed down, spume and spray arcing high, an unceasing mist encircling the whirlpool created by their sleepless frenzied feedback loop. Even in the silent hallways of Crypt Dun, this is what we fear most: one cursed spasms in sleep, strikes a wall, and the reverberation does not fade back to nothingness... but grows and redoubles itself... until the whole of that hill is clattering with the interred in as unending a chorus as this. It is a testament to our deliberate planning and engineering that the break-in didn't trigger such pandemonium. But to see this...

> "I don't know..."

... in all its horrible glory.

> "... where to begin."

Because this was what we were always fighting to stop. This was the panic that engendered our ceaseless work at Pauper's Pit. This is why we only whispered in graveyards.

Why we barely dared breathe when the carts were laden. This was the endgame we had no contingency plans for. We thought we were in control. But here, in Drowns, it waited:

Ground zero.

Ours is a wide, wide world made all the wider in our collective deaf-blindness. The message-runners keep us connected -- though with appalling and debilitative blindspots. That's... only in the province, however. What the fucking hell is out there beyond our piddling reach? And what about the Gap, those thousands of miles of emptiness that divide us from what we only assume is plague of pestilential scope? Is the unnoteworthy, miniscule orb hurtling through sun-scorched void that we call a home as blessedly silent as the grave should be, or teeming with this unrepressed display of turmoil -- such uncontrollable turmoil?

The world has ended.

But is it dead? Or dying?

"There's not enough," I murmur indistinctly to no one and without knowing what I mean.

My guide, the wordless ferryman.

I shake myself, and return.

"Has this ever slowed?" I ask. "When did it begin?"

"Can't rightfully say much, nor none that I've noticed," she admits, rowing us mournfully away. "Not hard t'miss, right? Appeared when winter was fixin' t'end, fair immediately, 'ad it. Like it were waitin'." Clicks her tongue. "T'shit on spring."

"At least they're stuck in their loop for now. Lake won't freeze that deep...."

"How d'yeh figure? Frigid ice cube it became at the heart a'deepness, whole damn thing."

"That's not... possible, is it? Lakes... don't do that."

"Do now. Or ours do."

"But... the whole...?"

"Near as can, 'ad it. The fish, they go down, way down, they'll live, but no matter the agitation those cursed makin' presently…" Her oar trembles an inch above the surface, grazing a thought. "…ain't stayin' liquid fer long come that deepness. And… winter…" Strokes through the water a fragile caress. "Deepness devourin' more and more a'winter yearly."

So that was our fixed timeline: the indeterminate start of deepness -- after which the gyre would solidify and we'd see firsthand what a Dun breakout would look like in real-time.

Arroyo was incapacitated. Would be for months if the operation was a resounding success.

Euliae was Euliae. I could count on her if I could count on her, and right now I don't exactly know what's going on there.

One single man, subjugated by time and tidal forces, setting himself up against visible oblivion? Sounds like some retarded shit I would do. Makes a fully compromised Crypt Dun and emptied Pauper's Pit sound like idealistic drunken babble ending in practically a dare.

Megs hardly needs to voice the scarcely-concealed dread rictused across her entire body when she witnesses what passes for professional emotion masking what was once my face a few seconds ago.

"We are the architects of our own salvation," I say.

She turns away, perhaps with more horror than hope.

As they say at funerals:

The Executioner is come.

#

If I wanted to do the impossible it followed that I'd need to know what my resources were, halve them (because events would surely fuck me in the ass reasonably hard) and assume my best-case scenario failed spectacularly. And yet I still pull it out in the end.

I'm trying to hold on to that dangling optimism. Good boy, Lethean; one person may live after the curtain plummets. Might be you.

Decided to hie myself to what passed for a city hall, or at least the attic of one, and learn more about what Echo Downs was like before the flood devastated everyone's plans: them back then, and us back now. It's strange. I've traveled all over the stretches of roads from Old City to Avershym, but feels like I haven't seen much of anything. Rutted earth, countless trees, vast barren emptinesses, and little but the outskirts of civilization.

I suppose I'm too married to this job.

"Making good time, Boss!" the imagined voice, resonating from a barely-remembered memory.

A smile I didn't notice I had falls.

"Not really," I reply. "The greater part of research is wasting time until you find the single thing you need." No one answers back. "Clearly haven't found it then," I add in undertone.

As tedious time dragged by, the eureka epiphany never sparked. This place was a city, nothing more special than that outside the exceptional shit circumstances under which it now wallows. I poked my head outside before I went cross-eyed.

A ragged tail of stratus was blazing along the edges, sun sunk behind it ready to get to sunset and get on with things. Time to gather the maps and architect plans into a bundle and strike out to Ricken's.

I didn't tell Arroyo about the site called Maelstrom. Though I suppose, as the drugs coursed through her throbbing then quietening veins, it wouldn't have made much a difference on the success of this operation. I am no slave of truth. Beauty, I think sometimes. Not truth. There are facts not worth relating even on the brightest, most horrible mornings. Focus on the important things instead:

continue to hold Arroyo's hand as each finger unclenches its death-grip, falls as limply as her doll-like head has against the pillow. Smile for her in a mirror reflection of the smile now slackened to a small, unconscious "oh" of surprise.

I planned to let go and move to the nearby armchair after Ricken tightened the straps and double-tightened the tourniquet. When the fine teeth of his handsaw began gnawing through the little Executioner's bone, I realized that armchair hadn't been sitting there earlier -- nor the matching one next to it.

"Oh," I said in my own mirror of surprise, and kept holding her hand up until the moment Ricken returned to his workdesk, palms cupping the bones that used to attach her leg to her foot.

Hours passed. No one came and went.

Arroyo slept, a line of drool trickling from the corner of her mouth the whole time. If a drop of blood escaped the tourniquet, I missed it in spite of my anxious vigilance. I glanced over at Ricken and leaned back into the armchair. He seemed like a master sculptor with his hammer and chisel, breaking Arroyo's ankle bones with such patient precision, with such steady hands, that I doubted whether he was only the dilettante he claimed to be.

Not once did he acknowledge my presence. Whatever he was, he was a professional. Hunched over the bench. Measuring. Studying a bone splinter in the light, rotating it appraisingly like a dealer of coin. He made a deep grunt, hunched back down, and pasted the splinter to the larger nearly-constructed puzzle piece.

His method was alien to me. Would my young charge be the cripple, ejected from frontline work and relegated to support? Didn't seem likely before Drowns. Seems less likely now.

My spine pops when I stand. Ricken doesn't flinch.

#

My third time knocking is aggravatingly loud. I fold my arms, noisily shifting my weight every handful of seconds so she knows I'm not leaving. But at length I do because I am not the asshole.

#

"And there was this massive, massive bunny! Big as a tenement! And he kept burrowing into the mountainside and pooping people out, but no one seemed to mind which was strange."

I'm not sure why that was the strange part.

But after the drugs defogged from her disturbingly creative mind and her babbling started making more sense, except not really, Arroyo was as chipper as ever.

"Bed rest forever," I say.

"Unfair!"

"For two weeks," Ricken intoned from what passed for a kitchen, "if you can manage."

"I can manage." Arroyo looked deep into my eyes without blinking. She couldn't manage.

Ricken returned with two bowls of the most peculiar smelling soup. I feared his talents weren't well-rounded, but leaned forward to accept his offering anyway. He ignored me and placed them both next to Arroyo.

"Hot piss!" she exclaimed -- in celebration I assumed, but she could have been adding a feisty commentary all her own. She devoured both bowls with such wanton gluttony that my spirits said our little Executioner was already mended... until a few minutes later when her body imploded and her face screwed up. "Pain!" she called. "Pain pain pain!"

Our ad hoc doctor trod across the room -- I damned his relaxed gait -- and administered the treatment. She was drooling soon again, this time with a silly grin. "Yer pretty, captain. Sometimes."

I rubbed her hair. She giggled, then choked, coughed, snorted and horked out a huge gob of something onto my lap. She seemed pleased with herself, then fell asleep.

#

Megs was to be an assistant of sorts over the next few days. She groused a bit which surprised me, but apparently there was also some friction between those two -- that is, her and Ricken. None of it was aimed at Arroyo, for whom Megs was touchingly protective.

One new complication had to do with Arroyo's training and freakish health: her damn metabolism was so hyper that the half-life of painkillers was worryingly short. And thus she would stay at Ricken's until a proper balance was restored.

"I'll try to deal with the pain," she winced.

I left the materials I had recovered of city records by her bedside. I doubted there was much in there, but poring over boring minutiae may glean a few potential demi-answers and, more importantly, distract her. "If you have the brainpower tomorrow," I told her, "study over these."

She reached for the topmost ledger. A maroon little thing. Probably budgetary. "Twenty-five bags flour. Two bushels oats." Lowered it, glanced up at me. "The heck's a bushel?" Glanced back down at the ink, quirked up and confused, then quietly to herself: "Oats grow on bushes...?" Flips the page. "... huh, didn't know that."

I took the ledger away from her and replaced it on the pile. "Most of it is probably bunk. See if there's dun prospects here."

"Why?"

Don't tell her why.

"That was Krohn's plan," I say, not exactly a lie.

"I remember." She takes another ledger, this one off-white. I pull it out of her hands and put it back.

"Get some sleep. Long day, yeah?"

"Not really tired, Boss. But if that's an order," she put on a stupid look, "I'll comply."

I pointed at her pillow. "Order."

She saluted.

I managed to maintain my forced smile up until the moment I shut the front door.

#

Set a bowl of nourishing breakfast at the door. Waited hours. No response. Left.

#

Arroyo is mostly out of it today.

"Our concerns about the painkillers are, on the whole, likely paranoid..."

"I like my paranoia."

"... as well as premature. Yes, I'm sure you do."

"She didn't want to wait yesterday. Not an instant."

"And today she begged not to have them at all, a decision made in sound mind that I respected until she began sweating profusely and digging her nails into her forearms unto bleeding."

"Stubborn."

"Inherits that from her father figure."

"Get off my back."

"Both a'yeh shush, 'ad it!" Megs storms in, pushes the door shut and latches it. Her cheeks raw red from the biting wind.

"Can you wean her?"

"There will be discomfort."

"Then, try to avoid it."

"Most certainly," he intones, "however, I suspect it will prove... temperamental." Even his shoulders frown. "How I wish you hadn't plied her so liberally at the start..."

#

Came back to an empty bowl. Cleaned up. Slept. Brooded out at gray skies of a morning that too did not want to rise. Set another bowl at the door. Barely waited. No response. Left.

#

Arroyo is better today, but hurting.

#

Another empty bowl. Cleaned up. Had a shot of brandy, only for the taste. For a brief moment, the antediluvian Echo Downs washed over me: carts along the cobblestone streets laden with apples for pressing; the conversation of businessmen; a handshake and jingle of coin; then in quicker succession: the juicing, the barreling, the aging, ultimately culminating after months maybe years into this bittersweet oaken taste burning the back of my throat.

But these were merely borrowed nostalgia from Old City. I have never been to Echo Downs.

#

Arroyo is good today, but hurting more.

#

Empty bowl. The cleaning. Sleep. Tomorrow came on the backs of corpses dart out of a grave at me. My fingers strangled air. I set out another bowl, though blearily I may have forgotten the bread.

#

Arroyo is bad today; the hurting won't stop.

#

An empty bowl.

#

Arroyo is worse.

"Do you want to play your graverobber game?" I ask.

She doesn't look up. "No thank you."

"I really don't mind. It's a useful perspective."

She won't look up. "No thank you."

#

An empty bowl.

#

Arroyo is worse.
I say words to her.
She doesn't look up.
I still say words to her.
She doesn't look up.

#

An empty bowl.

#

Arroyo is worse.
I hold her hand.
She doesn't mind.
There are no words.
She doesn't mind.

#

An empty bowl.

#

Arroyo is worse.
I sit next to her.
She doesn't notice.

#

An empty bowl.

#

Arroyo is worse.
I haven't stopped smiling.
She has no expression.

#

An empty bowl.

#

Arroyo is worse.
I've stopped smiling.
She doesn't notice.

#

The bowl was empty. The hallway was empty. I did not clean up. I did not sleep. I waited. I waited all night. I waited all day. I did not visit Arroyo. I waited until the next day.

At sunrise, I rear back and slam the heel of my boot full force one inch to the side of the doorknob the door cracking off the paltry partially-rusted lock and swinging on screaming hinges to rupture against the wall and creak back not halfway knowing sensing understanding I would tear the whole apparatus off without remorse.

She is awake, sitting on a chair in the corner of the room. A lance of dawnlight the color of scar tissue cuts across the floorboards, dividing her into a skewed space of her own.

She looks at me. When her expected scowl begins to crease her face, I bark: "Gather your equipment. All of it."

Her scowl, half-formed, miscarries into one of blank confusion. With only silent acknowledgement, she complies. Finished, she stands before me, backpack slung over both shoulders. Curious now, she awaits me to inform her the order of business. I leave instead. She follows.

My guidance takes her through every alabaster tower across practically every rope bridge to a distant cul-de-sac: an asymmetrical spike of roof overhanging nothing but drowning lake.

"You gonna tell me—"

"Give me your blade," I tell her.

Euliae lets out a bored exhale. Unsheathes the weapon, flips it, handing me the hilt. She walks past me and hunches down at the roof's edge. "It's all very dramatic." Humorless laugh.

"This isn't your new blade."

"So what?"

"Where is it?"

Jerks her thumb at the backpack.

I open the strap and root around inside. It's down at the bottom. I stand and toss the old blade over into the drink.

"What the fuck!"

"You'll be using this one henceforth." I throw the pointlessly-buried blade at her tip first. She snatches it midair and contemptuously shoves it in her sheath, then grimaces at its unfamiliar sound.

"Happy?"

"Get over here and itemize your resources."

"No. You don't order me around."

"I want a full list."

"I said, you don't order me."

I stare her down. Somehow, it works.

"You are so infuriating!" Like a pissy child she stomps over, drops to her ass, and sorts through everything and lists out each item while explicitly noting the quantity -- increasing the volume and ire of her voice whenever there is only one. "There! Nice and sorted and tidy! I sure am glad we took the time to have this by-the-book session, Lethean, I almost feel wet! Should we itemize panties too?"

"Take out the crossbow I gave you."

"Take out your cock and fuck yourself."

"Take it out."

"No."

"Take out the parts of your crossbow and place them in front of you, Euliae."

For a moment, just for a moment, I think she might gather her belongings and leave. But something about this now has the air of challenge and—

"I know what you're trying to do," she warns me in a flat undertone that has the implicit warning of undertow. "Don't fuck with Euly." Stares me down this time. "Euly fucks back."

I tell her to assemble her crossbow. She does. Competently, but without haste. She can do better. I stop her before the final step.

"Again."

Emotionlessly, she disassembles it. She pauses a second, waiting for me to observe that everything is within an inch of where it was previously. Then she reassembles.

Faster, but her heart is clearly not in it yet. She pauses before the final step. I say nothing this time. I wait. Like at the door.

"Not good enough."

Dissembling. Pausing. Reassembling. Mediocre.

"The cursed has beaten you about the head and upper torso. Useless."

Dissembling. Pausing. Reassembling. Decent.

"It's closing distance on you. You won't have time to slot the bolt."

Dissembling. Pausing. Reassembling. Passable.

"If you got lucky, you could get a bolt off. But your aim probably wouldn't be accurate."

Dissembling. Pausing. Reassembling. Nigh perfection, but not for her.

"Sloppy." I spit, legitimately disgusted. "Again."

Her shoulders tense and quiver. She disassembles the crossbow, slapping each piece down like a miniature impotent thunderclap. Doesn't look at me when she asks, "You going to shoot me with this?"

"No. I'm going to do worse than that."

The smirk doesn't leave her face. I painstakingly lead her through each step, ignoring the automatic command she has over the process, ignoring the twitch in her muscles that want to move on to the next step before the plodding gait of my words. We both know she can do this blind. Already proved it.

As before, we both pause at the final step.

"String it."

Without hesitation or imperfection, she does. Not a hint of the smirk slipping. It really is the perfect mask.

She stares at the crossbow in her hands, not even her eyelids moving. I wait, knowing my silence is replaced with the invisible torment of inner monologue. Because whose trapped voice can be more malicious than our own?

Execration

Some sadism must have finally rubbed off on me at some point. I wanted to echo back all the poison building up in our relationship for the past several years. Holding nothing back.

Instead, I told her to cock it.

Her whole body refused. The smirk was gone. I repeated myself. She shook. I kept repeating myself until her body stopped shaking and became a statue. I said it again. I kept saying it. Eventually, a bubble welled up from her chest and gurgled out something that may have meant "no" or "please" and I ignored it and said it again I ignored the hollow in my gut and said it again I kept ignoring it I kept ignoring it.

When she, at long last, managed to draw the string back, her fingers and palms were covered in a network of scarlet lashes.

The waters far below the roof were unmoving.

I saw it first out of the corner of my eye: the hand hovering above her knee opened and closed, then rose by inches towards my own. By the time it reached me, it was partially-yet-reluctantly-open and struggled to remain that way until it wrapped timidly around my wrist. A hesitation. Then one trembling finger lifted, ready to sign a word or a message or a sob.

I pulled out from her grasp and slapped the hand away.

"Do your job, Executioner."

And left.

#

After reading a fourth book from the growing pile to a barely-conscious Arroyo, who I pretended had begun to pester me about her boredom and pleading so annoyingly for me to at least make up stories for her so she could stop drug-dreaming about being trapped in a world of oat-bushes and vengeful dandelion-bunnies, Euliae appeared.

My absence the day before had gone unnoticed... which wasn't fortunate because, as Ricken noted again to Euliae, our little Executioner was having an arduous recovery. He related to her the general synopsis of the last week or so, giving a prognosis awash in his normal mannerisms. If only all dilettantes were so adroit and thorough.

And Euly?

Never said a word. Just listened. That's all.

Arroyo seemed to be stirring a bit. I could never tell when that meant the drugs were wearing off or she was dreaming her bafflingly uncomfortable dreams.

Took it as an opportunity to leave and catch up on sleep myself back at the Crow's Rest. My partner silently took over my vigil, only a careful nod of her head in my direction acting as acknowledgement.

Before I shut the front door, I looked back.

Euly wasn't focused on me at all.

Good.

#

Death darkness deepness entwined, hints of three more seasons our little secret that the jester puppet giggles in the ferry. She says it repeatedly, epic chant hymn of gaiety loss full felt void of meaning. She forgets the origin. Doesn't matter anymore. She cannot sit up without aid.

My arms are bone.

No stringy sinews to help.

"It's okay?" I ask.

"Not really," she giggles. Sighs. "Is this what we've come to? We've missed the harvest. Another year of starvation. You've done well for yourself."

I frown. But I don't frown because there's only bone.

"I do wish to be less than this."

"Given time, put yourself in an hourglass."

Which way will be upwards then and of another perspective it might not matter though one of us will spin laugh make love brood and either turn it upside-down or ourselves to headstand wiggling toes at a blasted sky where amber wheatfields are terracing overlooking seas of... that never happened. Did it?

"It did!" she screams while the wheatfield susurrus laughs for the emotion she can no longer form into a clay word not for lack of *need* for lack of *want*. The reason cannot exist in solitude. If it could.

"What a glorious waste."

She sits up without strings. She surpasses herself. She transcends by attaining the mundane. I weep.

"What a show," she sighs again. "But I will not perform the leading role. Keep me in the shadows and then, at the climax, I will play a different part. The desolate audience applauds with silence, the lanterns are unshuttered: there are no seats there are no walls there are no stages and we actors have not yet begun. I will not play the leading role, but one of us will. That one is not yet come. That one is not yet assigned." Then she turns away towards me one of us horizon-bound the inverse cannot be determined lamplight? firelight? The sun!

Ah. It ends.

"If you were assigned, I will be cross." Tells me true.

I shake my head, but without muscles it does not move. "I am not."

"Then who is on the stage? What is the name that sits on its head?"

The sun! A window!

"The name..." I echo. My ribcage hollowed out a space beyond bones where ossification is how eternal watchers are borne across a tide unlike this one where the liquids are either black or crimson or black. "There is none. I think."

The jester puppet is horrified terror terror terror surprise shock manic the panic panic panic it was supposed to be an easy answer but this this this—

The sun! A window! I cannot move?

—if the one has not been set then everything is in flux.

"If the one is not yet set then everything is in flux!" she cries aloud for the sky wheatfields that now listen and the hourglass turns is dropped it knocks hard and the strident reverberation shakes the world.

The sweep of the rough bristles of an errant broom against the rougher surfaces of stone do not echo the impermanence of all things, but rather they are the promise that everything will be alright because – despite our constant unending cries – kindness, we often forget, has always been the more powerful scythe than the malice of hearts.

She collapses unable to hold on to the thought and her body at the same time.

"Be at peace." My skull is smiling. "I can feel the sunlight and there are constants in a place even such as this."

Sight obliviates. Warmth expands. The flap of wings.

#

Although nothing at the city level is resolved or remotely started, we three are normalizing to our situation. Arroyo is progressively better each day. Not perfectly -- there are still bouts of pain and loopiness from withdrawal -- but any victory is a victory when rock bottom was a bed we settled into far too long.

I feel less frayed at every end, a state I'd been wholly ignorant of until I noticed its sudden absence maybe yesterday or the day before. The perpetual gloom of Drowns, to an outsider like me, is less affecting. Euly is currently practicing the ancient and humbling art of ignoring-the-overwhelming-situation-by-focusing-on-small-albeit-selfish-concerns. But since that is only my cynical way of saying she did the right thing, I'm okay with the outcome.

That being said... we've lost valuable time we can't recover and the moment has come at last for me to apprise her fully of how deep in the shit we are.

I tap her shoulder. "Can I borrow you?"

An unreadable expression passes over her like a noontime shadow, then is gone. Tiptoeing away from Arroyo's second naptime, she joins me over at the storeroom where I'm waiting.

This will be the first time we've exchanged more than the monosyllabic since...

"Thank you," Euliae says to me.

"Eh?"

She makes as if to make a frown, then sits next to me on the bench instead. Her hand takes mine. Tap, tap. Stroke, tap. Stroke stroke. Tap. Pause. Emphatic tap.

::Euly thanks Leth::

And she repeats herself aloud. "I said 'thank you'." Starts to look up at me, then glances away. "As opposed to..." Pauses, bites her lip. "... when I only..." Clears her throat. "... say the words."

Silence.

::Euly::

"Yeah."

::We need long talk::

"Hell, man." Gruffness mixed with shame. "What more is there to say...?"

I continue to hold her hand and let out about as long a breath as can be let out. That gets her attention more than anything. She turns towards me, leans into the wall, and swallows. Knows me well enough to know this ain't chitchat and it ain't about *us*.

So, I tell her about Maelstrom. I keep my voice low, near enough a whisper, probably in hopes that will blunt the reality. The currency of beggars, isn't it? Agonizing does not change no matter what methods you chose. It just is and you bear it unto the grave.

With each word, her head sinks farther into her hand. "I don't have any tears left to give this endeavor," she says at length, suffering a convulsion immediately afterwards.

"Damn it. Damn all this fucking…"

Pulling her close, I rub her back in gentle, even strokes. She doesn't stop me.

"Lethean."

"I know."

Head pivoting on her hand, one watery eye piercing up into me like the sharpest blade I've ever held.

"What the hell, Lethean?"

"I know."

"No one is equipped for this scale. No one. Not all of us. *No one*."

There is nothing I can do except let her mind run blindly in terror through the maze of thought I already have. By my reckoning, she has about two weeks of catch-up to do. But she's Euliae. She'll be beyond my comprehension in short order and jeering at me from the outside in.

"I… I don't know what to do with this. Shit. Shit!" Hands on my shoulders, wild-eyed, practically begging me, "Have you thought anything up yet?"

"The obvious solutions, none of which will work and all of which we'll be trying anyways because what other options?"

"And I was— for, like—? unghh! I'm such a bloody self-absorbed— nnghha!"

"We still have time. Maybe."

"I did that! *I* did."

"Humility doesn't suit you."

Scowls at me. Grins a bit, but scowls.

"Be a bitch already. I don't recognize you anymore."

Scowls more. The grin nearly slips into a sob.

"Come here," she tells me.

"Well? What do you think?"

"No. Come here."

She puts her arms around me, tightens the one across my chest. A tender moment when all is… I don't even know.

"We gotta tell Krohn," Arroyo complains diligently from the doorway.

Euly and I are startled out of hugging.

"It's procedure, you guys. Also, can I join this group hug too? I like it when you two aren't fighting."

"Sweetie, you shouldn't be walking yet or, like, *anything*." Admonishment though it might be, I confess the heavy relief in Euly's voice made me swallow the rising ache in my own throat.

Little Arroyo had propped herself up on a broom and hobbled over to us with that makeshift crutch. Now she leans against the doorway, face quirked-up to the side like she was considering whether or not to chew some tough dried fruit already in her mouth and couldn't decide if the taste was good, bad, or even had any.

"Rest and recuperation was the order," I say.

Ignoring us, she plows on ahead. A lucid Arroyo is a hell of a thing. "You two shouldn't fight. You're friends. You love each other." Shaking her head like the overbearing aunt she's trying desperately, though unconsciously, to be. "Honestly. I don't know what goes through your minds at all most times, not at all."

"Nothing if you're him."

"Fuck off, Euly."

Arroyo throws her hands in the air, immediately losing balance. She clings to her crutch, huffing and chuffing. "This is *exactly*," she mutters to herself, "what I've been talking about."

She wobbles over and drops next to me. Or at least, she would have if I didn't grab her overexcitedness by the trunk and lower her the rest of the way.

The huffing and chuffing are about to continue.

"I'm glad you're back." I rub her messy, unbraided hair.

Huff and chuff abort simultaneously. Mostly.

"We makin' a plan or gonna grouse instead, Boss?"

160

Euly leans into my shoulder, head pressed against mine. Not lost in thought, just lost. Arroyo copies her. I wonder what Ricken would say if he saw us. Probably pop in, vaguely acknowledge the tableau with a glance of one eye, take what he wanted from a nearby shelf, and leave without so much as a taciturn grunt.

Echo Downs, where do we begin with you?

#

Always consider your worst ideas first.

Yes, yes, farmers and smiths and any blessed normal bloody trade can ignore what I'm about to describe. Their lot is infinitely more stable, comparative to ours, regardless of finicky weather or broken tools. If I seem belittling in that, understand it's coming from the vantage of jealousy.

In those worst ideas is a kernel of brilliance, informed by the insanity inherent in our strange brand of artistry. We had two pragmatic solutions:

Bury the cursed in a dun.

"That sounds nice and cozy."

Go get Krohn.

"Let Big Boss deal with it."

In three months? Impossible.

"We are so *fucked*."

Anyone in this wide, wide, forsaken world could have said that. Arroyo had the honors, across the room and staring at a network of cracks in the wooden beam overhead. She readjusted the pillow on her pallet and shoved another molasses roll into her newly-defeatist mouth.

Hence the worst ideas. Maybe we could unearth *something* of value buried in their rotten husks.

"If I leave tomorrow morning, I can bring back everyone available and then some," I said, still not touching my leek soup. "But we'll return to deal with the aftermath of whatever catastrophe will be awaiting us by then."

"Assuming *that* can be dealt with," Euly replied.

"And if *you* get started now, you can inter maybe twenty percent of what's out there." I knocked the ledger I'd been having a lurid affair with the past hour against my thigh. For emphasis. Emphasis feels good sometimes. Feels almost like control.

"Heavily assuming we can even *recover* them," she said, groaning. "One at a time?"

                               "Fucked
                                     fucked
                                        fucked."

"Arroyo…"

                                  "Sorry, ma'am."

Euly frowned at my soup, then scowled at me. I started to eat. "We'll have to claim ownership of their farming hill, covert it into a makeshift dun, and conscript every able-bodied person who was too stupid to die the first time tragedy struck."

"We don't have right of conscription," I tell her.

"Well, I mean, I was planning on lying about evacuating them. They'd stonewall straight out, I'd act frustrated, they'd dig their heels in, I'd pretend compromise by saying anyone who's willing to help can stay." She tosses me a roll. "That's when I stonewall and it works."

I stare at the roll in my hand, wondering how much of the flour was replaced with ground-up opportunism before being shoved into a blistering oven. "Is this how you think about people all the time?"

"Menace…" Arroyo whispers.

"Not… *all* the time?" Euliae says carefully, considering the question while she talks -- as if the possibility that she was an unredeemable shrew had never once occurred to her. "Either way, main rule of lying is to not care if you get caught, dear Lethean. Doesn't matter to me if they catch on or not. We three alone understand the scope of the shitstorm coming."

"Eeef. Storm's already here, basically," Arroyo reasons. "Weathering it's the question. Or mitigating the damage. Uhghh, crap."

"Hmm?"

"You're killin' my idealism. Instead of seeking the solution, I'm giving up." Bolts upright as her passion takes over, faltering momentarily from moving her ankle. Wincing. "Boss, it's your fault too. *If* you do this… *if* Euliae does that… *if if if.* Whole reason we Executioners are going on is 'cause we're the ones who can help keep the world going on." Scrunches her face to the side. "Or at least the City and tiny stretches the province we know about 'cause the message-runners are kinda mostly—" The angriest Arroyo face I have ever witnessed pops into existence. "Aghhh! I'm equivocating again! Look!" She points at me. "We didn't lose yet! World died, but we're still here. Right? That's a victory. And that remains a victory until the game is over. So let's stop thinking about lesser scenarios where some things are kinda good and kinda bad and that's satisfactory and—" Now pointing at Euliae. "Come up with a plan that solves everything!"

Euliae's eyes go wide. Mouth hangs open an inch, then she grips her stomach and emits an insulting guffaw. "She's a tiny Krohn! I *get* it now!"

"Ma'am!" Arroyo's face, bright pink.

"She isn't wrong." I turn to her. "How?"

"'How'?" she mimics. "Um… We… uhhhhhhhh…"

Euliae stage-whispers at me, "Now we see the limits of idealism. All hail the sarcastic sacks of shit of the world!"

"Hail!" I stage-whisper back with a derisive salute.

"Bury them all at once."

We lose our mocking miens and stare at the teenager with a bandaged ankle and broom-crutch by her side.

She shrugs. "Just… inter them all. Same time."

Ah. There it was. The insanity I was looking for.

#

Arroyo insisted on joining us atop the Crow's Rest. Euly and I insisted in return that she nap or else we'd drag her scrawny ass back to Ricken's -- a bluff on my part, I'd never suggest returning her to that skillful bastard I suffered such begrudging gratitude towards. We were both well outside the room and closing the door when she lobbed some well-aimed guilt.

"We're a team for cu—"

To save the world, that would one day come after us, from inheriting an unkind, unloving, far-from-innocent Arroyo, we relented straightaway and took turns carrying her to the heights of our own professionally inherited folly.

A bleeding sunset cast a prophetical glow across the lake, making the vision of Maelstrom at once autumnal and malevolent.

I had no words nor do I now.

There are times when it is important to simply stand before what destroys you. And although we stood far away and high above, we could feel it towering over us and consuming each second of our future.

#

Fact-gathering woke at dawn with a sense of urgency that would, from this point forward, never relent until success or ruin.

Everyone agreed that Arroyo would stay on with the ledgers. I put out a call for the denizens of the drowned city to drop off any formal documents they knew about to the provisional headquarters we had made of Crow's Rest. Most records would be gone, but I wanted all that remained.

"This is so cool!" she piped from the dining room overlooking the harbor. Milk coffee in one hand, parchment in the other, leg propped on a pillow. Golden sunbeams cut lines across her face, reminding me vaguely of Euliae.

Our girl was feeling very official.

Euliae was already pushing off across the deep waters on Megs' ferry. Her guide raised a hand to me in farewell, expression unreadable under a large floppy hat. I raised my own hand, wishing them good luck. Euly was all business, but spotted me watching them go and flashed a silly grin, then returned to writing notes down.

The twine connecting the rear of the ferry to the dock slowly tightened as they went.

Her task was measuring distances. Particularly how far away Maelstrom was to the fraction of an inch. A bookish task for such an active woman, but to be frank I think she was happy to finally have something to do.

I hoisted my backpack and headed to the morning market, stocking up for the full day's travel ahead. Marveling at the variety of choices. Hardly seemed diminished from the packed stalls of Old City. There's a lesson on persistence and agricultural creativity here.

As much as their Underground was a boon, I saw other secondary sources of food while I hiked in the direction of the derelict eyesore called Windtower. Vertical farms, I suppose would be the apt term: iron fences had been repurposed, remolded into cages along the walls exposed to constant sunlight, filled with sod and happy growing vegetables who cared nothing for the law of gravity or even politely acknowledging it.

I stretch my arm over the bridge, nearly tipping into the lake, grab a handful of greenery and yank.

Yellow carrots.

"Huh," I say, as profound and incisive a comment as ever I've uttered.

In the end, the legacy of Echo Downs may well be a perspective on modern life: developing new ways of living in spite of the direst circumstances.

Perhaps the gloom I always feel is a self-inflicted wound. For all we know, maybe the world is thriving beyond the limits of communication. One day the message-runners will inform us if that is true or wishful daydreaming.

For now, we carry on.

#

I stare up at Windtower from the crumbled stone it has sloughed over the seasons and I'm struck by one simple question: why didn't I ever bother asking anyone what the hell this monstrosity is?

"Masochism awaiting its faithful servant," I mutter, scrambling over the accumulated detritus and searching for an entrance that I also didn't ever bother asking anyone whether such existed or not.

It does.

Somewhat.

An aperture slick with drooping, purple mildew burrows into the interior. Size of a window, not a door. I squirm inside, reminding myself that far more disgusting slimes have attached themselves to me in the past -- although at the moment I can't recall when or which.

Air humid, stench like rotten fruit, more of that grimy mildew splattering every wall of the atrium. I cover my face with a bunched-up cloth and make a mental note to avoid areas that would have grown stale and toxic without airflow.

Fool me, forgetting this is *Windtower*.

Sunlight only pokes gingerly through the remains of the entrance, but I scarcely require a torch. A network of golden webbing extends from the nearby columns, winding its way higher until it creates a kind of abstract tapestry upon the vaulted ceiling. Even so, the glow emitted is a precipitous drop from the awakening morning outside; I step carefully towards the staircase as my eyes adjust.

My task? The most wonderful of all, of course.

Climbing this damnable thing to its pinnacle and measuring the height. Now, I should think, you understand Euly's previous grin.

A breath of cool air flows from above, a gentle yet oddly viscous wave rolling through the megastructure pipes that perforate the ceiling, encompassing me transiently then drifting on down -- unperturbed by my presence -- through the metal grating that covers the entirety of the floor.

Place is certainly worth a visit with more light. Might have potential as an ad hoc crypt. The soothing wind alone, whispering secrets in my ears with every breath drawn from the apex of the tower and disappearing before I can decipher their cryptic syllables... such a peace may lull the most restless cursed.

Where do I derive my boundless optimism?

As I reach the next floor, many storeys later, my heel steps on broken stair and sends me sprawling. Fragmented stone clatters away, pinging against metal far below... several seconds later.

Accepting no blame, I grumble and reluctantly strike a torch. Well. That was dumb of the architects.

The final dozen stairs at the top are eroded to the point of taking on the appearance of pulped paper. The score below are hardly in better shape.

"Can always take the easy way down," I mutter.

But I manage to locate a solid anchor, wrap the first cord of twine around it and toss it over the edge.

Upwards he goes, the silly Executioner who's supposed to be down in the dirt.

Thankfully, the heart of the structure is strikingly preserved. I go up and down a maze of stairs and ladders without fearing for my life or creating a final punchline for Euly. Between these levels are interstitial layers of complex machinery; actual floors more like afterthoughts.

And surely there *is* complexity here, hidden from view behind inscrutable bronze pipework. I leave my measuring twine at the most logical junctions, but it's becoming difficult to understand where I am vertically.

Despite continual airflow, humidity increases the higher I ascend and the deeper I'm forced by convoluted pathways that certainly contain meaning for someone not me.

"Is this thing functioning?" I ask no one, unsure what I could glean from a simple yes or no.

Pressing my ear to a tube.

Silence. Then *thrummm*. Silence. Then *thrummm*. Like the lungs of a sleeping behemoth. So... it is working? Doing its... wind... thing? My ear aches from the cold metal. Another lesson in which I learn either nothing or something I don't understand.

I grab the rung of another ladder and climb.

The next room is a spacious, abandoned workshop. Golden webwork covers the farside wall, engulfing lathing equipment and storage shelves. As I approach, my torchlight reveals -- or perhaps causes -- barely discernable patterns of movement along each strand of web, as if light inside was hastening to escape me only to return in strength along other tendrils.

Removing a glove, I reach my fingers out and tentatively stroke a partially-detached tangle wavering in the breeze of my movement. Glow intensifies where I touch, sparks outward like a languid explosion, meat cleavers severing my wrist reattaching severing reattaching flaying.

My yelp of agony echoes throughout the building, repeating back until only a taunting whisper puts an ellipsis on the end of that particularly painful statement.

I stumble into a chair, clutching my throbbing hand, and swear off curiosity for the remainder of my probably short existence.

"So," I pant, "a break then. Good job, Lethean. An early lunch, yes, well deserved." But instead I feebly grip a bottle of tepid water and glare at the webbing, willing it to float out at me so I can stab it with a few choice invectives if not my eager blade.

The meal dulls my rage, but does nothing for the lingering shame. Being the only witness to my stupidity helps. I pretend not to be wincing when I tug the glove back on.

My ascent continues without further incident. I suspect I've reached the halfway mark. Cracks of sunlight are showing through the walls where damage increases in severity. The top of the tower, I remind myself, may well be inaccessible.

New friends reinforce that fact when I jut my head out of another countless staircase.

I had previously assumed the growing, now sweltering, humidity came from the warming of the day and my own exertion. Imagine my grateful and joyous surprise when I beheld a throng of dozing spiders curled in balled-up dreams all around a labyrinthine forest of gold.

Now. How much do I genuinely care about accurate measurements? If this is halfway, I do know a simple trick for estimations…

I sigh. Silently as I can.

And tread across a floor conquered by the empire of mildew in ancient days now passed into legend. It would, I think, be useful to know if these creatures are nocturnal. With the morning risen so high already, it feels likely. They certainly seem untroubled by the brilliance of their webs, the magnitude of which is either amplified by thick weaving or the fear I won't admit to experiencing.

I can't find the next staircase.

But there. In the center: two web-wrapped ladders bound more tightly than those interred in Crypt Dun. I inch towards them, creeping within the deadly tangle, carefully cutting through webs unattached to any sleeper that might feel its hammock shifting.

Thrsssss. Thrrissssss. The throng whispers, spindly legs twitching as I pass.

A tentative poke of the ladder. No excruciating jolt. One gloved hand over the other. Every few feet I stop to carve away the webs impeding my climb… but the higher I go, the more I realize that this is effectively a structural column supporting perhaps a hundred spiders. Above and below me.

This rung I cling to may very well be the better part of valor.

Ah!

I spy the staircase over a clump of younger sleepers, each no larger than a modest pumpkin. Hurrying back down from my perch, mindful of every inch of exposed skin. And I really do a marvelous job not screaming this time when Windtower inhales, the room-mass of web flutters, and the spiders hiss ignorant of the meal gritting its teeth biting its tongue clutching its neck as I do for a full minute.

Blinking away tears, I creep slowly. There are no pathways I can wend, however, that don't require careful chopping. After making a few risky excisions, always aware of my exit strategy, I manage to bypass the youngsters and reach the stairs.

It is fully enveloped in web.

Thrsssss. Thrrissssss. Sssshshhshhk.

Mercifully without inhabitants.

I chop straight down the center, web parting like an impotent curtain. Frayed strands dangle above me. Ducking where necessary, chopping, chopping, sawing the thicker cords, until I emerge into more rooms filled with the equipment of days long gone and sleepy squatters.

Before mustering the will to push onwards, I return the way I came and set up measuring twine to be collected on my way back down. And so my methodical progress goes, uneventful (though my heart rapidly disagrees), selfishly glad to be alone. More bodies would mean more chances to make fatal mistakes.

Best to risk just one fool today.

Windtower's upper levels cool rapidly as I leave the moist, festering lair behind. Sunbreak firmly owns the remaining floors, considerable though they remain, since one of the walls had so destructively sheared off. Those gaps between stone and metal scaffolding are bound with webbing, but not extensively. The wind refuses to allow them easy prey in its rarified domain.

Gentle breezes are a thing of the entry halls, dulled by the pipe-laden contraption lodged in the way. Up here, the inhalation of wind feels as though it is sucked downwards by an unfathomably massive and desperate bellows.

For all I know, my imagination pegs the technology I scampered around with complete accuracy. *The lungs of a city.* Could that be of use to us or is this simply the castoff dregs of the intentions of ghosts?

There is a calmness to the sound. A gentle sleep...

"I don't know what, but there's something definitely here... Something possible in this..." I say. Euliae will want to explore this idea. Her perspective would be invaluable.

A powerful gust shoves me towards the edge, broken floor waiting four storeys below. I grip whatever railing I can see, waiting for it to abate. This is going to make measuring a pain in the ass...

Once I mount the final staircase, I reach the summit of this monumental construction effort. Taking shelter in a portable alcove, locked in place on iron rails rusted from raw exposure to the elements, I sit and overlook Drowns beyond.

And yet, I only see Overlook. No lake and occasional ferry, but sprawl and a multitude of busy souls busying about their daily toil and pleasures. No windblown shore and decimated forest, instead: the ricefields, the shipyards, the clocktower -- blue-gray and shadowy in its distance from the glass-domed observation room -- majestically towering over Old Kingdom. A dead idea out of the living past.

The nostalgia fades. The lonely solitude, the longing, the urge to return, though tamped down by duty and patience and understanding, remains. My core of self. My space in the world. My roving nature. My nomadic wind of existence, settling only for a moment to become unsettled again by duty and patience and understanding. My home does not exist. My home is in myself. I am ever, ever seeking that place of belonging in which my shape of self is firmly fixed within the other shapes around me, in the hole that is always left behind when I go because it can only be filled by me.

For the first time since arrival, I feel the loss of Echo Downs. Of what it must mean for Megs, the surviving citizens, perhaps even Ricken -- damn the obnoxious uncompromising lout -- to see *their* home this altered and corrupted. The damage is, of course, not yet done. What nature, the death of the world, and other forces I can neither name nor understand have so wounded, we Executioners must now uproot.

Drowns may not exist when we are done with her.

I shove a hastily-prepared sandwich into my face. It is delicious. The meat is still juicy, the veggies crisp, the bread flavorful and yeasty. I can't stop myself from tearing up.

"Why is this so good?" I ask.

And the wind ignores my question. It continues to plunge, devoured itself by an inhalation that refuses to exhale. It will continue to hold on and never relinquish. There are some things that cannot relent, despite the building pressure or the pain.

#

Sunset finds a rattled Lethean and a shaken Euliae and a chipper Arroyo rather confused to welcome back her comrades in such states. We all eye the alcohol on the table between us with different emotions and needs.

We all avoid it for different reasons too.

"Rustle up anything useful?" I ask Arroyo.

"Tons!" she says, patting stacks of books set up around her commandeered command center. "Death records stop after, well, the obvious. Unsurprisingly not many moved about in the past two decades. Prior, I mean. Good self-sufficiency, right? And then when everything went south, well, like I say: the obvious. They holed up the same way we did, same way everyone did.

"Birth records we got. And population numbers, too." Picks up and waggles a drab-colored tome. The cover is peeling off and the spine is cracked. "So, uh, like…" Sheepish and self-aware of her professional excitement. Carefully places the book back, hobbles to her throne, and plops down -- but carefully, the way I taught her. "So, um, yeah. If we can trust these figures, we're lookin' at… like… maybe hundred-thousand dead."

Having already dealt with the emotional impact of the devastation itself, raw numbers barely faze us.

"I'm curious the percentages," she muses like some detached, dusty historian completely unconnected to the unfolding events.

"Meaning?"

"Isn't hundred-thousand cursed out there, is it? Not in Maelstrom, least. Might tell us the chance that a corpse becomes a cursed. Statistically."

"Her smarts are getting spooky," Euly murmurs.

"There's other interesting stuff I read, but what about you two?" Turning to me. "Boss, how'd it go?"

They *were* nocturnal, but I screwed up stepped on a little one twisted wrong ways then right ways as a rush of still-sleepy still-very-very-dangerous spiders chittered after me their eight dagger-like legs multiplied by throng and skittering after *thriisssss shrrrikkk thrsssss* blood drain distraction in a shock of web worked, barely, then down and down and down the lodged metallic contraption laughing in maddeningly gleeful survival and it was a lie feint millstone.

"Fine."

Silence.

"Oh, okay, good. Did you get the measurements?"

I pass over a sheet of parchment. She skims it, absentmindedly reaching for her notebook to add it with the rest of her work. "Interest— Uh. Is this blood?"

"A little."

"Um." Quirks up her face, glances at me, quirks to the other side of her face, then looks to Euliae. "Okay, blood, yes. Ma'am?"

Euliae passes over her own parchment. Silently.

"Oh geez, you went all over the city, didn't you?"

Her steely face says nothing. I assume she assumes it's rhetorical. Arroyo apparently doesn't, but is too occupied looking back and forth between our sets of measurements to press the question any further.

"Wefff. Now *that* is..." Arroyo mumbling to herself. "And that leaves... um..." Attempts a calculation in her head, failing multiple times. "Oh whatever." Picks up some discarded paper, uncrumples a sheet, and jots a battery of numbers on the backside in a half-assed barely legible script. I hope her notebook isn't this cryptic. "Huh."

"Huh?"

"Huh?"

"Yeah," she nods at the calculation and looks at us. "We can bury Maelstrom if we knock the Windtower over with plenty of room to spare. If your figures are accurate."

"They are," we say in unison, a speck of learned insanity in our tones, then a heavy weight of implication shutting our traps when we comprehend the solution our Arroyo so innocently so casually dropped in an almost offhand remark.

"That's..." Euliae, the first to regain her voice, shrinks in her chair. "... a huge gamble."

"Yep." Arroyo spreads her hands. "'Super-duper burial' -- your words, Boss." She winks.

My throat is dry. "That was…" I cough. "… me being glib and argumentative."

"And not wrong. Right?"

I haven't an answer. Euliae side-eyes me, spitefully I think, though when I glance over her expression is completely blank.

"Pass me Euliae's map."

Smug and smiling and self-satisfied, Arroyo hands it over. Her mood makes me wonder if she's been hitting the painkillers again, but this is clearly professional pride bursting through her myriad seams.

My partner's exhaustion is writ clearly in the prickly precision of ink. A long day's intricate effort. And flawless. "This is good," I say quietly to myself. I hear her grunt an affirmative yet uninterested something. As I scan the irregular blocks that better illuminate the positioning of accessible buildings, I relive my hikes past the various alabaster towers and their connecting rope bridges. Plenty I have yet to explore, turns out. Task for the week, I imagine, with this document in hand…

One hitch in Arroyo's mad plan is glaringly obvious: plenty of occupied buildings lie in the path of a dropped tower and, critically, so does the would-be-dun called Underground.

I don't hold back my critique.

"Can probably withstand impact without compromising our objective," she evades.

I give her such a look. "Oh balls, you can't know that."

"Weeellllll… 'til some expert tells me otherwise, I'm leanin' into not caring the details."

My look transmutes into an upbraiding glare. "The details are *all* that are important, budding Krohn."

She huffs. "Don't call me that." Now giving me such a look. "Not that I don't like her. I do. Lots to learn from her. Still. I'm me and this is my plan."

"Don't get lost under your ego over there," I mutter audibly, turning back to the map. "I'm no engineer. But let's pretend this provides sufficient raw material to bury every body churning that whirlpool...

"First: there's no Executioner care in this. I think the best it does is *press* the cursed down to the lakebed. Winter comes, then deepness and the lake freezes solid. So. Now we have -- what, thousands? ten-thousands? -- pissed off corpses beating through that ice like it's spoiled lard. With those numbers, plenty are bound to destroy the foundations of the remaining buildings. Goodbye, Drowns. Or else, hell," aiming this next bit at Euliae, "they all just escape?"

She's staring out the window as dusk fades its final scarlets into mottled violet. "I'm checking out the lakeside edges tomorrow. Full circuit." Bites her lip momentarily. "Half of it, a ways east and south, probably is gently sloped. This was rolling hill country, after all. That didn't change."

I nod. That would be a breakout we couldn't sort ourselves. But if we got someone to run a message back to the City, we'd have a modicum of support to deal with it. Theoretically.

"Second: I've poked around Underground enough to know it's not a proper dun. Potential, but not proper. No reinforcement. The weight of that construction... Arroyo, you haven't seen it yet. It's gigantic. Best-case scenario would squish the top three levels like pancakes and I don't know if the lower levels would even be accessible then. Because there would have to be an underwater entrance if that's the case."

Arroyo shakes her head in confusion. "I don't see what that has to do with anything."

"Because you're too young to give two shits about politics -- and long may it be so while you have us crusty old curmudgeons around."

"Crusty and dusty," Euly chuckles, tickled by the idea.

"Uhhhh… existential threat? Hello?" Arroyo is very quickly about to breach the area of sociopathy with her narrow-visioned drive.

"It's much more—"

"'All corpses fall within Executioner—"

"Oh, come on."

"—property. All vault construction falls within—"

"That is bullshit. You're—"

"—Executioner oversight. The Executioners may—"

"That kind of flagrant—"

Voice rising in force and speed, Arroyo plows on ahead -- reciting every single syllable by dutiful newbie heart -- heedless of my own stirring hackles and Euly's annoyed sigh as she grabs at the bottle of whiskey she's been avoiding.

"—create burial chambers, built to Executioner code, regardless of location.'"

Discussion has now taken a full turn and barrelled straight into argument.

"Who the hell—!" Stopping myself, lowering my voice and leaning over the table. "Who the hell do you think is going to help us with this? With any of this? Two Executioners—"

"Three." She crosses her arms, daring my rebuttal to correct her.

"*Two*. You're out of action, Arroyo, and you know it." Her whole face twitches. "Whatever we decide, it isn't about us anymore. It's us and the citizenry. If we could send out the clarion call to everyone back home, I'd agree with you that we *can* strong-arm this city. But that's not happening. If these people aren't behind us, neither death nor durance as threat is going to give us the manpower we'd need."

Arroyo's face contorts into various impossible shapes, but otherwise she remains unresponsive.

"Euly?"

She casually sips from the bottle.

After a long draught of consideration, she swallows and lets out a held breath. "Is the tower's stone Executioner grade? She asks despite knowing the answer."

"No, but it is thick enough to make the distinction academic. It'll do."

Eyebrows raising. "That *is* surprising." She aims the neck of the bottle towards me. I shake my head and she takes another sip. More silence. Then she considers Arroyo, who isn't hiding how uncomfortable she feels under the scrutiny of my critique or Euly's penetrating gaze.

"Arroyo's stretching it. *Legally*, that is."

"Letter of the law versus the spirit?" I ask.

"Basically."

Silence.

"No one will like us doing this," Euly continues after another drink.

"Oh, I can think of at least one person who will desperately love it."

"Then, we're doing this?"

Silence.

"It's necessary," Arroyo offers.

No one responds.

"Do we want to... vote?" I ask.

"Aw," Euly moans, "but I like my unilateral decisions best." There is no humor in her voice now.

Carefully, but confidently, Arroyo raises her hand.

Euly looks at me. "Well?"

I smirk. "Waiting to feel which way the winds are blowing?"

Her hands remain in her lap. "Already made my vote, haven't I?"

Reluctantly, I raise my hand.

Euliae nods twice, replaces the bottle on the table between us. "Alright. That's that. But let's not shout this from the rooftops, what's left of them. Be as thieves. Suss out who's pliable. More importantly: who's knowledgeable. Has to be at least somebody left what erected that thing."

"I'll make inquiries. Arroyo, you want to buddy-buddy around or keep hitting the books?"

Arroyo, perhaps feeling the weight of her proposal, is fidgeting strands of unkempt hair. "I still have some I haven't read yet…" A voice so low it could brush dirt from the floor.

"Also," Euly interjects, "can we commit that we drop it *only* as a last resort? I'm wondering if we can chop off the top, lower it onto Maelstrom." Demonstrating with her hands. "Like this. Move it over, push it down, make a freakish kind of… sunken mausoleum, I guess."

"Lot of scaffolding and ropework for that…"

"Lot of time."

"Not really, but we'll see. I have my reservations." I flick my finger against a glass. It peals a strained, sonorous tone then disappears. "Even so, we have a plan now." I give Arroyo a reassuring smile. "Want to make it official?"

"Um." More fidgeting, thinking. Arroyo sits up in the chair, looks at me, at Euliae, and back again. "Okay," she agrees, regaining her spunk and a newfound fire behind her eyes. "Operation Downfall commences at first light."

#

Our start was less dramatic than Arroyo's choice of words would indicate. We ate breakfast together, our host's cooking steadily improving as she figured out we wouldn't be leaving anytime soon. Highlights: marinated steak-thick mushrooms; runny yolked eggs; unidentifiable beans baked; stewed tomatoes. Lowlights: sausage made of not-meat; bitter leafy weeds best left in the ground a season longer; a plentiful lack of potent coffee.

It would be a long day,
week,
month at this rate.

179

As previously settled, Arroyo was already perched atop her yesterday-claimed throne and surveying her ad hoc kingdom of all things transcription. It was truly an office if I'd never seen one before. Manically organized in her own mind.

For Euly's part, she would continue circumnavigating the lakeside and logging worst-case scenarios. We'd be running up against a lot of those. If our quarry escaped, where were they likely to go? We needed to contain that and, although neither of us voiced such pessimism to our tiny fearless leader, contingency plans may lead to the only successful undertakings we might hope for.

Decry mitigation as idealism allows, but at the end of the day that is sometimes what is standing bulwark against the end of the day.

"If you have time, check out the Windtower and Underground. Not that you're not busy."

Euly and I walk out into pink dawn towards the dock. I put an encouraging hand on her shoulder and she immediately shrugs it off.

"What?"

"If you're not too busy."

"No," she frowns. "You're doing that thing again where you talk away from me and I can't hear you."

"Poke around in the Windtower and Underground."

"Oh." Considering it with an uncertain throat-clearing. "No time for that today. I'm trekking into the wilds outside the lake. Full circle of the strand and then some. But I'll— Stop towering over me."

Shoves me away a foot.

"I'm taller than you. Deal with it."

"… always towering over me."

Megs is sitting in her readied ferry, staring out at the weary sun struggling over a flat expanse of water. Hears us coming, turns and smiles.

"Fell mornin', 'ad it!" she announces, blisteringly cheerful in spite of what looks like soot rubbed prodigiously under -- maybe even around? -- her eye sockets.

"You don't mind trawling this lout around?" I ask, jerking a thumb at a pre-scowling Euliae.

"Nay, she's good people. A thinker, that 'un."

"A '*thinker*'…?"

Euly hits me.

"Aye, woman a'action too," Megs chortles. "But prior t'that, aye, much thinkin'." Without standing, she pokes her oar against an unseen support beneath the water and pushes the ferry closer to the dock.

Euly, about to step inside, stops and confronts me. Almost one inch away from my face.

"Are you okay?" she asks.

"I'm alive, aren't I? I can't be a pessimist."

No scowl, but it seems implied somehow.

She doesn't repeat herself.

"I don't know what you're getting at, but things are things, yeah?" A pause. "Are *you* okay?"

"There's something in that question," she whispers to herself, but consciously aloud for my benefit too. She half-smiles. "We'll see." Holds out her fist. I bump it and she full-smiles. "Good luck, Leth. Even I don't know what we've gotten ourselves into this time."

"Good luck, Euly. I look forward to you digging us out again."

I watch them set out -- a lingering soon to become tradition if I'm not careful -- before heading to the marketplace to pop a squat and chit some chat. After yesterday's climb? I'll need to ease into the day if I plan to last through the afternoon.

I'm the first person. It makes me wonder how I'll look as the vendors pour in: the lone Executioner waiting with evident intent. Leaning against alabaster stone, I wish I had taken up smoking. Might as well give them a resonating image.

But I'm here to speak, not spook. So I wind up the tower and across the bridge, essentially to spy from the other side until I can make a more casual entrance.

Creepy opportunist, that's me.

I get my chance an hour or so later when the sun has deigned to drag its lazy ass an inch over the horizon line. Good morning, you fat fiery bastard.

#

The honeymoon period was over.

Now that we had been here a while and were a known unknown quantity, old fears were resurfacing. I couldn't account for it. Public outreach we desperately need and never have, but I'd figure my daily presence at the market would at least make me an acquaintance of sorts.

Way to hurt a scheming guy's feelings.

I asked with careful tact, not blunt in the slightest, the baker who had always been lukewarm. But a pleasant and engaging lukewarm.

He shrugged. "We don't know what you're up to."

Could it be that simple?

"You make it sound like a conspiracy."

"Most sorts don't trust the Executioners…"

True.

"… name doesn't inspire much confidence either."

Also true.

"I like a warm bun," I say, taking a bite of the steamy mini-loaf. "Same blood courses through my veins as yours." This latter comment completely unintelligible with my cheeks stuffed with wheaty fluff.

"Do you lot literally kill people?" He stops wiping his hands on his apron, clenches it almost unnoticeably.

I choke on the bun.

Could it be that complicated?

I start laughing. "Oh hell, don't tell me that's what this is about. Superstition?" He nods, clearly offended by my outburst. "We're no arm of the law, friend. It's the corpses that won't stay corpses we're after. My concern," I point over his shoulder, "is that whirlpool of dead folks out beyond your homes. That's the lot you need to worry about. And one way or another, I'm going to inter every last one of them."

"All of them?"

I pop the last piece of bun in my mouth. "Mmmfff," I say, very committally.

"But we need to worry about them?"

I swallow. Taking my time. "Enough to help us strange out-of-towners out." I grin. "Can I get a few more of those to take with?"

#

I had many lunch dates that week. Some turned into afternoon snack, dinner, and crepuscular boozing dates. Fine men and women, every one. Most had interesting perspectives, but few were the specialists I sought.

No one who had built the Windtower had survived the flood. None of the administrative body either. The majority of the elderly, who I had hoped were aldermen or at least steeped in the history of Echo Downs, disappointed me. Professionally. They were simple old codgers, long of rambling digressions and short of temper. I liked them immensely.

Then, I found engineers. A core group, in fact, who had motley origins and appearances. One from Old Kingdom (had a minor hand in the clocktower). One from up Tallow's way (architect, but kind of a skitz). Three brothers from out east, miners by trade who knew loads about delving such that we might pick up a new trick or two (I suspected one was a sister, but didn't press my curiosity or my interest).

They created Underground under the leadership of...

"Ricken," I greet when he answers my knocking.

He curtly turns away, but leaves the door open and returns to his workbench. I step inside. Three seconds and I'm already pissed off. I have got to learn to deal with this better. Let's make this quick.

Thorough.

But quick.

"I suppose you must need something, loathe as I am to seem this casual or dismissive."

"Why don't you go fuck anything that has a cock so thick it has hope to fill the voluminous expanse you call your mouth?" I think very loudly at him.

Instead, I ignore the provocation.

"You do competent work," I say. "Arroyo is on the mend, although the question was always if the operation was necessary and if she'll recover to peak performance."

His bulk lifts and drops in an unheard sigh. "The way of your organization, difficult to maintain peak performance for any reasonable duration. The human body simply isn't meant to withstand that much force or stress."

I glance around for equipment that Downfall might require -- either to negotiate and borrow... or to sneak back in during the eleventh hour and "borrow".

"We have our training."

"This is rapidly devolving into a debate I tire of entertaining," he says, "and you aren't here to update me on the child's condition." He crosses the room, fills a pipe with pungent weeds, and creaks down into the folds of an armchair. "Though I'm heartened by her recovery, I had zero doubts." Despite saying so, the clouds are gathering across his face.

We talk.

#

I knew before starting that he wouldn't go along with our plan or encourage anyone to join in our destructive endeavor. So, I never once hinted at the true purpose of this visit. Over the coming days, I imagined that I'd learn how strategic his mind was. Did he expect the logistical gymnastics bounding around my mind? Or was I a dull-eyed, obstinate One-of-Them too wrapped up in my own cleverness to see how utterly stupid I was?

I feigned the former. I hoped the latter.

"It's mostly dirt and while the stone is thick in places for structural support, it is porous. I use it for filtering liquids. Your premise is weak." That was the judgement over which he presided.

In short, I was pretending we were turning their Underground into Dunderground. In normal circumstances, it would have been the best option: tunnel out much deeper levels, use a series of retractable ladders so the cursed were trapped wherever we laid them to rest, and forbid anyone's entry beyond a certain point. Oh but the city would freak out. No one would be able to harvest any crops without having heart attacks or suffering paralyzed necks from looking over their shoulders every few seconds.

We all face our occupational hazards.

The conversation felt as long as it was. I'm paraphrasing the event to avoid the testiness, snarking commentaries, and other puerile bullshit. His fault entirely. But I came away with quite a bit of context -- and dead-ends -- to take back to the ladies.

Mass exodus was out. Echo Downs died here. Drowns would die here, too. It's a proud people that live through the total decimation of their home and hang on. We are all trying to do the same in our own ways, privilege of locations and decimation notwithstanding. I wouldn't press the point... until it became unavoidable.

Empathy aside, I don't care a whit for this place. I'm not nostalgic about someone else's past. But its populace? Not dying on our watch.

When I left, and left the door open because I can be a dick too, I couldn't help urging myself to be responsibly irresponsible. Run back to Old City. Climb the rocky terrain to Overlook and shout everyone out of their beds and down to Drowns. But it wouldn't happen. No time... no time...

Winter and deepness whispering in the wind.
Hug your loved ones, mourn your kin.
#

"This subterfuge feels pointless and not at all my style, but I'll allow it," Euly said.

Arroyo scribbled some notes, tacitly omitting everything I had described and instead concocting a paper trail of half-truths. "We need to crunch numbers," Arroyo moaned. "If we're spending weeks faking it, those weeks need to give us a tactical advantage greater than... public relations?"

Neither were wrong.

Now follows Lethean's Proposal:

Our itching-to-work-on-some-project-that-is-challenging engineers would be employed in creating Dun tunnels built to Executioner code as far down as they could get. As locals, they would have the sway to get help carrying dirt back to the surface and in building ceiling supports. Underground dropped five levels, each getting successively larger the farther you descended. We'd plunge five levels deeper -- and also send an exploratory survey to excavate until they hit bedrock.

<u>Gains</u>
Legitimate tunnel network to use for interring.
Equipment to repurpose for felling Windtower.
Refuge if we failed to stop Maelstrom in time.

186

Now follows Euliae's Proposal:

After chewing me out at length about my failure to allude to the spider infestation in Windtower, she demanded an apology before saying that she'd be working with some weavers and farmers in the collection of the glowing spiderweb. Apparently, a seasonal autumn festival unique to this particular region was set to begin; the web could be spun into thread, then stitched into clothing. No one dissuaded her from the bafflingly brilliant idea of fashioning durable, nigh-indestructible ropes and nets.

<u>Gains</u>
Ability to mass-dredge any underwater corpses.
Equipment to decapitate the top from Windtower.
Barriers if we failed to stop Maelstrom in time.

Now follows Arroyo's Proposal which she had already actioned without consulting either of us:

Books were boring. Desperation for action was killing her inside. She made friends with seemingly everyone her age and younger. Plenty of ferrymen took a shine to her as well. She didn't have an army yet, but given a month...? These troops were busy creating detachable, floating bridges that could be interlocked into variable shapes. Considering the inefficient rope-bridge maze that connected the city, it was a wonder no one had thought to do this before.

<u>Gains</u>
Highly-adaptable and expanded logistical routes.
Equipment for supporting our other proposals.
Escape if we failed to stop Maelstrom in time.

#

There were problems.

"There are always problems," I would later note.

But there were problems with such immediacy that I felt the world was clucking its tongue at me from some deep and distant hollow, wondering aloud to itself how one of its sons had gotten it so wrong to think he could get it all right so quickly.

First came the miserable rime rains, freezing a thin sheen on every surface. The frequent winds, which were growing more frequent still, abetted in this trip-hazard annoyance. The bitter air was making Arroyo's ankle bones ache so painfully that there was naught to do, and naught for her to do other than pile under blankets before a not-so-roaring fire (proper fuel was another problem after the first few storms found a gap in a ceiling and trickled in until the woodpile inside was thoroughly soaked and rottenly useless).

She cried often.

Drowns citizenry became far less amenable to us. Everyone knew we were trying to help. No one ever believed in the effort or that it was necessary. Everyone was too inundated by anxiety, wrapped up in their own meagre lives, with a wish to return to the normal ways. Or pretend that they remained.

I knew the normal ways had never been a reality, but try teaching them that. I tried. I failed.

With people leaving our construction teams in droves, the timetable was a shade darker than grim. Once there were enough floating bridges to reach and retrieve more dry wood from the lakeside forest, those stopped moving altogether and masqueraded as a permanent route for the steady trickle of gatherers -- whose goal was nothing more than cooking stew that night and keeping their families passing warm.

Then my architect-cum-tunneler got roaring drunk one night, lost his way home, slipped off a roof, and drowned.

Fortunately, the dun effort continued uninterrupted and had, in fact, picked up a score more workers. Some people, to avoid the dismal weather or perhaps (I suspected) for lack of anything better to do, showed up with shovels and picks in hand and baskets on their backs. What could I do? I put them to work.

Two weeks later, marginal improvements. Arroyo was still tearful, but more talkative if not much more mobile. Euliae had ample spiderweb to fashion a prototype net. Turns out she hadn't a single damn notion *how* to make rope when she started. There's a lesson in there.

I feared I was starting to get hopeful. To combat that dangerous possibility, I had a sudden realization and asked, "Won't the jolt enrage them when it touches their skin?"

"Huh?" Looked at me like I had suggested we crawl into a potato sack and fuck each other's brains out. "Oh, you idiot! You actually touched it? Fool!" Went back to weaving and ignored me for a potent minute. "Any child could tell they'd do *something* to you with all that sparkle and shifting lights…"

"Glow-mushrooms don't hurt when you poke them."

Her blistering gaze didn't feel very warm. "Don't touch them either!" When she calmed down, she graced me with the pedant. "You need to soak them in brine and then hatchel the snot out of them. Once you're at the binding stage, you don't need gloves anymore." Seemed about to grin, then frowned. "Are you here to help or just be a fuckwit? Because I have time for both of those, but only patience for one."

And that's the story about how Lethean learned to craft rope. The end.

One day, the weather acted like it was ready to play nice again. Clear skies, brightest blue, a mirage of summer dreams. Did not trust it. That night my architect resurfaced, slightly drunk but very much alive. He refused explanations, gave only a haunted look that told epics, and apologized.

I take my good luck where I can without asking its provenance or catch.

And then Euliae got a major case of the frustrations. She may have been bleeding. For all I know, she specifically *waited* until she was bleeding and then very publicly, very vocally enacted a modified version of her bluff-blustering conscription plan.

It almost worked perfectly. But Ricken came out of hibernation from his hole in the ground, unofficial mayor and voice of reason, and barked at her and barked at anyone convinced by the "official" Executioner decree.

There's a lot you can do with paper and ink and a forged signature that no one within leagues can authenticate.

Ricken saw through the bullshit without blinking. So. My game he was blind to, but not loud-mouthed Euliae. That was interesting...

Looking back, we all probably fucked up something bad with the way we carried on. Now a legal threat of dubious worth hung over everyone's heads (ours too... thanks, Euly) along with the existential one that kept me up nights but didn't haunt a single toddler.

The stunt did net us more workers. Euly was pleased with herself, as she always is, and divvied up the conscripted into teams. Most went into rope-making, the rest into bridge-building, and I got a few dregs. Which was fine. I could hardly benefit from more, lest people start bumping into each other and creating chokepoints.

"We do have an easy way," I whispered in passing as she went to bed later, "of scaring them to death."

Her sober look didn't twitch. It was already on her mind. "Yeah. But no," she whispered back. "This was way too obvious. I got impatient."

"It would kill any doubts. Even Ricken—"

"No, he's a hardcase. And better informed than he lets on. Mmm, no, that's the wrong word. 'Worldly' maybe."

Pried her boots off, took off her pants, then just sat there on the edge of the bed. Chin against hands, brooding on some old unknowns and the new unknown tomorrows.

"Fear you see isn't so powerful as fear you learn," she ultimately says. "Unless they figure it out for themselves, their hearts will stay hardened."

Silence.

"Lethean."

"Yes?"

"You remember that anorak, what's-her-name, the goggles-girl."

Fogging over. "Goggles-girl...?"

"*Adison*," she misremembers confidently.

"Oh, the Technocrat kid. Um... Abi."

"Sure. Abi. Hey!"

"What?"

"Stop staring at my panties."

"I'm not. Finish your bloody thought so I can go check on my operation before I turn in."

Her offended expression dissipates as if it was never there at all. "Built that contraption, right? Decent analogue before the adjustments -- from a layperson's perspective, I mean. Didn't have a clue, did she? Not until the very last test." Takes off her top and lies down, staring out the window.

No moon tonight. Better borrow a lantern when I go.

"Fair point. See you tomorrow?"

Squeezes the pillow. "I'm starting tomorrow."

I stop reaching for the door.

Silence.

Make my way over to her bed and sit next to her. Her face is only visible, though barely, in the window's reflection. "Are you sure?" Doesn't answer. I rub her shoulder. She doesn't push me away. "What do you need from me?"

Her hand snakes out of the blanket and holds mine. For many long minutes we stay like this, saying nothing, doing nothing, thinking too much.

::Euly knows this threshold::

"She would," I agree softly.

::No return point::

I let out a long breath and repeat my question:

::What does Euly need?::

::Pull Euly back::

::If Euly goes too far?::

::When Euly goes too far::

::Okay::

::Leth::

::Euly::

::Promise Euly::

I chuckle quietly. "Now that's a twist coming from you." But I don't hesitate after getting in the easy quip.

::Leth promises::

She nods and pulls her hand back under the covers, but only after giving my fingers a final wordless squeeze. She bids me goodnight by settling into a curled-up position. I bid her goodnight by shutting the door so the latch doesn't click.

\#

We're all outside at noon. Morning was spent rearranging floating bridges until two dead-end pathways extended out towards Maelstrom. Megs and her fellow ferrymen are steadily waiting in the broad lane between both.

I watch from the end of a bridge while sitting on a small one-person cart, whittling a hunk of wood as I wait. I've no talent. This will remain a hunk of wood when I'm done.

Arroyo is much farther away, nowhere near the water's edge, distinguishable only because of the crutch she leans against.

Euliae, hurrying down the other bridge, directs the ferrymen and distributes bundles of rope to paired teams. There's a lot of chatter back and forth. Probably confirming her every single word so nothing is left to chance or misunderstanding. They're nervous. But she's remarkably patient with them. She's nervous too.

The ferrymen tie their ferries together in a network, the ones along the sides roping into the bridges for further support. Euly runs around, checking the minutiae of absolutely everything, until satisfied. Or, more likely, until she's worked up enough nerve to lead the vanguard.

Finally, she hops into Megs' ferry like always and signals at the two ferries flanking them. They gently move into position within seconds.

And the fleet sets out straight for Maelstrom.

"Good hunting, Euly," I tell her back as she drifts away.

#

The three vanguard ferries spread out the pride of Euly's daily craftsmanship: a sizeable net made of spiderweb. Prototype though she had called it, the sight was impressive. Brilliant sunlight caught the golden fibers, creating a dazzling display for anyone watching when Euly threw it high in the air towards the unstoppable whirlpool.

Someone dead was caught in the net instantly.

"Row!" Euly yelled, so sonorous that I heard it as though she were standing right next to me.

The ferry fleet rowed back towards the city with maximum effort. The worst scenario would rear its head now if she had underestimated the distance between her and her quarry and grabbed multiple bodies. We knew that would happen eventually, wanted or not, but this first undertaking needed to remain simple to prove the method and steel the hearts of our untempered laborers.

It worked.

We had our first corpse in tow.

When the fleet had pulled safely away from the churning void's ravenous influence, they came to a stop. Euly looked over everyone. The ferrymen were rigid, their spines unbending.

"Break!" Euly yelled.

Only the ferries that flanked her moved, rowing away in opposite directions and leaving her all alone in the center as the golden net stretched and began to rise up out of the water. I stopped whittling. The oak shavings that rested on the surface of the lake quivered. Some sank.

The net emerged, rivulets pouring off it like a cup running over, flecks shooting in every direction as the cursed inside violently thrashed within its confines. The city had grown as hushed as the graveyard it was. The only sounds came from Maelstrom, dull roar, and the captured body, wet limbs slapping and spume dripping.

Euly, never letting the cursed leave her sight, half-turned to Megs and said something. Megs hesitated. Euly half-turned again. Megs began to row towards the net.

The flanking ferries endeavored to continue heaving. The binding of the net constricted, preventing extreme movement from the captured, but not all. Their strength would diminish in time and from emotions, *its* would not.

Not until...

Euly stabbed at the cursed. She twisted the blade. I swear, despite the overwhelming crushing weight of that moment, I heard the neck vertebrae pop.

The body within the net went limp.

Her next stabs were methodical. Elbows. Knees. Done.

She did not shout out her next command. A single gesture, and the fleet glided back to its starting position as one. I don't know why I expected the ferrymen and the growing audience over in the city to cheer. I felt jubilation in my heart, as I do when any job is successful or nearing success, but the spectators were oddly restrained.

Silent celebration? I think… no one knew how to take it. Did they even understand *what* had been done? It is a strange business we shoulder. How much stranger to those on the other side of the day, curiously, fearfully, looking in? They had now caught a glimpse and knew naught what any of it meant.

"The end of the world," I whispered at the horizon beyond the drowned city, as Euly's ferry veered straight towards me.

Within seconds, she docks next to my cart. I help her with the corpse. We gently lay it on a bed of straw inside. I bind the hands and ankles. I stop the eyes.

My charge is ready.

Euliae is smiling at me through unshed tears. An image in my mind alights -- blindingly, an ablative force burning through decades of memory and evaporating everything but the present -- of a broken woman bowing low before the burden of an impossible task.

Euly…

… I want to hug you.

But with all eyes on us, I don't. And she doesn't. And she turns away, shoulders pinned back and chin aloft, ready, ready, ready, stepping back into the ferry and floating away, so slowly, so determinedly, silent, silent, the rowing of the fleet no louder than a forgotten touch, an ephemeral vision, a whispered regret.

#

Retrieval operation. Three cursed recovered.
No incidents. Cart fully loaded. Lethean on duty.
Destination: very much to be determined.

Four is my limit on a good day -- alone. This was an exceptionally good day, but I didn't want to get cocky. All that damned effort for three paltry, emaciated rotters and wouldn't it be hilarious if Lethean tripped, or the bridge had a structural integrity problem, while he pulled the cart and they went over into the drink?

I like a good anticlimax punchline as you do, but let's not and say we did.

The next few hours involved me painstakingly carting the dead throughout the city. I'll spare the boring details... Had thought to really make a show of it, take a route that would increase the visibility of my quiet procession. But that risked going by noisy areas and as Euly noted last night: best to let the rumor mill do our work for us.

Nonetheless, the direct route took a while considering the constant going up and down the towers. The rope bridges were particularly treacherous. Having a ferry on hand would have certainly been the most efficient option. For our first attempt, however, I needed to know how prohibitive going... "overland" is the wrong term and I fear if I take into account that I'm transiting rooftops I'll just coin some annoyingly cute phrase.

In any case, I needed to know if it would work. Besides, the ferrymen were going to be pissing themselves for a bit.

Give those stalwart women and men some modicum of time to recover and make this whole enterprise seem mundane in their minds...

The city is underwhelmed by the significance of Maelstrom. If they knew what our true emotional response was...

Follow me?

The dead sure were. Catatonic and unmoving right behind my back. The ingrates oughta thank us for that straw. Luxury we never use except to train the newbies. I take them to a building across the water from Underground, pile them in the corner, double-check that the windows are boarded up to keep all light out, and ever-so-gently shut the door. And bar it. And creep away with my cart.

#

The ferrymen were joined to us with knots stronger than their golden ropes. Must have bonded as those in battle are said to do, as I have read from the old tales when the world had the time and resources to play real-life board games with human lives, invisible boundaries, and lofty words like Primogeniture.

They stayed.

The majority of the rest of our workers fled. Our stunt had backfired spectacularly. Or had worked perfectly. I was too pissed off to tell the difference.

Euliae and Arroyo were complaining at each other. Both had completely divergent pivot plans. They sat cross-legged beside the campfire. We had ditched the city for an overnight camp. And to avoid all walls-that-have-ears.

"No! We are gonna thin the herd," Euly said. Slapping a knee for punctuation. She thought the momentum of the whirlpool could be slowed to a stop if we took enough bodies. The rest would sink, freeze over during deepness, and could stay down there forever. Fuck them for drowning and not staying drowned.

"You agreed to Downfall! We'll repurpose your ropes, guide the plummeting tower straight on them and bury them once and for all," Arroyo said. She phrased it more thoroughly than I can restate. She'd been the most on-task and dauntless from the beginning.

"Actually, she abstained from the vote and—"

"Shut up!"

"Be quiet!"

I'll leave it a grand mystery who said which.

#

An early winter came. Seemingly while we were bickering. As the weeks passed by, the edges of the lake began to freeze. Our timetable was thrown out. The wind was rising. We were miserable. We remained divided.

Euliae and I continued temporary interment. The centrifugal force and diameter of Maelstrom did not lessen. Arroyo reread every book, found a few more on her crutch-walks about the city that I asked her not to do alone, learned nothing new and certainly nothing helpful.

Miserable. Divided.

We made unreasonable demands of ourselves. I know I did, staying up more hours a day than I should have, eating less, smiling not at all, speaking little, focusing only on the individual needs of the present, the path of least resistance best choice mitigation of circumstance the settling always settling day night gloaming eternal still the wind picking up and moaning "*Fools… Fools…*" until I became so unfocused that my inability to stay the balanced connective tissue of our group nearly killed everyone.

I do not think I am being overdramatic.

One morning, I became aware I had not seen Arroyo in three days. At that point, I had no concept of a day. I'm using this as a way to make sense of my bleariness.

Luckily, her crutch-tracks in the dirt were easy to follow once I grasped the fact her goal was outside the city.

I discovered her crying in the twisted woods, thirty miles away, coincidentally near the site of her injury. I don't think she meant to double back that way. She may have been hopelessly lost.

I know she was lost.

During the hour I held her, my mind cleared in spite of the burnout. She kept sobbing, then fell asleep against my chest. I continued to hug and wouldn't let go. When she awoke, we talked for a very, very long time. Then we went back to the city.

But the important point is that we went back together.

#

Euliae had abandoned her side job on the Windtower. Scaffolding climbed halfway to its apex. Her brood of ferrymen were rapidly becoming a cult in their passion for any endeavor the woman set them against, although they had no idea why they were being focused on the tower itself. I think Megs had figured it out, but if she did she kept her thoughts to herself.

But Euly, when we met her dockside, had apparently reached the same conclusion I had.

"There's a festival coming up," she says.

Half of Arroyo's face smiles. "That would be fun."

"Is that why everyone who left us is still scurrying around as if the city was burning now too?" I ask.

Euly nods. "Yep. Preparations."

Previously, in some fairly justified paranoia, I thought all the carrying-on meant the citizens were about to reject us from their sodden burg. That they were rallying around Ricken who, with a triumphant grunt, would kick our asses out and back home with our tails not hanging between our legs but wedged firmly way, way up our assholes.

Turned out the colder weather meant everyone was hurrying to Get Things Done and set up long before the marked day.

We relinquished our burdens and helped out. No one was against it. Surprised. But not against it. I spent my time constructing stalls, leaving the nailing to Arroyo and any other small task that wouldn't require her to move from a single spot except to pee.

Kids, what few there were, popped over to chat with her and play a curious version of tag that somehow Arroyo won every time.

For long minutes, lounging in a bit of afternoon warmth, I sat apart and drank a sugary concoction that tasted faintly off though I couldn't say why. I became a little too absorbed with solving this when I spied Euly far off messing with the roof of an alabaster tower. She and her brood kept this up often and I wanted to ask what it was all about, but she was always too busy and never around. So she did her thing while I did mine.

And before my worries resurfaced and I started yelling at myself for not doing the bloody job I was sent here to do, the first night of the festival fell upon the city of Drowns.

#

The Ghost Festival.

A legion of wraiths drifted into the derelict city, seeking the joys of a life denied them when the pitiless deluge came and refused to recede. What griefs, what longings, what pains continued to pulse within their spectral hearts on a horrible night such as this? I couldn't know. They were all as silent as the tombs they escaped.

As I too floated among their endless ranks, I watched their shimmering passage. Tattered shrouds, now their only clothing after a year of sleeping underwater, glinted with threads of shining gold. Sometimes this inner light intensified for the briefest most fleeting seconds, causing the shrouds to take on a feeble pastel glimmer that, when it faded moments later, bled away to a hint of rainbow at the edges, then went dark.

"This is *so cool*," Arroyo whispers to me, wobbling on her muted crutch. She padded the end so it wouldn't make the normal *clip-clip-clop* noise that usually announced her passage. This was someone who always took playtime seriously.

And the citizens were of the same mind. Everyone played their roles perfectly, taking the utmost care to avoid making strident noises -- or any noises at all. Would this change towards the end of the night when the tired would sleep and the true revelers -- perhaps my architect? -- would laugh themselves roaring drunk?

Somehow, I doubt it.

A solemn atmosphere blankets us. This is a celebration. It is also a wake. All the smiles are heartfelt, but I cannot know their impetus. From soft memories long gone, or the very present scent of spicy stewed meats, or the fermented mosses turned alcoholic and bitterly sweet, we all find our reasons.

There is nothing mutually exclusive here. All are one.

On the rim of the horizon, a pumpkin moon is rolling into view, but uncertainly so. The earlier dates meant the full moon would not usher in the festival's opening as planned. Personally, I prefer that it will now watch over us on the final night. The jolly sunburst glow will seem more comforting at the close, I think… more… optimistic.

And spookier.

Wind caresses my shoulder. I turn and see the ghostly Euly handing me a fistful of scone-like substance. Spongy and…

"What…" I ask no one specific, mouth perplexed by the illegal taste.

"I *know*," she hisses, but not genuinely angry.

"Where the hell did they manage to get honey?"

"*Who* did they *acquire* it from?" Euly corrects.

Arroyo gobbles my portion before I can react.

"Eeef! The *best!*" she cheers, too loudly. The wraiths around us laugh, untroubled by the happy outburst.

It's good to see her normal hyperactive energy returning. I keep trying to disappear from her sight so she can enjoy as much freedom as possible. Each time, I last minutes at most before her hand reappears from the crowd or the fog or the shadows and holds on to the crook of my arm.

"Hey, Boss," she'll smile.

The food and drinks are the main attraction, especially to a glutton like Euly. She samples everything, sharing with me the choicier bits, and always impatient to see whatever surprises the next stall has in store.

Paper lanterns, pastel oranges and pinks and greens and blues, hang above us. The drapery on every stall is much the same. Only the alabaster towers, smothered gray in the dark, have their tops lit with blood-red lanterns.

Everyone is avoiding those areas.

"Oooof. Moss is hittin' me."

I give Arroyo an appraising glance. "How many?"

"Oooof. Umm... two?" She thinks. "Three." She thinks further. "Got no idea, in fact."

There's a quieter corner near the closest dock. I sit her down with a flagon of water. "Sober up, kid," I order. "Night is young and so are you."

She salutes, a happy little drunk. And munches on a bag of snacks.

I go for a stroll.

But Euly waylays me next. "Shit, did you try this yet?" She shoves a steamed bun into my face. I chew before she takes her hand away.

"Mmmff!"

"Right? That's not even meat, man, it's mushrooms." Furiously gnaws the center from her own. "How did they do that...?" And then she demands of me, "How do they do it?"

"Only the dead know what the living do not."

"Cute." But she smiles. And shoves another in my face.

"Mfff, yes, but… I'm going to pop. Need to fill in the cracks."

Her eyes widen in shock. "Have you drunk any of this?" Passes me a wineskin. "It isn't the greatest thing ever. New distillery. *Impressive* though. Whiskey. Of sorts."

While holding the spout away from dubious lips, I ask, "Of sorts? Or it is?"

"Just drink it, man."

It has a harsh kick off. Perilous impact. Doesn't bloom, it explodes in my mouth, slinks down my throat. I almost choke. Instead of laughing, Euly's eyes continue to widen and she nods up and down like a berserk rabbit dancing with a spider.

"Geehhhhh!" I sputter.

"Stick with it!" she encourages.

The taste spreads out across my tongue. The intense peaty overtone remains, then softens to allow other flavors to blossom. Blackberries and chocolate, then cinnamon and coffee, now caraway and vanilla apples, each new layer revealing something buried deeper as it digs down to a foundation of some complex flavor I cannot identify nor describe as anything other than a memory of a dream I may or may not have ever dreamt.

"No lush, me," I say, taking another sip, "but I'm thinking about it."

"Seriously…"

"I'm for a stroll," I tell her.

"Sure." She tags along as I leave the main festival grounds behind.

Life carries on. Alcohol might drag the philosopher out of us all, long and sleepy draughts turning into longer and sleepier thoughts. The city puts me in this mood, constantly. We don't talk about it, though it weighs on us both.

Silence is preferred this night.

We perch up on a nearby tower, gazing down at the swarming glimmering ghosts.

"As good as Old City's, isn't it?"

"Better," she breathes. "The theming is perfect. Depressing and perfect." She drinks.

We cross bridges, aimless and comfortable in spite of the stirring breeze. Warmth, a natural quality of spiderweb threads woven into the fabric of our wraith garb. Peaceful night, as much out here in the unlit obscurity as back with the others. At times I hear a low hum in the air that fades before I can place the source. Walking was a good choice.

A lonely wraith stands in the middle of the bridge before us, craning its neck up at the Windtower now crisscrossed with golden rope pulleys. I'm not sure if I'm seeing their residual innate glow or a reflection from the moonlight.

The figure regards us.

"Ah. Hallo, outsiders," Megs says. We greet her and she makes room for us to pass. Euly goes on, but I linger for a polite moment.

"You're far from the celebration," I note.

"Mind too busy spinnin', 'ad it..." she says cryptically, then explains, "Rememberin' som'un."

Part of her old story bubbles up inside me. "Sorry to hear."

Shrugs. "Story a'ever'un, yeah? My turn t'be maudlin. Ain't no unique character. I'll go back... in a tick." Long exhale.

I hand her the wineskin, then remember that I had already given it back to Euly. Drop my hand, leaving the unspoken and confused gesture behind as I tromp after my tipsy partner.

"Was good," Megs calls after me, "a'y'all t'pitch in." Twists a long sleeve between her fingers. "Don't think none would mind if'n yeh wanted t'settle down here." Twists tighter. "Not the settlin' type, I imagine."

"We are," I say. "Or, I am," I correct after a belated second. "But we roam. It's the job. *Things*... need to settle down."

Another exhale. "Mm. 'Things' is it? Mmm." Shakes her head. "Can yeh fix this situation? I see yeh tryin', 'ad it. Ways I don't much understand, but... well..."

"I aim to till I can't."

"And if'n yeh can't?" Stops twisting, stands stock-still.

Now it's my turn to pause and eke out a sober thought beyond a string of monosyllabic. "The way I reckon it, this world is doing its damn best to bury us all. We're giving it the finger and burying it back." Snorting at myself. "Ffff. This philosophy stuff again... Listen." Pulling my hood back so my face is plainly visible in the glow of my outfit. "At the end of winter, I don't think many people are going to be happy, no. Our options are dwindling -- and we had hardly any to begin with. We are doing what we can, but we're what you see we are. Three people." The liquor must be working. I feel endlessly tired. "Three. That's it. We can't force you into anything you don't want to do. *I* can't make you care. *I* can't show you the vision I have in my thick skull about what six months from now looks like. Twelve months. Eighteen. *That's* where I am right now. *I'm* dealing with that debris and hoping I'm doing exactly what I need to do at this exact moment to minimize that burden. Because I know there's going to be more work to do elsewhere that none of us are conscious of today. So, yeah, if you all want to help yourselves, I'm really, really, really running out of time that none of you have."

It started professional. I think at a certain point the aggravation came out, then rolled up into misplaced anger as I tumbled with an uncontrollable gravity.

Leastwise... that's what the stricken face that stares back tells me.

"You've been a blessing. I'm not pissed at you," I say.

Despite my meaning those words, she turns away and leaves. Somewhat hurriedly.

I finish crossing the bridge. Stronger breezes buffet it to swinging. Euly is sitting on the topmost stair, looking up at Windtower with a stupid plastered grin.

"Nice pep talk."

"Thanks. I think it cost you your workforce."

She finishes off the wineskin and chucks it into the lake.

"Fuck it," she decrees.

"Fuck it," I repeat.

Silence.

Then, I realize I have no clue why there is scaffolding of any kind around the tower or the nigh-endless ropework. Is that ours or did the spider denizens come out to graffiti their home? Euly explains: she hadn't given up the possibility of lobbing off the top levels. Borrowing my engineers had given her confidence, but now...

"It's too late. I'm gonna run out of material soon and we still haven't solved the counterweight problem." Sighs. "Decapitation is no go. It's fucked."

"Downfall, huh?"

Silence.

Her head sinks against my shoulder. "Downfall..."

Silence.

In a quiet voice: "Leth, I'm not sure it can be Downfall. It's like... those dorky spiderkin know what we're thinking. Or maybe they're replacing the web we stole. Yeah. I shouldn't be paranoid... still... I think the new weavings they pooped out are reinforcing the internal structure that... ahh... hell..."

"It might not fall," I finish for her.

"I don't know. Maybe?" Looks up at me, our noses brush. "Maybe, Leth, maybe..."

"Maybe is all we need right now."

"A life built on maybes is a shoddy structure, man."

"Welcome to the world, Euly. Leave your hopes outside."

She barks a disgusted laugh. "Accurate."

\#

Wind rises. A song begins.

It blows through the hollow arches of the towers.

It whistles along the rope bridges.

It rustles the water, grass-like whispers.

Wind holds its breath. The music fades.

"Did you hear that?" Euly asks me, many long moments later, starting me from my dozing.

It's just the wind… give me a few more minutes…

Wind flows faster this time into a new song, the same notes blending into new patterns. Euly bolts to her feet.

Blood-red lanterns, cut from their moorings, sail overhead. And then I hear a swell of stringed instruments taking over the night. Rising and falling, shifting patterns again, bound to the wind, singing beautifully and now without pause.

Euly yanks my arm and drags me, almost twisting off the swinging bridge a few times, until she finds the vantage she was seeking. Squints into the shadows, then stiffens. Points at the alabaster tower we had been sheltering under.

"That's a bass!"

Resonant notes hum from an instrument affixed to the tower's roof, barely visible as the blood-red lights of the lanterns retreat into the sky. And all around us, close and far, we hear a chorus of new pitches entering the song as the entire city becomes one huge instrument for the whims of the wind.

"Is this what you were doing all those days?" I ask in a hushed voice.

"Yes and no," Euly breathes in awe. "Apparently I installed what those… wind harps are attached to. No one told me it was for— They said it was a surprise and then I—

I guess I forgot about it with everything—" Shakes her head, dreamily. "This is wonderful. I must have told them about my music and they wanted to impress me." Shakes her head again, more dreamily. "Worked."

We spend the remainder of midnight wandering. Each quarter of the city producing different melodies, a continual song that never perfectly repeats itself. Even Maelstrom sounds less intense when we stand out on the edge of rooftops, then walk the span of the floating bridges and stare out towards where we hear it, but cannot see.

So ended the first night.

#

Sunset comes with much buzzing expectation. Arroyo was already slavering by gloaming. Euliae was literally trembling when true nightfall descended, a manic energy frissoning as daylight fled, darkness spread, and brighter colors were finally set alight. Among those, this second night: violet lanterns strung up above the wind harps.

Then I thought about the city before, of Echo Downs. How glorious was the symphony that would have existed when the majority of the buildings were not underwater? I made no mention of my thoughts. I didn't want to spoil Euly's crazed grinning.

She is getting into this a little too much... isn't she?

"Pace yourself?" I ask Arroyo as she starts wobbling off to the now-opened stalls.

Innocent, so innocent, half-smile. "Boss, my metabolism is killer. I, like, don't even *know* what a hangover is."

"Take care anyways."

"'*Take care anyways~*'" she mocks with my voice, except slower and a lot more stupider than I actually am.

I clop her on her dumb little head.

"Ouch," she pretends it hurts.

"It's fine, Boss can chaperone the child tonight."

"*No!*"

"Yes. Arroyo is not old enough for booze. She must learn. She must be taught."

"Noo! Taught *what*??"

"That Boss has power. Arroyo has none. No food tonight either. She must learn. She must be taught."

"No way no way, he can't do that, can he!?" she begs of Euly, who we both notice at the same time has disappeared into the crowd and left no trace.

We come to a truce. The child will pace herself.

Around midnight, the violet lanterns take off in the rising wind. The music begins anew. Several hours later, Euly reappears directly in front of me. Freaks me out, the suddenness, that instinctually I thought: shit, a real revenant has crawled through death to claim me.

I don't think the common language has an apt word, or enough of them, to describe the terrifyingly insane grin I see within the shadows of her hood. The pulsing glow of her costume illuminates the scar bisecting her face until it seems like a living thing with its own fears, dreams, agendas, and hatreds. Had I seen her exposed face, I may have likewise been scarred for all the rest of my days.

#

The third night. Halfway through.

Euly has taken me away from the crowds. I have not eaten. I have not swallowed a drop of anything except salival confusion. Maelstrom is before us. She is trembling, her eyes will not move. She death-grips my hand. My fingertips are numb. My palm is tingling.

The third midnight. White lanterns take to the wind.

A new song: dull, clumsy, a mountain uprooted and rolling, an earthquake transmuted into atmosphere.

A dreadful...

a dreadful...

"Shhhhhhh," Euly whispers to still my racing thoughts. A quarter-hour passes. My hand is hurting so much, but she won't relinquish it. I look at her. "Listen... Lethean... Listen... Whisper me what you hear."

Nothing... just... the song, the silence, her breathing, the song, the silence, her breathing, the—

"It's quietening," I whisper.

Tears pour from her eyes, still unmoving and staring out at the churning moonlit whirlpool. Maelstrom is slowing. She lets go of my hand, extends her arms out towards an audience of perhaps tens of thousands.

Euliae sings a dreadful lullaby and Maelstrom slows even further until the constant noise of it is very, very nearly drowned out beneath the lyrics she is weeping by the end of her aria.

#

For us the festival has concluded. The Executioners are back at work -- pay our unwraith-like behavior no heed. While the rest of the city languidly drifts about, you may spot two-point-five wights flying haphazardly every which way. That would be us.

My current task is to keep Euly from believing she can sing underwater and prevent her from diving straight into the lake to perform.

She is that fired up.

Turns out there are plenty of unused wind harps in storage. We've been spending the day attaching them to any stable base we can find and even jury-rigged a few atop some of Arroyo's bridges. Right now she and Euly are detaching a section of bridge after tying it with spider-rope.

"Carefully," I say.

Excitement and tension are charging the air. No "aye aye, Boss!" or "yeah yeah, man..." from either. The ropes are secure... extending one wind harp as close to Maelstrom as we can, right at the limit where its pull shifts from a gentle, disturbing tug to a ravenous and lethal yank.

There's as much art in genius as there is in stupidity.

When night comes, my stomach reminds me I haven't eaten all day. I tap Arroyo's shoulder.

"Hmm?"

Jerking a thumb over my shoulder. "Going to grab some grub. Want anything special?"

Her eyes light up far too brightly.

"No. Alcohol. Tonight."

The light is gone.

"Mushroom buns, obviously. Get a bunch for Miss Euly. I'll eat whatever." Nods, then does her face-quirk dance. "Also, one of those curious orange-berry pie-thingies." Nods, satisfied. Then remembers something. "Oh oh! And those fried veggie-stuffs." Nods again. "Ah! And—"

"I'll pick up a hoard of different things," I say.

Reassured, she smiles and laughs.

"Keep an eye on her. Don't let her start without me."

"Yeah, no worries, Boss. She's itchin'. I can tell." She calls out, "Miss Euly! Boss is getting us dinner now. Come take a break with me."

#

Tonight's less-impromptu performance will start later. Euliae filled up so much, she was on the verge of puking. Calming her nerves by eating... a poor idea, but I don't blame her. We're at the threshold. Maelstrom could be dispersed within the next few hours, leaving the final night of the festival for true, enduring revelry.

Damn me. I dare hope.

Sinking these corpses would create a new problem, but one far more manageable. One that *might* last long enough for those reinforcements, roundtrip notwithstanding. Pros heavily outweighed cons for the first time.

I casually salute the Windtower. You may live through this too, friend.

Yellow lanterns take flight. On the edge of hearing, the prelude begins to hum. Euly stands up and opens her mouth.

#

She was laughing. She was singing. She was twirling. A vision of the girl she had once been before adolescence, confusion, adulthood, and trials hardened her moods. Except for one stark fact: she was drunk on something Arroyo and I could not partake of. Our headquarters could not contain Euly's exuberance and I was relieved everyone else living and sleeping here was out festivaling in their own ways.

"A grand performance! Tomorrow! The closing night!" Euly decrees.

Arroyo is sucking her inkstone dry on slapdash posters. The pile is growing with every passing minute.

"This was the answer I was *always* searching for!" Laughing again, wiping her eyes. "I'm so happy. The whirlpool slowed even more than last night. I'm so happy…"

Arroyo was too. The mood was so merry that no one took note of the taciturn, glum Lethean with a smile so flat it could be mistaken for a frown. Maelstrom did slow, but not as much as last night nor as long.

Euliae was wrong.

Arroyo hadn't been there, so she couldn't have known.

#

I lighted out before they woke up in the morning, after having plied them with many "celebratory drinks". I took the flyers with me. Thought to junk them, but couldn't bring myself to do what was necessary. Not fully.

"Nay. Maelstrom came after the last festival," Megs told me, confirming what I knew.

I hated having no precedent. Euly saw it as the oblique route we had missed while stumbling forward, her instincts justified after years of wondering.

"Never seen a cursed with my own eyes," the lukewarm baker told me. "I don't think Echo Downs had any prior."

Unless someone more worldly had an eye on things.

"Intriguing hypothesis," Ricken told me, turning his back and leaving the door open.

As I thought, active Executioners had been through the city when it was dry, but long before our last group. The Ghost Festival was an even longer tradition. *If* the music worked, though, as Euly was convinced... if the wind harps *could* lull the cursed back to sleep... no one may have detected them otherwise. False negatives buried normally and forgotten.

"I should temper what you're planning," he said after a long think, pointedly and without flinching away from the for-once-solicited critique. "Consider the overlooked possibility: it doesn't always work. It might not work at all, but if it does the reliability of the result is questionable."

"Because there are always more factors to take into account than acoustics alone."

"I have no memory of the festival being a safer time. Nor was it more dangerous. The music may not be a factor, as you mention, but a mistaken corollary. Wind has always been the first denizen in this valley. Perhaps that is your 'lulling agent'."

We were witnessing something we wanted to witness, was the short of his point. I could accept that. I didn't know how to suggest Euly accept it.

#

She was sitting on the dock, running a bow over the strings of a few more acquired wind harps. Testing their timbre, resonance, and sustain. Tact would have meant she'd ignore me, so I told her bluntly she was losing objectivity.

Two points of data aren't enough. We need much more. Then we can have the concert. Agreed?

Oh, but she refused to agree. Kept testing. Pretended to ignore me, but she was clearly agitated. Kept testing. When I left, I placed the flyers next to her. This was a choice she had to make alone.

#

New floating wind harps were arranged on the edge of Maelstrom. There were four notes that Euly had become partial to, a simple ascending arpeggio of three in sequence and one note a half-octave higher. Even steeped in my doubts, I had to admit that it was a hypnotic blend.

By sunset, the only audience consisted of us three and the dead. By nightfall, the wind rose. Gray lanterns took off, hovering above a full pumpkin moon that shone brilliantly along the lake, a sparkling strip that extended from the grassy shore to us.

Euly sat and listened. After an hour, she rose and added some wordless vocals. She sat and listened again. The alternation continued another hour.

"Be honest with me," I pleaded.

Her scarred face was torn. "I'm telling you, I think it's slower tonight more than last."

I didn't agree. It sounded, it looked, like diminishing returns. I said nothing of my biases for fear of coloring Arroyo's opinion.

"It's super hard to figure." She was all balled up, a defensive wraith, absentmindedly playing with her crutch. "If it's better or worse, not by much. Not enough to—"

"I *know*." The torment in Euly's voice killed any conversation for the rest of the night.

#

The Ghost Festival concluded.

Clean-up began around noon the following day when hangovers had abated to the extent that no one would kill themselves or each other by staggering into piles of used lumber and nails. For my part, I surveyed the city. A little aimless. Very frustrated.

Ferrymen were taking down the scaffolding surrounding the Windtower. I didn't spot Euliae among them.

After satisfying myself that our dredged cursed were still secure in the storage building across from Underground,

I meandered my way over to the nascent dun and headed downwards into the restricted section. I was astonished by the diligence of my meagre crew; give a man a shovel and a directive and eventually he'll dig to antipodes. Presently, the total space here could easily house thousands of bodies.

My architect, cheeks smudged with loam and skin going sallow from all the time avoiding sunlight, showed me another surprise: a bricked-up burial vault set in the wall at the lowest level.

"Please tell me you didn't find this down here," I say.

At first, he thinks I'm serious. Then he releases the heartiest belly laugh I have heard since and likely ever will. It would have echoed throughout the tunnels had the walls been more solid. His explanation simply amounts to: it seemed like a good idea at the time.

I can't dub it amateur work. Amply professional such that I call him out as a closet Executioner. He laughs again, denying it.

Giving myself a short sprint for momentum, pivoting, I slam my heel against the vault's center. Nothing. I do it again. Cracks appear, but their veining is fine.

"The hell did you make these out of..." I hold a torch close, basically grazing the wall with my eyelashes.

"Mudbricks," he states.

"The hell you say, mud."

Astonishing yet true. He shows me a pile of several hundred in the adjoining room. I test a few at random. Not Executioner grade stonework, but damn close. And mud? What the hell!

"If you tell me this is a trade secret, I'll haul you before the magistrate until we yank it out of your tongue."

Mud grins, like a kid caught stealing and not caring, and explains far more geological information about the province than I can retain. But the short is this: if we need to inter, we now have the legitimate resources.

If not the time. Or corpses. Or manpower.

Before departing, I inform my equally-busy miners that I'll be putting their equipment to new use within the fortnight. Downfall had to happen soon or it wouldn't happen at all.

And she may have been right when she said that that bloody erection might not drop. I poked my head in Windtower -- and that was about the extent of what I could do. The spiders had gone all crazed abstract artists on us. The interior was practically blooming with webwork, glowing with such magnitude that I wondered if these spindly bitches and bastards had climbed into the sky, plucked the moon from its firmament, and flensed the poor thing to absolute shreds.

One dinky spider, the size of my fist, clearly insomniac and territorial, hissed at my intrusion.

"Oh piss off," I told it, stomping in its general direction until it got the hint, or got bored, and skittered away. An organic reverberation shifted multiple floors above. I could feel its force travel down the walls, shivering the very stone slabs beneath my feet unto pregnant silence. Perhaps the insomnia was contagious. That gave me one of those thoughts I know is only a possibility, but my feelings murmur that it is true.

Things are going to get worse.

#

Explicit plans needed to be made with my engineers. The whole group had to have the loyalty of a family and the resolve of a conspiracy. Arroyo and I set to work on seducing them. The weight of "Krohn's" decree would, as it always did, only get us so far. Invisible threats are no threats if they stay permeable. Legal force does not mean squat when it's over the horizon and in the future. Most people don't see that far ahead.

I hated that I always had to.

"Sugar over vinegar!" Arroyo announced plainly. Another plan, a new directive. We required the benefits -- from whatever aftermath would be -- to make the coming shitstorm feel like a fart in the middle of the night. Barely wake up. Turn over. Go back to sleep.

Money would be involved. Money is always involved even in a city that switched exclusively to a bartering system fueled by goodwill and a bit of wholesome socialism. Besides, we represent order wherever we roam. People miss the system when they remember all it did for them.

I'm being cynical, it's honestly not so underhanded. We all miss when things worked as we expected them to work. We miss connection. Literal connection. We've become too isolated from one another that trade and communication are luxuries, but mostly poorly-recalled dreams. I'm exploiting nostalgia and plenty of other emotions.

If there's any justification that assuages my abhorrence of manipulating the innocent, it would be this: I really do want to help everyone.

In the end, my pragmatism and Arroyo's jubilance won each and every able body over. They understood the gains and the risks and the threat to survival if not for themselves then for others. Of all that we offered them?

Well...

I have to give you some plausible deniability, don't I?

#

Two weeks were in the passing. Much of the foundation of what would come next did come next. My crew and I, under the cover of gradually darkening nights, transferred from the dun most equipment that could demolish the "base" of Windtower. I had to keep reminding myself that the real bottom lays fathoms deep. We would be jamming the chisel into stone, so to speak, a few feet above the waterline.

The spiders were going to be a pain in the ass, mostly because Mud insisted on climbing to the spot where I did so he could survey the angles and distances with his fellows.

"How many of you need to be up there?" I asked gruffly.

Everyone wanted to. Those perfectionist blighters.

I talked them down to the engineer and Mud alone -- who instead insisted on the plucky miner from out east I still fancied, who apparently was banging my architect.

Mud, you ingrate.

#

So.

I've been avoiding talking about a certain important someone, haven't I?

Let's discuss Euliae.

This is going to get... complicated.

Messy.

I think I'll keep avoiding this a little longer.

Yes.

That's surely for the best.

#

There were two deaths. One inevitable, one stupid. In some ways, neither could be helped.

An elderly woman had decided to take the easy way out of life by dying in her sleep. It was scarcely dramatic; no heart attack or suffering to speak of, simply shuffled away gently and quietly, not disturbing anyone, such that it reminded me of the festival and I found myself smiling sadly. No family. Not in the city at least. I never learned her name. They'd given her a water burial, forgetting to invite us to check if she was cursed or not.

You'd figure *someone* would understand we're here for a reason and the one I keep going on about.

Sarcasm aside, it was more muscle memory in their mourning than spiting me personally. And I am not worried about the addition of a single new cursed at the bottom of the lake if that's how it is.

Not yet.

The other was a damned unfortunate setback. The engineer who worked on the clocktower back home? Yep. Thought he could scale the thousands of steps and veritable maze of ladders within Windtower on his lonesome. Why? No one will ever know. To impress me? Inspired autonomy? Madness?

All I know is that I have to go inside to check whether *he* was cursed or not. That's what I need: some murderous, unstoppable force beating the spiders to pulp while I'm trying to surreptitiously destroy where these eight-legged squatters took up residence.

I haven't mentioned what will happen to the spiders when this place crashes down across the length of Drowns, have I? I haven't because I don't have a fucking clue.

That's Future Lethean's problem, that poor forsaken luckless boy.

#

I locate him five floors up. Shitlick is cocooned like a baby in smothered swaddling by a mom who had a change of heart. As far as I can tell, not a cursed.

I leave him there.

His real name was Claron Bonz, sometimes called "Clarion", but he'll always be Shitlick to me.

#

Deciding to get the real ascent over with, the next daybreak saw myself, my architect and miner, reach the top of Windtower. Interior was indeed bursting with webwork. Felt like I was cutting through a forest infested with brackenweeds and bramblethorn patches. Very unpleasant.

They made their measurements, double-checking several of my own from months prior, and independently verified each other's work. Nice team.

"Will get squashed real good," his miner told me, inclining a head in the direction of my fledgling dun.

"You can't go around it?"

That earned me a sympathetic, pitying look.

Ffff. Mud, you ingrate.

The uneventfulness of going up was inversely proportional to the descent. No, I will not describe it. Suffice to say that one reason I picked these two included: the muscles in their arms, legs, and between their ears. I armed them with cudgels and strict orders -- and they complied exceedingly well.

At the bottom, we were bruised and bleeding in places, but alive. As I defended their unflattering wriggle of an escape through the entrance bolt hole, I caught sight of spider-part fragments dropping through the huge metal grating in the floor. Even the larger chunks didn't splash. In fact, I heard nothing at all.

#

"Oh. Well, it's the Windtower, isn't it? Tunnels for the wind to go all over beneath the city," the other miners told me later with sympathetic, pitying looks of their own.

Huh.

#

About Euliae.

On the practical side, nothing was amiss. Her pivots surpass the grace of a dancer. She is not one to bash her head against a wall until the wall decides it's had enough of that and moves on. That's my method. Or so she tells me often.

The prototype net, having proven itself for dredging, was expanded upon now that the scaffolding project was defunct. Larger nets were woven including one enormous piece that made the maddening loom of the spiders' home look like casual embroidery. I thought that alone spoke volumes of Euly's current state of mind and I was moved to be complimentary for positive reinforcement's sake until learning Megs had gone full bore with a score new recruits.

None ferrymen, but all diligent and impatient. I did not abstain from the compliment despite the new source.

While everyone else worked dockside, Euly was out on the water towing herself around on an utterly bizarre network of poles and ropes. The puppeteer madwoman had become a spider herself, obsessed with incremental adjustments to wind harps -- whether this was their physical alignment, their amount, or the quality of their harmony.

"Give me a second," she told me.

I gave two seconds. Nothing. I gave minutes. Nothing. Every time I approached or called out to her:

"Give me a second."

She wasn't even an ass about it. Or distracted. Sounded completely rational and each time, maybe it was gaslighting, I believed that she really did need one more second and everything would be perfect.

But it never was.

I brought lunch because obviously she would have forgotten. Refused. Same excuse.

Euly was going to drop and if it happened out there, I'd be powerless to reach her before the current pulled her into Maelstrom and I lost all desire to stop the fucking thing.

Thought about hauling Arroyo over here to play upon her vestigial sympathy. Felt too cruel after... that day. Instead, I managed to trip hop climb fall over to her position, grab her shoulders and say, "Please stop."

She didn't. Not really. But somehow I managed to get her back to the bridge and sit her down. She looked normal. Completely normal that I expected ire or a dressing-down.

"When have you last slept?"

"Oh Lethean, we sleep when we die. You know that." She laughed, but it sounded like it came from the underside of the moon. Also, her eyes never shifted focus once.

I handed over some bread and fake meat. "Please eat while I talk."

"No time, man. I'm nearly—"

"Eat and listen. I have problems I can't fix," I lied.

"Oh. I see."

"Need your input."

"Okay. Well. Ah. Yes. I can help you."

Much of what I related next was utter bullshitting distraction and went down enough circuitous pathways that I cannot completely remember now everything I rattled on about. I'm sure it was topically engaging though vaguely astute.

I name-dropped the city's major points of interest for that extra poke at verisimilitude. Euly didn't flinch. Secretly, I wanted her to.

After my droning went on for roughly a quarter of an hour, pausing for her unengaged input, her eyelids began having better sense than she did. She contracted a chronic case of the wobbles, ending only when she lit off from consciousness, leaving me alone to my thoughts and a dead-weighted woman. A cart happened to be nearby and thankfully she's physically easier to move than a corpse. I might have should have dumped her down in the dun to teach her a lesson.

Took her back to bed instead.

#

"Stay around her for the next few weeks," I ask of Arroyo. "You'll understand."

Puts her journal down. "What doing?"

"Just stay around her, please."

#

A refreshed Euly headed back out, Arroyo clomping by her side. Tonight was the new moon and my headstrong partner refused to stay away from her experiment or be delayed. That part of the story was clearly over.

It was overbearing, but I shadowed them later. Concern makes it hard to let go and let be. Although I'm conscious of that personal flaw, I can never shake it. As she says: Lethean. Head. Wall.

Arroyo was official notetaker, seated under a lantern.

In the near pitch black, Euliae was once again out on the water. Only an obscure shadow that fell on a cord of rope here, now over there, then back again, now far off, whispered of her presence. Whenever I saw nothing for long minutes on end, the hollow in my chest echoed.

This was a live performance. Maybe a dry run. The reedy music was familiar, not dramatically altered from the last I had heard it. She was still relying on those favored four notes, but... entirely concentrated on their tempo. The willfulness of the wind might have been anathema to another composer; she used it to her advantage in ways a non-artist like myself can neither understand nor adequately describe.

One hour later, her shadow had not appeared anywhere. I was a nervous wreck. Then good sense offered me the suggestion to angle my eyes somewhere other than where I thought she was -- because she had long since flitted away.

She was sitting next to Arroyo.

She was fine.

And Maelstrom was very, very, very quiet.

#

Arroyo does the talking. Euliae stumbles up the stairs to bed, even more drained than when I forced it on her yesterday.

"The light was the problem." Face scrunched up, Arroyo taps her journal to indicate the data set being referenced. "Full moon screwed things up good and proper at the end of Ghost Fest. Glowy ropes may be a problem too, but we can shroud them if— *when* the harps are perfectly aligned."

The search for perfection: everlasting rest for the dead.

Is that a mirage or are we, at long last, truly on the brink of... This might be that new and bountiful harvest of success that Krohn herself had given up on as childish twaddle after the massacre of Sarcophagus.

We call it "Harmonious Repose". No one believes in it.

Euliae believes in it.

#

Two more weeks pass.

I spend solitary days clearing out spiderweb from Windtower's lower levels. I've been up their pointy asses so often they avoid me, not out of fear but because when they don't get in my way I don't get in theirs. Mutual disrespect.

It was cute when they left a human femur waiting for me once. I thought it cuter when I left them fifty pedipalps.

Euliae continues with the wind harps, though the bulk of her work is nocturnal... which doesn't work well for Arroyo who's become more of a morning person. Dutiful little helper, she is acclimating. Even trying to walk short distances without her crutch.

Too early days for that, I'm afraid.

I wince when she does.

Warmth is fully behind us. The weather turns worse. I've begun wearing my wraith outfit under my normal clothing for the potent self-generating heat it provides. So wrapped up in preparations, I forget to check how it's affecting everything outside my narrowing scope.

The forests outside the lake masquerade autumnal, a matting of dead leaves and needles proclaiming their coming fate. All vibrant, clustering bursts of orange and red are for show. Pure leafy bluster. Edges of the lake, the full circumference, are thick ice at least three feet down already and extending towards the heart of the city by another six.

"Our bridges are going to get stuck where they are," I report to Arroyo.

She allays my worries. "No, no. I had them built with precautions in mind. We'll detach them when the worst of it hits, then pop! Drag them back out atop the big freeze."

"One path for escaping into the wilderness, right?"

Arroyo goes mum. Her expressions do not.

"That was your plan," I press.

"Yeah, yeah, I know, Boss, but…" Gestures frantically at Euly's brilliant madness. "Things came to freely pass."

And they'd have to pass soon if they didn't work at all. Eight weeks, then the whole lake would solidify. That gives her two new moons to get this thing right. If the song she's composing fails both times, if Downfall goes wrong and likewise fails: we bunker down in the dun or make a dangerous pilgrimage.

Either option makes me uncomfortable.

Which reminds me to get to the interring I've been putting off for over a month.

"Were you inducted into vault security yet?"

"Crap, no, are you kidding me? I've been horny for that since ever."

That's the attitude I like to see in my recruits. But…

"Boss." Pokes me out of reverie.

"Hmm?"

"You can't keep babying her."

"I don't want her out here alone."

Waves her crutch in my face. "The heck you think I can do anyway? Scream really loud? I mean, crap, we all *know* I can do that pretty freaking good."

She's right.

"You're right."

"Don't like that I am, but that's how it is today." Stands up and starts hobbling onwards as if she's leading this expedition.

Perhaps she is now.

Tiny Krohn.

I laugh.

"Stop making fun of me," she pouts.

How did she know…?

Definitely Krohn reborn.

Catching up, I give her shoulder a squeeze.

Euliae does not notice our departure.

Equipment Manifest

Two (2) braziers, mid-height
Four (4) squares kindling
Six (6) logs firewood, cedar
One (1) experimental Technocrat torch
One (1) trowel
One (1) bucket mortar paste, non-Executioner grade
Six-hundred (600) mudbricks, non-Executioner grade

Burial operation. Twelve cursed to be interred.
No incidents. Four cartloads. Lethean & Arroyo on duty.
Destination: newly established dun in Echo Downs.

Preparations Made

Ten floors down under Underground. We cart in the first batch. I do the manual labor; Arroyo clomps ahead to keep the way clear. That padded end of her crutch is worth its weight in… whatever happens to be of value these days, I wouldn't know.

The two braziers flank the far ends of the designated burial space, blazing cobalt and dampening our quiet passage. A sizeable selection of the most dependable workers from my group are assembled opposite the twelve gaping holes in the wall I had them delve.

There happen to be twelve workers in total. I swear that's a coincidence, but the nervous atmosphere will keep them sharp. Plus, I told them that anyone who made a peep or ran away would have to deal with me later. It must be a credit to whatever image the city has developed of me because that vagueness kept them literally in line.

I pull the cart all the way down the hall, nodding to everyone in greeting. The new torch that spits out tongues of azure fire is affixed above the heads of the cursed behind me. This stark color makes of us all the appearance of ancient sentries -- or statues yet-to-be-carved in an unimaginable age ahead.

Everything would be pure observation for my team. Earlier, I instructed them what I planned to do and expected them to remember that and the demonstrations to come. Arroyo was a teensy bit miffed by the audience. Thought to be the sole focus of attention today. Wanted quality Boss Time, I suppose. A high-maintenance child. Normally that might bother me, or especially Euliae, but the fact that our protege is such a dependable and passionate dork about everything concerning work, we just think it's adorable.

Lethean has an eye ever-fixated on a future that may or may not be there. Most people aren't bashing down our doors or trying to steal our clientele to get our attention. Arroyo was the vast exception. We don't spend much time with the normal populace and -- blatant confession -- our stay here has opened my eyes to the foolishness of those blinders we've been running around with.

Krohn declares "transparency", but have we ever *really* done anything to demystify ourselves?

Hence my proactive outreach.

Eventually, we will leave. I would wish, in the best of circumstances, to leave a piece of myself behind: terrified peasants yesterday, fearless Executioner-material tomorrow. I've done worse.

Under an Inviolable Command of Absolute Silence

First: lay bricks as a slab for where the interred will lie flat and supine -- basic but essential.

Second: construct the interior wall, working outwards with a focus on symmetry -- this is crucial for later, so get it correct now before needing to strip out and redo.

Third: construct the ceiling, holding each brick in place until the mortar sets enough to move on -- this is painstaking and a pain in the ass without Executioner grade materials; I suggest vaulting the ceiling for a slight arch to hold and disperse the weight evenly, or using accurately-sized wooden planks with support beams as a temporary inner structure until the mortar has dried (I'm doing the former option).

Fourth: double-check the fires -- cobalt color strong? Good, proceed along. Color failed or wavering? Not so good, add more kindling. One at a time, too. Don't waste.

Fifth: gently transfer the cursed from cart to resting place -- fuck this one up, it will fuck *everything* up. Either prior to or immediately afterwards, make sure the bindings are tight around the limbs. I prefer doing this first to avoid having to drag the cursed back out to rebind. This is also a good opportunity to determine if the neck or lower spine vertebrae are still separated (*if* the cursed had to be stabbed), same with the elbows or knees. For my purposes, that happened so long ago it already healed. The lesson here: these are very dangerous cursed.

Sixth: brick up the exterior wall -- probably the simplest step and the easiest to mess up in the promised relief of finishing, going home, and getting dinner. Wow, Lethean, distracted much... Anyways, make sure at least one brick has the telltale X marking that means Known Cursed. This is usually a bit redundant, but it's one of those protocols to observe. Why?

Why...

Huh. Good question.

I mean... I think it's in case, one day, they stop being cursed and we can track the data? We're... figuring things out as we go.

Obviously, I didn't tell *that* to anyone. And Arroyo of course knows.

Oh right, before I forget: add any bricks listing who the person was, if they can be identified. And another where they were recovered. And the date of interment. Date of actual death doesn't particularly matter (we think) and that's rarely available.

It's a lot.

Like I say: we're figuring it out.

And that's the first vault constructed. Not completed. Technically, that won't occur until the mortar fully hardens. It'll take a day or two with the quality of these materials. Executioner grade would be within five hours or six hours -- ideal conditions will get it in five.

I help Arroyo construct the second vault. Then oversee the third. Then do nothing other than a spot check with the fourth. Along the way, of course, I move the cursed themselves. No one touches them except me. Unless she experiences a second growth spurt in her twenties, Arroyo will probably never be able to move any corpses by herself. That's fine. We work mostly always in pairs.

Finally, I waggle my finger questioningly at the workers I hadn't forgotten. Who's game? And lo and behold, all but one raise their hands. I send them off in pairs, then work with the odd man out. Arroyo finishes the exteriors.

Burial operation. Twelve cursed successfully interred.

One incident: someone got confident and talked; two cursed stirred (one had to be stabbed and rebound); no casualties; reprimand given.

Potential recruits identified. Prospects: optimistic.

#

There's a commonplace maxim here about fretting over the small things while ignoring the big ones. I think it's a ribbing about stupidity. I call this being overwhelmed and avoiding burnout.

More's the pity, either way.

Thousands of miles away a new ending is crossing impossible distances atop a flat drab wasteland draped in a burial shroud fashioned from broken hopes. They crunch like glass, *krrshhk krrksstk*, but stick into the earth and not the feet that trample them. This will be an end it is not the end so much will break and the hopes will be the least of these will be an end they are not the end.

The eternal sloughing.

"Do you think we could help?" I ask, craning my neck to find the way, but it doesn't move because my neck is bone.

No answer.

The jester puppet is silent without strings. It is glowering at a ground it cannot perceive.

"Are we safe here?" I ask next.

No answer.

A willow tree is on the horizon. It approaches us from the mountains that have also appeared on the horizon. Crinkly crimson leaves are vomiting from its mouth creates a carpet underroot as it reaches me bark grown into a smile that cannot frown. The willow tree is as small as it was on the horizon.

I return the smile, but there are no lips my jaw of bone.

"They cannot come here," I say, making the decision no one will make.

"No. They will."

Curling inwards backwards, the jester puppet summons indescribable anguish to enforce a will of sorts mostly a puffing up sigh and to then and also there was a decision once wasn't there a single hole but none would fit we were too cowardly. Hollow puppet eyes meeting my hollow sockets where my inverse dreams of bone.

"They will not," I maintain.

In the air, I see it now: the gargoyle perched on a black cloud of void and staring at where I will one day fall.

"You forget, Lethean," the jester puppet tells me, "we're already here."

\#

The full moon wanes.

Maelstrom roars less angrily with every passing night. By daybreak, it renews its protests. Our impassioned and revitalized Euliae keeps at it. I worry. Arroyo returns to her sentry post. She writes. She has now begun to draw. Her sketches are good. Light-hearted and fearless.

Megs and I are becoming better friends. The friction is gone. We've come to appreciate, at our own pace, that life has permanently scarred us both in vastly differing ways. Commiseration of sorts. Existential armistice. Her brother's death is a weight she does not know how to shrug off.

"If you could absolve yourself of the grief," I ask one afternoon, "would you do it?"

Stops rowing briefly. "I say 'aye', 'ad it." Pushes her oar back into the water. "Hurts so much, y'know? Holds me back from livin'. Holds me back from... feelin' other things."

I nod. Her back is turned, so she doesn't see.

"I've heard tell that makes me a heartless creature," she admits, minutes later. "But I can't agree with that. I *know* he meant plenty t'me. Cuttin' off the pain wouldn't... cut him off. He's always important. He don't... need t'stab me all damnable day t'make that known, 'ad it." Slaps the water with the oar. "Damn dead bastard."

I don't think Megs could be an Executioner with her hang-ups and one foot always stuck in the past. Perhaps a message-runner. Probably always someone never straying too far from home. The one kind of person I can never help: the ones that simply have to figure things out for themselves the hardest way possible. Come what may.

"Come what may..." I whisper, reaching my fingers over the side of the ferry and into the water.

Ten seconds, then the ache becomes too much.

The ferrymen and I have found a way to dredge the cursed during the day, while Euly snores, without disturbing her careful preparations. Their efficiency is so laudable that I start trusting them with simple transportation runs to the dun -- provided Arroyo is waiting on the other side.

Of their own volition, my workers had constructed a temporary morgue with her disability in mind: the loaded ferry coasts into the building (covered with blackout curtains); a simple yet ingenious pulley system attaches to the cursed's bindings; a modicum of effort lifts it out of the ferry by way of a lever, and she need only guide it by hand to an empty pallet.

Everyone involved knew emergency protocol: run the fuck away (as quietly as possible) and get Lethean (as quietly as possible).

On a good day, I can safely inter around a dozen cursed. On a better day, I don't even think about how ineffectual this is in the face of the coming disaster. On the best days, I stop asking myself why I'm interring anything in a place I'm planning on mostly destroying, or at least making nigh inaccessible, while killing time I don't want to kill waiting for my partner's plan that I have extreme reluctance believing in let alone supporting.

Today is one of the bad ones.

But it's coming to an end. I have only now finished slotting the final brick, sealing off another vault. I stand. Stretch. My spine pops. I hear fingers scratching at the interior of the vault directly behind me. I wait for a few minutes, but it doesn't repeat.

Then I make the customary walk down the hallway, checking for any damage that no one has yet surveyed and listening for any worrisome changes. Everything passes inspection and I go to leave, thoughts of spiced potatoes and our dwindling liquor supply pulling me by the stomach.

Mud flags me down before I ascend the ladder.

"What are you doing down here?" I ask.

"We forgot about Asa and Giri."

"Meaning what? I told you guys this level is restricted. None of you should be here without my say-so."

He nods, sheepish. "The fact is: we really forgot about them. They've been digging nonstop even after the rest of the tools were transferred out. They hit bedrock down in the wind-tunnels."

I know every word, but I don't understand a thing he's telling me. So, I have him lead me. We make for an extremely distant area far outside the safety supports such that I'm wondering what idiots I'm employing who somehow disappeared, took our equipment (things I never detected were missing after the prep work at Windtower), and kept working on...

Then I remember the exploratory survey team that I originally sent off to plague-knows-where. Well, now we do. At the bottom of a dizzying, burrowed, spiral staircase I recognize their dirt-covered faces the instant I see them.

"I thought you two ditched me when everyone else did."

They both stare at each other like the thought had never crossed their single-mindedness. I suppose the joke is on me when I told them from the start to keep excavating. They did. Corkscrewing down into the depths until they found a massive rock tunnel.

The walls were unnaturally smooth, appearing like marble until the feeling of grittiness under my palm dispelled the illusion. What had caused this? A silly instinctual question and one that had already been answered to me twice, once by Mud just minutes ago and weeks back by the miners. In case I needed a more obvious hint, a breath of wind rushed around me and flew headlong into the darkness beyond our torches.

"Huh," I said, ever the smart one.

"Huh huh," my echo said, managing to sound smarter.

I poked around a bit, walking in the direction of the pulsing breezes. Occasionally they would grow in intensity, at the most unpredictable times, once shoving me head over ass. I think I laughed, until my torch expressed how it didn't share my sense of humor.

This was an oddity. The possibility space felt endless as I stared into the nothingness down one tunnel, then the other, and yet I couldn't think of a single use for them. More obdurate stone for more secure vaults, yes, though without the manpower at present to make much headway -- Asa and Giri's obsession notwithstanding; plus, I was sealing up all the mudbricks about as fast as Mud could produce them.

The wind makes a pleasing, toneless music that if it didn't lull the cursed back to slumber certainly wouldn't rouse them. What would Euliae think of? Run a system of brass instruments upstairs? Piped-in music? Classy. This feels like future work, not now work. Maybe I've merely stumbled into tomorrow's corpse road to Old City.

"Good job," I tell them. "Let's install a few sconces and everlast tapers down here. When that's satisfactory, get yourselves topside for a while so no one thinks you've died. And get some sunshine already before you turn into rocks."

#

The days were long. The days were short. Today, when I dipped my hand in, I tore it back out after three seconds. Fingertips white and throbbing. I cancelled retrieval operations that day and asked Megs to take me around the lake's boundaries.

We didn't make it very far. The ice hadn't crept up during the night, it had advanced with a declaration of war meant to trigger a preemptive and unconditional surrender. I managed to stay in denial until afternoon when a bank of clouds appeared on the horizon: sickly pale and faintly green.

Only one month into winter and deepness had come.

We have lost a new moon.

I spot Euly over by Maelstrom, setting up for the night.

"When's the trial run?" I hurriedly ask.

"Whoa whoa, still asleep here, man." She grips a rope for support, losing her balance in surprise.

"When is it?" I press.

"Ehhh, I don't know. Look at the moon." Shields her eyes from the sun, gazing around. "Ah nevermind, doesn't come out until night these days. I forgot."

I tell her.

Arroyo bounds over to us in time to hear the tail end of Euly's recitation of every bit of profanity she has ever heard. Coined a few new terms as well. While she gritted her teeth to dust and throttled a rope for want of someone to throttle, I informed Arroyo of the turn of events.

"Cunt-fucking shit!" Arroyo spat.

More colloquially that translated to: we did not have three new moons to get this right, we did not have two new moons to get this right. It was now or never.

Windtower loomed in my vision.

"I know," I said. "I know."

#

Fortunately, Euliae was born to work under maximum pressure. It took Arroyo another day to unfrazzle herself and return to usefulness. In the meantime, I took her place on the docks and studied her meticulous notes.

And daydreamy sketches. Lingering on the one with stick-figure Lethean and stick-figure Euliae holding hands with a heart over our heads atop which stick-figure Arroyo was dancing and singing: "Best Bosses~!"

It was so precious I wanted to tear it out and plunge it ten fathoms deep so no generation to come would ever be tempted to forge such tight bonds themselves after being this inspired.

No good could come from it.

Tonight is a sickle moon, its sharp edges more than sufficient to puncture expectations. Euliae pops over to me after an initial inspection of her setup -- the winds and rolling waters have a tendency, even after her tireless afternoon adjustments, to mess things up in minute ways I don't understand.

"Just realized, I might have to do this in the blind."

"Meaning?"

She points. "What if that glimmer alone could piss them off?" The golden ropes are what she means.

It's true, we could shroud them as Arroyo suggested, but how would Euliae do a live performance? Without a doubt, we would order the city to a full lights-out for the main event. Had she practiced so much that she could feel her way about, loosening a rope here, pulling another tighter on the opposite side, all around this network of poles, ferries, ropes, and wind harps?

"Yes. I can."

The confidence in her voice bolsters me. But the unspoken was:

"You don't want to."

"Definitely not."

I squeeze her hand. She yanks it away.

"Not now, Lethean."

After a quick catalogue in my head of our meagre resources, I offer one solution that she offers at the same time: use all our remaining kindling. We don't have enough to last the night, but if we ignite a batch whenever she needs to move around out there... that could work.

I can tell she's been second-guessing herself a lot over the course of... well, probably since the moment we approached the lake's edge that one night. Working her projects definitely exacerbated that anxiety. I don't want to ask what I'm going to.

Friendship requires it.

"Do you need to make any more adjustments?"

"No."

Again, that innate conviction strengthens my own wavering. In this. In her. In every decision we have made along this tortuous journey that has inexorably led us to this possible present, sitting next to each other -- staring out at a whirlpool we cannot see -- divided by a few inches of empty darkness, hands close to one another yet not touching.

"But..." she starts, chiseling away at that confidence straightaway. "But the forces that are working against me, they *always* move something out of alignment. Sometimes it's okay! Sometimes, happy accidents. That's art, right? I'm not mad. I'm... the limiting factor."

I wait for her to explain that.

"The music is the best I can make it. But me, *my song*, the lyrics... I don't know. That might be subjective to the cursed. They may not respond collectively. Individualistic, like people. *I* could be the only instrument out there that..."

"What choices you make are the right ones at the right times," I say. She folds her hands, hunches over a bit as though the falling night is pressing down on her. "Because you're you. Things happen, you respond. If things happen in a different way, you'll respond a different way." I bump my shoulder into hers. After a long delay, she bumps back. "Stop living your life in the negative space."

Nods, gripping her hands tighter.

"Okay..." Exhales a shuddering breath. "Time for a dry run."

"Your audience awaits. Go put them to sleep."

Barks a laugh, forcing it through layers of wound-up tension. She hops off the bridge and scurries between the ropes. Before she becomes a shadow, flitting beyond my sight, she turns and bows to me -- as if the performance was already over and a success so resounding the entire dead world was aslumber. I stand and I clap.

#

Tonight is a sliver moon, thin as a strand of hair and brittle as porous stone. I join Arroyo about an hour after the dress rehearsal began. Adjusting my schedule and consciousness towards the nocturnal is not usually so difficult.

It is no colder this night than has been the case lately, but the breeze off the water cuts through all of my careful layers. I'm relieved that no one is relying on my being out there tonight or any night.

For once, Arroyo does not have her journal with her. She is bundled up, buried in a blanket she stole from bed. Not a bad tactic.

Out in the darkness, the wind harps are faltering erratically. A chill breeze blows, not a strong or consistent one. I ask if this has been going on the whole time.

"Yeah." Blanket Arroyo nods. "Don't freak out, though, this happens occasionally. The night wind always comes."

A firm fact, stated with such a casual tone that had she fished her journal out of the comfy mound of herself, shoved it in my face, slapping dainty fingers on the exact page listing the exact calculations, I would not have been any more persuaded.

Not long afterwards, the night winds do indeed sweep down and stroke the wind harps to singing. Then, high above them all, somewhere dancing between the dreaming world and colder doom, sings the voice of Euliae the Executioner.

#

Sunset.

Opening night of the final performance.

After yesterday's flawless dress rehearsal, I expect to see Euly still beaming. When she had stepped off the stage, returning to us, her smile was the first thing I saw: stretching across her face nearly as long as the bisecting scar. Now she is stoic. Passionless and expressionless.

There are no more dry runs.

Her clothing is tight, almost constricting. Leggings tucked into boots. Bust wrapped beneath a tunic laced to her neck. Long sleeves tucked into leather gloves. No equipment. The whole ensemble pure black, tinged crimson by the ensanguining skies. Ruinous hair, so often frayed and curling at the edges, is bound behind her skull, held in place with two sticks and an obsessive number of pins.

"I'm ready," is all that she says.

And we wait for the daylight to snuff itself.

When I think back on the flyers we had made after her first grand epiphany, it feels so naive. Or maybe that's nostalgia contrasted against the seriousness of the now. Only Arroyo and myself will be in attendance. Out amongst the poles, ferries, ropes, and wind harps there is a new brazier set center stage; our humble collection of kindling in a secure box underneath. Shrouding the ropes turned out to be a poor idea; it inhibited the muscle memory of her hands which, even gloved, knew the network of rope far better than her sight did. A fine layer of charcoal paint was the compromise, dulling the innate glow of the fibers and leaving her conscious mind focused on everything else.

We have done all we can.

Night falls. One by one, the fires of Drowns are extinguished. First the lanterns in the alabaster towers; then the torches atop the buildings, the docks, the unused ferries that have been tied to stationary poles; then the markets and the trellises and the porches; and finally the candles glinting on windowsills until every window reflected back the nothingness surrounding us.

As if in respect for our myriad preparations and hopes and solidarity, an unseen curtain of cloud remains drawn against the starlight. I have never experienced such a total darkness aboveground. A hazy, milky white floats in the center of my non-vision. Euly is somewhere there.

I let her go without a word.

Arroyo, too, does nothing. I am sure she would want to at least give an encouraging embrace. But this moment is far too fragile to disturb with even the slightest touch of affection.

Maelstrom's dull, eternal roar is more monstrous in my blindness. Churning waters, countless limbs of the cursed breaking through the surface and slapping down, spray of violent mists. Before them all, defiant of this cacophony: the soft padding of Euliae's boots as she marches to the end of the bridge, then jumps off onto the nearest cluster of ferries. I listen to her passage as long as possible, until the overwhelming background noise drowns her out and becomes the whole world to me.

The time has come to silence the discord.

It may be my imagination, informed by the past week of nights, but every minute or so I think I can hear the protective coverings unlatched from each wind harp. Unboxed they stand ready, as Euliae, for what must surely happen next.

What words can describe this anticipation?

An energy thrumming through the air, unsounded, building, unseen, replete with possibilities within the emptiness that surrounds the thrust stage, within the pressure that swells outwards into the auditorium of this strange found space theatre made of a dead and dying city.

It begins.

A single note, steadfast, suspends itself in crystalline clarity from the throat of Euliae. Pure, undiminished by its loneliness, full of resolute faith despite the void. For an instant, it feels like it might fade and disappear forever from this world, unsupported, unloved, untrusted... until the wind rises upon the face of the waters.

The harps join the song.

And this is what they sing:

Darkness, darkness: Favored Guide.
Transfix…
Waiting, waiting for the night.

Blindness binding, feet falter.
Transfix…
Journey's end, nigh paralyzed.

I walk in fog, moonlit tears.
Transfix…
Firelight illusions mired.

Is where I go where I am?
Transfix…
Always stuck in this moment?

Maelstrom is listening. The brazier sparks to life, burns low, muted cobalt yet bright enough to reveal the scene. Arroyo shivers, pulling the blanket close and grabbing hold of my leg.

Euliae gracefully repositions herself, exiting my sight. The harps continue to play in her absence. After a long pause, her voice emerges from downstage right. She repeats the same set of lyrics, adjusting her tempo and pitch to match the changes in the wind.

Always stuck in this longing?
Transfixed… transfixed…

She adlibs without hesitation in this easeful manner when an unexpected gust shifts the notes dramatically. Instead of a distraction or impediment, she flows into the intensity, transforming it into a slight crescendo suffused with grief.

Sleep now, sleep now: Death Wakened.
Transfix...
Famined hearts released from blight.

Deeper, deeper, yearn no more.
Transfix...
Dreams forfend the lack of rest.

Euliae returns into view -- languidly crossing towards downstage left with her hands gliding atop the ropes -- and disappears again.

Sinking once more underground.
Transfix...
Return in peace as it gloams.

No more sunrise, sunsets fail.
Transfix...
Within silence our downfall.

Maelstrom quietens further. She repeats the lyrics, three times, then pauses to listen to the changing winds. One harp opposite her has faded near enough to silence; she hurries to its position, then sustains a wordless tone in support until its singing returns. This carries on for many long minutes all around the stage. Once the wind seems consistent again, she lets the brazier go out and starts back at the beginning in total darkness.

Maelstrom is as quiet as I've ever heard it. But is this its limit? It is still nowhere near silent. The performance feels stuck, though her mournful voice continues to penetrate the gloom. For an hour this stasis remains, punctuated by new tongues of cobalt fire.

Thinking back, Arroyo must have suspected the climax. She stiffened, let go of me. And everything went wrong.

The idiot dumps all the kindling into the brazier, throws in the box itself for extra fuel. Then she strides downstage center, gets in a ferry, and starts rowing in the direction of tens of thousands of fully awakened cursed.

On instinct, I dash for the end of the bridge while she restarts the concert from the top. The fact that her ferry is elaborately roped to the stage instills in me no confidence. She completes the first set of verses by the time I manage to slink along the rope and get my feet back on vaguely solid ground. I hazard a glance.

All the ropes tied to her ferry are taut.

I haven't been out here in the depths. It's a labyrinth. I'm tripping and cussing, nowhere near her, by the time she finishes the second set of verses. Her ferry is within feet of the yawning whirlpool. A stray limb, if it reaches, will crack the fucking boat in twain.

Let be, let be: Sundered World.
Transfix...
Time stretched my life, rutted roads.

Storming straight ahead, knee knocking wood palms cut and raw. Reach! Reach! Torment torrent silence screaming.

I am not lost, now depart.
Transfix...
Relinquish me, my last hope.

And I grab a hold of rope and yank against the force of legion. Euly whips around, still singing. Eyes screaming at me. Maelstrom is lulling. Maelstrom is lulling. Still singing, she signs at me. Even without her touch, I understand.

::Stop::

She is singing. She is begging me.

::Stop::   ::Stop::   ::Stop::   ::Stop::

I cannot. Hauling straining, involuntary aching laments, muscles severing from each other or at least preparing to be so permanently divided. I fight for every inch and refuse to give back a single one to the ravenous pull of the inevitable.

Disappearing horizon.

Her voice is breaking.

Transfix…

Grips the other end of my rope.

This moment no longer stuck.

Frantically grabs for the blade at her side she realizes she isn't wearing. Maelstrom is lulling… Maelstrom is…

I force myself to look away from her hands that continue to plead. Hearing changes in the crying of the harps, in the churning and slowing waters, in the new roar that is now inside my head blood pounding out the staccato of a more furious, more intractable crescendo.

Euly, shoulders trembling, turns her back on me. Steps towards Maelstrom. Mouth open, arms spread wide, but nothing comes out except a sob that only I can hear. Shakes. Stamps a boot. Tries again. Her ferry lurches as I tie off the loose slack.

Where I go is where I'll love.

And she's safely out of Maelstrom's influence. One foot in my ferry, one foot in hers, I wrap my arm around her waist and forcibly hoist her out.

Transfi—

Kicking me.

Transfi—

I won't let go.

"Transfix!" she wails at Maelstrom. "Transfix!" Fighting me -- her only enemy -- struggling to steal my blade and go back out there -- her only hope. She fails. Every time, she fails.

I don't remember anymore how I managed to return with her to the bridge at all. The tears of blood and the gashes and the welts that covered our bodies by then must surely have told the whole story, though only one bruise remains after we have long since healed.

Not once did we come to blows, but her fervent need to escape me was equal to my own in bringing her safely back. What factor placed a finger on the scales afforded to me, I will never know.

Once it was over, she stared outwards at the roiling darkness. The cobalt brazier blazing, the wind harps harping. But it was over. She made one more attempt to sing -- to finish the song -- to project her voice and her very will at that forsaken pit. But it was over. Maelstrom was already roaring that same damnable intensity we were familiar with. The same liminal undercurrent that is always, always present wherever we go.

Arroyo hobbled over, stroked Euly's face twice and, perhaps not knowing what else to do, offered her crutch. But Euly was seeing something else entirely. Something she had seen before. She collapsed to her knees, hunched over at the edge of the water, and began to cry.

Nothing has changed. And I may have ruined the only chance we ever had.

#

She didn't lock herself in our room this time, but the end result was the same: I stayed away, feeling a shame that may or may not have been justified. A repeat performance the next night, or more ongoing experimentation, could have been justified. The cloud cover, though sparse, remained present and the sliver moon's power might be negligible.

But as I stood at the base of Windtower, turned towards where I thought she would be, I heard no music carried on the wind.

If not tonight, then she had given up.

And I did feel shame.

#

I walk the length of a wind-tunnel below the lake, below the earth, lost in thought. It is my customary habit now, days out, when I cannot sleep. As I delay the unavoidable. The lake continues its freeze, the fogs have begun to gather, and the nights will soon be deadly.

How can I bring down the tower on her boxed-up instruments?

"You're well into self-loathing as it is," I tell myself. "Be done with it all, damn the consequences."

"Be done with it," my echo reminds me, moments later.

As far as I can tell, these tunnels run for miles beyond the city limits. I've a fair bit of mapping complete, though little context. Still haven't bothered to ask anyone as to the purpose. Cooling off the city during summertime? Running mills I don't know about? That's a silly idea... using wind from a tunnel when they could as easily use the wind on its own to—

"Ah," I say, surprised.

"Ah ah," my echo repeats, making the connection first.

Daydream-walked myself to a source of light, far above. Squinting up at the golden shine and, before I make sense of things, a perilous deluge of wind floods down, pushes me flat against the ground, and pisses all over my poor torch.

I hear it hissing at me when the downward rush has tapered to a contemptuous breeze.

Apparently, my brooding has taken me to the origin of all wind -- at least, that which travels underground. Though from strength alone, who knows, maybe this is the one spot in the world where it is birthed.

Or comes to die.

"Huh," I say, upon insight's threshold.

"Huh huh," my echo repeats, having since crossed it.

Recognizing the pattern of the distant metal grating, I satisfy my obsession for details and hurry away before the next downfall.

Huh.

Now that's an interesting unconscious slip, isn't it?

#

Every worker is down in the wind-tunnels today, exploring and sketching for me the most accurate map I'll ever want. I cross the paths of various survey teams on my way back out from a twenty-mile roundtrip. I have no idea how far these extend.

For once, that's not a blindspot that matters.

#

"It's been verified by three teams," I say, all the maps spread atop Arroyo's mess of a desk. "I don't know if we have the tools to burrow upwards before the big freeze. My engineers are on that question even at this hour. They *are* optimistic."

Arroyo is subdued, as she has been, though intrigued. "Eeef. This could drain the lake."

"But do we want that side effect? We're storeys above the old street level. There's no knowing how the foundations have weathered after the last deepness."

"Give architects their due, Lethean."

Euly sits apart. Wasn't certain if she was listening. That's the first I've heard her say tonight. Though Arroyo

247

insists she is eating again and helping with the work to be done.

"So…" Arroyo awkwardly rearranges the maps, once more diffident about her 'leadership' role in the proceedings. "Are we saying we're shifting Downfall away from felling a tower to digging a pit?" Then mutters to herself: "Can keep the same op name, I guess…"

"The plan with Windtower was never cure-all. It's nostrum. At best, were it to work, we haven't solved the underwater cursed problem it creates. They freeze up, and then what?" Rhetorical though it is, I lay the question out before us. No one takes the discussion up. "They start breaking their way out, plenty of them -- law of averages -- travel up the banked hillsides and out into wilderness where we three *cannot track them*." I fold my arms. "Ladies, let's talk about what we're talking about: Maelstrom is Crypt Dun failed." The silence suffocates. Even the candles are somber. "We've all thought it. Now we need to admit it."

"Admit failure," Arroyo says, "is what you're saying."

"Yes."

"Mitigation…"

"Yes."

"We could make rope-fences around the perimeter."

"Could. Or we can bury them down in a new pit and wash our hands of it for several seasons."

Arroyo stares at the closest map. "More fitting to what we normally do, sure, yeah, but… that will create an 'unknown variable'," she quotes.

"Report me."

"I mean… I gotta, Boss." Leans forward, elbows atop the desk. "I mean, look at this." Indicting my sketches. "You went ten miles down this tunnel. Where does it end? And that's just one! Unless we map all of them, it's… wefff! It isn't Crypt Dun failed, it's another Pauper's Pit! But this one we got no control over!"

"That's the negative view."

"Well, okay, maybe. We got a positive one?"

Counting off each on my fingers. "Dark as pitch underground. Walls are extremely durable. The tunnels can be known. Points of egress can be bricked up, monitored, fortified. The wind is consistent. Music might work."

Euly perks up at that part.

"The theory's sound, I guess," Arroyo muses. "But if something messes up, we'll know the number of our days."

"True."

"'Cause this is quickly turning into: drop the tower, fix a problem; dig a pit, create a new one."

"Honestly?" I say. "I think we were always screwed on this one. But I'd rather go with what we know works."

Euly flinches.

I turn to her. "I'd like to repurpose your ropes for the new construction efforts." She doesn't respond. "With your permission."

"Hardly need that," she says.

"But I'd like it."

"Do whatever you want."

Arroyo, slipping into leader mode, was going to bring up the idea of a group vote again. I agreed in principle, but the stipulation had to be this: the community that lived here would need to make that decision. As far as we had come with mostly-coerced volunteers, any subterranean work would require the whole host of Drowns on our side. If not that, then it was to be Downfall as originally planned and whatever that aftermath would be.

For the city.

For its denizens.

For us and our future work throughout the province. To say nothing of the current works we know nothing about. It is too easy, stuck in our own problems, to forget that our comrades must also have their backs up against the wall.

Enough of the constant lies and subtleties. Enough of public outreach and manipulations. We will have a dialogue. Probably arguments. It *is* going to suck. But at this point, I don't know what will dig us out of our collective miseries other than a healthy, bitter draught of truth.

#

I became the voice of the Executioners from that night forward. Power doesn't interest me, though I confess a lust for results. I joked repeatedly that Arroyo speak in my stead: youth will win their minds and injury their hearts!

"What!? Boss! NO."

Why is her face draining of color so amusing? I mustn't tease...

We had a series of discussions with the community, but the impact of that first meeting was staggering. Everyone currently unaffiliated with us was vehemently against everything I suggested. Ricken's unending intransigence was the mortar that filled every crack, hardening before I could begin to chip it away -- only to discover another heaping I had to strike at immediately afterwards. The lack of leadership structure did not help our cause -- which is ultimately theirs, I tried to make them understand.

I had to play the pedant. Because they refused to see with their eyes and would not open them once shut off from reality. I suppose, at the end of the day, that's why we're all in this mess of a city in the first place.

"The dead must be appeased," I told them, trying to rephrase things in a way that might make sense of the senseless. The word 'cursed' just confused them. But, of all points, I drove this to the hilt without compromise: extreme conditions rouse these corpses into sources of limitless violence. Sunlight exacerbates this. Noise and physical impact exacerbate this, hence the self-perpetuating problem of Maelstrom. The only reason why the lake freezing through triggered our doomsday scenario was because it meant the whirlpool would solidify, the cursed would pile up, and eventually start ferociously and mindlessly breaking through -- either towards populated buildings or out into the countryside.

That is a perfectly reasonable explanation.

The unreasonable responses that followed built an impasse. I won't countenance them by listing any, but they're what is always spoken by the powerless to the powerful. Fortunately -- and this is a credit to our hard work these past months rather than my lacking persuasiveness now -- some local voices came to my defense. They meant to galvanize the unmoved hearts of the crowd, if not mollify them in the slightest.

For that latter point, I concede, there is nothing to be done.

Megs spoke for the ferrymen. She expressed an insight into Euliae's methodology that I, digging down my own pathways, had neither been privy to nor conscious of. Rather than describing practicalities alone or the wind harp plan, she kept shifting the topic back to my partner's character.

"Seen her exhaustin' herself composin' that tune," she told them, "fer us, 'ad it. But also... fer... *them*... in a way."

And then, weaving in personal grief, she testified to the life and death of her beloved brother. I am not unsympathetic to the loss of others, though it must be said that I have become professionally detached after witnessing scores of funerals and unearthing hundreds of corpses. However, when she reflected on our plans to inter the dead -- whether her missing half slept in the deep or had been swept up in the ongoing torrent -- I became moved. By the disquiet she felt not knowing. Of the peace that even a strange burial may bring. Ricken too, I noticed, was not unaffected by her words.

Other ferrymen, succinctly, gave their own affirmations after a silence no one was comfortable breaking.

"She's an angry bitch, but I surely like her," one said at the end, which definitely sounded like her and I caught myself smiling and glancing around. Euly wasn't present.

Mud spoke for the diggers. Ah. Let me amend that, lest it infer support for a group it does not. He spoke for the engineers, miners, and sundry that had been burrowing like vengeful rabbits in the dirt. The most gripping moment was, unsurprisingly, his account of the interment of cursed we had fished out from the lake. His explanation, I thought, bordered on the overly-detailed at the risk of losing the audience that Megs' emotional entreaties had won.

Sometimes, past all the negativity and intractability of my thoughts -- the dimmer porches I return to constantly out of habit -- people will surprise me.

His description seized their attention. Rapt with wonder. A horrible wonder, certainly, but one no less amazing. He did in mere minutes what my bavarding the past hour could not. He made us real.

"You have heard the name Crypt Dun prior to tonight," I finally rejoin the conversation. "That is our main success story. It proved our concept. We're constructing new duns wherever we can. Our efforts here are pathetically modest by comparison. However, and this is my idealism speaking, the safest future for your homes -- if you intend to stay -- will be for us to inter all the corpses in Maelstrom—"

"And we ca-can't do that by... *ourselves*," said a meek voice behind me.

I turned. Arroyo had snuck up, leaning on her crutch with one hand, spastically clutching me with the other. Her eyes were frozen on a weed poking out of the floor, the point that was furthest away from anyone else's eyes.

Grinning, I pat her waist reassuringly.

"No one can reinforce us before spring because no one knows the situation here. And there's been no safe means of communication, as you all know from your attempts…"

"De-deepness… wi-wi-winter…" Arroyo stammers, so quietly that only I can make out the words.

"We will be surviving the deepness with you," I translate, "and staying through winter. I won't preside in judgement and say Maelstrom will be the death of us all, that I don't know, but the chance remains if we do nothing."

And now the voice I wished to hear from no more:

"A false corollary. You mistake inaction as surrender to circumstance and action as moral imperative, that needs must compel the doing of *anything*," Ricken tells the assembled by way of me. "Action has a way of… precipitating a string of reactions that none of the wisest may foresee. And a worse outcome than the original problem brooked."

I think if we had publicly butted heads on that point as early as a week ago, I would have reflexively stabbed that argument and profaned the corpse of it. For whatever reason, I find myself conceding the point without a blink of ire.

"It's true when I say 'I don't know'." A reaper moon is poking over the horizon. I should end this meeting before tired minds determine on a course of action that won't go in my favor. "I really don't. If we *had* dropped that tower months ago… maybe everything would be fine now. I'm not sure why I hesitated so long. Yes, you'd probably despise me my unilateral decision, and I'd hide behind the curtain of legality the proclamation confers, and no one would be happy except me that my job was done." I stand up in such a way that Arroyo is beside me. "That *might* work. Or it *might* delay the inevitable. It *might* give my organization time to lend many, many needed hands. And all those statements apply to this new plan as well. My instincts say 'burying' the dead in such a manner is that best outcome."

"Mitigation," Arroyo says.

"Exactly so," I say. "The best of a bad situation. And on your consideration of that, I take my leave."

Dramatic stuff, Lethean.
Get this boy a wider stage.
And a heftier cut in pay.
It worked.

#

The majority were for us and would be sufficient to the monumental task set before them. My engineers had determined to an inch the exact center beneath Maelstrom. My initial elation sloughed into paralyzing responsibility when I saw the host of Drowns assembled, whose working safety fell heavy on our shoulders. Felling a tower would kill no one. A mistake made while digging upwards…?

At least we had a backup plan if I lost the nerve.

For now…

The rest of the meetings we had concerned the logistics, the shifts, all the boring minutiae that required full concentration. I only appreciated how resilient a lot these denizens had been become through their suffering when I beheld the fearlessness they displayed, grim and determined, as they bore a hole through the ceiling of the wind-tunnel towards awaiting calamity.

That gave me confidence I hadn't realized I needed.

#

Vault construction. City formerly known as Echo Downs.
Multiple incidents. Tunnels converted into mass grave.
Incalculable interment operation required in near future.

There were plenty of injuries until the foremen of each shift, on continual morning-afternoon-night rotations, synced the transition of replacement workers to an art. In spite of the efficiency we attained after a while, progress was grueling. The roof had to be checked at regular intervals to ensure it would not crack open before we wanted it to. That date was the very heart of deepness, when not a single drop of water would remain unfrozen.

Specialized masks to withstand the coming fogs were being created topside. The ingenious use of spider gossamer created a product of such quality I saw visions of exports all across the province -- provided we survived.

The consistency of Windtower's airflow meant we would not have to worry about those fogs seeping down here, as can often happen in the lowlands. That meant my other operations went unhampered.

We were bricking up the tunnels, of which there were five, extending outwards from the centerpoint. Permanent catwalks lined their upper walls. Those were for the Executioners that would return, to observe and coordinate the extraction of the cursed far below.

I had no illusion of the horrors that awaited them. So many cursed piled up in one single location? The churning violence above us would continue down here, regardless of the darkness and the quiet. But perhaps we could make their jobs easier if we did everything perfectly now.

No one has ever done anything on a scale so colossal as this as I am today. I do not like setting precedent.

#

A month is ephemeral when stress is high.

I was burning out so visibly that Arroyo threatened to tag along and help with the digging if only to watch over me. By and by, one evening after hitting her own breaking point, she followed us out to the streets and declared, "I'm coming too!"

Euliae and I were going to shut her down so damn hard until it became clear that her rebellion against us was pure bullshit and she simply wanted to know what it would feel like. Then she left, barely using her crutch. I asked about that before she was out of earshot. "I do this when no one is looking," she said. I asked when she started that up.

"Um. Just now."

What *was* this rebellious phase?

Today is one of the rare days when Euly and I are on the same shift.

"How is your harp setup going?"

"Huh?"

"Your harp setup."

"Oh."

Silence.

"I haven't heard it much. Wasn't sure if you finished."

"Huh?"

"Did you finish?"

"Ohh. No. No."

Silence.

"Do you need anything?"

"Oh. I see. No, it's— There isn't anything doing yet."

"You've been digging?"

"A bit. It takes my mind off— You're going the wrong way."

"Ah. Yeah. That's the scenic route."

Silence.

"Holler if you need me."

"Yep."

"Or if you don't."

"Heh."

Silence.

"It's too funereal," she admits after a long delay. "Too much the dirge."

"Really?"

"Of course. Oh, I mean for the workers. It freaks them out, I think. So, I abstain."

"Makes sense."

Silence.

"Euly."

"Mm."

"Serious question."

"Please let's not."

I point out at the lake. This will be frozen through in less than a week.

"This is our last chance to drop Windtower."

"You said the community had to decide."

"And I've been second-guessing myself since my mom popped me out of her womb."

She doesn't smirk.

"You said they had to."

"I'm asking you."

"I don't want to be asked."

"I know, but I am."

Silence.

And then she walks past, leaving me behind. "I can't do this," she says, I think not to me. "I cannot do this."

That may have been the last time we truly talked.

#

Deepness came in full force, worse than I had ever experienced. It's rare for us to be out in the wilderness when it settles in for, what more and more feels like, the duration of winter. I know too many teams had it rough last year. A few people didn't make it back home. We still record them as 'missing'.

I haven't given up my scant hopes.

Nor here, though my frequent brooding admits otherwise. My mask has become permanently attached to my face as I pass through the fog, brandishing a torch that is likewise permanently attached to my hand. The evening winds help disperse the mists, but not by much. I'd have instituted a curfew if the city hadn't done that already.

My workers have informed me that little digging is left to do. It's time to crack a hole so wide in the earth that it swallows catastrophe and will -- my final hope -- take nothing else with it.

At the entrance to Underground, I pause and stare out at Windtower. Its hulking decrepitude pierces the roiling fog and so upwards into obscurity and out of sight. A rusted nail struck into the heavens. But what exactly am I beholding? A final regret? Or an attempt to experience what a different version of myself might be experiencing, staring down at me and questioning choice?

I cross the threshold and enter.

Warmth from braziers and body heat. Chatter, subdued yet not pessimistic. Camaraderie. All the things that should comfort me instead bolster the rising anxiety. I nod to everyone in passing. Megs says something supportive that I miss. Mud clasps me on the back.

Good folk.

#

The din of all those pickaxes echoed so stridently around the inner chamber that I wondered if the noise would annoy the cursed above into going away just to avoid us. My engineers were stabilizing their machinery against the tunnel's roof before making the last adjustments; pistons the size of corpse carts would slam upwards into weakened rock. Didn't like how precarious everything seemed up on that scaffolding. Looked like obese, armor-clad people on stilts. The whole spectacle completely lacked humor, was horrifyingly predictive of inescapable calamity.

One engineer, on a break, allayed my ignorant concerns. The other workers, sitting around waiting for their turn to come for the rigging of explosives, made them worse.

#

Now is a harvest of plenty in Underground. Much has been gathered and more will be soon. I gave the farmhands a day's break, though it may last longer after I do what I've come for. At the last level -- or, technically, what was the last before we arrived -- I cross through a field of wheat. Aside from the rustling I cause by moving down the main pathway, each unreaped stalk stands sentinel. So does Arroyo, at the entrance to the forbidden catacomb sections.

"What's the good word?" I ask.

"Got a lot of those," she jokes, "but all's quiet."

We smile at each other and I pass on by. Pausing. Then returning.

"Ehh?" she squeaks, muffled against my chest the next moment as I embrace her.

"Glad you're off the crutch, kid," I say, the huskiness in my voice catching me off guard.

Still confused, she laughs, then squeezes me back. "Yeah, well. Had to happen eventually. Geez. Aches, though, from the cold. And the rehab. Be nice to get back to normal. Whatever that is anymore." I ruffle her braided hair, until she swats me away so I don't ruin it back into its normal mess. "Stop teasing me and go finish this, Boss."

#

I literally kicked in Ricken's front door, busting the lower hinge and making a twisted mess of the top one. Black inferno was raging through every crack in my mind, I was as much at a loss for words initially as the shitheel himself. Then I found a few choice ones. Shortly afterwards, I started making sense.

"You gave us the wrong formula?" I shouted. "Knowingly!?"

"I did. Which is why I sent the rest of the ingredients over this morning."

"That negligence could have wrecked a month of preparations—" Again I returned to less constructive phrasing.

"I had a change of heart." Crossing his arms. "My error of omission has been rectified."

"*Barely!*"

For the first time in months, Ricken seemed about to erupt. Instead, he merely stated, "You *are* a hot-headed one."

I left, and left the final word on the matter to the whining, broken hinge swinging forwards then backwards.

#

The vaults are silent. No stirring or scratching. I descend farther, down the spiral staircase, to where Euliae awaits, back firmly fixed against the wall and legs casually crossed. Beside her is the hole that will take me to the lowest point. We had previously gutted out the last three twists of staircase, once the work in the inner chamber was complete, to make room for a detachable ladder. Cursed are not entirely inept when it comes to stairs, but they are thankfully incapable of climbing things.

Always take advantage of any advantage.

In silence we stand, punctuated by our alternating shallow breaths.

I realize there is no harp music playing down in the tunnels. When I comment, Euliae shifts her weight uncomfortably. "Let's not with that variable yet. Major shit is about to go down and we have no clue the— Listen. They may home in on the noise of it in the absence of anything else to focus on. Once things settle, we can carefully add it. Until then…?" She shrugs.

If things settle, is what she means.

I nod and pass on by, gripping the top rungs of the ladder and stepping down. I pause before dropping out of sight completely, but she returns to crossing her legs and staring at her own dancing shadow on the torch-lit wall.

#

I walked out onto the lake towards Maelstrom where twisted spikes of ice had spiraled around like the scales of some primordial monster trapped in rime. The churning waters were audible, though I could no longer see beyond the static, wintry hellscape.

It might be one day too early to break the bottom open if there remained more water than the sluices could handle.

It might be one day too late if too many cursed had become frozen in that twisting mass.

Our experts pegged today as the best chance for success. Lest I seem hiding behind their expertise out of cowardice in accepting my own responsibility in events: my instincts whispered that same refrain. *It is time.*

#

Sconces light the burial chamber to afternoon brightness. The candles within will flicker and die within the half-hour. I will scarcely need that much time.

I climb the scaffolding towards the cracked, buckling ceiling. The next minute will be the point of no return: weaken the roof, detonate the center. So simple. So much opportunity for failure.

One final deep breath.

I jam the activation lever on the first machine. It pounds against the stone above me, scattering stone chips like shrapnel. And I kick off, flying over wooden boards that pound underheel, jumping and arcing high over terminal gaps in scaffolding. The next lever. And the next. Sky of stone convulsing next lever then earthquaking next lever next lever the womb desperate to break open in killing its—Blood! Petrified blood raining down, clattering on a pit of stark maddening nothingness of boot skidding to halt at the next last lever push push push scream and jam the blade in the corpse of this forsaken dead world.

No conductor possesses a scythe keen enough to end this song that I now sing.

What a small creature, this one, who at the risk of breaking every bone vaults to the floor, rolling impacting only air and pulls out every crossbow part from the supply pack when he lands dizzy-eyed heart-pounding malevolence.

Assemble it.

String it.

Cock it.

Load it.

FIRE, DAMN YOU, FIRE!

Execration

<pre>
                    Into the
                    pulverized
                       sky
                the paste-coated bolt
                       flies.

                       "Ah,"
            his bleached mind says so clearly
              that he almost misses it,

                      "this
                       is
                      what
                       it
                       is
                      like
                    to die."

                The world cracks open.

                    And
          all   of
                       the
      dead   lost   cursed
             rain
                            down
          down
                   down   down
       down   down
                   down
    down   down
             down
                            down
was the earth weeping

                            or was that only me?
</pre>

262

#

Burial operation. Unknown cursed temporarily housed.
Estimates between five and ten thousand. Barriers hold.
No incidents. Harps seem to lull them. Work ongoing.

As expected, there were clean-up tasks. Some cursed
were indeed lodged in the frozen lake surrounding the
gaping hole where Maelstrom once writhed. We excavated
them, stabbed the fuckers to immobility, and shucked them
down into new vaults.

"Why don't you toss them down with the others?"
Arroyo asked often.

A fair point. One more down in those dark, agitated
depths was the proverbial drop of water in the ocean. Still.
Habit, you know?

The hardest remaining labor was to roof over the wound
rent into the lakebed. Teams that once burrowed in the dirt
now burrowed through the ice -- which gave me an
appreciation for the concept of a glacier, though I have never
traveled so far north to see their grandeur let alone hike
within their frightening crevasses.

Every rope we had ever created was woven into the
largest net that has ever been woven. They lowered me first
down into the burial chamber -- as a test of its safety and at
my own masochistic request. At noon, the sun shone down
into that horrible darkness... uncountable cursed...
uncountable... the shadow of the net cast an illusion of a
prison across their frenzied mass. I could hear their limbs
slamming against their own bodies, the ground, the broken
machinery, each other. But, for now, the bricked-up tunnels
were secure and at night they did sound... quieter.

With careful use of the net, a reinforced stone roof was
created. Durable and well-sealed to withstand the melt of
spring that is coming.

And it will come.

So, I am waiting out the deepness beside the cozy fireplace in the room that has been Arroyo's office. It is a lounge again, but still tacitly ours. The harvest of apples was spectacular this year and, for another countless evening, our host's spiced cider is putting me to sleep, buried in comfort.

Arroyo is lying on her stomach before the crackling flames, the rug beneath her messed up from constant fidgeting. How she can draw in her sketchbook stretched out at such odd angles must be a secret beholden to youth.

Euliae is passed out drunk near the staircase. I am not sure if she was going somewhere or coming back. But she seems without a care in the world, curled up on a pillow that is gradually collecting too much drool.

Green-tinged clouds are overhead. Tonight's hailstorm will require our help in the morning to patch up the damage. This will be our lot until winter briefly returns as a prelude to spring. I look forward to the mundane.

Time will go quickly.

And I am finally going home.

#

Dozens of storms arrive and depart, queuing along the rim of the horizon for their turn. They conceal dozens of sunrises and sunsets. This is the birthing of a bleak gray time. The rainstorm directly above me is fierce, pounds against my thoughts for months compressed into a short moment until my brain is drowned waterlogged.

I stare up at the lancing spears of rain I cannot avoid. Droplets running along the sides of my empty eye sockets reveal themselves as someone else's tears. Collect inside my skull. Numb. My mind slows down. Grief. When someone sits me up, I sit between the gargoyle and jester puppet. The campfire embers breathe lightly.

"I did not mean to come here," the gargoyle moans.

"If you are going, now is okay," the jester sighs.

"Is this a dream?"

"I don't know," they say.

The hunk of wood in the campfire looks like a mountain, crumbling to dust made of leaves. A tiny tree that was growing atop it is engulfed down to the roots. My heart does not cry out because my chest is hollow behind my ribcage. And willow branch shadows cover me like a blanket. I find that comforting, knowing it is behind me. I find it upsetting that I cannot turn around to look at it, to embrace it, to say my goodbyes properly.

And then I question its existence, and mourn an illusion I can neither confirm nor deny.

Smoke continually rises from the flames, collects into a miniature mockery of the storm cloud overhead. When I try to stand, the water collected inside my skull pours out and douses them both.

"Will you remember this when we wake up?"

"No, but neither will you," they say.

#

Spring infused warmth back into the bones of the world, each ray of sunlight a tender caress. An apology for a prolonged absence. We could tarry no longer.

I threw responsibilities around like candy, knowing certain stomachs were going to get sick in very short order. Fortunately, there were some hardy bellies I thought we could rely on. Those I specifically tasked with maintaining the daily inspections of the burial chamber. Given our lacking equipment, they would be perfunctory inspections out of fear of overturning our great success to an accidental unmitigated failure.

We simply did not have the kindling necessary to visually survey the interior for damage without rousing the cursed with light. I did hand over that experimental torch...

"For. Emergency. Action. Only." I said.

... but with so many additional caveats I doubted it would get much use.

Candlelight was the limit. Go in quietly, check the brick walls, and leave. No catwalks. No entering the actual room with the cursed. Exterior surveys only.

Same went for the exits to the wind-tunnels -- which we had eventually identified, although they were in such absurd and remote locations to be nigh unapproachable. New task for the less hardy stomachs: brick those holes up to six feet, leaving the airflow unaffected, and check for cracks and signs of escaped cursed every end-of-week.

Overkill saves lives.

That was it. We thanked our host, I shook hands with Mud, parted ways with Megs in high spirits, and tromped along the permanent addition of a new bridge that connected the city of Drowns with the mainland.

There was, oddly enough, one final farewell that I, oddly enough, decided to make. He was waiting outside, watching the morning clouds streak west. I think they meant to accompany us. Salient. Because my question to Ricken was:

"Would you return with us? Even unofficially, you propped up a dead city. That's a talent we sorely need these days."

His shoulders rose and fell, a full foot it seemed. He snorted. It was not contemptuous.

"Two points," he said. "The Executioners have their own methods. I continue to disagree, your victory notwithstanding. The second thing is that the Technocracy knows how to watch the omens of environmental collapse as well as anybody else does, perhaps a little better, certainly no worse. I would have little to contribute."

I took my leave, but not without telling him the offer was standing.

But even that, after a weighty pause, he rebuffed in the most understated words possible.

"Long time gone," he said.

#

The first footfall on a new journey.

I suppose that would have been when I got out of bed this morning... but hell, it's good to feel my worn boots on dirt roads that I have never before traveled.

After striking west for ten miles, we all came to the same conclusion: the direct route we had taken would be too dangerous. Significant hailstorms had forced a multitude of trees to bow, then took advantage of their vulnerability to dismember their limbs. Who knew how agitated were the beasts lurking within those traumatized forests?

We went north, breaking out of the treeline by midafternoon and ending the day on grassy plains too lazy to roll as they do around Old City. As the days blurred into one eternal hike, I started to comprehend how bone-weary our time in Drowns had genuinely been. The weight of near half-a-year disappeared from my spine. I walked a little taller, a little faster, with a purpose without much actual purpose. Going somewhere else, that was the cure.

Our map proved, as we had been warned by last year's teams, "of questionable value". We meandered through every town along our route to shelter for the night, but few remained inhabited. The ones that were tended to be cloistered families of farmers, paranoid of anyone without blood relation.

Reflexively, we checked the few graveyards nearby too. I figured burying as many as we had this year was a new record and we had earned our rest. Euliae agreed by staying silent and not disagreeing. Arroyo was... Arroyo.

So, while we "lazy, bad examples, I cannot believe this" squatted on tombstones, the overachiever among us dashed around to ensure everything was secure. She got pretty excitable after rustling up evidence of gravediggers, for which we did move our butts a bit, though it turned out to be a hungry burrower which we left alone.

Arroyo gave it the finger before we set back out.

I had grown accustomed to the wildflowers and sweeping plains once we reached forest again. It was a pity to leave behind such wide vistas, full of daydreaming possibilities. But I soon became entranced by the new sprigs on every pine branch, so lime green they were nigh fluorescent.

Even Arroyo slumped into lazy mode with us, enjoying the perfume of the natural world and the nights of camping out. Good food, day hikes, and evening board games. Not a bad repetition. By the time we reached all the way up to Crossroads, our morale was fairly high, our feet tired, and our asses wanting chairs. We would rest before the final leg.

We met with our fellow Executioners, each of whom I knew in varying degrees. Vrigg, eyebrows growing bushier every time I see him, was in charge of the whole operation here. The graveyard was a more active hub than I had ever heard it was planned to be.

"Necessity," he told me one night as we perched against the railing of one of the many squat towers used to combat deepness fogs. "Supplies were stretched that thin out east, there was a mass exodus."

"Every place?" That was hard to believe.

"All but Avershym. Had to feed the starving until winter was over, then send them back out." He let out a belly laugh. "We all lost a few pounds."

I regarded his stomach. "You did all right."

"Benefits of oversight."

"Leadership, you mean."

"My active days are behind me. You and that witch of yours are the ones with necessary energy to burn the world." Lifted his bottle in salute. "To your myriad adventures yet to come, Lethean."

I took the well-wishes gracefully -- and the bottle once he passed it. Then his leader quality pushed through his puffed-up chest, or maybe a bit of surrogate fatherly concern. He, like everyone, is surprised by Arroyo. A teenager? Out here in the graveyards? Grinning like a dork? It never stopped being confusing to everyone not assigned to her development.

Visually, Crossroads was a mess. Busted gravemarkers and buildings everywhere. Like someone had a party and forgot to clean up for over a year. Turned out, that description was uncannily astute.

"This is all last year's," he said, gesturing down at the wreckage. "This year treated us much better." I passed back the bottle, knowing where he would shift the conversation next. "What about you?"

Where do I begin telling a story about a drowned city, left for dead, that the world had somehow ignored for the better part of a year? The message-runners, unless they had some sort of perfectly-formed excuse, were going to be *reamed* by the Sovereignty when we reported back to Krohn.

For Vrigg's part, he was amazed. And complimented our professionalism for not scattering this story around. "A morale-killer," he proclaimed. Then, surprising me, he lunged for my exposed neck. So to speak. "But you didn't stay, or leave one of the women? That's a very poor decision, sir, though I'm loathe to come down hard on you." Shook his head. "Who could fathom this?"

"The stress of managing until relief forces came would be too detrimental," I said. "I know I can't handle that right now. All three of us were put to the breaking point in different ways. I don't think they could manage either." I refused the bottle, wanting to think clearly for the moment. "If things go to shit down there, one or two or three Executioners won't make a damn difference." Sighing. "Which reminds me, any message-runners scheduled to come through?"

"Had you arrived a few days ago, yes. But no one on the docket until next week. Best head on back yourselves.

Make about as good a time than waiting." Smirked. "Though we're happy to have you bum around. Nice seeing new faces. Also... Hmm." Leaned in, worried and serious. "I surely should send someone down there."

"Thought it myself, too."

"I might could spare ten. More if you stay."

I considered it, but declined. "We shouldn't. Mental health, and all that follows."

Slapped my shoulder. "You're one of the good ones, sir. But a smidgen of advice from one man of oversight to another: stop taking so much damned work on yourself. Share the load and the good times."

It was sound advice.

I wish I had listened more closely to it.

#

We stayed over two more nights, resupplied, and headed west along reasonably well-maintained roads. Although great wilderness would continue to surround us, having a little strip of civilization underfoot was heartening.

I was glad to know the rest of the teams out here had survived winter -- and also that Arroyo's pouting was over. It came on abruptly and hadn't lasted long, but she really, really wanted to make for Avershym just because it was there and she hadn't been yet. Such a trip would add months to our schedule. Plus, we didn't exactly have permission to head that far east.

"We can send our request through the runners." This was Arroyo's last stand.

"*Our?*"

"And if we're denied, we go home."

"The time lag alone will doubly piss Krohn off." I shook my head again. "Not happening. Sorry."

Euly put her hands atop Arroyo's shoulders, gazed soberly down into imploring eyes, and stated: "You will *never* get to Avershym. *Never.*"

Apparently that was supposed to be a joke, but clearly a shitty and ill-timed one because Arroyo, right on the spot, started tearing up.

Thankfully, everyone cooled off by lunchtime and that was to be the biggest upset we'd have to endure on the remainder of the journey.

Our route kept to the forests. When the trees thinned, the jagged mountains rimming the northern horizon made sporadic appearances until we fully stepped out onto the grasslands. The ancient clocktower down Old Kingdom way came into view first, a familiar needle that unfortunately made me think of another tower first. But then a dumb bunny flopped over to us, wiggled its cheeks around in a display of total dominance over the defeated blade of sweetgrass in its mouth, and then flopped away.

Nowadays, that's about as official a welcome ceremony as you can get in these parts.

With every last mile trodden, Old City spread further into view and then the crystalline waters beyond. Afternoon sunlight gleamed off multicolored sails zooming about on fish business. Which was specifically the kind of thing my voracious stomach wanted to know about, and urged me to hasten my steps.

"I'll race you!" cried the cheating Arroyo who already started running.

Euly and I exchanged glances, did nothing but watch the little Executioner take off oblivious of so many things right now or at least able to discard them when they weren't the most important thing in the world. That, for this particular moment, was to be a happy weirdo and enjoy simply being here in this place at this time.

Some bunnies did start chasing her, however. Which was cute. Which did make Euly laugh. Which did make me smile, too.

Home is a special refuge.

#

The wide streets are bustling with repair work, bookending our leavetaking such that I scarcely detect the pounding hammers at first. Part of the background noise of city life. But now that I'm aware of it? I can't escape it.

We make straight for our favorite after-mission stop, but the stall is nowhere to be found. Checking adjacent sidestreets in case it moved. Nothing. I ask around. Nothing. It is gone though the ongoing repairs up on the scaffolding remain, seemingly unabated since autumn.

Sometimes, things just disappear.

After a detour to the small outdoor marketplace nearby, our stomachs are filled with fresh bread and cured meats. But… it's not the same and, although full, I still feel hungry.

There are less trees on the route to Overlook, but the glass dome continues to gleam high above us. At the base of the rocky peak, I see a glaring new addition: some mechanical monstrosity squatting amongst littered debris, extending a huge arm towards our headquarters. One of our own is dithering about on a platform, as confused as a clueless turnip. He notices us and eagerly waves us over.

"I think I figured it out," he announces. "Ah. Yes! Here it is. Stay on the inside of the railing."

"For what—?"

The metal platform beneath out feet shudders and begins to lurch off the ground.

"Oh cool!" Arroyo cries out, leans over the railing, looking every which way. I yank her back. But, drawn by instinct and interest, she returns to the railing over and over. Eventually, I join her.

Old City drops away. We ascend to Overlook. Up near the entrance, someone is jumping up and down. Very animatedly. Arroyo waves back cheerfully. The person stops jumping. Stunned. Then starts yelling. Once we're nearly halfway up the hillside, the racket becomes audible.

"—every time! What is wrong with you ignorant people!? I said 'no one'! No! One! And here you are, again and again, like it's some sort of fun times ride. Why!? This was installed for a specific reason and that wasn't for you sods to avoid exercise. Get off my machine this instant! Jump over the edge! I don't care! Get off it! I am absolutely tired of—" And so on. I'm mostly paraphrasing. Several of the word choices became extremely creative.

When the machine stopped moving, we disembarked and the frustrated Technocrat hurriedly closed and locked the gate.

"That's it. That's it. I'm going to have to hang up a sign; there's no avoiding it now!"

The tents that used to line this pathway are gone. Apparently with their masterwork complete, our guests went away -- and accidentally left someone behind.

Nothing has changed within the interior of Overlook. The scent of cedar furniture welcomes us, along with the distant echoes of movement through the gauntlet of stone hallways. Naj, too, is sitting at her desk and not even trying to look busy. Legs kicked up and chocolate in her mouth.

She does do us the courtesy of pretending, however, once she spots us.

"Ah, you're back! Welcome home," she pipes up, reaching for baskets.

"Did we miss anything?"

"Nothing what filtered down to my ears." Pretend fury. "I never get told anything."

I turn to Euliae. "No scuttlebutt. Something must be up."

She shrugs back. "Happens."

"Krohn around?"

"Sure, sure," Naj replies, stacking the baskets once our equipment is inside. "Chatting with the techies. Need anything? Something big happen?"

The three of us say nothing.

"That's a *yes*…" Naj murmurs anxiously.

What myself, Euliae, and Arroyo are silently debating is how much of an emergency is Drowns? We've been traveling for weeks. It's difficult to call what we have to report break-down-the-door-and-get-her-attention stuff. And yet it is.

I lead the way to her chamber, hoping her initial reaction isn't to send us on an immediate return trip. If no one else is around to help that's a very real, very tiring possibility. While we wait outside her closed door, that idea grates on my nerves. My room is so close. I want to go to bed early without the looming prospect of another journey counted in hundreds of thousands of footsteps.

An ending. Not the start of something worse.

Fifteen minutes later, Euly -- who has been zoning out -- politely knocks on the door. A knock? When she would normally barge right in? Another fifteen go by when I hear chairs moving and muffled voices drawing closer. The door opens and two Technocrats take their leave, trading goodbyes with Krohn and "we'll let you knows" and "appreciate your candors".

For her part, our dear leader extends diplomatic grace towards them… all the while giving us a scathing eye that says "there better be a damn good reason for your unannounced return."

Once we settle into her room, door definitely closed fast behind us, she starts pouring tea for herself and is slightly more blunt than I had expected.

"You three look like shit."

Arroyo makes a lot of embarrassed and apologetic faces, starts squirming beside me. I want to believe Krohn is expressing that she can tell we've been through hard times. I think she's just livid and refusing to show it.

"Echo Downs flooded last year. The city is under a lake. Hundreds of thousands dead. At least ten thousand cursed.

We mass-buried the ones that were accessible, probably thousands more isolated and submerged. Post-deepness: no signs of them, so we may have gotten lucky. We're on good standing with the survivors and—"

"Tell me about the burial space," Krohn interrupts.

I tell her. The whirlpool, the wind-tunnels, the explosives. Whenever my report strays towards details and context, she interrupts and sets me again on the straight path for whatever dread simplicity she seeks.

What team will have so bizarre a tale as ours? Spiders, Ghost Festivals, a concert for the dead. Yet, by her questioning, she is infinitely more interested in the mudbricks, the length of the tunnels, the depths of the fall, the durability of the ceiling.

"That's an echo chamber," she says at last, "not a solution."

I can't tell if she's criticizing or merely confirming our own understanding that this is a temporary solution. Rather than fall into the backpedaling trap of self-justification...

"We stopped by Crossroads on the way back. Vrigg is sending a few people down to keep an eye on things. But this is—"

"Another fucking Pauper's Pit." Krohn finishes her tea, sets down the cup, and folds her hands atop the table. "And another problem we don't have the capacity to handle." Sits back, hands in her lap now. "You did right by meeting with Vrigg. He'll know what to do until we can confer." Shakes her head in dismay, the first physical display of emotion. "This lapse in communication is going to do to the message-runners what Crypt Dun failed to do to us."

And now we get the homestead update:

Crypt Dun is secure, stronger than ever after the attempted break-in, and retains its vaunted status of 'impenetrable'. Parkside Dun also benefited from the upgrades in defense -- which apparently had quite a bit to do with the Technocracy's new toys. Somehow, Krohn had managed to unlock more funding and we now had a new dun of sorts down Old Kingdom way: a bullshit honeypot trap that has already caught two diggers. I suppose those rumors I heard way back when weren't entirely full of it.

Considering her outburst, or what passes for one with Krohn, I am sure that you can guess what follows. Pauper's Pit was an unmitigated (there's Arroyo's word again) disaster. They evacuated multiple times and suffered not an inconsiderable amount of casualties, largely due to a few critical failures from the technology our benefactors were installing. Apparently their "small scale tests" hadn't accounted for some technical-whatsis I can't follow, but the short of it is that I'm worried about that experimental torch I left in the hands of Mud.

"Right," Krohn says, ending that particular topic. "Had you been able to resolve the Echo Downs situation permanently, I'd be putting you on the Pit fiasco. Your fledgling expertise could have provided insight they're lacking. As it is you didn't, so I won't."

I glance at Euly, who says nothing.

"We may have stumbled on some actionable insight," I say as a lead, receiving no supporting comment.

"Truly? Actionable today or…?"

After another pause, it's clear my partner isn't going to offer anything freely. "That answer is measured in weeks at minimum, I'd say. Longer, most like."

"Hm. Doesn't sound urgent, then." Crossing her arms. "Anything else I need to know this very minute?" Scans our faces carefully.

Over time, I've gotten used to this scrutiny… though for whatever reason I feel like I've screwed up majorly. Even though we did the best we could, right now I just want her to dismiss us. And she's about to when…

"I'm suffering burnout," Arroyo says out of nowhere.

276

Krohn's face softens. "Are you?" she asks, a subtle undercurrent of amusement surfacing.

"I'm constipated," Arroyo continues, "and my mind keeps wandering and the hours disappear and I don't realize they're gone until I realize that." Symptoms listed, she returns to dutiful quiet.

"Are you exhausted?"

"No."

"Having fun?"

"Yes."

"I think you'll recover." Krohn chuckles. "Anything further?" She waits many long seconds. "Euliae," she says of a sudden. "You are being uncharacteristically silent."

"It'll all be in my report," Euly replies.

Krohn's expression of sternness is renewed. They look at each other, revealing absolutely nothing to us bystanders. Something seems to pass between them. "See that it is."

And then the moment ends.

"Now," Krohn says, ending the debriefing. "By my reckoning you have several hundred miles underfoot since summer. Take the next few days to do anything or nothing of value." Now who's uncharacteristic? "You can pen your reports by week's end." That's nice of her. "But I expect them not one day later." That sounds like her. "And Lethean."

"Ma'am?"

"Don't spare the details. In writing, I will want everything."

She waves us out in that manner of hers that creates the appearance of being eternally busy and yet not exactly dismissive. It can be difficult to ascertain when her good graces are present or on whom they're bestowed.

For now, we go our separate ways. Me to lie down, Euliae to eat, and Arroyo to bathe.

#

I slept in a lot those first days. Always the last arrival in the mess hall, poking at the vaguely warm leftovers and swallowing all the bits that no one else wanted. Food is food and I am not picky.

Euly's absence was felt before I was conscious of it. Normally we'll ghost into each other at home. As winding as the many hallways are, we tend to share the same daily routine and interests, and keep much of the same company. As was common more nights than most, whenever I returned to my dorm, she had already rudely invited herself in for lazying about and I could find her, lost in thought, staring out the bubble window -- or up in the loft, ruining her sleep schedule by napping on my bed.

Seemed to become habit for her at some point.

And I got used to the imposition.

Now whenever I take a route that passes by her dorm, the door is firmly closed -- though it doesn't seem like anyone is inside.

Today I bump into Arroyo within the library. If it can be called that. It's mostly a little side room adjacent to the glass dome. Two floors, modest, and quiet.

"Did you know..." she speaks very carefully, enunciating with a focused quirkiness, "that the *bunny* is a na-tu-ral in-hab-i-tant of every known province?"

"So that's why the plague is everywhere. Those fuzzy bastards are the carriers and killing us off, but they're too cute for anyone to suspect. Their plans are *insidious*."

"What? No!" she says. "Oh, it's you, Boss."

"Yes, it is. Wait," I say, "were you planning on telling that fact to anyone who walked through that door right now?"

She thinks. "Maybe?"

I start flipping through the reference books, assuming that what I'm after isn't here. Most of our materials are permanently on loan from Archives and if we don't have it,

I'll need to make the long trek down to Old Kingdom. Because I don't want to put *that* much effort into this… I'm assuming that's precisely what will happen.

But the reverse psychology of my cynicism pays off and we do, in fact, have a copy. I rummage around the upper floor for the tome. In my mind I pretend it will be dusty and neglected, pages falling from binding peeling from covers. In reality, whoever is assigned to take care of things here obviously has.

"Whatcha lookin' for?" Arroyo calls.

I flop onto the couch next to her, our legs kicked up on the same table. Hers are atop a fluffy pillow.

"History of mass burials," I tell her.

"Oooh, that's a quality topic."

Anyone outside the organization would ask why.

Remember that self-justification comment? Before I put my thoughts to paper… *many* papers… I want to reassure myself that every call I made was the right one. For all I know, there's been a total meltdown in Drowns and the countryside is currently filled with the breakout we were trying to contain.

I sincerely doubt that. But there's this nagging—

"Why are you sighing?" Arroyo asks, concerned.

"Did I?"

"Mm. Yeah. You're getting moody and stuff."

"And stuff…"

"Mm. Yeah. Lots of stuff."

Doubt.

There is so much doubt and disquiet within me.

Closing the book and my eyes… this is supposed to be an interlude and I'm actively choosing to run myself ragged. I should be irresponsible like Arroyo and poring over the history of rabbits. Can there actually be so much information on that subject to fill the contents of a single book?

That's so… *bizarre*.

"How is your report going?"

"Oh. I already finished that," Arroyo states.

Because of course she would have. In fact, she wrote the whole damn thing her first day back after our meeting with Krohn. It was inspiring. It was embarrassing. For whom, I can't say. But it is. Both.

Now she was sitting on it, convinced she had forgotten things that were best shared. Couldn't remember. Decided to relax. Then: bunnies.

She flips the page. Accidentally flipped more than one. Flips back. "I mean, sure, I was going to turn it in immediately. Not like I can't cobble together... an... addendum." Fidgets, holds the book out to me. "What is this word?"

"Severe or strict," I say. "Or if it's talking living conditions, harsh. Or plain."

"Plain like..." Flutters her fingers, makes a swooshing sound like wheatfields.

"Plain like boring."

"Got it." Page flip. "No, but, like, Euly was talking to me and I thought maybe I should think things over more."

"Is she here?"

"Dunno. She may have run away." Looks down her nose at me, imperiously. "*Temporarily.* Think Krohn is mad at her. Or going to be. I mean, *you* will probably try covering for her, but *I* need to be forthright about some of the bullshit we pulled." Page flip. "She pulled." Points at a word. "What's this one?"

"You know what that one means."

She laughs. "Maybe."

#

Managed to write a first page. Took effort of will. The rest became scratched notes along the margins which meant I'd have to rewrite everything again. So... I did what I normally do when frustrated. Gave up for a bit.

But not without leaving a bit of organization behind: high level outline of preparations from Overlook, the journey to, arrival and personnel recovery, plans upon plans and their complications, the burial, the journey home.

Then, berating myself for doing that much half-assed, I grabbed my scarf and headed off to anywhere else.

#

Checked on Crypt Dun. Liked what I saw. Same with Parkside and Pauper's. The Pit itself, as ever, I did not. But none of us do. I was a quarter of the way there, intrigued as all hell, to poke around that fake one only referred to unofficially as Apiary -- as these things tend to go, I imagine that temporary appellation will stick around until it is indeed official -- when I spotted I was doing it again:

Not. Switching. The. Fuck. Off.

Married to the job.

Lethean. Please... *stop*.

And I confess, as I stand here, telling myself to stop, knowing I need to stop, I am totally at a loss as to what that looks like.

Spring is glorious today. The swaggering, puffed-up clouds are limned on the edges in gold by a sun eclipsed by their interfamilial squabble; in seconds, that ends in an all-encompassing embrace. As irrational as it is, especially in this warm and swarming street, I realize I'm isolated and growing increasingly upset the more I think about that.

Perhaps I'm the one of us burnt-out, but never noticed. Or never had the time alone to notice.

So I walk. No destination. Lived my life in this sprawl of city, but there are so many areas yet to explore. I've always been looking outwards, wanting to be somewhere else. Frustrated in retrospect: the collapse of society, the inward huddling all provinces did with each other, and then all cities did of each other. That was before my time, though. Something for the old and forgotten generations to brood on

281

what was lost to my generation. For me, this is simply the way of things. Becoming an Executioner was, I think in some ways, an attempt to reach into that unreachable past. To know, what was it like to travel the world?

Today, I cannot reach the corners of this planet any more than I can walk on the moon. I will probably never reach antipodes of where I now roam. I do not even know where antipodes is or how I would recognize it. But, for now, I can see and live in this place in which I exist.

This is what I find...

#

Tiny market stalls, secluded away from the normal commotion, in the shadow of the old theatre house. It seems like a poor business location. Then, I sample the products.

I will rave till my dying gasp about the spiced sausages of undefinable origins, but the cheese... The *cheese*! So many variations, it feels as though the cheesemongers in every land known and unknown have managed to reach us when no one else could.

Yes, I remain embarrassed how much I pushed the limits of free samples. But I left the happier with two sizeable wheels, taking them back to Overlook -- one in my room exclusively for me, one in the common room for everyone else -- before setting out again.

#

A keg-carting merchant by the busy lakeside taking advantage of the sweating laborers, his apparent surplus of pewter steins, and my need to inure myself against any negative reactions I may have picked up to large bodies of water.

Almost literally bumped into him as I strolled through the docks, past racks of drying fish, and the ever-noisy shipyards, before dipping back into the merchant quarter.

A brief respite under a spreading chestnut tree, and I watch the ships float as effortlessly as the clouds. This amber ale is helping me to float too. I glance back at him. Carting beer rather than corpses?

Poor scut doesn't know what he's missing.

#

Technocrats pretending to be farmers in the terraces down south. Come autumn, we will know the quality of their bewildering efforts... is my initial reaction until I see they are harvesting, not planting.

This... grew over winter? *And* survived the deepness?

"Better than last year's experiment," one Technocrat tells me, sunlight glinting off her goggles, "by a factor of at least twelve-fold!"

I had heard that experiment was a resounding failure, so I'm not sure if the comparison merits the optimism. But witnessing their buzzing activity, her bright voice, this small vista into a vision of tomorrow... it does feel like better days are here at last.

The stems and leaves are autumnal scarlet, the panicles shades of orange from an endless summer dusk. A breeze jostles the field to whispering.

Golden rice.

"Exactly what we call it!" she laughs merrily.

#

My stomach demanding a real meal, and not this perpetual snacking, by the time I reach the edge of Old Kingdom. Perhaps I'm easy. Perhaps I'm a bore. Any food will do, hence the favoring of stalls and outdoor marketplaces now and ever before.

I walk into a grand establishment, but that might be my bumpkin ignorance speaking. Long tables spread out with ample room to be social or secluded depending on one's proclivities, with a central balcony that rises four floors.

Fond of an overlooking view, surprise surprise, I take to the very top where barrels stand around as makeshift tables and the patrons are far fewer. The bar is up here and—

Goodness, where did this caraway schnapps come from? I best have a second so it doesn't get lonely.

I jest. A truly disgusting amount of food will be had before the next drink, nursing the first until the arrival of roasted duck with onion jam, pickled cucumbers and olive berries, stewed venison bursting with garlic and forest mushrooms, and the most amazing bread -- so dark as to be black as the molasses baked within -- slathered generously with lard.

When more schnapps did indeed appear, I surveyed the damage I had done and felt much (and an abiding) satisfaction. And then I filled in the cracks with a helping of rose pudding.

Down below, preceded by raucous cheering and thunderous applause, a band begins to play. I recognize that reel straightaway and arch over the balcony. The stage is covered by a torch-lit overhang. I wonder if I will hear Euliae, but the singer opens her mouth, and it's someone else's voice, and the song is joyful, and then it ends.

#

The Old Clocktower, as imposing and impressively ornate as always, towering over the expanse of Old Kingdom. I crane my neck -- mindful that I'm not craning nearly so much as I did with the Windtower of Echo Downs. When I was a kid there was a nominal fee to climb these many (what then seemed like) endless steps. These days the tower is open to all between sunrise and sunset, though some special events allow for nighttime views.

Bastard that I am, I muscled my way into staying past closing by flashing my Executioner colors. Perks of the job. I repocketed my scarf before I reached the top -- a perfectly reasonable and easy-to-say sentence which truncates a climb that takes me ten minutes of spiraling up staircases not wide enough for two people standing abreast and gripping ropes to cross an interweaving of catwalks overhanging precipitous drops. Older, if not much wiser, I wonder if that fee may have been a collection to pay damages for anyone who happened to fall.

There's an apocryphal tale about a madwoman architect that I'll relate another time, but I tend to lean into its apparent truth.

My time in Echo Downs must surely have strengthened my knees and thighs and butt because I reach the top without any part of me complaining except perhaps a stomach asking, "Now? Really?"

When I mount the final step into the belfry, most people have long since departed. I passed many of these evening stragglers on the way up as we awkwardly squished ourselves against opposite walls to inch towards our conflicting destinations.

Here the belfry opens out onto a platform that wraps around the tower. There are secret rooms some floors higher I've heard about, but my curiosity isn't such that I'd break the law simply to jut my nose where it doesn't belong.

Waning twilight is transforming the huge bronze bell into a ruddy fist, ready to fall and melt into the earth below. It's tradition -- this, by the way, started way before my time and no one knows when or why or who first did it -- to stay here when the bell gongs with such force as to announce the very fracturing of the sky, cover your ears and shout out towards any horizon anything your heart desperately needs to exorcise.

A love confessed.

A hate buried.

Swear words and curses.

Poetic gibberish.

Whatever needs purging.

For me, tonight, there is nothing I wish to so express. Besides, the bell is stilled until daybreak and I am not a loon. I lean against the eastern balcony and listen to the final footsteps echo down the winding stairs and into the obscurity of anonymity.

Night settles in. All the kingdom, all the city, all aglow in comforting patterns. I pick out the familiar constellations below me, lingering on the frenetic walls that surround Apiary due south and then, up north, the glinting nostalgia of Overlook's cracked dome.

Nothing has changed. And home never honestly noticed that we were ever gone.

#

Inspired after my many small adventures, I had hoped to take Euliae around to a few of them. Felt necessary for us to relax together and reconnect. Had been a while since. She remained scarce, however, and no one could locate her. That wasn't like her. Fortunately, worrying was never a consideration.

Euly takes care of herself.

#

"Oh that sounds fun, yes!"

My partner being absent, I asked Arroyo instead. She dithered about, poking her fingers together, scanning an invisible schedule in her head for conflicts. Not that she's a socialite. Likes being organized, this one.

As a certain other someone does, as has been noted.

In the end, it all clicked and she was zooming around her living quarters, amped-up on an inner energy I want a bottle of.

"Come in come in!" she calls, voice muffled in the closet.

One of the better aspects of Overlook is the abundant space we have. Everyone picked up gets their own room pretty quickly. The petitioners bunk in far less personalized dwellings, of course, until proper vetting and hiring. Arroyo popped out of shared dorm life earlier than most, though this is the first time I've been inside her place.

It's a lot more colorful and fluffy than I expected. No loft like mine. Smaller studio. Overall, we have a lot of room throughout the complex, but individually we kinda get the shaft.

Arroyo has fully moved her personality in here and done what she can. Her desk is as chaotic as was the case in Drowns. Yet everything else is presentable, her bed made, and a squishy stuffed toy poorly hidden beneath the blanket. I can't tell if it's based on an animal or person, and despite the growing temptation to tease her about the childishness, I'll let the opportunity pass.

For now.

"I'll just be a sec, um, you can sit on the sofa. Umm... Oh!" Disembodied head appears. "Do I wear this?" Her work clothes appear, thoroughly cleaned after soaking up the muck of all things travel and Arroyo.

"If that's more comfortable, sure."

Thinks. "What about this?" Extends her scarf.

"If you want to unnerve anyone, sure."

Blanches. "Oh geez, Boss, no." Puts everything back. "I mean, I'm off the clock." Hangs up the black-and-crimson. "In-cog-ni-to," she proclaims, brushing it lovingly with her fingertips.

I hear sounds of her rummaging around, bumping into things, then changing her top. She emerges in a white tunic, thick laces on the chest and wrists, cut and formfitting, over dark red leather pants. Still mostly looks like an Executioner.

"Smart," I say.

"Think so?" Scrunches her face side to side, tugging at the hem. "Haven't worn it. Found it at this cute tailory shop last year. Been too busy." Scampers to the bathroom, scrutinizing the mirrored reflection scrutinizing her back. "White is a commitment!" they declare simultaneously. "I won't eat like the slob I am when I'm traveling~!" Quieter voices. "Better not be..."

And then, reaching back to undo her braid that is already getting quite a bit messy and sticking out on the sides... "Eeef, whatever!" Leaves it alone and heads towards the door to put on her black boots. "Let's go!" she cheers brightly.

#

We set off in the early afternoon, meandering a variety of places that I wanted to show her. She took me on a lot of detours too which tended to be as unexpected as they were eclectic, much the same as the turns she took in the conversation. Arroyo's mind exists in multiple places at once even when constantly insisting we sit for a while.

Turns out she was originally from Old Kingdom, about as far west as you can get in the boonies and still see the walls on a clear day. A foundling. Picked up by some common merchants who had come from another province, got stuck here roughly a generation ago, and stayed. They always wanted to go home. Never happened. Too old. Now they're in the ground, same as her real parents probably.

Silence followed, the kind that is difficult to peg as awkward or not. I studied her for a bit, more to get a read if this was a tall tale. Felt like the other boot was about to drop.

"Stop staring," she laughed.

It was all true -- and made a lot of sense, thinking of her as a street kid. The awareness, self and situational, the personal grit, her fascination with anything and everything, the way she injects herself full force and with all emotions into life. She didn't have an abundance, so she clawed into its depths for meaning.

Suck on that marrow.

Then she got all inquisitive about me and my upbringing and the like, but I barely had anything interesting to relate. Normal kid from Old City. Things only got interesting once I fell into this line of work.

"I feel that way too most of the time," she said, again drawing my stare because how could she mean that after growing up in such an active way with no passive options ever available? Especially when it didn't harden her heart like so many others.

I asked.

She didn't know.

Fell silent for a long time. Tried answering in different ways, stumbling over words that went absolutely nowhere except another attempt to answer.

"It's fun," she stated by and by. Nodding. Satisfied.

By dinnertime, we had worked up the appetite necessary to do some serious work. Her eyes spasmed at the grand entrance to The Tipsy Troubadour. Torches blazing between each window, live music piping from within, both doors propped open in wide welcome.

"This is a freaking castle!"

So maybe not my bumpkin side after all.

Arroyo was overwhelmed. I have never in my life seen a slack-jawed yokel nor someone who was literally gawping. Now I have. One step over the threshold and she was mute. It took minutes to get her to focus so she could say where she wanted to eat.

"The bar the bar the bar!" she chanted.

"Have I raised a drunk?"

"No! It's—" Wiggling fingers inexplicably, arms gesticulating in ways no one could translate. She strains to describe in words what her limbs have, I'm sure, somehow perfectly conveyed. I just don't know this quirky language of hers yet. "I like the... *bottles* with different colors and the way the *light* shines in them."

That's genuinely way more rational an explanation than the one alluded to by her spastic dance.

After reaching the top floor, she hops onto the stool and practically keeps bouncing until bread arrives to snack on. The packed crowds below mean our meals won't be coming any time soon.

"Some of that," she says between steaming rolls, "sounds like Euliae's stuff. Not that I've heard her outside, ya know, the dirge thing, and, ya know, practicing alone, but it's, like, *how* I've always heard it in my head."

"I thought it was her last time. Similar style, for the most part."

"The genre."

"Yeah. But she doesn't lock herself into anything. I wouldn't say there's a true style that *is* hers."

"Maybe she's looking for one."

"Maybe."

"Maybe she's trying to make one up."

"Her own genre?"

"Someone has to start it, right?"

"Makes sense. She's on her own path."

"You reckon," more bread getting in the way of her mouth, "we'll be leaving soon?"

"Ready to go already?"

"No. Yes. No. I don't know. Ahh!" Throws her hands up. "Stop interviewing me!"

I laugh. "What are you on about?"

"I get nervous! When you guys ask me these questions. Probing." Angrily points with the half-eaten bread. "Always so probing!"

I try to stop laughing. "No, I'm serious. What are you even saying?"

"That's what I'm *saying*," she moans at the bread -- which remains half-eaten and uninterested (yet resigned to its fate). "I just want to give the correct answers."

"None of us are psychoanalyzing you."

"Oh, hell, Boss, yes you are. Yes you all are. I am under considerable pressure to kick ass and not explode. And you are all talking about me about how much I'm kicking ass and not exploding, but maybe *she will* 'cause she's *tiny*."

She's average height... and now talking in third-person.

"Kid, we're open about everyone and no one is especially worried about you. Trial periods are over. You're one of us," I say. "I mean. Listen. Is *that* what bothers you? That you're technically an Executioner, but haven't accepted that internally yet?"

She sighs. "Going~ to~ need~ me~ some *booze* to think through those complex words, Boss." Shakes her head. "No, this isn't a self-confidence thing." Face instantly paralyzed. "Unless it is."

"I think you're working yourself up into a tizzy."

Stops blinking. "A tizzy?"

"A lather."

Stricken. "A lather?!"

"Yeah."

"Stop making words up!" she fumes and I think she means it.

"You're stressing yourself out for zero reason. Everything is fine."

"Okay. I can accept that." Finishes off the bread and lard in one bite. "Report has me pretty introspective lately. And I worry I messed up. And didn't do much." Adds something else I don't catch. She doesn't repeat it until I press. "I *said*: 'and that it was all my fault'."

"What was?"

Our huge feast arrives, each plate and bowl covering the length of the bar as they pile up, every knock of porcelain on countertop interrupting a now truly awkward silence and preventing her from answering.

"Being broken."

It would be difficult to convince her otherwise in any situation, but out in public doesn't make it any easier. I do the best I can -- and encourage her to eat while I talk. Food enters her mouth. Hyperactive, happy-go-lucky Arroyo makes sense to me. Hypercritical, glum Arroyo does not. I suppose I'm naive if I ever thought she only had a single facet. Even coins have twice as much. I start unraveling the knot she wove with the practical view: shit happens and it wasn't her fault. But no one ever finds that angle helpful, so I describe more of my story... of how I eventually joined, of meeting Euly -- I talk about her a lot -- and our partnership, of our trials and how we overcame them, the various injuries we got along the way. And as I do, I realize my tale isn't necessarily as boring as I think it is because she perks up with a shine in her eye and spoon sticking out her mouth.

We stay till closing and finish every plate. At the end, her clothing remained untarnished and her easy smile had returned.

#

My report is finished.

Two days before the deadline means I can continue to screw around without consequence. Free time will always be the tireless worker's only reprieve... and bane. So much freedom and I transform into Arroyo when she beheld The Tipsy Troubadour.

I thought to keep up my local adventuring, but a slight storm crept in from out of nowhere overnight and decided only one of us was going to stay and the other had to leave.

Picked up a book from the library that Euly had recommended ages past. She's not the reading type so I was curious *what* story would have captured her attention, and decided to spend the rest of my break sussing it out in a comfy chair under the dome, tinkling from the rain, and with a steady supply of hot drinks.

Oddly enough, or maybe not since I didn't know what to expect, it was a historical epic. The prose pushed up against the melodramatic so closely that it nearly dove over the edge into "I can't deal with reading another page of this silliness." But I persevered. And chided myself for the gut reaction that might have cost me a new experience.

This was not histrionic.

This was raw and without scar tissue.

I would come to view that as the main theme of this piece. The protagonist could not find safe haven anywhere in the world. Her trials were unending. Rest was impossible. Is this how Euliae viewed herself? I'd often set the book down in my lap, daydreaming at the gloomy sky, putting myself into the pages between the stained, well-worn covers. My imaginary character was always the companion she was missing, offering what she lacked: a shield against a blow, a kind word in the silence, a bandage for a wound.

Her consummate shadow.

After that first reading, there was still three-quarters left and yet I wanted to discuss what I'd read with Euly. But she simply was not here. Nobody had seen her once following our arrival earlier that week -- and I have long since wearied of knocking on the door of a room that is probably empty.

Arroyo herself had become scarce. In fact, I think she was avoiding me. My encouragement must have dissipated and she was stressing out again because once when I waved at her from across the room, she pretended not to notice and hurried onto wherever she was heading.

I shifted in my seat. Reached for a mug that was, I tasted too late, down to dregs.

Once Arroyo stops sitting on her report, I think whatever is legitimately bothering her will disappear. My own is quite the chronicle, so thick that I dropped it off as soon as the ink had dried. That moment was liberating.

But, oh so suddenly, too suddenly, my final unfettered days have disappeared as well and I'm scheduled for a full debriefing with our dear leader. Krohn or *the* Crone? I will soon see.

I knock on the door. Without hesitation, she bids me enter by name. Firm face. Tight gloves. Fingers interlocked. No tea. Definitely the Crone. And then she says it:

"There have been complaints of harassment."

What?

I don't understand where this—

Oh.

Oh. I get it.

Nevermind.

I've been brought in as a character witness.

Euliae has been bullying Arroyo.

That's why she's upset.

What the hell, Euly.

"Okay," I say.

"You've been making some of your female coworkers uncomfortable."

What?

Wait.

What?

"What?"

"A lot of it is, on its own, innocuous. But it's the repetition we're concerned with today. The not listening."

The what?

"Euliae has been setting clear boundaries with you. You're someone she expects a lot from. It is why your partnership has been seemingly as solid as it has been for the past years. You work well together. When you work well together."

Right. We do. So then, why—

"She is someone who needs space. Maybe more than most. Arguable, but I'd say that is a fair statement. And yet you follow her around. Constantly."

We're partners.

"Outside of work. Even throughout this week, I've heard about you knocking on her door. Every day. Sometimes multiple times. Why? You aren't on assignment."

We're... friends.

"She's good at switching off. Too good, frankly. I don't know why that hasn't rubbed off on you. But it hasn't."

Old messes.

"Euliae was very affected by the condition of Echo Downs. Very upset. Instead of helping her, you repeatedly sought her out. Again, the constant knocking. Despite -- despite, mind you -- the note she wrote to you, asking you for some distance."

It's weird how closely you monitor me.

"Asking you to stop."

You don't order me around.

"I appreciate you were all under duress. An entire city destroyed and no viable means of communicating with home. That's an isolation I wouldn't want for a team thrice your size. But your conduct? You know she remains— I don't care how much she refuses to show it or admit it, but *traumatized* by what happened to her face."

I said, you don't order me.

"That was cruel, Lethean."

I know what you're trying to do.

"She trusted you."

Don't fuck with Euly.

"Is that how we treat those who trust us?"

You going to shoot me with this?

"I don't know what to say. The rest of the operation seems to be unilateral decisions on your part. Euliae tended to express reservations. Instead of a debate, you tended to strong-arm Arroyo into agreement and stifle a proper vote. That's all in your report, by the way. You often make mention of Arroyo being in over her head. What else is she supposed to do when she so idolizes you? And now I'm jumping ahead, but what is wrong with you that you're ignoring her physical impairment and forcing her to walk across the length and breadth of the city when her ankle is hurting her?"

My throat aches.

"She... never... said..."

"Of course not," Krohn snaps. "Why would she ever do anything to risk disappointing you of all people? The best she could do was request to sit and rest whenever the pain became too much."

"I didn't know."

"And this is what I'm describing," she sighs. "Missing unspoken social cues. Lethean, are you trying to court her?"

"No!"

How can she ask that?

"Because you had interest in Euliae early on. You went on a date."

"One," I say. "We went on a single date. She declined the second, and that was the end of it. And that hasn't gotten in the way of our professional relationship." Silence. "Or our friendship."

Krohn pauses. "Euliae tells it a different way. Hence the issues with your constant presence and attentiveness." Waves at a stack of papers on the desk between us. I recognize my report, but she's gesturing at the other pile that is much taller. "Following her. Bothering her. Food gifts—"

"Food *gifts*?"

"Yes, that's what I said."

"We're *friends*. We share food with each other all the time. We've always done that. It's gotten to the point that if she has something she doesn't want, she just gives it to me. And vice versa. And we do that without speaking. That's one of our quirks. That's not damning. That's how…"

Intimacy?

"… it…"

Intimacy?

"… works."

Krohn considers that.

I press on. "Arroyo was fading out. Euliae refused to come around. *I* was breaking down. I was alone in the middle of a shitstorm. I *needed* my partner to back me up. Of course I'm disgusted with myself for hurting her that way, but I needed her to wake the hell up and get back on her feet. And she thanked me for that."

"She *thanked* you?"

"That's not in her report, is it?"

"No."

"Well, she did. Meaningfully, too." I look down at my hands. "I bet she didn't inform you I went with her to visit the Technocrats last fall either."

"Not that I recall. Though you claimed to be present."

I want to laugh, but the stabbing in my throat aches too much. "She requested it," I say, "and afterwards she was a fucking mess. Sure, Euliae the Executioner, showing off her shiners and bruises at the meeting. But you didn't see her kneeling down in the middle of the road twelve hours earlier, puking up blood."

"If true, she omitted the fact. I'd have to check the infirmary's records."

Which would say nothing because Euly never went. I feel ill. Can we end this and I go back to bed and sleep for a year? Krohn, stop looking at me like that.

"She omits a lot when the truth erodes her infallibility, huh?"

"Perhaps. From my reading, however, there's enough of a criterion of embarrassment that I'm inclined to believe her. You remember we have talked about you two before. I would hope it wouldn't astound you to learn that I do the same with her." Rain is silently streaming down the window. I hadn't realized it had started again. "And if it were merely that, I might ignore it. Chalk it up as… personality differences. Stress and tension. Maybe try splitting you apart." Shakes her head. "But now comes a last-minute addendum from Arroyo and I am left wondering if I'm ignoring the root parched for water and pruning a branch. Sod the analogy. Lethean. I think I need to let you go."

> Go where?
> My place is here.
> *With...*

"After what I did for Echo Downs?"

"Because of what you did in Echo Downs."

"But that's not—"

"I know it's not fair. What did I say at the outset? We cannot do everything, we cannot be everywhere, hence I can't play a numbers game. I have to keep the organization running irrespective of any of our personal feelings." Frustration mounting. At a loss. "Do you want me to reassign you out in the sticks? Hole you up somewhere? Alone? With another partner? Honestly, Lethean. Would you ever accept that kind of situation?"

I...

"*That fact* that you're hesitating... isn't that an answer? You're so attached to Euliae. And I think you're deluding yourself if you don't see how it's infecting more than your periodic squabbles."

"She's not blameless."

"Nor am I. Neither are you."

I can't see the rain anymore.

"Out of courtesy for your successes and in light of some... information you've illuminated, I'm going to investigate this." The subject is closing. I have no idea what I'm supposed to be saying. "I have a few more people to talk to. I'll inform you of my decision."

Dismissed.

I ghost away, numb, towards my room. Mind racing down every memory, lost... lost... that year of sleep I asked for, now I beg. It won't come. I stay awake. I stay in my room. A closed door that I normally leave open. In the dead of night I poke my head out, listening, satisfied that no one is around and sneak to the mess hall like a thief and stock up on food. I feel embarrassed about everything.

Two days I avoid everyone. I drift around my room half-conscious, expecting to find Euliae napping on my bed, sitting in the crook of the window, perched on the desk, smiling at a bad joke gone too far.

Doesn't happen.

Then Krohn does what we expected. What she said. I'm asked to leave. She shakes my hand. It doesn't feel like anything. Everything I own is in a backpack strapped against my back. It isn't heavy. On my way out, I half-heartedly try to be willful and reclaim my blade from Quartermistress. But she was already informed, apologetically declines, making me more embarrassed. And I leave Overlook. I walk down the hill. I look back once, at the midpoint. The windows are vacant. No one is watching me go, not even to mock at a bad joke gone too far.

I don't know where I'm going until I find myself outside the tailor we use. I ask for a replacement scarf. He doesn't ask why, so I don't have to explain why I don't have mine anymore. It works. I feel embarrassed. Afterwards I find myself outside the cutler we use. I ask for a replacement blade. He does ask why, so I have to lie about why I don't have mine anymore. It works. I feel embarrassed.

Where am I going?

What am I doing?

Why did this happen?

I walk. On straight roads without detours. Not knowing if my future is tugging me towards the sunrise or sunset, in indecision I go south. I pass familiar locations filled with strangers who cause me to feel embarrassed for no reason and then I feel even worse.

When will this stop?

I keep walking. Out of Old City. Out of Old Kingdom. I lose track of days. Weeks. Months. I kept walking. I am still walking. Today, at long last when I raise my head at the edge of civilization, I see a place that is called Gallows.

#

The "city" of Gallows is one among several shantytowns along the southern border. I do not believe many remain inhabited after the province's economy collapsed and the mass migrations northwards where food and the semblance of prosperity were rumors if not fact.

Whoever left must have trickled back here, incapable of reaching that destination -- or escaping. The roads are lined with crumbling brick buildings with about as much prospects as their occupants. Blessed are the visitors.

Which am I?

Night is falling fast and there aren't many more miles I can manage before collapsing. A powerful amber glow is reflecting off the low bank of clouds and some of the taller structures at the heart of the city. I turn towards it, having long forgotten warmth.

A dull roar vibrates the air. At first, in my bleariness, I think it's one of those events I've read about where the very earth shudders. But it clearly originates from that source of light I have nearly reached.

One incomprehensible voice rises high above the din, hanging there like a dead weight ready to drop. When I enter the square and behold a throng of vengeful silhouettes thrashing around a bonfire, it does so with two words.

"KILL HER!"

The mob crashes around, exhorted by this screeching voice that is cracked and bleeding as if a rod of brambles was raked down its throat for hours. And from across the way, out of an alley, the victim is carried -- lashed to a pole, so tight as to be immobile, and thrown into the flames.

Their celebration, their joy, their catharsis in this display of abject cruelty. Shadows whip and twist about a madman's dance in the amber light that stains the scene. The voices of the revelers are hoarse, but no less insistent, all their vilest hatreds strung together in an unending chorus of filth.

And then I hear that squelched voice from before, the most fanatic, rise up again and strike the air.

"BURN HER TO ASHES!" it wails. "BURN HER TO CINDERS!"

I stand a safe distance apart from the hundreds or thousands that surround the poor, burning wretch. She may have already died. I can't see her moving. No writhing, no screaming. Does she disappoint her rapt audience? They hardly seem to care.

No distinct faces can be seen in the intense glare of the bonfire, nor between the flaming torches waving like an engulfed wheatfield. Only undulating pink skin, dark holes where eyes should be, and sometimes tears.

The bonfire fades to coals. They leave, almost dutifully, in a silence I hope to never hear again.

I alone remain.

And so does the dead that I approach.

Sounds of my bootsteps echo throughout the abandoned square, tamping down what few tongues of fire are not yet sated while the embers breathe the nighttime air.

The head of the burnt figure sags down to its chest. The poor fool. The poor fool survived this ordeal only to witness me staring straight at her and doing nothing to help. And in that instant, that fleeting instant now gone where two human beings acknowledge one another, my existential daze lifts and I finally, finally, too late, return to myself.

"But who will inter her remains?" I ask no one.

Beside me, the shadows stiffen. The last reveler unnoticed till this moment. Waiting for the death rattle before departing with the others? Now offended that I offer pity. I can hear a tongue being chewed in this person's mouth. A stream of spit splatters the hot, blackened wood. The hiss and the straggler fade away as one. I wonder aloud whom the insult was meant for…

The dead girl refuses to say.

While trudging down the poorly-maintained and barely lighted roads, I aimlessly seek shelter. It's rather fitting that I stumble upon a cemetery instead. Not a horrible place to camp. Sleep undisturbed, if nothing else, unless cursed or critters are about.

This sight, so common throughout the land, is becoming anachronistic under our watch. A graveyard within a city? Pointless risk. We've exhumed most of them regardless of whether any cursed lie buried. And if that horrible spectacle which welcomed me here is any indication, these ignorant fucks probably have a crematorium.

I hoist my ass on the cheap granite wall and try to make sense of senselessness. Everything. Up north. My death march. Down south. But my thoughts are all muddled, jump around haphazardly, and I come away with zero insight. Just a persistent, unchanging gloom. At some point, I realize I'm absentmindedly passing my blade back and forth between my hands. Never used to do that.

#

Even the ugliest settlements have at least one spot where its denizens search for peaceful oblivion, either within the confines of a glass or in the talk of distant lands whose people endure comparatively greater bitterness. The intoxicated philosopher in the dusky corner of the room will stir the cobwebs about his head, lean into the half-light, and be the first to jokingly inquire if that means the people themselves or the quality of the beer.

In the cramped space of The Gagged Skeleton, there are no such characters. Everyone is grim, with expressions propping up thoughts they do not wish to think nor share. Perhaps I'm projecting. The only laughter comes from a skinny waitress by the cellar, toasting a spot in the corner of the room where no one is sitting.

I brood, expecting reports. News concerning the province (though how could they know down here?), talk of what pit of a city I've found myself stuck in, idle grumblings or personal grievances, all the kinds of anything that let a stranger understand the subtle pulse of a place, but... No one speaks about the girl that was put to the torch, her flying in the fire.

Am I surrounded by none of the revelers? There has to be someone. There has to be. And yet the locals, every one, hunch low beneath invisible burdens.

My own, barely pushed back while consuming what passes for edible food, washes over me. I pay and ask after lodging. The barman scratches himself. There are no inns in Gallows. He kindly lets me snooze in the basement where mold congregates along the walls and the casks smell like turpentine.

#

At dawn I spill out into the streets behind the public house to vomit. Doesn't make me feel any better.

Now stained in the growing daylight, the city becomes even more grotesque. Streets appear the slop-ridden paralyzed rivers of mud they truly are. The walls around me, black-caked with years of muck, are diseased flesh ready to slough apart. At once the name and the extreme distance from home make a perverse sort of sense: it is as if someone kicked open a trapdoor beneath Old Kingdom and all the detritus of prosperous civilization dropped straight south -- and this is where it fell, still reeling and choking and grabbing for support that was no longer there.

My journey would have prepared me for that knowledge had I been aware of my surroundings during the past weeks. Dim memories reappear. Paved roads giving way to overgrown brush. Craggy hillsides with less and less towns. Plains of nothingness, brown and weedy fields. Acres of panic grass a color uncertainly alive but almost certainly sickly.

A land that has never been graced by spring.

What...

I look around, bewildered.

... season is it?

A non-temperature. Neither warm nor cool.

The streets, city, and sky likewise merge into an unidentifiable, monochromatic mess. I cannot get my bearings and it feels like I'm trapped within a maze I never noticed I had entered. Eventually an isolated gatehouse appears, down a road that inches out from the cobbled yet perpetually-squalid muck.

I... think I passed under that last night?

Whether true or not, somehow, by instinct alone perhaps, I return to the site of last night's bonfire. The blackened husk that was a girl becomes my bearing. It alone is understandable. It has a beginning, a verifiable present. The ending belongs solely to me -- though no one cares, especially not her.

No one is here. The windows all around are latched tight, eyes squeezed shut. Only a small stone gargoyle watches over me, silhouetted by the gray sun peeking over the roof.

I don't know what precipitated this horror. But, probably instinct again, I felt a few truths last night: that she was the innocent victim; that Gallows is lawless, in spite of the scant guardsmen and women here only to ensure the city does not immolate itself; that the citizens do not much care about anything; that even in death they give no civility; that I am the only Executioner within hundreds of miles.

Ah. Technically, that is... not true.

But no one is coming to dispose of this corpse. And in my heart I haven't entirely given up on everything. My role follows me, no matter how far I flee from myself. My true nature, as I fall even unto Gallows, bears me back up again.

So I will be her Executioner and carry her the rest of the way.

An overpowering scent of smoldered wood scratches my nostrils, choking me as I walk atop the coals. Before cutting away her bindings, I wipe the soot from her bowed head, her withered head, the poor fool's faceless head, made from a pumpkin.

The gargoyle drops from its perch gracefully to stride the ground between us. Its bare feet make no noise. And I see immediately that it is actually a woman wrapped all in grays, surely no older than me yet carrying a premature age in her stooped shoulders.

She stops, face deliberately inches from mine. Ghostly pale. Defiant. But her irisless, pitch-dark eyes are not what bind me, nor the lips bleached the same color as that pallid skin. Splotchy, irregular patches of her face and neck are completely blackened and bleeding black blood.

And I become aware that the windows around the square are gaping wide -- as well as the throng of people slowly trickling in from the streets.

I take a step away.

She slaps my face, then points straight at me. More black blood is bleeding from her wrist, dribbling down her arm and disappearing into the folds of a shawl.

A twisted smile flashes. "I mark you as my consort!" she shouts, loathing spilling through me to encompass the assembly.

The stillness in the square fractures. Like sheet lightning she is gone, flies down the nearest alleyway. The crowd storms towards me. Now they scream for my death and this time their effigy will not be a bloodless doll. The mud beneath a multitude of stomping feet squeals with sadistic delight. Delirious, I chase after the retreating gray figure, following its terrible laughter as a guide from the mob.

Headlong panic. Run! Run! Her glowering faces regard me flatly, doppelganger sisters pasted against the walls. I rip one violently away and turn down another alley.

THE
GRAY
GIRL
OF
GALLOWS

That's what the paper says.

The sketch is hardly accurate except for the pitiless gaze. She is wanted for theft, arson, torture, murder, rape, and a myriad other monstrous sins that I can't decipher in my blind terror of the countless pursuers behind me.

Her swiftness is unimaginable. Only my training allows me to keep up. I exit the alley into an intersection, catch sight of the gray shadow slipping down a new alley. I try to catch my breath. The adjoining roads, both ways, are empty. I could make my escape.

My reflection stares out at me from a window framed by two of her posters. My cheek, that she slapped, is a poisonous black. A primal fear expands in my chest -- more than from the onrushing mob -- of the unknown... of an answer to a question that rumors whisper up north.

Is this...?

I run the direction she went and find her patiently waiting for me, almost annoyed, at the dead-end of the alley.

Head cocked. "You still want to inter me?" she sneers.

"If it calms this mob down," I pant, "then yes."

Grinning. "Are you going to chop my head off? It shall grow anew! I will not die. I *cannot* die. They burn me night after night and I return the next day!"

With animalistic precision, the Gray Girl scales the brickwork behind her. I rush after, but the handholds are barely an inch deep and I struggle the entire climb to the roof. Call it luck, call it determination, I manage to pull myself up and over the very second before the yelling masses coverage at the mouth of the cul-de-sac.

She and I clatter along the rooftops, the swarming streets pulsing around us, sniffing for us, yammering slavering following our flight. Their clamor is deafening. I cannot hear my boots pound the shingles.

"Do you hate me yet?" she calls lovingly over the din. "Or is this our postnuptials?"

"I don't even know you," I yell. "This isn't my home."

"An outlander!" she laughs delightedly, clapping her hands and hopping back and forth, then over a gap to the next roof. She twirls. "I shall tell you who you have fallen for!" Points at herself. "A ruiner. I ruin. I ruin everything." And with a demonic expression and darker laugh, she flees.

I follow.

"They're going to kill you!"

"They can try, but I shan't die!" she sings. "Maybe you will be better at this thing, yes?"

I'm gaining on her, mostly from her ditzing about and dancing instead of seriously trying to make a break for it. I think she could if she wanted to. But this is all clearly a game. A mock. A performance.

Who is meant to be the audience?

A bit of shock flashes across her face when she turns and sees me practically at arm's length. She isn't used to the kind of velocity I, an Executioner, can attain. Frightened, cornered animal for only a second, she bolts towards the edge of the roof, lowers herself to spring across the street and over to the next.

She jumps.

I snatch her wrist midair and her momentum arcs her high, then sends her careening backwards into the side of the building. She impacts with a pathetic yelp.

I yank her higher, leaving her dangling over a three-storey drop, and press my blade against her throat.

"What would you do with me?" she asks emotionlessly.

"Cast you to them that want you, I imagine."

"And who is that, my love?"

"All of Gallows, Gray Girl."

Grinning again. "That is a fine answer," she whispers, apparently to herself. And then louder to me: "And why do that, my love?"

"It's your face plastering the walls of this shithole. I give them their kindling, they leave the stranger -- *me* -- alone."

Clucks her tongue three times, each with thickening pity. "Oh, did you not hear me? Or see my blood what darkens you? It is there. Right. There." Juts her chin forward. Licks her lips. "No, no. You are not, and cannot be, a stranger to Gallows now. Soon your face will join mine down there, as it is even up here." Mouths the words with relish: "A perfect match."

"I can see you're just having fun. I don't care. Take me out of whatever game you're playing. Anonymity and sleep are my goals. I really don't care what yours are," I admit.

Her voice takes on a dizzied, faraway lilt. "They... beheld blackened skin. Disease. You are a part of this thing, too. We are the same. They *saw* it. You are a plaguer," she croons. "Same as me."

Black blood starts to leak from her bandaged wrist. An agonized expression twists her previously joyful mask. My grip is loosening. She strains to get away, frantic, mouth half open in either an unformed scream or curse. The drop will break her legs, but she doesn't care. Needs release. Claws at me. Frenzied. Wraps her long fingers around my hand, squeezing with such excruciating and unexpected force that I drop my blade -- which she snatches out of the air unconsciously.

Then, she slips.

I lunge over the eaves, somehow managing to grab her again. Our eyes meet.

"What did you do to me?"

"I have said. I have marked you."

"Unmark me."

No response. Her deathly pale fingers are clutching the hilt of my blade so tightly that the tips are growing blue.

"Give me that back."

"I cannot."

If I keep holding on to her, she could kill me.

"I'll let you fall."

310

"Release me."

But I can't. If she falls, she'll die. And then I will never know what is wrong with me, never know how to cure it. If I let go of her, I will die too. She has to live long enough to give me an answer.

Some rough voice calls out. We've been spotted. Tendrils of the scattered mob reform, wrapped together like overly-knotted rope. There is no street beneath us anymore, only a road of red faces and unlit brands. The Gray Girl's head lowers. She starts slipping again. I try to haul her up, but my hands are covered in her cold blood. The more I lift the farther down she slides until I'm barely clutching her. Unless she relinquishes the blade, offers her hand…

Instead, the pits of her eyes are full of grief.

"I marked *you*," she says, plants her feet against the building and kicks off.

Back she flips, then down, down, downwards to doom. At the last instant, the crowd parts for fear -- which proves their undoing for her landing is as adroit as a fallen leaf, and when she stands she spins like a howling storm. A silver arc glints in dawn's light. She cuts a path through the mob as they avoid the blade whistling about their stricken faces. The empty circle surrounding her widens. Her attacks become a graceful dance, a ward against the dark and dangerous world.

But as she nears the alleyway that must be her goal, something catches up with her. Arms no longer bend fluidly. Quickness turns sluggish. Footfalls falter, stumble. The mob senses this; the circle starts to contract, slowly, to close the gyre. And once they draw well within range of the weapon, the Gray Girl panics.

Blood streaks across windows. Terrified expressions. The long blade itself. Blood pours from mouths. From necks. From hands held up in surrender. Blood is in the Gray Girl's eyes. Boiling, frenetic hatred. She stabs and slashes and hacks at anyone in her way, that pitiless gaze focused on nothing but the alley. When she reaches it, a final member of the mob is blocking the entrance and she breaks her silence with a baleful shriek -- and pounces. Stabbing stabbing wounds opening one by one to sing praises sing stabbing sing devotion to the Gray Girl of Gallows.

Then she scrambles to her feet, flies down the corridor into the obscurity of the city. And her shadow -- as dark as she -- flits across the rooftops, running alongside her, still watching from above, still faithfully following as it had from the moment it was marked.

#

Hers is the darkest domain.

It is a simple task to locate where she dwells once night has fallen: no fires burn in this quarter. No sounds of life, no breeze. Sometimes an occasional drip of water from somewhere, but that is soon suffocated by the oppressive atmosphere. The darkness and the silence are one indistinguishable curtain and her dearest allies.

I poke along the edges, torch aloft. All signs of her trail have vanished. It's stupid to delve further. She'd slit my throat in a reflection of her own depraved grin before I knew she was there -- if she thought that plot twist was exciting, if it magnified the fun she was having.

… but would she?

It's a fair question.

For someone fleeing the death sentence of a city, she certainly took the time and risk to announce that I was somehow different. After hours of giving chase, my rage has cooled off and I can't help lingering on that word.

Consort.

So, I'm to be the diseased lover of a diseased queen?

That sounds like too much responsibility. I miss sitting on my cart, staring down an endless road, and daydreaming about the warmth of home.

Home...

I miss having a home.

For the sake of desperation, again expecting a different outcome, I stare at my face in the broken glass of yet another abandoned building. No matter how many times I wash it, that black mark remains.

Stories of plague in the north are always on every rumormonger's lips. As it is, we know it has never crossed the thousands-mile Gap... if it's down there at all. But Gallows straddles the southern march, is the furthest point from Old Kingdom, the heart of the Sovereignty. If plague bred anywhere, where better a pit than this destitute shantytown?

#

I sometimes glimpse her from afar in the afternoons. Always on the rooftops. I too favor them now as the streets are dangerous during the daytime. What she does, I cannot determine.

Like me, she doubtlessly scrounges for food and fresh water. In a place like this, those are the most valuable commodities. Since her darkling throne is unthreatened by anyone -- save me -- she probably keeps an eye that the city won't convince the guardsmen to come knocking down her door.

I have yet to spy these guards directly. Only the momentary dimming of torchlight whispers their presence at midnight, pacing away the lonely hours in solitude. I see their tower-flanked battlements rising throughout the city. As with the manic nature of Gallows' construction these gatehouses are sporadic and unconnected, each scarcely the length of a dwelling. Why they were built in the middle of roads, as opposed to protecting someplace important, is beyond me.

My gray prey is likewise without pattern. All my skills as an Executioner, aside from resolve, are useless. I can neither catch nor trap her. The closest I come is when I observe the nightly cremation of her pumpkin-headed sisters. I am surprised their pumpkin-headed consorts aren't yet burning alongside them.

I almost feel insulted.

#

Respite doesn't last long. It ended the minute I had finally stockpiled much needed goods and found a dry space to hide with multiple exits.

I jolt from another fitful night of sleep. Something immense is crashing against the roof, reverberating down into my bones. The drone of the approaching mob has me reflexively reaching for my emergency supply bag... only to see it, and everything else I gathered over the week, is gone.

I'm out of the upper crawl-hatch and clawing at the shingles when I see the Gray Girl standing on the adjacent roof. Unceremoniously, she tosses my belongings into the onrushing sea of torches that flood past her victorious form.

"You are ready now, are you not?" she calls. "I do not wish to wait longer. Yes? It is time for us to play."

This is how she began the dance. Her partner was selected. The floor cleared. The music swelled up. She took the first step.

Of course she did.

There was never any doubt that she was the one leading.

#

The circles around my eyes must surely be as black as that damnable growing splotch. I can barely locate a single place to rest before she raises a clarion call to rouse the city.

"Why lie there, love?" she cackles. "Did Gallows slay you already?"

And food is scarcer. Wherever I find a door or cellar ajar or a rusty lock easily dismantled, I find her peeking around a corner. She flings mud and discarded objects she picks up from the ground. Other times, atop the roofs, she hurls shingles and -- worst of all -- food she apparently doesn't want.

"Oh," she says. "You wished to eat this thing?"

At those times my ire plunges to its furthest depths. Starved, head pounding, I struggle after the Gray Girl. Flashing images of a helpless girl, no longer able to run, watching in horror as I gnaw the flesh from her bones. But she knows I'm in a weakened state, takes full advantage of it in her taunts. The more my energy drains and the more mistakes I make, the more fun she has.

Pushing away the foggy overreactive hatred that threatens to choke me, I feign a last-ditch effort to give chase. Just as she is bounding ahead... one block away... two blocks away... I duck into an alley I know passing well and make for a section of Gallows far opposite her abode. I focus my adrenaline on observation instead of killing intent, hide my tracks, stick to the most unseen pathways unless it's absolutely necessary to cross the street.

It might be useless. No matter where I've gone this week, I'm easily found. But I've only been fleeing the mob up until now. Maybe if I flee the Gray Girl instead... maybe if I run far enough... I can double back around and catch up with her when she's distracted by another amusement. I smile for the first time in a long while.

"Yes, Gray Girl," I say. "But this time, let's pretend that you know *which* corner you're backing me into."

#

It struck me, during my preparations, that I was actually leaning into my Executioner training. That honed my mind in a way I deeply needed. Though still famished, and aching from memories very present in the peripheral vision of my mind's eyes, I found satisfaction in that. Professional pride. And a concrete foundation to build from.

Cursed abhor light as they do noise. My would-be love is drawn to the same. So. If I cannot escape... I can lure.

#

I carry the flaming effigy of the Gray Girl over my shoulder. All of Gallows is after this beacon. I doubt even she would be so brazen as to steal the night's offering. Sleep-deprived, malnourished, mad, I dash straight towards the heart of her realm, that place that has surely never seen such fire. And I won't declare victory until I see its light reflected in her hollow eyes.

I burst through the dark pall that weighs heavily upon this forbidden quarter. I scarcely need glance back. The city played its role admirably and predictably.

"I didn't think you'd want to follow me any further," I tell them. "Well. This is a spat between lovers, after all."

The shadows in this domain recoil as I hold the effigy aloft. I don't know which derelict structure she dwells inside, but I'm certain this has all roused her attention. Which roof do you perch from? Which window are you peering out? From what quiet space, untouched by any but your own bare feet, do you watch this spiteful, irreverent, crass procession?

I plant the stake deep in the mud. Only two words must be spoken to summon the Gray Girl. My chest is shaking; each heartbeat pounds like a knell. Have I really yearned to shout these words so much? I can't hold them back. They gnaw at my spine, grating, shredding, horrible desires clawing towards my throat to make them real. Shout them! Scream them! Make her know exactly what you have come here for!

"Kill her!"

"A bold display," she says mirthlessly.

I spin. There stands she, the Gray Girl of Gallows, just outside the firelight. Smiling as ever. The thrilling insanity of the moment paralyzes my resolve for one, brief beat. What if all of this is merely playing into her game again?

No.

316

There's an edge to that burnt voice. An irritation she hides well, but hides nonetheless. An unspoken tell I'm used to hearing someone else make. This, then, was not what she was expecting.

"I wondered where you went," she continues, walking in a predatory circle, voice lilting back to normalcy. "I knew you would not abandon me, but it hurts to see you spending more time with my subjects than with me."

"As you said: they aren't capable of killing you," I explain. "That task falls to me."

She pulls my blade from the gray rags she is wrapped in, starts tossing it up and down in merry arcs. "Seems you have history with duties like this, yes? Such a strange dagger. Hilt long enough for two hands. Slightly too wide. More like a stake, or the end of a spear. But this…" Deft, vice-like fingertips snap out, clutching the blade itself mid-spin. It stops instantaneously. "Three edges curving almost into a spiral. What a *nasty* wound this can open." Grins at me. "What *were* you, love? Brigand? Murderer? Torturer?"

"Executioner."

"Marvelous~" she giggles. "I like that word. What a marvelous thing. *Exe-cu-tioner.*" Quietly, to herself: "I did choose well." Then back to me: "And is this why you have brought me here?" She gestures at the effigy.

"No, your fake sister isn't fated to burn tonight." I knock the figure over, extinguishing the flames in the thick mud and with the heel of my boot.

The tense scene disappears. I can hear her shallow breathing… in… out… in… out. My eyes adjust to the wan moonlight. She is motionless.

"It was very stupid of you to mark me," I say. "Not knowing who I am. Or where I came from. Or why."

Ignores me. "Why did you put out the fire?"

"Because I tire of the theatrics. The subtext. The double meanings. The fucking lies. I want the truth. Raw. Bleeding.

Real. And that means you and me, and nothing else. One little Gray Girl splayed out in a ditch and me leaving this cesspool of humanity far behind forever."

"Tch." Composure close to breaking. "I have the patience of the dead, my love. Trying to annoy me is *their* role. You are better than that. You are so much more." Shakes her head, as if I'm a child missing an obvious point. "Now, let us not fight like this. You are mine as I am yours. Yes? Relight my body. I must be fully consumed."

I lean down, inspecting the pumpkin-head. "Don't you think it's odd they carve your likeness?" I ask. "Poorly done, obviously. But they make effort. Why bother? Why not simply... pop on the pumpkin and be done with it?" I yank it off the stake.

"PUT IT BACK."

Her gaping eyes look like sockets.

A memory of cut strings.

I choose to say nothing.

"Reattach my head."

Silence.

"Prop up my body."

Silence.

"Burn her! Burn the forsaken bitch!"

"If you honestly expect this thing to go back on script," I tell the Gray Girl, "you're deluded." I squish the pumpkin underfoot. Her expression spasms. "Here's my revision: I hide my mark, identify myself to the guards, work with them to end the burnings at the stake, bring some decent societal order to this place -- I'm resourceful, picked up a few new tricks this year -- and then depart for anywhere else. Probably as a hermit in a hovel out in the middle of nowhere until I die so I don't infect anyone." I laugh at the absurdity. And at how lonely and painful that will be. "But I leave you this city. A calmed city, without superstition, that will no longer care about some homeless brat running around.

Whining and acting like she matters. Pretending she isn't a worthless and anomalous statistic the records of Archives may one day pen as a footnote: one plagued woman, indeterminate age, resident of Gallows, deceased. No plague outbreak to report. All is well." Now it's my turn to grin like an idiot. "Do you like the ending I wrote? I kill you by killing your reputation."

Momentarily, I think she'll run away. That this farce we have between us is over, its illusion shattered. My partial bluff and gambit failed. Then she stamps her bare feet wildly, as if crushing unruly grapes, splattering glops of mud all over while an unrepressed groan rises from the back of her throat. Black blood leaks from her eyes.

"Fine!" she shouts. "Fine! An empty death is more valuable to you than I am! Why, then, should I not give you what you want, my *love*? Let us see which of us mourns over the other at dawn!"

I dash off into the twisted guts of the Gray Girl's domain. And she follows.

Now the week of planning will either succeed or be all for nothing. She knows the entirety of Gallows and, more so, this dread place where none dare tread. I have scouted and mapped in my mind a small section of these buildings. I have repeatedly sped through them, gathering an unconscious feel for their layout. If she takes other routes than those I wish her to take, no matter: they all wrap around to a single point. A single corner.

Her singular end.

#

She is a predictable girl once you get under her skin. She does not think in a linear way, but does tend to become obsessively stuck on certain obstacles. First the effigy, now in chasing me.

She is not a fool. I wanted her after me. She does understand that -- she must -- from my familiarity with the rooms we bolt through, the stairs we vault over, in these places I clearly should not know.

But she cannot turn back.

Unlike my refusal to play her game, this is a game that she must play. Whether as consort or adversary, I cannot be allowed to win. At this very second, one relentless thought must be consuming her hell-bent mind: if she stops running... if I happen to lose her... *I will get away*... and what if I cannot be found again? What if I leave Gallows? That was the vulnerability created when she marked me. She needs me to be here. To taunt. To mock. To chase. To be chased. To kill or either be killed.

My escape won't be an outcome of this. She's faster than I am. When I spring at the wall, kick off and shoot down another corridor, she's right behind me, rabid and snapping her jaws, grazing my back with desperate fingers.

How can she keep up like this? I'm an Executioner and the physical strain I'm putting on myself is brutalizing every muscle in my body. Even the cursed aren't this driven.

Little shards of glass I embedded in the ceiling reflect shattered moonlight. I'm almost there. It's coming. The pit she has never seen before... because until the other day it never existed. Its entrance is covered in a perfect fitting of wood, as perfectly rotten as the rest of this place.

Around the corner is the real hallway. The one she believes I'll take. The one she expects.

Just a few more meters...

Two more...

One more...

Now!

I skid to a halt, immediately turn and wrap my arms around her -- and the momentum hurls us into the false wall I hollowed out. We break through the partition; I push off the ground. We twirl at just the right second, and I throw her against the other side. The Gray Girl cries out. But her reflexes are bitterly sharp even when taken by surprise. She goes tumbling, narrowly missing the grave-sized hole, desperately using her remaining velocity to clamber away. Before she can, I fling her against the wall and jam my fist halfway through her stomach.

"Gyeuh!" she sputters.

I drag her towards the grave. She kicks; my leg buckles. She leaps atop me, snaking fingers around my neck and clamping down. Eyes screwed up in pain, voice hissing as her lungs shriek for the air I knocked out. I fight, but hers is a frantic battle. Losing is no longer the binary outcome of a game. If I subdue the Gray Girl here and now, she dies.

"I... I... I...!" she wheezes.

But I can no longer breathe and her spasming breaths are enough to keep her going.

"I... I... I...!" she shudders.

The pressure in my head is going to burst. Unconsciously, I clutch my sheath. Fool! Of course it isn't there. She stole it. Where is it? Across the room, scant feet away: silver gleam, twisted metal.

"I... I... I...!" she chokes.

I try to roll. She resists easily.

What is this creature?

Kicking. Hitting.

Nothing injures her, nothing stops her.

What *is* she?

What *are* you?

Back and forth we rock, my vision is fading, my face is going to explode. And somehow I crawl, inch, inch, inch, suffocating under the Gray Girl of Gallows. All this time, all the pain, the lies, the pain, the lies smiles laughter carts meals campfires plans conversations adventures suffering joys idle thoughts holding hands smiles laughter carts lies laughter carts lies laughter lies and I clutch the hilt of my blade stabtwistpop stab twist pop S T A B T W I S T P O P.

A thin, chill breath crawls down my throat.

Bit by bit, her fingers weaken. Cold, wet ooze drips down my neck. Shaking. Smiling. Laughing a despaired laugh. The Gray Girl's visage shifts between the deepest hatred and weariness imaginable. She falls back. Slumps in defeat. Glances at the barren room. Glances at the grave. Glances at the dusty moonbeams beyond the rafters. Glances at my blade which remains on the ground.

Finally, with hesitation, she lowers a pitiless gaze at the black blood seeping through her bandaged arms and pooling upon the floor.

So.

This is what it means to have the plague.

#

Is it victory? Can I call it that when all the fire in her eyes is doused, replaced by two dulled spheres of coal?

"They wouldn't fear you," I say, "if they saw you this way. The Gray Girl is just a girl. Dead and dying."

"Dead… dying…" she moans.

"Makes me wonder how long you've lasted like this, in this place."

"How long…" she moans.

There's clearly no need to bind her limbs as I had originally planned. The pain she endures binds her there tighter than anything I could tie. From the way she doesn't move those arms, they must be completely paralyzed or, at the very least, barely useable. By now a thick pool of blood surrounds her, making it seem as though she is melting little by little and will soon disappear into its depths, and the only proof of her sad existence will be the remaining tattered gray clothing and unwound bandages.

Killing her would be a simple matter. Provide no release.

I feel no elation.

I am not looking down at my vanquished enemy; I am staring into the abyss of my own bleak future.

"What do you... wait for... little man..." she pants. Lucidly, neck arched backwards. "You spurn... my love... you spurn... *me*... don't... you?" Her leg spasms. Or maybe she's trying to stand. "You know... how to fight back... too...!" She coughs. Or maybe she's trying to laugh. "Clever... *clever*... we are... matched... evenly you... see? Maybe in... another try... I would be the... one to... to... to..." Shakes her head, only an inch. "If you... wait you... know I... will flee. Don't you want... to... to... to..." A glint, a flash, some instantaneous light reappears in her eyes, then snuffs out. "Don't you want to... inter me?"

I sink down to her eye level. "When were you infected?"

"Yesterday," she says, "or an age ago. What... what does... it matter? It is... happening now."

"You marked me."

"Yes," she hisses.

"Tell me the symptoms."

"Are you blind?" she spits, a voice of such dripping bile that I unconsciously flinch away.

"How will it start?"

"I don't know," she says, "I don't know. Most everyone... they..." She swallows. "It could be... anything. You'll get... weak. You will... sleep. But one day. *One day*. The pa... *pain* came first... and then th... th... bleeding. I do not know."

She is helpless.

Those eyes... no longer search for any way out.

She is helplessly trapped.

She could be locked in this room. This building. This city. She could be sealed in a grave. A tomb. A crypt.

She is helplessly trapped inside.

But it doesn't matter. There is no -- can be no -- escape.

She is helplessly trapped inside her own body.

"Oh," I say to dark and empty grave, and realize that what I came here for was not what I came here for.

#

The trail her bare feet make is faint. The mud appears to flow together purposefully, hiding each footprint and leaving behind the impression of a half-smile. The avenue opens on what was once a plaza, a massively skewed and broken-down tenement squatting in the middle like some sour, unreasonable drunk. The Gray Girl of Gallows totters towards it uneasily.

On closer inspection, the building is actually comprised of two different structures. Some time back there must have been an enormous landslide because the tenement collided and merged with an old stone watchtower. Broken, unwanted, they brace each other, likely because they haven't any other choice.

Inside, little muddy footprints are everywhere. Flaking apart like dead skin. Black spots and streaks are on the walls and floor and ceiling -- and on every timber piercing through each one. All these signs of whatever contagion afflicts the Gray Girl: the accumulation of years of not disuse... but her body.

It's a confusing labyrinth, but she waits for me, back turned, and staggers ahead once I catch up. Wading over collapsed rafters, we reach what could technically be deemed a basement. She descends the steps into that rectangular, confined void without pausing for light.

I creep down carefully. After a full minute of staring over the threshold, my eyes adjust to guttering candles haphazardly set around the room.

Her living quarters are the most contaminated. A pile of rags and ratty cloaks masquerade as a bed. A rusted copper basin is nearby: bathtub or perhaps water tank. Above it, a broken crack in the ceiling lets in a trickling stream the color of storm clouds. The wall opposite the entrance has been pasted completely with papers smeared in shadowy monochrome. A bizarre, strangely compelling pattern.

She awkwardly gestures. "Welcome to… my bastion."

The Gray Girl shrugs off what clothing she can without the use of enfeebled hands, then uses her teeth to tug and unwind the tight bandages wrapped around her forearms. Clad only in a simple, knee-length gray dress, I behold the full extent of her condition.

Ruinous, streaked splotches cover practically every inch of pale skin. Her arms are by far worst: the night-black limbs of an obsidian statue, bleeding night-black Gray Girl blood. She continues to stare at me listlessly, then hobbles off towards the basin. Black droplets trail dutifully. At the water's edge, she either quickly kneels or trips. I can't tell.

She rubs those bloody, partially-submerged arms against the basin.

Down, then up.

Down, then up.

Down…

"Why did you… come into my kingdom?" she asks after a moment.

"I was trying to disappear. I think."

… then up.

"Being an outcast is… like disappearing."

Eventually, all the blood is washed away revealing only splotches that were hidden underneath. The cleaning appears a futile exercise, but… somehow she seems… pleased.

Unsteadily rising, she staggers towards the wad of blood-soaked bandages, cradles them shakily between fists that cannot unclench, and returns to the basin. She drops them in the water and tries to step in after.

Stumbles, hits the floor hard. Stays there, gawking at nothing. Tries to bend her arms, tries to push herself up. Neither work. Then tries to push with her legs. Her feet tread water. I watch her impotence with the morbid curiosity that one might regard a flipped rolling bug. How? How could this stricken girl make me an outcast in an instant -- a carrier of some horrible and terminal disease -- and yet lie here so powerlessly with that non-expression across her face?

I prop her up. Bony shoulders two icy gravestones.

"What a kind... thing for my... Executioner to do," she says without a whisper of emotion.

"Who are you?" I ask.

"The Gray Girl," she replies.

"That's your name?"

"They call me other... things too."

"But what's your name?"

Her legs start churning the water. "Your name," she repeats faintly.

"You do have one, don't you?"

Pointing with a fist. "Do you have... a torch with you?"

"Yeah."

"Kindle it... to blazing."

I do so, wondering why. She nods.

"Good. Bring... it closer to me."

I hold it next to her, away from her chaotic, tangled hair. The fire reflects off the opaque waters of the basin. A memory of a drowned city surfaces, then recedes before I can focus on it. The Gray Girl hardly reacts, stares straight and unblinkingly into the licking flames. Her eyes are obsidian orbs, the dark sclera imperceptibly churning in syrupy patterns that could be her thoughts.

She shuts them. Breathes deeply. Shivers. Leans in, listening to the crackle of a tiny, restrained inferno. Faraway humming echoes in this corner of the room, the fragile song of the Gray Girl of Gallows blending with the burning of oiled cloth and split poplar. Each note hovers around every tendril, rises and falls, a cadence that nurtures the flames. They relax. She relaxes. Fists uncurl, fingers flex gently. She slouches, making her stoop more apparent.

Eyes opening, she removes a cleaned fabric strip from the basin and winds it around her forearm a tight bandage.

"Call me what you will." She reaches in for another.

"Do you bleed like this often?"

Glowers at me. "That is *not* what you say next."

"Huh?"

"You express the bond in turn."

"Um…"

"Your *name*."

"Oh," I say. "Lethean."

She finishes wrapping the other bandage. "Hi."

It seems such a laughably stupid exchange after everything we've done to each other these many weeks.

And yet…

"Hi."

"I am very tired. You should light candles before you burn out your torch." She goes to the bed-heap, collapses. "Are you planning to Executioner me while I sleep because if you are I shall sleep elsewhere."

For some reason I say, "Not right now."

I think she nods.

Unlit candles litter the basement. "Won't they notice?" I ask while lighting.

"I painted the windows black," she says. And so she did, painted over every pane so not a single person on the outside -- no matter how close they were or how diligent -- could perceive the slightest flicker or squirm within.

"Is there no cure?" I blurt out.

The Gray Girl lies quietly, every limb splayed at uncomfortable angles. "Yes, you will have to die," she says at length. "Gallows thinks fire works best."

I stare at the papers along the wall with their twisting motif, their unknown story. The melted candles upon the windowsill make the edges glow, almost like it is breathing. I douse my torch and hear it smother with a sigh that is barely there at all.

#

I might have slept. Time stretched consciousness thin, making imaginary scenes and creatures jump seamlessly from my thoughts to my eyes and back again, fading once I started to scintillating phantoms along the wall. At one point I was convinced they hid just on the other side of the papers. I peered behind them, but only saw half a dozen Gray Girls giving me half a dozen quizzical looks. They must have been sisters.

One of them was kneeling over me for a time. Another whispered to herself. One drank water. Most of them sat, doing nothing. The other whispered to herself again. The last one crept around me later on and she told me that she was going outside.

"Where?" someone protested with my voice. "The city is full of demons."

They all laughed in genuine amusement. "This thing is exactly true. Perfectly true."

#

The Gray Girl was nowhere to be found and she had taken my blade again. I wondered with complete detachment what her intentions were given the capital crimes listed on the posters strewn throughout the city. Decided I didn't really care.

My ankles, when I stood, cracked like bedrock splintering, at last giving up on its burden of everything above. I wobbled a bit, light-headed from lack of food and crashing hard after the continual spikes of adrenaline from the day before... or day before that, whichever it was.

I searched her "bastion" first for something to consume and then, failing that, out of idle curiosity. There's a lot to be learned about someone from the place they stay and the possessions they keep. But I didn't find much. Didn't learn anything new. Her home's arthritic bearings are so destroyed that I can't imagine how it remains standing or why she feels safe here. Maybe that perception is what she likes.

Within the center of destruction, or as close as my warped spatial awareness places it, there is a staircase carefully camouflaged among the wreckage. It winds upwards, canting at angles, disintegrating and apparently held together by sheer will or spite alone, spiraling in such a dizzying manner that I wonder if I'll ascend to the highest throne of the sky, step off the edge, and plummet.

I'd see the walls of Avershym cored into the eastern mountainside, looming in judgement over the cemetery at its base. Unkempt roads would stretch into wilderness and out into other provinces we have not spoken to in all the silent years since civilization collapsed within a hair's breadth of unrecoverable ruin.

There would be Crossroads, the extensive hub now smaller than a pinwheel. Below, a giant lake with an epic tower now no wider than a toothpick jutting from a puddle. So much forest, dark dreary sage carpet, dwindling farther west until the verdant grasslands on its eastmost side... the amber plains on its southern border... and there in its sprawl, in every direction, there it is... *there* it is... my—

She is gazing out over the surroundings from the top of the watchtower. Whether it is the same night or the following, I cannot tell. Perhaps there has only ever been one night and she and I have been circling each other repeatedly without end. A sudden gust blows thick cords of hair in her face. She brushes them back. Far in the distance clouds hang in resignation and farther still the ashen moon. Its mute glow pulses across the edge of my lost blade at the foot of the parapets.

"I figured you had stolen that again," I say.

"Ah," she says, noncommittally.

Beyond this unlit and isolated quarter, the whole of Gallows is dotted with light. From here, if it were seen, the hateful festivals must seem inviting, even warm, spectacles. But if one were able to maintain that illusion, the screams would carry on the night breezes and be a drab reminder that not all flames give comfort when seen.

Another gust makes a violent riot of her hair. She does not shiver. "I know you hate me," she says after a while.

My hand stops momentarily, then retrieves the blade.

"My life collapsed when I left home," I say. "Coming here didn't change that."

"Will you leave?"

"I don't know," I admit. "I won't go back after what..." My voice trails off. "And now that you've..." Again the words dissipate. Bound for no destination. "I don't think there's anywhere I can go. Unless—"

From this height, you can see it to the south: that vast stretch of absolutely nothing, a land treeless and desolate for thousands and thousands of miles.

"—the Gap."

"Madrigal," the Gray Girl whispers at the moon.

"But I probably wouldn't make it very far."

"You might," she says, "but it would not matter. Nothing is there."

"No reason to stay either. It's impossible to blend in." When I woke, I found that the splotches on my skin had spread farther down my neck, had spontaneously blossomed on the backs of my hands. To hide it with bandages would be, to the city, a death warrant rather than disguise. "So much for hiding my mark," I laugh joylessly.

"Le..." She puzzles the foreign word over her tongue, betraying a lilting accent I can't identity. "Le... thean."

"Hm?"

"It might be different for you."

"What would?"

"Your plague. It might be different than mine. You might not hurt or bleed or... or any of it. It might get better."

"Did yours?"

"I thought it did, once. But... no."

"So it isn't likely," I mutter.

"This… This is… beyond my ken. But," she presses on, "Le-thean, it might. You are already here. If everywhere is the same as here, why leave? There are ways to live, you have found it, and… I can teach you."

"Because I'm your consort?" I joke.

"Yes," she says. "Because you are my consort."

No matter where I've been in this decrepit city, whether behind or before, knowingly or unknowingly, I have always been chasing the Gray Girl. It is strange then to be standing at her side now, to smell the coppery scent of her skin and hear each shallow intake of breath. This is an interlude, I tell myself. This is a truce. There will come a time -- there will come a time soon -- when darkness falls. I will suffer from this infection. There will come a time -- there will come a time someday -- when I will no longer perceive any hope. Each star blotted out one by one until the afterimages evaporate without the faintest hint of smoke.

Gallows, some of your candles will not last the night.

Things fall apart and yet…

"It's almost beautiful."

She looks at me, then looks back out beyond the tower.

"… is it?"

"It may be."

"… I see."

"You don't think so?"

"… I did not know."

Silence.

"I don't believe you."

"I know."

"There's no cure."

"I know."

"There's no way out."

"I know."

Silence.

"Then, I'll stay."

"You'll stay."

"If you don't kill me, I won't kill you."

"Okay."

I extend my blackened hand.

She faces me. Rather than taking it, she partially unwinds a bandage and wraps it around both of our wrists. Then, placing delicate fingers against my palm, she nods her head.

"You'll stay," she repeats, this time saying it to me instead of the impermanent lights of Gallows.

#

If I came here in search of respite, I cannot be sure I've found any. I have an ally now -- she would say consort -- but the barbaric denizens are restless. They were slow to react to my presence, probably from surprise; however, she assures me that this place will no longer be as it was. For anyone.

Even though she says that, stretching her back and preparing a few items to take with us, I don't think she understands the heavy weight of those words.

Two diseased plaguers.

Finally there's a tangible reason for people to believe in the dreaded Gray Girl of Gallows: infection has crossed the thousands-mile boundary and its host has claimed a carrier. Who can say how the soon-to-awaken world will react?

I can.

But I won't.

For now, I live in spite of it all. I think, with her guidance, I can learn to live to spite my disease too. She transforms that which is horrible into something of a... well, what she and I have done from the start, I suppose... something of a game. If it's possible to say that the dark isn't dark, why wouldn't it be possible to then believe it? I think back on what I said:

Can beauty truly be found in ugliness?

Something is exciting me. I'm being pulled along by her again, and this time I don't think that's a bad thing.

I ask her what comes next.

She slips her bandaged arms into the torn-out sleeves of a patchwork shawl. Dramatically flings the long ends over her shoulders to trail like the draggle-tailed mantle of a spurned monarch.

"What," she says with a smirk, "a silly question."

And so began our game of terror upon the board of Gallows.

#

One.

We vault to the rooftops, my preferred way to traverse the city after mimicking her. As with the unlit quarter from whence we emerge, the citizens of Gallows shun this unknown place of darkness. It is a road, a bridge, a tunnel with an open ceiling of stars and night and possibility.

Two.

There are many loose shingles. Sturdy, but weakened by poor craftsmanship and frequent rain. "The storms come to pay me homage," she explains. "I thank them for the bounty they leave us." With a well-placed kick, she snaps a shingle in twain and passes me the larger half.

Shingles make great missiles as she once demonstrated to me. And now she does so again on a vulnerable window, then the face of the frightened man that gapes out through the jagged hole for answers, then the wailing woman that flees out the front door -- whose wail turns immediately into a feeble mewl. When her husband, nursing a gashed forehead, comes to her aid, I aim for his prodigious and flabby gut.

The Gray Girl compliments my form.

Three.

The candlemaker has two bubbling cauldrons of tallow that vomit their guts all over the shop floor after being tipped over. We dump every completed taper into the mess and watch them melt into formless blobs, wicks sticking about impotently. I can hear them cry out, as they submerge, lamenting the fact that they were never actually candles in the first place.

Four.

The blacksmith has many finely-crafted implements: of carpentry, of forestry, of gardening. This includes shovels. The shovels make our task of shoveling molten metal from the furnace onto the many finely-crafted implements much, much easier. The Gray Girl finds an axe hiding under a table.

Five.

The candlemaker and blacksmith now share a doorway.

A brief intermission.

We laughed and rested for a bit. This was good exercise. This cleared my mind. Merrymaking in catharsis. I ate unleavened ash cakes. She had a yellow apple, then a second. It crunched loudly between her teeth and juices were dribbling down lips upturned in a cautious yet unrepressed grin.

Six. Seven. Eight.

This is when I honestly begin to enjoy the game. It's like the comfortable simplicity of being an Executioner on those rare eventless nights, having a target and ending it well. After weeks on the road I'm starved for focus and I gobble up every instruction, each and every word and sneer and gesture of contempt, losing my worries deep in the world that only a Gray Girl could have invented.

We rush into areas crowded with people on their way to the bonfire. They scream and scatter. We give chase until they either disperse or bore us with their pleading for mercy. Those deplorable kinds are given special treatment: covered top to toe in street-strewn slop.

We rush into taverns, ostensibly to greet the less savage citizenry abstaining from the Gray Girl's latest flying in the fire. She doubles over in a hysteric fit every time. We do nothing except block the entrance and the patrons whisk about in total paroxysms of madness.

She counts aloud how many flee out the windows.

I count how long it takes.

Both are impressive figures.

We rush over to the square where first we met, this time scaling a three-storey building for an elevated view. She sits on the eaves, perched giddily over the edge and watches the swelling mob gather around the flickering flames. Her whole body is trembling.

I sit next to her.

She claps her hands silently: a child waiting for a show.

When the effigy is hauled down the main thoroughfare into the sight of all assembled, their chanting for the death of the Gray Girl of Gallows expands from one voice to dozens to scores to hundreds. And when the stake is finally positioned into its fated hold and ignites, the mob loses its sense of self and becomes the mass embodiment of Hate.

But of the real Gray Girl?

She is no longer trembling. Stares, unmoved and unmoving, at the fire. Out of the corner of my eye, I can see her mouthing words that remain unspoken. When the burning is complete, the square becomes as silent as she, and she rises.

The last to leave.

Her vigil concluded.

#

The Gray Girl chittered to herself, pleased beyond description. Rocking back and forth on the garden wall of an abandoned home, finishing a third apple -- stem, core, seeds, and all.

Dawn crept across the sky. Color inching back into a colorless world. While I yawned, stretched, and sat beside her, I found she had surreptitiously stolen my blade again. Wasn't doing anything with it. Didn't seem conscious of it. Just held it loosely in her lap while licking the remaining juices from her other hand.

"You really like taking that from me," I said.

"Yes?" Apparently confused.

I tapped the twisting steel.

"Ah," she said. "Yes." Wiped her hand dry on the side of her dress, then held the weapon reverently up to her face. That lack of visible iris is disconcerting. I never know exactly where she is looking. "I value your gift dearly."

"Does pilfering someone else's belongings count as such where you come from?"

"This was your first present to me," she declared. "I shall retain hold of your armaments as a keepsake of your love." Smiled, a little dreamily. Perhaps our night of work had tired her out too. "As a show of your devotion."

Not sure how I felt about that. It made me feel naked, as it did when I walked downhill from—

"Here."

"Ah!"

I dropped the sheath in her lap. "You'll need this then."

"How wonderful!" she said. "A matching set!"

"Well, not really. They're part of the same—"

But who cared about the specifics? Why explain it? She's happy. Let her be happy. Some are pleased far less with far more.

"How extraordinary. It makes no noise when inserted or withdrawn!"

"And now we both understand why I scarcely noticed your quick fingers," I said. "My consort, the master thief."

She laughed, rocking back and forth on the garden wall. "This is not so. I am the Gray Girl. Thievery is beneath me. I merely claim what is mine by rights."

I wanted to laugh too, but now that the sun had peeked into her domain exhaustion had me in its clutches. It was time for us to hide for the day. I said as much and she nodded, following me with only half her attention -- if that.

"Is it so silent…" she asked slowly, piecing her question together nearly one syllable at a time, "… so that your victims do not hear you approaching before…" Face full of innocence. Eyes black as tar. "… you slit their throats?"

"Executioner doesn't mean I kill. Fact is, I'm protecting— I was protecting normal people. Do you not know what a 'cursed' is?"

"What is this? Magick?" she perked up. "I have a great interest in the magickal arts!" Then began listing superstitious subjects that do not exist and haven't been believed in for well over… a century, at least. Longer I should hope. "Haruspexy. Chrysopoeia. Pyrophoria. Prescience. Transmogrification. Enchantment. Conjuration. Visions. Tyromancy. Metamorphosis." Running out of fingers to count on, she struggled to continue.

"I can teach you potatomancy."

"Can you!?"

"Do you have any potatoes in your cellar?"

Deflated, she hugged her sheath. "Alas, I do not." Shook her head, mournful. "Not a single one."

"Perhaps another time."

"Yes! We will add this to our next objectives. Potatoes will be gathered and then *you*..." Dancing with her arms. Thrusting the blade's point at the dead center of my chest. "*You* will teach me this thing!"

Part of me believed the Gray Girl would sever our alliance when she learned all I was offering was my spiced potato recipe. Part of me believed she would be overjoyed.

It felt good not knowing.

And feeling something new... that felt good, too.

#

Her zeal was boundless when I awoke fitfully, clawing paralyzed fingers through dreams I couldn't escape and didn't want to remember. But there she was, sitting patiently a foot away, watching me, and peppering me with questions on what a cursed is and why I spoke of it as though it were commonplace knowledge and would I please teach her to Executioner too so she might expand her skill set and we would share a special bond -- and other things that spilled out of her mouth's excitement that a trickle of drool being wiped away was the only punctuation that showed she was done expressing herself.

"You are a singularly bizarre woman," I mumbled, sitting up and picking sleep dust out of my eyes.

She just grinned wider, as if I had stumbled upon an arcane mystery of an age long past and had yet to grasp its importance.

I told her the simplest version I knew: at some point, seemingly between fifteen and twenty-five years ago at our best guess (which it has to be because we have no firm evidence), certain corpses became unrelenting, violent beings of destruction.

"Why?"

I told her no one knew. We only assume it is due to the world ending, how plant life is dying, how the natural order is breaking down in ways we are barely capable of measuring let alone halting or reversing. And so, maybe completely at random, a corpse will be a corpse or it will become a cursed. Executioners are tasked to inter them safely away from what remains of civilization.

"Why?"

I told her we've found methods to lull them -- since destroying them is impossible and stopping them is always temporary. We're trained to be stronger and faster than our bodies should, theoretically, be capable of. It falls upon us, then, to take care of the cursed. It's our lot. So, we house them in the darkest and quietest places: the Duns.

"Why?"

Graves are too shallow; graveyards too widespread and unmanageable. Mausoleums are too expensive. Crypts are too maze-like, although we do borrow some of that design and organization for our burial spaces. Crematoriums are stupid and therefore outlawed.

"Why?"

Fire pisses the cursed off like nothing else. They become something worse. Something *more*. Something, I have heard, nigh unstoppable.

"Like me!" she announced, clapping in darkling camaraderie.

I smile. "Like you, I suppose."

She frowns. "But my dagger will not stop them?"

"Only disable."

"'Temporarily'," she quotes.

"Correct. And only if you stab and twist here." I touch her elbow. "Or here." Her knee. "Or here." Her other knee. "Or here." Her other elbow. "But this will incapacitate that limb and that limb alone." I tap her spine at the neck's midpoint. "This is the spot. Hit this right, the cursed will collapse like a worn doll."

"Yes, I see. Very good." Nods in appreciation. "Then the inter begins."

"The Gray Girl is a swift learner."

"She is," the Gray Girl says mostly to herself. "She has to be."

Deep fog was subsuming Gallows when we went out. It might have been midday, but it looked almost night or that the sun had stopped caring. We were able to move about the streets, avoiding blurry silhouetted shadows whenever they formed from the mists. We committed very petty vandalism along the way towards whatever goal she had in mind. That became obvious when we passed the first tombstone.

"You will induct me in your ways," she ordained. "It is good and proper that I understand your strengths that I may best support you and adopt them as I may."

"Are you ordering me?" Wasn't sure if the correct response was amusement or frustration.

"No. We are as equals," she clarified. "But I will not make sense of your queer oddities until I witness them. Is it not so?"

"I suppose I understand that logic."

She nodded in triumph.

But what really could I teach her? I'm neither equipped nor that competent. Even when we were joined by—

"My love?"

I lost myself somewhere else.

"Are you angry with me?"

My tongue didn't move.

Wilted. "Why are you angry with me?"

Shook myself. And returned. "That's not it. You caught me off guard."

I smiled.

She smiled.

"Caught me off guard," she repeated.

"I can tell you some more. Demonstrations probably wouldn't be safe. But let's try to stay quiet, alright? No need to draw another mob or any cursed if there are any."

What a shabby plot this was. Worse than unkempt. Gravemarkers crumbling... when there were markers. Who died? Who knows. A nameless field of death stretching away perhaps to the horizon; the fog had erased all boundaries.

I described common pests that fed on corpses. Signs of cursed. Risk factors. Preventative actions. Disinterring, stabbing, binding, carting. The offhand comment about gravediggers confused her the most and she pressed for much explanation.

"Money... buried... with the dead..." Folded her arms. Stared at the ground. Frowned. Looked up at me. Frowned deeper. "I do not understand." Shook her head. "I do not understand this thing." That faint hint of accent started pushing through again.

"Where are you from exactly?" I asked.

Avoided the question. Turned away.

"This makes no sense," she muttered quietly to herself.

"Cultural artifact," I said as way of explanation.

Turned back. Even more bewildered. "Now what is this? An artifact? Is this more of your magickal knowledge?"

Who the hell is this woman?

"Umm... 'cultural artifact', it's a concept. It's not real." Her face hardened into stone. I think the confusion had reached its furthest limit: paralysis. "A tradition that has lost its original purposes or meaning, but people still do it for whatever reason. Coins given to the dead. A gesture for saying farewell to loved ones. It's the meaning behind the action that's important, not the action... that is, giving the coins... that matters."

"I... see." Expression chiselled itself back onto her features. "When the gravediggers steal these coins, they are stealing the farewells and love of the mourners."

"Um. No. They literally just want the money."

Her face fell. None of this was making any sense.

"Do you want to see how an Executioner can move?" I asked to change the subject.

"Yes," she said. "Please honor me with this."

But we had to wait. The fog remained so thick that there was no way I could attain the needed velocity without disappearing from view. I started milling about randomly, she followed, then I purposefully stalking down the uneven rows of the buried dead, she followed.

"What are you doing?" she asked.

And that was when I realized I was making an impromptu inspection of the grounds.

"Here. Let me give you something."

"Yes?"

I pulled the scarf out of my pocket and wrapped it around her upper arm. The crimson line was the only color on her.

"You're an Executioner-in-training today."

Gleeful. "Yes! I am!"

Then I went on explaining what our job entailed in cemeteries, both for maintenance work and loitering around on guard duty. She had a habit of interrupting with questions, but most of them were fairly astute. She even identified a false positive sign of stone-rot, but that and lichen are difficult for me to differentiate at times.

Eventually the fog thinned, revealing stone pillars that may have been cenotaphs some decades back, but weren't much more than collections of rubble that refused to sunder. I kicked their bases hard. Seemed durable.

"Stay here and watch."

"Yes. I am watching."

I backed off a ways, then dashed at the first pillar. Jumped, slammed my heels into its side, pushing off in the direction of another pillar. Slammed into it, pushed off, vaulted over the next, then repeated the process until I returned the direction I had come.

For effect, I was going to try to land right in front of her, but in the last split-second I remembered she had my blade and I didn't know her well enough yet to know if she was the jumpy type or not. As it was, she was sufficiently impressed such that she was stomping side to side in, what I assumed was, the approximation of a Gray Girl dance.

"This is very artistic!" she declared. "Enchanting!"

"I suppose it might be," I said, considering. "For us, it's raw pragmatism. Cursed are lethally quick. We must be as quick, if not quicker."

"That is a thing I understand. The Gray Girl must also be fleet of foot and sharp of claw."

Her dainty hands were limp at her sides. "She has claws?"

She grinned normal teeth. "And fangs!"

I knew she was bullshitting... but she easily outpaces me in a chase and my neck has a phantom memory of asphyxiation. With the proper guidance and environment in which to thrive, she could be better than even—

"My love, will you watch me?"

I jolted a bit. "Doing what?"

Took my hand in hers, led me further and further from myself, my thoughts, my—

On the outskirts of the graveyard, a gnarled and towering birch stood. It had not known leaves for a generation. Water droplets, left by the dissipating fog, clung to each bare branch. A dead tree with leaves of rain.

The Gray Girl released me and flew towards that very birch. She was either laughing or growling. It was hard to tell. I wasn't sure what she intended, until she jumped as I had and struck the trunk as hard as can be struck with a body. Dazed, she looked over her shoulder at me. Water droplets were cascading all over. Her eyes went wide and she cowered from their touch, but only for a moment, uncertain what the liquid was. When she understood, she did that odd dance of hers and beckoned me to join her. If she meant to jump off the tree, it was a miserable failure. Yet she seemed pleased.

Why?

"Now I am an Executioner too," she said. Unsheathed her blade. "Observe! This is how I dispatch cursed that hide." And with total grace she climbed the tree and pounced from limb to limb, stabbing at imaginary figments, and springing so upwards until the treetop was sagging under her weight, a glutted crow.

The Gray Girl sat on the highest bough, clutching her knife and sheath, rocking back and forth. Her hair fluttered. The dim light somehow caught and magnified the crimson line on her arm.

My voice came out rougher than I intended.

"That's enough," I tell her.

She hurries down to me.

"I said that's enough," I tell her again.

Slowly, she sheathes the blade. It makes no noise.

Silence.

"Are you going to strike me?" she asks carefully.

I unwind the scarf and put it back in my pocket.

"You can strike me," she says gently. "It's okay."

There are other phrases like that she continues to speak on our way back to her lair. The fog is gone now.

#

"I'm not supposed to be here."

"Nor I," she says, "but it is my kingdom now." Smiling. "I've made it my own."

My expression doesn't change. Her smile drops away.

I'm sitting on the far end of her bed-heap. Surprisingly comfortable. She is propped atop pillows on the other side. One of her episodes of paralysis is beginning. A trickle of blood drips from her bandages into a bowl held awkwardly between crossed legs.

344

"Why did you forsake your home…?" Her voice is barely audible, each drop of blood louder. "Le-thean."

Glum.

Heavily accented.

Remote.

Staring at my hands, I ignore the question.

This hurts her.

"I confess," she says solemnly, "I am a monster."

No, she isn't.

"This is truth," she continues, head bowed low. "The Gray Girl may be who I became and who I am now, but that is what I am.

"I earned my home here and my rule through trial by sufferance. There are, I will tell you, countless miles beneath my feet. Do you see? They are as rough as the Winter's wind and as enduring as the core of the world. I understand what is mine by rights now. I do not ask. I take.

"Who has survived more than I? Countless miles and countless pains and countless deaths. Who can press their soft soles in the indentations of my footprints and extract them without cutting themselves? I shed myself of that skin. I am free."

Another lie.

"There are none who can say how long the Gray Girl made sojourn. The sun itself lost count of how many times it dragged its bleeding form from a horizon-cradle to a horizon-grave. The moon too would know nothing, sleeping as it did and turning away in shame and hiding its face for incessant days at a time. Sobbing. Sobbing in the dark.

"She did not countenance either their rejection. No! Not once! She disdained their prison. East to west. East to west. Disgraceful! Disgusting! East to west. East to west. She would not be like *them*. She would escape. She would not self-slaughter as they each day! And so she strode the edge of forever until the south became the north and she came here."

345

"You crossed the Gap?"

"Yes."

"That's impossible."

"Not for the Gray Girl!"

"It is impossible."

"No!"

"You *walked.*" I wiggle my fingers facetiously like legs. "Across a barren *wasteland.*" They fall off an invisible cliff and land with a thud in my lap. "For *thousands* of miles."

"I did."

"What did you eat?"

She doesn't answer.

"Where did you find water?"

She doesn't answer.

"You're full of it."

Confusion. "Yes? Of what?" Again, the accent.

"No one crosses that way. They go around." I arc a curved finger in half a circle. "It's three times longer, but there's infrastructure— *was* infrastructure for trade. A generation ago, yes, but merchants would take that route. Not even a large caravan would go straight north to Gallows. It's retarded. Cost prohibitive. The more food and water you would need, the more people you would need, and so on. It's impossible. There'd never be sufficiency. You came by the roads," I tell her. "If you came at all."

"I walked!" she shouts, gesturing wildly with wooden arms, with paralyzed fingers unable to bend. "No one will take that suffering from me! Not even you! I bore those many agonies! No one to speak with, no one to comfort me, no one to encourage me. I did not even speak to myself because my voice had become so monstrous that I wept to hear someone else speaking with my mouth. Only now have I the strength to accept her timbre. Her voice is mine."

"And you crossed the Gap alone?"

"I was alone," she maintains.

"And you lived."

"Yes, I lived."

"How?"

She doesn't answer.

"How?" I press.

"Somehow," she says, tiny and defeated.

"I can't believe that."

"This is not what I am asking of you." A fierce tone, but a placid expression. "I am hoping that you will listen."

I pause in thought before I say, "I can do that."

Her proud, emaciated chest relaxes.

"Thank you," she breathes.

And means it truly.

"Tell me your story, Gray Girl of the Gap."

Closing her empty eyes. Inhaling shakily. "Of this," she says, "I shall not speak." Reopens her eyes: black solid pits, churning with dark viscous memory. "Of Madrigal I alone will relate."

"Madrigal?"

"My home."

I've never heard of such a place. I think there's a kingdom far beyond called Arq Chi Seng. Is that her name for it? My familiarity with maps ends at the Sovereignty's borders. This is the farthest I have ever been from my own home.

Huh... the same must be true for her.

"Madrigal, the famous city of circles," she whispers. "This was a difficult seat of power to hold on to for any reasonable length. I slipped off the throne many times. And there were many thrones. Mine was for the artisans, for that was myself in my prime: the artist. I was never the best, but I was... very determined." Swallows. Endures a spasm before continuing. "Then the plague struck. No one knew at first, such silent creeping dormant death. Once, and only once since I was a scrawny damsel, there was a vacancy upon the empress's throne. I should have left my self-built prison earlier, clawed ever upwards and claimed it for my own. I could have once." Nods. Spasms. Continues to nod, lower and lower, chin nigh to chest. "Once. Yes. Once. Could have. Almost escaped that once.

"Everyone was more powerful than I. Tried associating with them in the hopes of..." She remains quiet for a time, unmoving. "Something too much of this, Le-thean. I will move forward. Perhaps to return after. Yes. Perhaps.

"The plague," she carries on, "was a wasting disease. Plants withered. People withered. The roads and buildings and walls withered. Mm, I think you will think me lying about this. No. It is hard to describe to one who has not experienced it. This is not an infection as you know it. Not a... very bad flu?" Looks at me in question. "These are your words?"

I nod.

"I see. Yes, not that. It is a... *force*. As if the very world has..." Struggles for the proper phrasing. "... given *edict* against life. Against living. Do you... understand me?"

I shake my head no.

"This is well. You should not. None should. This is a thing that is that should not be." Remains silent for a while longer. The trickling of her blood has turned into a constant stream. "Such suffering. Such decay. One of the few things we knew was that it came from outside Madrigal. They closed off the outer rings of the city to stave it off, contain it. Quarantine, it was said. But the plague... did it come on the wind? Some said this. I said this, too. Others thought perhaps someone climbed the unscalable walls and brought it deeper. Because... because..." Takes a long minute to breathe deeply. She has started moaning, softly yet painfully with every exhale. "Ring after ring was closed. The plague halted. Days later, it had breached a new ring. All the circles of Madrigal were then shut. Never before had this been done.

Yet, it crept. Yet, it infected. I think now, perhaps, if the wind was... harbinger, this would have occurred much more swiftly. Widespread... Unstoppable... Unassailable... Does not matter... much. In the end a... city full of plaguers."

The stream is quickening.

"Did they look like... us?"

Her body jerks forward, shuddering for an extended, excruciating silence. When it passes, her expression is limp. Emotionless clay. "The plague of... the Gray Girl is... exalted. These... people looked... tired. Only... tired. So... tired." Eyelids drooping, only a thin cut of black between them shows me she's looking at me at all. "She hurt... she bled... but she... did not decay. Disease gropes for... us even here. The Gray— Gray— Gray— *I* am the... messenger. It will... come, I... was merely... I merely... mm— mm— mmm!— came— h-h-here— fff— ff— fff!— first!" she gasps.

There is much more to tell.

But this is all she can manage.

After replaying this history in my mind again from beginning to premature end, I say, "Later, I should like to hear of your home before the plague came." And then I tell her my story, the one that you too have been following.

My tone is somber. When I speak of happy memories, there is no joy in the recollection. No uplift. Nor do I paint myself as better than I was. What I say is plain-spoken; I have no reason for varnish. If I did once, certainly not now. Who would I impress?

As I reach the conclusion, where there is little left to tell that she does not know firsthand, I physically curl up on myself. Cradling my head. A rush of loss, of betrayal, of defiance and outrage transfixes my throat with such *aching*. And I can finally say aloud what I couldn't say before.

"I didn't deserve *any* of this."

Between spasms, she asks me: "What was her name?"

"Euliae."

And now that that word is out of my chest, hangs in the air briefly to disappear -- I think -- forever, I cry. For the first time. Since everything. Wracking sobs that uproot long years of tender joys and endless abuses. It is over. It is over. It is over. This is gone.

But... something happened next that I did not expect. Something I had no hope for. Something I didn't know I wanted. I needed. And it happened so quickly after I broke down that it was nearly simultaneous.

The Gray Girl was hugging me.

Had I been talking so long that her episode had finished? Or had she pushed herself, in spite of disability, to endure such pains as I cannot conceive... simply out of a desperate need to cross the gap between us to offer comfort?

I wrapped my arms around her, crying into the crook of her neck. She was exerting herself, panting in anguish, and I understood why when I felt how rigid her arms were while pressing against my spine.

Not ten seconds had passed from the start of my tears.

The steel bowl was still spinning in ever-contracting spirals on the dirty floor, its contents splattered everywhere in a pattern I will always remember. When it stopped moving it was upside-down, noiseless, while blood leaked out in every direction the indentations in the ground would allow.

#

Water was gushing through the pipe that pierced the ceiling, gathering in the copper basin. The Gray Girl busied around her lair, cleaning, cleaning, cleaning. Managed to mop most of the spilled contents back into the bowl.

What was it for?

"Secret," she told me.

Good or bad?

She paused, considering. Shrugged with one shoulder.

"Beneficial," she said at last, providing little to no clarity.

I stoked the fire, cooking the ash cakes she had taught me to make. Kind heart, she had insisted on doing everything herself. I needed to explain that having a mindless and mechanical task to do would help me.

Only felt numbness inside.

It was too uncomfortable to bear.

Distractions... need distractions...

She understood that with such an immediacy that a blunted split-second of grief flicked my heart. At one point, I asked if I could clean her bandages for her.

Was that overstepping? She was horrified. "No!" Sudden recoiling outburst. Took a while for her to relax and unpack that. "No, please, you mustn't. My blood is... polluted. Exposure will only sicken you worse... more swiftly." Frowning, the irony of my marking not lost on her. It was always on her mind. "Avoid it as best you can. I recognize... it is... everywhere. But when it dries, it is safe." Flexed her fingers, hesitating to continue. "You could... help me... bind them? Later? My arms? The tighter they are, the better I feel. It is... awkward... to do so myself. Though I manage." Nodding. "I manage."

"Echo."

"Yes? I repeat this thing?"

"That's your name."

Wildly bewildered. "I am sorry?"

"I mean, that is true," I explain, "you do have this odd quirk of repeating yourself on occasion, or echoing what I say when it's a phrase you're unfamiliar with. I don't know, I just... I don't know how it's been for you when your life was normal, but I've always felt like I'm reaching out for someone and no one is reaching back. And I don't even care who it is, but no one is there. So I shout and cry out and: nothing. Except now. Except here. The request for companionship is fulfilled. My words have come back from the other side of the world in an echo that is you."

"This is weird, Le-thean."

"Is— is it?"

"And sweet." Laughs. "Very well. I am now your Echo."

"Then the Gray Girl of Gallows is no more?"

"Oh no, she is I." Pulls the cleaned bandages from the basin and approaches me. "But now she has a name."

\#

While I bound the bandages around her gray-stained arms, she told me tales of Madrigal before its collapse.

"There mossy fields surrounded me with flowers like miniature sunbeams caught by greedy clumps of emerald, then wrapped into little baubles. Forests on every horizon. And when I stood upon the highest walls and heard the trees within the city rustle, it was as though I heard those faraway trees whispering to one another." She smiled. "Eavesdropping on an ancient language that made me feel warm inside though I knew naught the words nor why it made me feel so. I miss the wind," she sighs, "and the dreams that flew upon it."

To hear such colorful, rich language from Echo... Her grayness disarms me to the fact that once her life was as vibrant as mine prior to—

I look at the gray dress that hangs from bony, asymmetrical, stooping shoulders and wonder if the wispy black patterns were not on some lost yesterday nemophila branching throughout dandelion fields, but now endlessly sullied over the years by bloody secretions. A pattern like vines... or veins.

I finish with her left arm.

"Wind is here too, you know."

"It is not the same. You are silly. Gallows knows only the eternal season Moribund -- a fifth season wedged somewhere between Autumn's fall and Winter's death."

I pause.

"Do you know what season it is now?"

Her head bobs in loops, more a dance than an expression of anything meaningful. "Now? This is the Summer."

"Summer…" I start on the next bandage. "Did I travel so long I completely missed spring?"

"Worry not, my love. There is never the Spring here. You missed nothing of value. Only a lighter shade of brown." Shoulders shaking with repressed mirth.

"What's south of Madrigal?"

The mirth evaporates. "Sister-cities, dying siblings." Rubs the hem of her dress between forefinger and thumb. "South… is without words. Empty. Silent. Void."

The lull in conversation lasts a while.

"Shall we throw shingles tonight?" she asks excitedly.

"Yeah… hmm, that's a question," I mumble to myself. "I'm thinking you're going about this wrong. It's fun, but I question the effectiveness. Diminishing returns."

"Yes?" Confused, as ever. "We are returning… this thing?"

I finish with her right arm.

"It means the more effort you're putting into this, even with my help, it's hardly changing anything. Does the city really take you seriously? Have you honestly done the things they accuse you of?"

"I have."

"Murder?"

"Yes."

I remember that arcing dance of silver in the streets.

"Rape?"

"Yes."

It's possible. But…

"I don't see you having interest in that. Especially with the red-faced lot out there."

"The Gray Girl has needs," she says simply.

"If you say so."

"I do." Imperious. "They burn me nightly. Need you further proof of my effect?"

Crossing my arms. "I've thought about that. It's more like a cleansing ritual."

She mimics me. "Explain this thing."

It hardly needs any explanation. So much of this showing of hatred is theatrical. Routine. Literally occurring once a day. Without fail. Without end. Is it for the populace? To purge themselves and achieve catharsis? Or is it for the Gray Girl herself? Appeasing her baser needs for attention, acknowledgement?

For "an effect".

Because -- might be my city boy nature and what extent I've been law-enforcement-adjacent that pokes me at a suspiciously funny angle -- the guardsmen and women do not give a single shit. Not one. And no one employed directly by the Sovereignty is that defunct of purpose.

Or that stultifying lazy.

Getting stationed at Gallows? Surely not the best and brightest. Nor the ambitious. Nor the ones that genuinely wish to make a difference. I'd bet my dwindling stash of coins this is a place that's fallen through the cracks of both bureaucracy and hope.

Which tells me two related facts:

They aren't taking this seriously.

So *Gallows* isn't taking this seriously.

Where are the search parties and their torches? No one is uncertain where my little pissy consort lives, who is growing pissier still as I lay out a case for her -- it's my nature to be blunt -- failure. Mobs there may be. Mob rule there is not. How long has this play been performed?

Her fury is so monumental, a touch of color is actually flushing through her deathly pallor.

"Three," she spits, "years."

Tact is one of those traits I've never picked up. Loses its lustre when days and nights are as existential as clinging to a blanket on a death bed. Long since cast that away. Though, a hint of politic conscience tells me to tread with care.

This rut is not hers alone.

I make a suggestion. Simple and, no modesty needed, very probably effective.

"Don't do anything for a while."

She broods.

"Let them wonder where you went."

She is bursting with complaints.

"Then do something bigger than you've ever done before. Never let them rest. Randomness for randomness sake, that's your new axiom. See what they make of that. Especially if your consort is across the city doing his own magnum opus at the same time."

She shuts up. Remains statuesque for so long I start squirming under those unmoving, unblinking eyes. An imperceptible smirk grows as the possibilities swim inside her darkling imagination. It's uncomfortable to watch. That leer she has for me does not help.

I suppose that too is something I'll have to grow accustomed to in this new life, damn the consequences.

#

The Gray Girl of Gallows was officially on hiatus. For the first few days, she was clearly agitated in the way I have seen people who abruptly quit the pipe. There is a violence in her. With no outlet, it turned inwards.

Which did show me more of her deeper character than anything previously. I would have been an easy target. But not once was there a sniping comment, a rough word or look or grimace. And that showed me a significant piece of my own deeper character as well:

That kind of response was the one I had been expecting.

And in its absence, I felt confusion and even neglect.

As silly as it might seem, I took Echo camping. That did clear her head and outlook on our nascent plans. We trudged south until Gallows was a barely visible smudge defiling the landscape and no one would detect our campfire. Without hills or tree cover, we had to travel quite a distance.

Echo shared more stories about life beyond the Gap. Twice I tried to wheedle out an account of her journey across it -- and twice she refused. Not angry, not upset. It was simply a part of her past she did not wish to give voice.

Couldn't help but be morbidly curious. It tickles us all on occasion and, technically speaking, my butt was sitting in the Gap this very moment. I did wonder what it was like. During the day, I saw a flat plain of unending beige. It was as though a great sword had cloven a flawless cut across the face of the world, leaving no weeds, no cracks in the ground, no shifts in elevation. Of distinguishing features: none at all.

Thousands of miles? It could not be believed.

"Somehow," she had said.

Where was I five years ago? I think that was a lull of a year. More logistical than anything else.

Echo lost her home.

And four years ago? That was a busy one. Overlook was under construction and the Sovereignty's eye was on us -- if not yet its favor.

Echo walked alone.

Three years? Prototype dun creation. Sorting out graveyards. Making better friends and people to care about. Settling into a nightly routine. Feeling connected to something greater than myself.

Echo's corpse was burned.

Two years... Some idiots failed to break into Crypt Dun. Our authority and esteem skyrocketed.

Echo's life was spurned.

Last year... out east. Field work. Mostly carting.

Echo was reviled.

Today she smiles.

Eats a sugary mass I had cooked on a stick until it bubbled and crispied into a fragile, golden skin. She savored its gooiness -- which in her haste was plastered and hardening on her lips, cheeks, and fingertips.

I asked if she was ready for tomorrow.

Her strange bobbing dance ensued.

#

Pandemonium reigns.

No one is prepared for the terror we unleash.

Gallows has enjoyed its time in the calm of the storm in our absence, but now the squall we bring lets them know they were merely in the eye of it -- and that reprieve over.

Echo has set an entire block aflame. I can almost hear her maniacal laughter all the way over where my more subtle work is being unveiled.

Bones and skulls are nailed to the doorways of homes. Rotting corpses litter the streets, posed into tableaus of utter depravity. Some murder each other. Some commit suicide. Some devour themselves. Some fuck each other. Some fuck… other things. And on a broad wall, high up, visible from practically every angle, I have painted the following demand:

WORSHIP YOUR GRAY EMPRESS

In the coming weeks, I have other phrases to test out for maximum effect. Graffiti that will become more pervasive than the posters everyone thought would aid in catching her:

MY CONSORT WATCHES

and

THE EXECUTIONER IS COME

and

DEATH REMEMBERS

This is going to be a hell of a show.

Her fingers dug into my clothing as she laughed into my chest to the point of delirium. She could scarcely catch her breath between fits and used each giddy inhale to joyously complain how much her stomach hurt and how she couldn't stop and how wonderful I did and that she undoubtedly had chosen well.

"I fail at— art you have— true creativity I feel— such jealousy though— it's amazingly— ha ha ha! it's— it's— hurts so much— Le— thean— ha ha! did— you watch— them run away— left their— homes my realm is— now twice— as— as— ha ha! twice— the size!"

Atop her dark watchtower, we roared with laughter. It was true: the omnipresent candles surrounding the abandoned quarter had been snuffed as the occupants fled.

Where?

Certainly not where she had kindled inferno.

Definitely not where my disinterred were posed.

An exodus with nowhere to run.

It was marvelous.

Weeks of glorious tension in the streets were stretching everyone's wits to snapping. The Gray Girl of Gallows and Her Consort had disappeared.

Why?

What did it mean?

What should be done?

Where is this graffiti coming from?

It appeared last night.

But we were patrolling last night!

We may have missed it.

Impossible! How did they do it?

We may have…

We may have…

Unleashed something.

Yes. You did.
    I say.
Yes. You did.
    She says.

They are coming.
They are coming.
They are coming.

#

The burnings had stopped that first night. Seriousness suffused the air like leaden rain. We spent our nights hoarding supplies and digging up bones. I didn't want to dilute the use of corpses, but a few more would appear soon at random. Smaller tableaus. More intimate scenes. The *smell* would draw the audience.

Certain mornings, I played the pragmatist. Donned my hood, covered my markings, and chatted with the guards of the watch up on the battlements. I convinced them that the rumors they were hearing were fake -- some asshole teenagers were simply playing pranks and whipping the aldermen into frenzies of superstition.

"Blaze put scores out homeless," one rebutted.

Nodding. "You say very right. Thankfully, it's summer. No one will freeze to death. Plus, I get the feeling that just got out of hand. That... stake-burning ritual ended that night. I tend to figure the fools yet doing that childishness dropped their nightly offering."

His partner spat over the wall.

"These fucking people," she growled.

Smiling to myself, I nodded farewell and continued carrying home my backpack full of skulls.

#

Worth noting no one had died. Echo didn't particularly care, and that was fine because they really had had it out for her for years. One unexpected bout of paralysis or a single misplaced step that plunged her off a roof and into their clutches, and she'd have been kindled to blazing herself. And they, dusting off their ashen hands, would go back to living those same pointless lives they had before senselessness had given them a hate to whittle and sharpen.

For my part, I insisted on the psychological torment. Of self-defense and defending Echo? I would cross that threshold. But not unprovoked and not unless the last resort. Monster though I might also be, I am a monster yet with morals.

#

The Gray Girl was attempting to learn subtlety. It was not her style. She screwed up a lot. Invariably, a moment for dramatic flourish would present itself -- and she'd chase on after it, brandishing all her violent talents and driving mass panic to the hilt.

Later, her head lowered in a modicum of shame. "I become... *very* excited," she said with self-awareness and self-reproach. "These things take me over."

But it was no loss and there were no lectures. I hadn't any criticism or judgements. If anything, I'm a lazy bastard: why do any work when your prey can work for you? Like luring a cursed instead of wasting the energy to hunt one down. That made more sense to her.

Somewhat.

It's hard to tell once the machinations are pulsing through her veins. She's a distractable sort. Narrow focus. Dubious attention span.

I'm trying to direct that stubborn mind. If she can switch trains of thought a little more quickly, she'll gain an adaptation that -- I have found -- is necessary for thriving.

"Yes. Your Echo has one idea she would like to attempt. Will you watch after her?"

#

Hardly needed my help. She got it right the first time.

Tiny fires.

That was the idea. No great conflagrations. No Gray Girl erect on an adjacent rooftop, silhouetted against the dying light of sunset and proclaiming the doom of the world. No, she simply made small smoldering piles all around the city that were, more or less, miniaturized campfires as I had taught her to make while camping.

The rest of her "subtleties" flabbergasted everyone. Including me. When did she make the preparations? I never saw it once. It's like she never sleeps -- or only lights out of consciousness for an hour or so, sees me drooling next to her, creeps away, works on projects, creeps back, sleeps a little more.

Probably has to be that. Whenever I'm awake, she's attached to my hip.

A portly townswoman with an overhanging, oversized lower lip hurried towards the fire in an absolute tizzy. Thought to save another tenement from going up in smoke. Smashed her heel up and down. The fire went out.

Or so it seemed.

A swarm of wiggibugs, young ones without wings, probably at least a dozen, spewed out of the ruined pile. Their carapaces were aflame like flickering capes.

"How the hell—" I started to say.

"Ha ha ha!" Echo rolled next to me.

The woman screamed.

The bugs started crawling on her mindlessly. A few were climbing the building, but other than the spectacle they weren't likely to cause any real damage. The rest scuttled into the middle of the road where they were seen by the people roused by the woman's writhing and thrashing about. They stood agape, then tried to help in spite of their disgust.

Other scenes such as this were playing out everywhere. On our way to an early dinner, Echo explained a bit of brilliance on her part, though she was inexplicably frustrated with the compliment I gave it. To her, it was an obvious thing. The short of it was this:

The boxes she had crafted for the bugs were fragile things such that, even if someone didn't stomp the fire out, her many-legged helpers would eventually begin to burn and burrow their own way out to freedom.

"Same outcome no matter what," she reasoned.

I was proud.

#

Our next hiatus came and nearly went without a hitch. Our brainstorming sessions were such the height of arrogant creativity that she would become so excitably engaged I literally had to calm her down. It was a problem. She did not know how to turn off. When she started waking me up in the middle of the night to blab about anything, I struggled to convince her that her limitless energy was not a trait I shared, marked or unmarked.

"What if I forget?" she asked.

"Write it down."

"This is a boring thing."

"Writing is supposed to be boring. It's a thankless, shitty way to waste a life."

"Are you angry?"

"Tired. I'm going back to sleep."

"Yes. Very good. I shall go walk the length of the realm. Good night, my love. We will make convocation in the morning. I have such plans. In addition, we shall cook biscuits."

#

An episode afflicted her. It was no worse or easier than normal, but she fussed more than usual. Going a bit stir-crazy, waiting for the next phase of our game I suspected. I held her hand and read bedtime stories from some children's books we had found. Her pained smile...

It made me wonder if she had lacked a childhood.

Like other questions, this was one of those apparently rare forbidden topics that caused her to feign ignorance and go deaf.

The sound of crackling fire.

Simple tales.

Fun pictures.

My voice, speaking low.

These were what alleviated whatever anguish she was enduring. Perhaps there were more remedies... *distractions*... we could discover now that I was here. Now that she had a new perspective other than the one she had been trapped inside for so long.

"What is the— meaning—?"

"This?" I tapped a word on the page with my thumb.

"You are stroking my— fingers in a— pattern—?"

Oh.

"Trying to comfort you," I say after an awkward pause.

#

A wasting heat blankets and suffocates me.

Each breath is scorching. I inhale slowly, shallowly. It is no help. I labor. She labors. Something is wrong with the weather. Something is ending... again... something is beginning...

We creep outside, off-balance, both of us holding our heads to fight against the pounding of internal hammers. The back of my neck is a cord of rope petrifying an inch higher with every passing minute. Bursting decapitation.

The sky is pure white. Unmoving air shimmers in blurry haze as if my migraine has externalized. I want to vomit.

I do vomit.

Echo retches, stumbles back to the false comfort of the basement that is the same temperature as the outside world. I follow. And when we awaken the next day, the heat wave has passed, but the ringing of real hammers throughout Gallows signals a different kind of death knell.

#

I can't see anything from the watchtower. Echo strains for higher vantage, tiptoeing atop the parapets. I grip her dress as a compromise since I didn't want her up there being so exhausted as she is today.

Neither of us slept.

"Let's scout it out tomorrow. I'm dead to the world."

She hops down. "I disagree. You are strong as I. And we must know what this thing is."

#

Our simple investigation hits an obstacle within minutes. On the edge of her territory, the road is bisected straight down the middle with cables fashioned of an unidentifiable substance. Tight as metal yet flexible, swaying minutely in the breeze. Three tiers, each cable divided by roughly six feet.

I approach and regret my lack of caution.

The cables hum, then wobble, then hum louder until the air is thrumming with an energy that rips the breath from my lungs. I stagger back to Echo -- who disappears as everything goes non-white infinity. Out of nowhere, her frail and powerful arms grip me, her body propping me upright. I pant. After a minute, vision tunneling… a concerned pale face… and nothing else… infinity to edges, growing, and then within seconds I'm back to normal.

Like nothing happened to me at all.

"This is a weapon?"

I shake my head. I have no idea.

"I must know its purpose and power."

I try to stop her, but she slips away and carefully inspects the cables. Once she reaches a certain distance, the wobbling begins. She stands firm. The noise increases, reaching the intensity of a bell. Is that what this is? An alarm? Echo crosses her arms nonchalantly, determinedly.

"Vexing!" she shouts at it, then stomps away.

"Did it blind you?" I ask, noticing her balance is off.

Waves her hands about the sides of her head. "This is impudent tripe. I am unimpressed. This pain is nothing. I shrug it off as I would my dress when I bathe." But she isn't answering my question, nor focusing on me. Debating with herself in a single voice. As though she forgot about my presence entirely.

"Echo."

"Yes, I see, yes yes." Stares at me, black sclera churning, hands still waving. "My peripheral— very fuzzy, but this is nothing. I am insulted. Come. This needs more information. And then a response. How dare they!"

We parallel the cables at a safe distance, ultimately learning that they encircle her territory -- even dipping into what is well and truly her quarter at a few intervals. Each new violation infuriates her, but she keeps her inner monologue (usually always so outer) to herself.

We're trapped.

… is what my instincts say.

But a Gray Girl would know better; it isn't long until she spots a place where we can vault from roof to roof. The only problem is… it's from a four-storey height to a two-storey landing. We'll get out, but how do we get back in?

#

A multitude of robed figures swarm around Gallows. Uniform white robes, edged at the hems and sleeves and hoods with non-uniform gold and brown and black -- as if these parts had been set out in the sun until they caught fire and were haphazardly extinguished.

Whoever they are, they are expeditiously constructing walls of stone that extend straight down the middle of the roads -- exactly as the cables had -- from one disconnected gatehouse to another.

For the first time, I note the guardsmen and women down in the streets patrolling. Spears over their shoulders.

This sight is the same everywhere in the city near as I can tell from our explorations. Progress is difficult and there are plenty of routes no longer accessible.

"We should gather supplies," I tell her.

"No. We must attack, lest they think themselves in control."

"They *are* in control."

"We shall see at that."

#

Neither opportunities present themselves.

There are archers on the gatehouses. And I have a strong suspicion that if they detect us traversing the roofs, they'll either begin patrols up here too or erect lookout towers to watch over them.

Quarantine is already in effect.

I've never seen it before. Only heard about it. Imagined what it might be like. Figured roaming the wilderness would always prevent it from affecting my life, but here it is... the first stages.

All townspeople shut up indoors.

Patrols with purpose.

Wall construction.

Someone in charge *and* being obeyed.

On the sparsely-populated outskirts we find the guards of the watch knocking on doors and passing out food rations. Not knowing what the days and weeks to come will be like, I favor assaulting this group and grabbing a bag of flour and wheel of cheese if nothing else.

The nocked arrow on that bow gives me pause.

Even Echo wordlessly demurs her initial impulse.

"How much food do we have?"

Frowning. "Little. I do not like to store abundance. When I cannot attend to matters, they spoil. I dislike waste. I will not rule a wasteful land."

I could have done without the embellishment, but...

"Follow my lead."

"Yes. She follows."

We drop into an alleyway. I don my hood. Echo does the same, but she's unmistakable regardless. If she stays behind me, though, all should go well.

The guards are still around the bend. I slow my pace as I exit to the street. There's a window beside the front door of the nearby home. I peer inside while passing. No movement. No voices. Good a place as any; better if it's deserted.

I knock.

Seconds pass.

I knock again.

Nothing.

Good good. Smiling victory at Echo. Her teeth creep into a mirrored grin within the folds of her hood.

I reach for the doorknob the moment it starts to turn.

Dammit.

A young man, plainly fearful, opens the door cautiously. *Very* cautiously. They must have orders not to open for anyone except—

"Take this one. Don't make a mess," I say over my shoulder.

I pounce through him, knocking him to the side. Scanning quickly. No one. Rushing to check the adjoining rooms. None. None. N—

Old man.

I bind and gag him before his wits are about him. Echo carries in her charge, subdued and unwounded, tosses him on the bed. As we leave I glance back at terrified eyes, put my finger to my lips, and shut the door.

#

The wood shudders under the pounding of a gauntlet.

I open the door *very* cautiously.

"Name?"

Shit…

I make something up.

A fairly common family name up north.

Echo knows it isn't mine.

Out of the corner of my eye, her fingers curl around the hilt of her blade. She sits, back turned to us, watching me in the doorway's reflection on a dusty glass. Back hunched, pronouncing yet hiding her telltale stoop, and wrapped in blankets to play her role.

"Did father give the wrong one before?" I ask, hoping to cover my ass since I surely guessed wrong. Fucking probabilities.

The mustached guard consults a list, then scrawls something on a line with a few random symbols that mean nothing to me. I tense my arm, ready to knock him out cold in a single stroke. Five of them... shit, six. Where did she come from? Two archers? Okay, if I dash through the center I can— if they aren't expert marksmen— they're surveying their surroundings and— we had better move before—

"No, no," the guard's bored voice laboriously rolls downhill. "There was never a census taken, so we're ordered to do double-duty now. We appreciate your understanding, citizen." He signals his seconds. One deposits a bag of flour in my arms— shit, what if *he's* playing *me* now that my arms are— the other plops a fat dull wheel of cheese atop, and they all turn away.

Except their leader. He has a funny look on his face.

Oh hell.

Does he see my mark?

"You have..." he starts to say, *laboriously*. "A copy of the rules, correct?"

Shaking my head no.

"Ah. Here then." He tucks a scroll tied with off-white twine between the cheese and my chest. "Good day, sir."

Adrenaline makes my voice warble. "Excuse me."

"Sir?"

"Who are they?"

"Ah. The bigwigs." An opaque glaze passes over him like a fog in the night. "Damned if we know. Bloody cagey lot. But them's the ones with the writs of seizure. Sovereignty-backed, so it's legitimate sure as it rains from the sky." He nods politely. "Sir."

When they were three more houses away, we untied the two men back in the bedroom, and lighted the hell out to safer territory.

And in good time too. Echo had started to bleed heavily.

#

We hide out in the graveyard. Piss poor location, but the best we can manage. Broad-trunked oaks provide decent concealment, more than the straggly brush that pokes out of the ground in fitful and random intervals. Now I know how diggers feel.

The bastards.

I stare off into the distant sky, waiting for nightfall.

Echo paralytically writhes, waiting for relief.

Something of a curtain surrounds the city limits. Orange cloth, saffron or marigold. Can't tell in the sunlight. Appears to be one continuous fabric until a gust brushes over it, whips up a section to flap like a banner, then languidly goes limp as an unused noose.

How was this all assembled seemingly overnight?

I need not inspect the curtain wall. The cables I see underneath when the wind passes on by tell me all I need to know. Gallows is on lockdown. The hammers, which have not ceased once, continue to pound from the heart of quarantine.

"How long do you reckon?" I stroke Echo's matted hair.

"Mmm— mmm— mmhour—"

An hour meant it was starting to taper. "Hang in there."

"Nmmg— thamngk— mggn— rrrrreeead—"

I pull off the twine and unroll the parchment.

The city of Gallows is hereby declared a potential threat to the province due to an alleged outbreak of plague, and therefore will be put into strict isolation until such time as The Bearers of this proclamation determine or ensure:

(a) The threat of plague is erroneous.
(b) The threat of plague is contained.
(c) The threat of plague is eliminated.

The Sovereignty grants executive and judicial powers, superseded only by Sovereignty directives alone, to The Bearers in the accomplishment of this task. Further, per exigent circumstances, the Sovereignty endorses the following set of rules after consultation with The Bearers:

1. *No resident of Gallows may leave city limits.*
2. *No persons may enter Gallows city limits without approval of The Bearers.*
3. *All local government is immediately suspended.*
4. *Residents must not leave domiciles during lockdown.*
5. *When lockdown is lifted, curfew will extend from sundown to sunrise.*
6. *Additional proclamations issued by The Bearers, not limited to this writ of seizure, must be obeyed.*

Any instance of disobedience will result in swift, extrajudicial punishments. For the sake of saving as many lives as possible, Gallows is implored to comply without exception to all future instructions. The Bearers retain full right to grant abeyance and abrogation.

Definitely Sovereignty. Everything from the artsy professional font to the meticulous use of legalese. We got one of our own a couple years ago. I think someone framed it in the common room. Probably Krohn.

And absolutely no identification of the harbingers of these tidings. Not a name, signature, abbreviation, or otherwise. "The Bearers" meant nothing. Message-runners when granted temporary legal authority to enact measures on very specific occasions receive the same moniker.

It was a generic term.

The undercurrent of my thoughts said "Technocracy", but nothing about this screamed goggle-wearing bobbleheads who seemed more like a club of nerdy dorks than...

Ex-military?

Possible.

There is no army. Hadn't been in... I mean, that was before I was born. Abolished and blown to the wind. This new lot didn't seem militaristic. Outfits alone looked more like costumes than regimentals.

I was clueless. And clueless I would remain.

#

"An invasion."

Echo, nonplussed, observing from the lengthening shadows. With her energy replenished, despite refusing to eat, she kept dragging me along on a scouting party. We needed to think about escape. Ignored that. Wanted to draw up stratagems and battle plans as if our kid's game had suddenly turned into bloody constraint between kingdoms.

In her mind, it had.

If she really was a foreigner, it was true.

My failed, vengeful empress.

With difficulty I cut (more like pried) a wedge of cheese from the wheel. An Executioner's weapon is not meant for slashing or severing. Her face, so full of conquest, curdles to see the slimy tan mess along the length of the blade.

"I feel you are not taking our situation seriously," she complains with a lilting resolution.

"Am," I manage between stuffed cheeks. "You aren't."

371

"Not so." Frantically cleaning the cheesy gunk off with her shawl. "No, indeed. We are disadvantaged in this thing. Outnumbered, outresourced, outmaneuvered. Yes? I must understand my enemy if I am to be victorious." Satisfied, plays the blade's tip against each finger. "My people were unruly, this I will admit. I knew how to chasten them. And yes..." Sidelong glance, reluctant. "I mistook the... repetition."

I shrug. Swallow. "You've been in over your head. Needed to come up for air."

"Yes? Yes, fresh air. I understand this. Your counsel has been much appreciated. And needed."

Now that I have her attention, I try convincing her again that we need to escape the city. Nothing good can come from being here. Not that I know where to go or what to do. This just... doesn't feel like a... throne she should fight for. She becomes, unsurprisingly, indignant and insulted by the tactless opinion.

And then, hopping to her feet, she hurries away with scant a word. I ditch the bag of flour in a dry hidey-hole en route. My lumbering around was already ridiculous enough.

#

We found the outsiders' headquarters where Echo had burned down the whole block. Ash and rubble had been cleared and in their place: orange tents and temporary-to-permanent structures. And, true or no, my consort maintained she'd found their leader.

Which seemed accurate. This person was sought by many and hadn't left the general vicinity for hours. Echo insisted on referring to her as the Executrix, saying it was clearly the one who had betrayed me.

"My past isn't fodder for your fantasies," I grumbled.

Her deafness resurfaced, conveniently.

This "Executrix" may not even have been a woman. Feminine body, wrapped in the tight robes as all the others.

Fairly indistinguishable I would think, though it's possible that… those are rounded hips and… those are small breasts. The false connection Echo tried to develop made me uncomfortable for another reason: none of the outsiders spoke. Vow of silence? Intimidation tactic? Instead they used…

Hand gestures.

Jive.

Esoteric movements.

I couldn't read a word of it. Wasn't our special language which we had invented in isolation. This was formalized. And where a word or phrase or idea or intent started and ended…? Beyond me.

Certainly beyond Echo.

Who, reckless idiot, is now standing awash in residual firelight. "Identify yourselves, you that dare to enter my sanctum!" she shouts down at them. "I have not given permission to so alter my lands! To quarter thus! To trample my authority! Bespeak yourselves, then begone! So says the Gray Girl of Gallows!"

Rapid arm gestures flash.

Polished mirrors refocus firelight on us.

Echo does not flinch as they scrutinize her black eyes and the blackened patterns covering exposed skin. The "leader" exits a tent, stares up at us. Makes her own hand gestures to various people; they disappear: some to tents, others down the streets and away from the unfolding scene.

Their fusillade of arrows has faultless aim.

At least a dozen pass through the air where Echo and I just perched. If not for our instincts, that would not have been the case. Call it a benefit for leading such dangerous lives as pariahs.

We fled.

Echo groused.

The cheese did not survive.

#

"Whoever gives the first shit loses!" I snapped at her.

Echo had absolutely no idea how to take that. "What do our movements have to do with these things!?"

"What I mean is, if you care *too much* and end up screwing us, it's your own damned foolish fault!"

She blew up at me. First time. A crack in the mask.

"Your phrases are very confusing!"

The anger oozing from that crack was real.

So was the unrepressed accent.

Idioms are going to be the death of us, I think.

#

The wrong kind of relief awaits us at home. The robed outsiders have replaced the townspeople that used to live on our border. Watchful eyes along the perimeter of Gray Girl territory. Like us, they avoid the cables -- except for an occasional poke with their blunted spears. Adjustments? Testing for faults? Their ways are not mine.

I creep close to a group intent on playing sentry at an intersection. Their eyes are alert and the only visible humanizing features. Covered so thoroughly, they are nearly wrapped in burial shrouds.

Unnerving anonymity.

And the silence...

I hear not one whisper. Only the periodic rustle of cloth sleeves when someone communicates with another. If we could have enlisted this group... the efficiency of our disinterments! It is impressive, and inspiring, and—

Sharp shingles rain from the sky, faster than arrows, down upon them. Echo flings them mercilessly, unconsciously fighting through my attempts to stop her from revealing our position.

In the end, once the assailed have retreated, collapsed from bloody gashes, or both, she smiles in pointless triumph. Reinforcements bearing torches are coming and we still have no understanding on how to return to the safety of our den. And can there be safety when they know where we hide? Luckily, the cables form a wide enough boundary and even if that broken refuge were dead center we'd be in no urgent danger of being ferreted out.

That said… now they know we can escape.

As we flee back into the city proper, I wonder if that's in any way an advantage or not. The fact that Echo hasn't thought that far ahead gives me more pause. Her gamesmanship thinks one move ahead -- if that.

The Executrix is clearly ten.

#

Sleeping atop a roof is, perhaps, the worst bed I have ever had. At least it is warm at night…?

Feh.

All of my bones snap when I stir, surely waking all the dead in all the world.

Echo seems fine. Awake already. Perched on a chimney, chin on fists. The consummate sculpture of brooding.

"We must attack cruelly today," she reasons, not looking at anything specific. "They have made mockery of me." Snarling like a newly feral beast, believing in its own egocentric regression over the unfathomable crush of reality. "This will not happen again."

I ask if she has food.

"I do not." Puzzled, as if I were the weird foreigner here. I tell her nothing is doing until I get a proper meal. The fact frustrates her. Had sleep, feed, and shelter become unheard of concepts?

This distractable woman…

Is her objective now simply to be a pest?

"Aren't you hungry?" I complain on our way.

"Not particularly. No."

And yet she ate even more than I when we managed, by noon, to secure vittles.

She is right about one fact, though; we do need to gain some sort of edge on the outsiders, and soon. There is only so much reconnaissance we can manage, the two of us. And those bloody willful outbursts of hers mean I feel less confident splitting up than I am staying with.

Barely.

Our highway will quite literally be blocked within a fortnight. The construction efforts are that efficient. No wonder too, for the heartier townspeople have been enlisted. Likely the ones deemed safe from infection.

And that constant fucking *hammering*—!

"Love?"

Echo pops into view as I clutch my head. Interlaces her fingers between mine.

"I'm not doing well," I admit.

She thinks for a curiously protracted moment before speaking the words with care. "Hang them here."

Takes me an even longer moment to comprehend what she's trying to express, then I start laughing.

"It is correct, this thing?" she asks, uncertain if she should be offended and add my name to her death list.

"Well," I chuckle, "if anywhere that's appropriate, it's here in Gallows."

#

The next days we spent on the lam.

Observation. Larceny. Creating caches.

I was rather proud of our temporary hideout in the graveyard, a spacious hovel we had tunneled under the roots of the largest oak. This would be the waystation and our last stop on our way out. The world beyond the curtain wall beckoned me with every errant caress of the breeze.

But I remembered my vow.

And Echo had no interest in being run out of her kingdom. According to the lofty backstory she continued to embellish, that would make this the second time.

Totally unacceptable.

I shrugged to myself as I shrug now. We all have our reasons.

#

One section of Gallows was entirely lost to us. This was a small yet significant defeat. The high, narrow wall -- now patrolled by normal officers of the watch -- was out of reach. I couldn't jump the distance. And the mortar-work was so smooth and to the very edge of each brick that Echo found it impossible to climb.

This was that residential area we had assaulted. For our pains, we gained a writ of seizure, a cheese we had promptly lost, and a bag of flour thankfully recovered.

I can't guess what's beyond that wall now other than an omen of what is to come.

#

We had some luck sabotaging other construction sites. Ruining containers of mortar was about the extent of it. Echo wanted to melt the stones, especially those newly erected, but we hadn't the means and I didn't have the know-how. Boiling pitch, would that have worked?

I asked if she knew where those types of craftsmen may be located. She had no idea and asked me what "pitch" was. I tried to explain it. She still had no idea and, although she never admitted it, I think she was clueless about what I was trying to explain.

#

The night remained our time. For what that was worth. Felt more and more like we were pissing on the leg of a behemoth, whining at the inevitable. It was demoralizing.

I sat Echo down.

"What is our objective?" I asked.

"The expulsion of the enemy."

"I don't think that's possible."

"They win when you say this thing."

Why do I understand the dead more than the living?

"Do you suggest we slaughter them?"

Turns away from me. "Violence is a show of weakness." Turn back. "That is not my strength."

"I've seen you attack people before."

Sniffing, annoyed. Not at me, though. "This is different. I was provoked. And scared." Looks hard at me. "That is not a weakness."

"Then what does the endgame look like?"

She crumpled in on herself. Like I had beaten her. Without reason. Without warning. "You want this to end?" Her hand wrapped around her wrist, clutching desperately.

"I mean, how can we be effective? Once the sun sets, every wall is a little higher. Our stomachs are a little emptier. If this goes on, we are going to be so overpowered that—"

"The Gray Girl will think of something," she said confidently. "She always does," she maintained, but the confidence had already wavered enough to be audible.

#

The plan was infiltration.

It was an idea we had flirted with, never quite courting, but never quite breaking ties with either. Had far more disadvantages than... well. As an extension to intelligence-gathering it seemed worthwhile despite the risks. Echo was ridiculously keen for it.

Why?

Then I remembered all the dramatics and thought, oh, of course, she's the theatrical plays-a-role sort. And then I remembered how horny she is for always having an audience. That made me think this plan was suicide. Which certainly would not have been the first time this year and with a scrap of luck would be the last in the best way possible.

Optimism has gotten Lethean this far. Right?

But am I learning their gestures correctly? The role of mute is not a necessity I have never donned. Yet... their language is only one we can mimic. Echo has visible trouble with the finger movements. Seems part physical... nerve damage? And partly mental... new things confuse her. It's a problem.

We're working on it.

Still, replication is not comprehension.

This... could mean "hello there."

But...

It could also mean:

"I'm switching positions with you.

Good luck on your watch."

In which case...

I wouldn't know *where* that watch was supposed to take place, nor for how long, nor any other manner of deeper information implicit in the understanding of...

Sigh.

Now I know where she's coming from.

"Yes?"

"Can you stand up straight?"

She does so.

"I mean... your stoop. Is it permanent?"

Confused.

I try manipulating her body to look less abnormal.

"That's... somewhat better. Walk over there."

She does so.

"Can you stay upright like that?"

Returns to stooping. "Very painful. Unnatural."

Well. Ignore that. Probably a detail that won't matter much. More importantly: we need to subdue two outsiders that are our size and shape, stow them somewhere, and explore as extensively as we can before they're missed.

#

Tonight our best opportunity arrives on a new moon.

Auspicious, despite the bad memory attached.

"Them! Them!" Echo points repeatedly. Her excitement, for now, isn't worrying. I had admonished her endlessly on the need for silence once we actually committed. In response, she regaled a story about the time she squatted in the citadel's pantry for weeks, hiding out from some problem or other, and was neither found nor looked for. That latter part made me question the tale's relevance, but it seemed to mean she would behave.

Two outsiders are sleepily finishing their rounds. This particular pair among those few out after dark. That's one good thing about their organization: so damn efficient it's predictable in parts.

Of our ambush, there isn't much to say. I knocked mine out flat; Echo kept hers from squirming away until I could do the same. Figure in binding and gagging (a worthwhile precaution) and it was over in less than two minutes.

I feel rotten stowing them both, naked but for undergarments, in barrels. Feels a bit like premature burial and that bugaboo creeps us Executioners out more than the general populace.

Fortunately, the robes fit us -- or we would have just been assholes for no reason. Echo would get kicks from that, but I'm not so much the joyful sociopath. I tug at the stretchy cloth at my waist. A bit tight. Awkward. Turned out my target was a lady.

Echo is already in costume, trembling in the way that means she desperately wants to do one of her odd dances yet is so far managing to suppress the urge. Good girl.

She turns to me.

Ah.

We overlooked this issue.

"Yes?" Her tone says smiling, though I can't see her mouth. Cloth literally covers everything but—

"Your eyes are too noticeable."

"My eyes," she says, tone lowering into a frown, "are beautiful."

"Well. Your beautiful eyes will give us away."

"Then, I shall change their coloration."

Pause. "You can do that?"

Black eyes rolling like tumbling stones. "Of course not."

I adjust the hood. With her stoop, the results are mixed. Maybe it's my familiarity... still...

New instructions: *Don't make eye contact with anyone.*

The Gray Girl bristles. Mutters what passes for expletives with her.

"Agreed?"

More muttering.

"Echo?"

"Yes yes! Your Echo will obey."

And yet the muttering continues while I retrieve the fallen spears and hand one to my acting partner. Having a prop shuts her up.

Keep her busy, keep her focused. My new mantra.

#

While their semi-permanent headquarters is the more tantalizing target, its density and our ignorance of the unknown keep it out of sense's reach. Instead we maintain the plan and approach the least built-up section where the walls are merely foundations and easily hopped over. The outsiders are clearly aiming their efforts most where they knew we had been previously.

In reality, we'd been everywhere. But here? We had done nothing grand here. Nothing memorable.

Guards are upon the gatehouse. Bored. Yawning.

Outsiders stand sentry at its entrance. Alert. Silent.

Echo grips her spear a little more tightly, staying behind my back, averting her gaze from everyone watching our approach. I casually plant my spear in the ground, leaning against my shoulder, and give what I think is a standard hail.

The outsider with amber feminine eyes signs back what I think is a standard response, indecipherable bits tacked on the end -- hopefully only details of their own report.

I sign nothing to this, betting everything on it not containing any questions. That's apparently true because the other outsider knocks his or her knuckles against the wicket gate which, after only a few seconds pause, opens from within.

We pass inside. Echo is trampling my heels.

The watch officer closes and bars the gate behind us, sighs wearily, and drops onto a cushioned stool. He returns to snoring a moment later.

Echo begins wandering off. Probably has always been a mite curious what the interior of these places is like. One of the few areas she couldn't ever breach. Nothing special. Stone and wood. Standard as any guardhouse or barracks.

I tug on her robe to get her attention.

Hmm? she probably signs.

I guess we leave these here, I try to sign.

Slotting my blunted spear into a rack of many others.

But I want a weapon, she probably signs.

Tough crap, I try to sign.

She glowers. Then complies.

Time to get to searching. Ground floor seems to be mostly supplies. Equipment and nibbles. One larger room with a broad table... prominently-displayed proclamation on the door... large map showing the layout of the walls, nothing we don't already know... but might be worth copying this down...

While I'm scribbling on a blank parchment, Echo waits by the doorway. On watch. Head cocked.

Plenty of other documents stacked around the sides of the room, but nothing pertinent. All guard materials. Manifests. Reports. Incomings, outgoings. Duty rosters.

Mundane. Mundane. Mundane.

Creeping upstairs. Softer light: candles not torches. Hallway of closed doors. I lean my ear against one. Then another. And another. Dorm rooms. Hmm...

Echo squeezes my shoulder.

Maybe don't? she probably signs.

Got to know, I try to sign.

Very, very discreetly I crack the door a sliver. There! In the corner. A dozen outsiders. Likely more if I stuck my head in to look around.

Echo tugs me away and shuts the door.

Bold yet dumb, she probably signs.

Bold and done, I try to sign.

The next staircase will lead up to the battlements. But the footsteps coming down make me lose my nerve to double-check. We hurry on to create some distance.

The person reaches our level.

Starts following us.

Coincidence, that's all. Keep going, Lethean. Time to leave. Or pop into the privy. Even outsiders need relief.

This floor has run out of doorways and we're heading back down by another set of stairs. And down. And down. And—

One-way hallway. No entrance in sight. And the footsteps continue to come our way. I peek at Echo. She shrugs and pushes me forward.

I go, not knowing where I go. It isn't long before I figure we've crossed a distance more than twice the gatehouse's length. Where the hell are—

A guard is coming towards us. Boots clomping stridently on flagstones like sledgehammers on anvils. Passes on by with a curt nod for both of us. With the footsteps still approaching from our rear, I have no idea if these groups nod at each other or...

I return the gesture, using it as an opportunity to glance backwards, and see black stains covering Echo's outfit.

That won't be conspicuous, not at this distance. I hurry our pace. Could be shadows. Could be dirt. It's fine, it's—

Another guard ahead. Then another, trying to catch up to speak with him. They're probably chatting about nothing, but I freeze up. Does Echo know that she's—? Five outsiders appear, in my rising panic, I think, out of nowhere. Like a visual trick: here's no one, now here's the end of your world, son.

Nothing for it nothing for it.

"Echo," I whisper urgently.

Stiffens. Taps me in acknowledgement.

"*Bleeding.*"

Long pause, made too long by the approach of seven—

Tap tap.

I have no idea what that means, but it doesn't feel anxious. Carefree. Friendly. She might be saying everything is okay. She might be claiming everything is okay so I don't break character and fuck everything up.

The guards pass, heads together, conferring.

An outsider leader hails me. I hail back, ready to move on by. Another rapid gesture, apparently the universal sign for "stop moving, please, I want to screw you over by asking you questions you can't answer because I'm Life and I'm here to *collect*."

I tell myself to not stop moving. I stop moving.

Quick jive, mostly finger movement. Arm gestures at the end. I pick up nothing familiar. He could be randomly flailing and I'd have no idea that it was meant as a mock for my hubris that this would ever work.

My dumbfounded stare. My want for a spear.

He starts to gesture again.

I am going to fuck you, I think he means.

Echo pushes me aside, clutching her head like it's about to explode. She stumbles on down the hallway, looking like a loon, staggering into things, but a damn good distraction.

The group watches her go. And they *have* to be seeing the dark black splotch on the small of her back. The leader, however, hasn't graced her retreating stooped form with anything more than a bored glance.

I begin to start gesturing nothing intelligible, pretending to be so distraught by the condition of my friend, and flash a quick farewell -- hell, I think that's farewell, I don't know I don't know I—

Hurry after Echo, blocking view of her body with my own. For a split-second, it feels like our foolishness worked. The next split-second, I hear us being followed and this time *they are definitely following us* and I have no clue where we are except underground *somewhere.*

An involuntary noise rattles in my throat. Echo unconsciously reaches back, grips my fingers tightly, and speeds up. Another split-second of respite, to hope, to relax, and the sounds of boots behind me likewise quicken.

I squeeze back so hard my nails dig into her flesh.

She lets go.

And we run.

We just *run.*

Bolting for all we know into a dead-end where the Executrix is standing, hands on hips, head thrown back in uproarious silent laughter. We ignore everyone we cross paths with. Enemies, enemies everywhere.

There's a crossroads.

Echo alters course, takes us to the right.

Why!?

Where are we?!

Light is dimming down this corridor and then: a staircase she flies up. I stumble after. And my senses return enough to recognize the interior of another gatehouse. The architecture is identical. Maybe it's even the one we had left, doubling back around to fuck ourselves up our own asses.

Pounding heels behind, spiraling up up up and—

Alarm bells trigger.

Carillon multitude announcing tidings of doom. Too late for us to blend in by slackening our pace. Outsiders, roused from deep sleep, pour from their rooms. We are fucked we are fucked we are—

Now at the staircase leading to the ground floor. The fact that no one is shouting disturbs me more. I have no idea how they're coordinating, what they are planning, how to defend myself, hearing only the swelling cadence of mute silence punctuated by feet slamming into the ground exactly like—

when her back was pressed against mine nowhere left to hide or run misplaced ideas failed trap but her back was pressed against mine we were sweating tang of pine needles and tar that ballet of stabbing there were too many to handle she handled them I handled them in the end her back was pressed against mine and I reached around to—

Snatch up a spear. Echo has already slammed the witless guard's face against the wicket, now she is struggling -- legs straddling the moaning dazed woman -- to unbar the only thing between us and—

Outside, I recognize nothing. The street is not empty. The outsider sentries are alert. They are more adroit with spear than I, but my instincts and training, speed strength will I'm an Executioner they are like still images spread across—

The ground.

I lie there, twitching.

The shaft of the arrow that hit me, rolling away. Its fat flat head covered in crimson cracked skull brains leaking with thoughts I turn on my back black silhouette atop the gatehouse battlements kneeling between crenellations and nocking another—

blacking out to a memory of a battered puppet that would not fall down -- witnessing this time there were many puppets that, when they hit the ground, did not move again.

#
Dull noise.
Someone crying out. Panting. Screaming.
Such silence.
Sleep. A sleep eternal…
#
They were binding my arms. They had bound my legs.
The crying panting screaming.
Duller now.
Silence. Silence.

Silence.
#
Eyes beholding the birth of a godling.
Rites   of   passage,
rites   of   ascent.
Rites   of   pain
and she transcends.
Glory
Glory
Glory
to
the
Gray
Girl
of
Gallows
on
high.
#
She is above me. She severs my bonds. She stands me up.
I fall down. She grips my hand. She drags me away. She is
steaming. She has eyes of shadow.
We go back. We go back.
She is covered in blood, none of it black.
#

Time did not stop for me in the echoless void.

Only now am I returning to it.

Where everything is pain.

We are in the basement. There is nothing that comprises the body and mind of Lethean that is not aching, pulsing with my weak heartbeat that is practically in sync with the hammering of hammers that are so close they might be inside my head.

I languish, unmoving, on her bed for hours. She does not move. She is hunched over, staring at nothing. The hammers stop hammering, and I can hear more distinctly the rainstorm they were drowning out.

She stirs only when I do. Face partially turning to meet mine. The mask is gone. And now I see Her face. Whatever name was once attributed to Her is gone too, cast away alongside the named dead who rot thousands of miles south of nowhere now here, exposing Herself to me the face of whoever Her was still is.

Not Echo. Not the Gray Girl.

Not the monster persona of dubious sincerity who had wrapped itself up in a labyrinth of its own creation pleading loudly silently loudly for someone anyone please someone anyone see me please find me please end me, who now clung to a new life she hadn't been expecting. The twist in a story she had already written inserted by an author with his own set of values and intentions and needs.

A new perspective before the denouement.

"I'm not a plaguer," she admits.

I try sitting up. The pain is too great.

"I'm *not* a plaguer," she says with finality. "So neither are you."

Silence.

Her accent is thick. There are no more barriers.

No stage. No audience.

Nothing but her. Nothing but me.

She unwraps a bandaged wrist, wipes a finger across the black blood, then smears it gently on the palm of my hand. Wipes away the excess. A mark remains.

"Whenever you slept," she chokes, flinching away. Swallowing, swallowing, swallowing noisily. "They will fade," she says, "from you." Rewrapping the bandage painfully tight. "Le-thean, you are *free*."

Then she unsheathes her Executioner blade, places the hilt against my stained palm. "What am *I*?" she asks, turning her back. "I am more than my *skin*. More than this *flesh* that pinions. It makes me *it*. Discards what is *me*. Everyone else can change their skin. You change your skin. You remove a scarf and are Executioner no longer. Not me. Not me. The skin changes *me*." Shivering. "What am I? What *am* I?" Raising her head to expose her neck. "I do not know. Perhaps a new kind of cursed. And perhaps we are all cursed in our own ways. Tiny ways, but our own."

I crawl towards her, feeling nothing now, and pull her fragile body into the tightest embrace my weakness will allow. "I don't hate you," I tell her.

And rain shakes the blackened windowpanes.

#

Both of our ordeals were heavy, but she recovered first. Kept me fed and rested, such as I could with the ceaseless pounding racket that started at sunrise and ended at sunset. Cleaned my wounds and changed my bandages.

"Medicine is beyond my ken," she had said.

My skull may have been fractured. Felt like it. I was covered in ugly bruises. Are there attractive bruises? Yes. They are the ones I've had before that don't feel like my body is decomposing prematurely. The outsiders had beaten me into submission after that arrow cracked against my head.

Somehow I had lost the city sketch in the tumult. Which meant all we had gained for our efforts really was just pain.

Then Echo sat me up by piling anything behind my back she could find strewn around the basement. Her old unfinished masterpiece had been torn down, scattered at random all over the floor. A new plastering of posters took its place, broad black lines perfectly replicating what we had seen.

"You truly were an artist," I say.

Nodding. "I remember." Nodding again. "Perhaps another curse." Walks over to the map, pointing areas out as she speaks. "These are not the walls. Though their masquerade is effective." Running a finger down a long, nearly unbending line. "The tunnels. Yes? Their walls... yes... they *mostly* parallel these what lie beneath the ground."

"And I'm guessing you were unaware of them."

"This is so. I was hoodwinked," she says. "Truer still that I had no quarrel with the guards. We had a... peace. Tacit armistice, yes?"

"Yes."

She nods. "Had we fought earlier, I may have learned of this thing." Taps the paper, the entire thing trembles like a wave is passing on through. "Today I know they have efficient access throughout all of Gallows, below ground and now above. This is..." Dithering. "Problematic..."

"But you know where the walls and tunnels are running in parallel and where they aren't?"

"Yes. Yes. I can perceive this most easily."

It felt like information, though. Just information. Nothing we could use, nothing that meant anything other than a cataloguing of a fact that simply *was*. Then Echo sat down, frowning, very serious, struggling to ask as I did:

"What... is our objective?"

"I think," I say cautiously, "it must be escape."

"Yes. Escape..." she repeats, defeated yet unable to accept the words. "That is asking me to abandon my..." Accent pushing through. "... worthless kingdom."

That isn't anything I can have an easy answer to. Glib statements, platitudes, certainly. But comfort? On this? I let out a breath, knowing exactly where on the road of life she is standing... that place without guideposts or any orientation because the sun has stopped rising and the moon is too much the coward to defy it.

I suppose the only acceptable answer to the Gray Girl of Gallows is to be as dramatic as possible.

"Why settle for a kingdom? Have the whole world."

A blank stare.

Thin line of mouth.

In her throat, a low rumble.

Boiling... boiling...

... into delighted giggles.

Echo rocks back and forth, a hint of gleeful childishness at the very heart of the character-breaking outburst. And then she does that dance of hers, but bouncing on her haunches and clapping her hands.

"This is so!" she exclaims. "I have looked inwards for far too long!"

#

Am I ready?

The daily headaches are gone, replaced with soreness to the touch. There is no more seeping blood for the bandages to soak up. Nonetheless, I finish wrapping and tying off new dressing, preferring the look since it reminds me of hers.

Is she ready?

Well, she's certainly overstuffed my pack with supplies; it sits ready to pitch over the bottom stair and flop onto the floor. Her own patchwork rucksack is swinging to and fro, a tail trying and failing to swat itself, as she paints across the length of the basement wall the following phrase:

HERE RULED ECHO,
EMPRESS-IN-EXILE

Finished, she flashes me a defiant smirk.

She is ready.

The way the candlelight flares, sputtering down into the depths of many years of melted wax, I catch a glimpse of the girl who was and the woman who will be.

Then I feel my hand clutching something in my pocket. I pull it out. The Executioner scarf crinkles open in my palm like a weary flower at false dawn. How strange for such a small and simple thing to feel so rough. The candle's flame caresses it, unsurely. I smile sadly and let go -- and the black-and-crimson ignites.

Echo approaches, flickering with its color.

"It was never even mine," I say.

And I laugh.

Now I'm ready, too.

#

Smoke is in the air, the night sky obscured by wispy brown. Without any wind, it hangs and gathers into a lumpy carpet engulfed in mold. This is the first time I've seen the completed construction work walling us in: the boundaries of Echo's domain now the borders of internment.

Assumed internment. We plan to leave.

We scout the perimeter, avoiding reflected searchlights. I can't help feeling responsible for letting them finish these walls. But I was too broken to do more than moaning in my sleep and Echo too attentive to leave me alone.

Fully-implemented quarantine stands between us and freedom. A bit of pride bubbles up that it took *this* to stop us. Each bubble pops, however, unable to sustain itself.

Unlike the gatehouses, there are no doors breaking up the monotony of the walls. The outsiders never intended on sweeping through our streets. So much the worse for us: no structural vulnerabilities to be found.

Whether we were spotted or timing betrayed us I can't remember, but that was the moment the inferno ignited.

One building inside the border explodes, then another directly opposite: pillars of fire supporting a roiling ceiling. And there, and there! Our territory, in seconds, an open-air crematorium.

Without a word, Echo sprints down a sidestreet. I recognize where we're going after the next turn: the building we used to vault over the cables back before things had gone too far.

We are halfway through its gutted interior when the roof explodes high above us, blowing a hole in the center and sending shingles plummeting down on our heads. Echo, in one gracefully violent maneuver, rips her shawl in two and throws half at my face.

"Soak with water!" she shouts, emboldened by the flames and speeding up to meet them.

Our most precious resource...

I cuss vibrantly at my upturned waterskin, then push the sopping shawl against my mouth and nose. Ignoring every instinct, I dash upwards into cloying smoke and searing heat. Echo is a gray shadow, dancing between burning walls and floors that buckle the instant she crosses.

The rooftop is about to collapse when I exit. And Echo is already arcing through the air and falling.

Three outsiders are ready for her atop the wall, two with spears and one with a bow. Before she lands, and before they attack, she seems to hang in suspension -- hovering atop shadows somehow at her command -- and her blade sparkles with an inner fiery fury of its own.

A scream folded into the twisting metalwork.

And that is the only scream that speaks, for all three are dead before her bare feet touch stone.

Then, collapse.

I was too slow. Incinerated timber gives way, balcony supports scorched to sneering cinders, and I'm hurtling downwards at a precipitous angle. Jumping is impossible.

Echo calls my name, reaching out instinctively, but I'm much, much too far away to do anything other than impotently watch her disappear behind the parapets.

Being good at falling is the only talent that saves me from a broken leg. I'm ashen, dazed, and covered in warm mud, otherwise still alive and able to hear a thrumming that resonates from the base of the wall. I spring backwards, into falling and flaming detritus, as the cable snaps up in front of me. Mud flings in all directions, mockingly, and the hollow noise of the cable and the pressure in the air squeezes my innards to jelly and I puke up half-digested food, bile, and a gout of blood -- in that order.

I fight for consciousness, crawling away from sensory onslaught and a four-storey pyre bent on a suicidal plunge.

Echo has begun another melee. The sound of her blade ringing. Her guttural growls intensifying as the wobbling of the cable fades. I reach an alley, using the side of the adjacent building as a crutch to stand. It starts catching fire.

A spear flies over the wall and lands at my feet. Echo's wrathful face peers at me. "I will seek rope!" she calls out.

For want of a rope and all that follows...

I try poking at the cable with the spear. The outsiders were adjusting it that one time. Maybe it can be disabled? Must look like an idiot, messing about with things I don't and can't understand while the Gray Girl's quarter burns.

She reappears above me and throws a rope down. I'll reach it with a good jump, but not without crossing the cable's threshold. I could black out this time...

Another building bursts into flame.

Fuck it.

I run and -- with a flash of inspiration -- jam the spear into the ground and vault up and over the cable. It almost becomes a living creature momentarily, shaking itself in rage and wild ululations. My vision tunnels. But my hands grip the rope, tying it around my wrist in case I—

Apparently I'm only unconscious for a brief moment. Echo is slapping my face. Hard.

"Stop I'm alive fuck woman stop!"

"Yes yes," she says, triumphant. "We monsters are most difficult to slay!"

She helps unwind the rope from my wrist -- which I suddenly notice are outsider robes tied together in thick knots. Every garment is covered in gaping, blood-stained holes.

Stealth will not be an option this night. Two groups, on opposite ends of the wall, are converging on our position. I gather up a quiver, bow, and as many arrows as I can scavenge before either are in range. Might not be a crossbow, but by damn I've missed shooting at shit that's trying to murder me.

"Direct me, my love." Oh, how she wants to be unleashed. Stooping almost so low to the ground as to return to an atavistic state, ready to bolt, slavering to dodge between spears, pouncing into masses of exposed flesh and goring them. Bloodlust. *Such bloodlust.*

I nock an arrow.

If we can stay atop the walls, our advantage is supreme: full access to everywhere in Gallows. A highway dwarfing anything we have ever slunk over, wending our way through madness, strife, and death.

Yet more outsiders are en route. The odds disfavor our survival. I rest my hand on her shoulder. The tight cords of muscle relax.

"This is bad ground. Let's cross to the market."

Stands up immediately. "I go, love. Come!" And now she springs from wall to roof, her shadow at her heels. We'll reposition ourselves. It's safer, we can—

Two more quarters of Gallows have erupted. Up north and far east. The purge is begun. Whatever comes of our flight, of this conflagrative hymnal, it ends at first light.

Though the final moves will be ours and those of the Executrix, the citizens of Gallows are clearly uninformed. They shriek about the streets, having fled their homes, and cry unto a sky above that has long since covered its eyes to their peril. They are alone. No one will save them. Dawn is coming and it ushers no absolution to the mob, consumed in a bonfire out of which their hatred was borne.

Is there pity in a single beat of my heart?

Time was, perhaps.

For their ignorance, if nothing else.

But the blood that careens through my veins is now dyed in Her color. And all my vision is gray, though the whole world immolate itself to a more radiant red than crimson and into writhing shadows darker than black. I am Her Consort as she is mine; I am cursed if I break the covenant.

Echo seems to hear my resolve.

"Yes, love!" she rejoices. "This is so!"

We dive to the ground, darting through the mindless throng. The outsiders atop the walls will not be able to spot us. Echo takes me across the main thoroughfare, passing the empty market, then cutting due south and every minute at oblique angles. The headless mob is far behind, their moaning and pleading background noise... a sickening verse to a song nearly done.

She pulls a gardening spade from her rucksack. "Dig under here!" Puts the spade in my hand, nods happily while pointing at the intersection of two walls. I'm not given time to protest the absurdity of the request. "I shall return!"

I'm able to move a decent amount of earth by the time she comes back, protectively carrying a cooking pot against her stomach and looking upset. "The digging implements... in the blacksmithy... they are..." Sighing.

"*Still?*"

She kneels down and uses the pot to scoop clay out with me. "We are victims," she says solemnly, "of old successes."

Our tunneling is arduous. Many times the outsiders dash across the walls above, going this way, going that way, but our progress is unmolested. We burrow a claustrophobic passage, then wriggle our way through the muck and out the other side. The recent rains may have been unwitting abettors, but we won't have time to toil like this again.

City center. More chaos.

Echo wields it like an extension of her violence, exhorting everyone into frenzy -- and into fleeing towards the nearest gatehouse. Guards watch in horror from atop their fragile perches. Then the crowd parts, frozen water bisected with a searing knife, and Echo approaches the gate and seems to darken with every step until a massive shadow expands from her arm and smites the thick oak to splinters.

Everyone recoils in terror. We stride inside, unopposed.

And I think it's over. We climb the stairs to the top of the road of walls, all abandoned of guards, no outsiders to be seen anywhere, and only fire and smoke and freedom ahead of us. I really, really think it's over. We leave behind the city that was our playground and our prison. Passing haunts and caches and hideouts, graffiti that has never been scrubbed away, the places where my tableaus terrorized each and every viewer, and reach the graveyard beyond which only the curtain wall stands in our way.

Until the Executrix reveals herself.

A flaming spear of coiled iron in her hand. A look of bottomless disgust in her pale yellow eyes.

Echo positions herself between us as if to say this is her fight alone. With a flare of dramatics, she flings her blade at the Executrix -- who knocks it away without thought. It is her undoing. For Echo has unwound her bandages, black blood seems to congeal into serrated wings, she flies, cries out victory, and stabs a spear made of black blood through the Executrix's chest, transfixing her to the cemetery's oak.

"Follow your empress into darkness," Echo whispers.

That is all, of course, without surprise, it's true, the version that, we trust you already understand, Echo always firmly insists that I relate. And so that is how I shall leave it with you, since the curtain wall part wasn't very exciting and I am still recovering.

In fact, I'll admit, I'm thoroughly exhausted.

#

An environment that cannot be perceived blurry in focus out of focus beyond all bound for nowhere. This is a good thing. This is where the true beginning begins. And where it is true, there can be no fear. Let go.

My spine is pressed against the back of the jester puppet. In awareness, vision clears: a vibrant land, but with colors remembered. A forgotten perspective. A lens of glass. Striations in the craftsmanship. Beloved imperfections.

We are sitting.

We are seeing opposite horizons.

The location of the sun is indeterminate.

The location of the sun does not matter anymore.

Wind puffs against us. My bones whistle. The jester puppet's strings sing then sigh. We do not speak. We sit. Time winnows thought, yet I hold on. It is...

It is?

Yes.

It is

so

comfortable.

I can feel the burnished sands atop which we are sitting back-to-back for a moment. Only a moment. I surpass myself, as she once did. And for this: gratitude, full felt, devoutly blossomed. Such warmth. In each grain, I reexperience a single memory. So many. Such warmth. Gratitude. Was it always so warm? How wonderful.

"I know *what* you did." My voice wind-weaving across a whispered distance between us. "But I don't know *why*."

Warmth. Grief. Warmth. Grief. Let go. Warmth. Grief. Warmth. Grief. It's time. Warmth. Grief. Warmth. Grief.

Love.

"I forgive you."

My words reverberate through me and into her. We cannot turn our heads to see each other. We want to. We cannot. I will drift away now. I will go from this place. Then I hear something on the edge of hearing. Tapping. Stroking. And I realize: her hand is lying atop mine. Tap tap. Erratic. Stroke tap. Insistent. Tap stroke tap. Determined. Again and again. And I think I understand what it means, but my hand does not have skin so I cannot feel the words. Her strings go taut for the last time.

And I feel the weight of her leave.

#

"I believe," Echo says, "that this direction will produce a great bounty!"

The idle days are peppered with such colorful language. I smirk. This optimistic change in her is like pristine air cascading down from the mountains -- things that she has never seen. But we'll find them. We'll find them...

Our journey continues to be randomly punctuated by her episodes. She claims they are easing, that over time they are becoming less intense. That's encouraging. Neither of us are under the illusion they will ever cease, but perhaps one day... perhaps one day not so far away, we'll figure out ways to make them more bearable. Holding her hand and smiling for her really do seem to help.

She hurries back to me, runs a finger over her neck, then paints four black lines across my cheeks.

"Were they fading?" I ask.

"But now no longer!"

"Will they ever fade?"

"Take the question to the graveyard!"

She laughs. She is beaming. Our empress-in-exile.

By the next new moon, we will cross beyond the edge of our map. Out of the province and into lands I have only ever heard about. Rumors, rather than cities. Legends, rather than kingdoms. Places yet unnamed. We are both ravening to create our own stories together to replace the pain of yesterday.

Things fall apart. But we won't miss the missing pieces.

How does this adventure end?

Who knows.

Life is a story without pause, for it is a tale made real only in its telling. Our dead world reminds us that we live our lives in passing. In that passage, perhaps something will justify us. And all the cries spread throughout history -- from the womb of our humanity to the birthright of our oblivion -- will finally become the song we always meant for them to be.

Do you hear that, Echo?

It's almost beautiful.